AND YESTERDAY IS GONE

AND YESTERDAY IS GONE

A NOVEL

DOLORES DURANDO

INFINITE WORDS

NEW YORK LONDON TORONTO SYDNEY

INFINITE WORDS
P.O. Box 6505
Largo, MD 20792
www.simonandschuster.com

© 2015 by Dolores Durando

ISBN 978-1-59309-666-3
ISBN 978-1-5011-1818-0 (ebook)
LCCN 2015934976

First Infinite Words trade paperback edition October 2015

Cover design: mariondesigns.com
Cover photography: © Keith Saunders / Keith Saunders Photos
Book design: Red Herring Design, Inc.

10 9 8 7 6 5 4 3 2 1

Manufactured in the United States of America

For information regarding special discounts for bulk purchases, please contact Simon & Schuster Special Sales at 1-866-506-1949 or business@simonandschuster.com

The Simon & Schuster Speakers Bureau can bring authors to your live event. For more information or to book an event, contact the Simon & Schuster Speakers Bureau at 1-866-248-3049 or visit our website at www.simonspeakers.com.

Blessed am I for my family...

My daughter Marilane, who has taken the time from her busy schedule to guide me through today's mystical technology, and whose shoulder was always there to cry on.

My daughter Dori Anne, who thinks I hung the moon and makes it so, and for her husband, Bill, a fisherman who would shame Moby Dick.

My son Bill, who is always there for me, strong and steady, and his wife, Cathy, who is all a daughter could be.

For my son Michael, who has listened so patiently and critiqued so gently over cold oatmeal and burnt toast.

And for my "other son" Matt, a big man with a big heart. The keeper of the keys.

This book is dedicated to my family, who have made this journey with me.
Without them I would have lost the way.
My daughters, who plan that I should lack for nothing.
My sons, who help to make it possible.
I am blessed.

ACKNOWLEDGMENTS

My deepest appreciation to Barbara Holiday, my indispensible, elegant editor. A salty San Francisco Margarita with a twist of Oregon.

I am thankful for the Rogue River's Writers Guild, who has cheered me on, showing no mercy. You know who you are, Emma Jean.

CHAPTER 1

Held by his stepfather's big beefy hand, the collar tightened as he hung suspended, his dirty tennis shoes barely touching the scuffed linoleum.

His head swung from side to side with each backhanded slap, delivered with an almost hypnotic rhythm.

He heard the screen door slam and looked past the man's upraised arm to see his mother pick up the knife lying on the counter, the old wooden handle worn smooth from years of use, the blade still razor-sharp. The chicken-butchering knife.

The man paused, turned his head to look into the eyes of the woman who held the knife just below his rib cage. His gaze dropped to the indentation of his shirt, to the trickle of red that grew to flow freely as though searching for a way out of a bad situation.

The young girl who followed close behind her mother whispered, "Do it, Ma."

"Put him down. If you ever touch one of my kids again, I'll kill you."

She spoke in a low, almost friendly tone, almost as though it was an ordinary conversation.

The man released his hold on the back of Stevie's shirt. The boy nearly crumpled to the floor, but regained his balance against the cabinet. He wiped his bloody nose on the back of his sleeve, smearing red across his face.

She held the knife steady, as though undecided. The big man stood motionless, his arm still upraised. Then slowly, her eyes never leaving his, she dropped the knife. It left a splatter of red against the white porcelain as it clattered to the bottom of the sink.

He turned without a word, pulled the bloody shirt from his pants with a look of shock and disbelief as he held it against his side.

The door closed behind him and they heard the pickup start.

"Well, Stevie, what brought that on?"

The boy's eyes teared and he tried to steady his voice as he answered. "I asked him for the fifty cents he said he'd give me if I washed the pickup and I did, but then he said he'd apply it to my rent.

"I told him that the fellas were waiting for me out front, that we're going to the movies. He yelled, 'Not on my money you're not, you worthless little shit. What in hell are you good for?' All the guys outside heard him.

"I said, 'Good for nothing just like you, you lying bastard.'"

Her resigned voice said, "Get it out of my purse. I think there's two quarters there. Sis, run down to the barn and bring that last chicken up and then we'll be done."

A week later Steve met Ollie on that dark, rainy night driving on a lonely road that led him down a slippery path to another world.

That was the beginning of a process where he learned who and what he really was. The tough shell that he had built around himself rotted off really quickly there on that godforsaken ranch. Out there cleaning sheep shit and digging postholes, he figured he'd start from scratch to find the real Steve McAllister.

There was no one to intercede for him or give a damn if he made it or not, with the exception of the skinny Mexican kid who was worse off than he was, and it didn't matter to anybody that it showed.

The skin that eventually grew tough became his own, and he was stronger than he ever would have dreamed. But he didn't know it then.

CHAPTER 2

I lay there in the dark listening to the rain splatter against the window. I pulled the covers up higher, hating the thought of going out into the wet darkness. I'd been thinking about making a run for it again—I'd run off once before, but the cops caught me and brought me back. Of course, I was only fourteen and dumb enough to take his pickup. Ma said I could go when I was eighteen, but I knew I couldn't last another year.

I slipped into the clothes I'd laid out last night and felt around for my backpack. I knew he was snoring on the couch in the living room—had been since Ma had taken the knife to him. I grinned as I thought about the look on his face.

The night-light in the bathroom showed me his pants were hung over the back of a chair; it was payday so I knew he had money.

My hands shook as I dug in his back pocket, pulled out the wallet and inched my way to the door.

The wind hit me and blew my hair over my eyes as I stepped off the porch steps. I put my head down, cut across the pasture and headed for the highway. Walking fast, the drizzle of rain felt good on my face.

Stumbling along, my mind wandered back and I thought of the years since Dad had died; how it seemed that everything had spiraled down from there. My self-esteem was at point zero, eroded from years of my stepfather's hateful words that hid beneath my fear. The bruises healed, but the scars in the inside needed more time.

I took it all to school and acted tough.

As a hyper, mouthy, overachieving troublemaker, I was also a straight-A student. I had a photographic memory and retained every-thing I read—and I'd read every book in the school library. I was captain of the debate team. Sis said I'd never have to repent my sins, that I'd talk my way into Heaven.

I never did a moment's homework.

After three years as editor of the school paper, I was kicked out because the principal maintained that I had questioned the Bible and cartooned the prophets. That was a deadly shot to me. Writing was my love and becoming a journalist was my dream...some day. I knew even then that writing was everything I wanted to do with my life. Because of Ma's tearful pleading, I was reinstated and graduated with an unsigned diploma—to which I promptly signed the principal's name. Better than he could have.

I walked a little faster and pulled my collar tighter, laughing to myself as I remembered how the fermenting mash had blown up in the chemistry room. The odor of beer hung in the air for a long time. That this happened shortly after my expulsion was no coincidence.

My cheeks were wet with more than rain when I thought how Ma was going to feel when I wasn't there in the morning. I was also scared and was wishing I could go back, but knew the die was cast and there was no way.

After I'd been walking a couple of hours, I saw car lights moving up behind me so I hit the ditch. When I knew it wasn't the pickup because of the diesel sound, I stood up and stuck out my thumb.

The truck stopped and I could see by the headlights it was pretty beat-up—looked like an escapee from a junkyard, so I was really surprised to hear the smooth sound of the motor.

A man rolled down his window, stuck his head out and asked, "Where're you headin', kid?"

That's when I heard the bleating of sheep and smelled wet wool.

"Where're you going?" I answered.

"I'm goin' home. I own a sheep ranch up at Camptown, right close to the Calaveras Mountains. So far back in the boonies that God has to look twice to find it. Wanna ride?"

"Yes, sir."

He leaned over and opened the door and I crawled in—scared to go, scared to stay.

My wet clothes seemed to emphasize the odor of wet sheep and the unmistakably pungent smell of marijuana.

"What are you doing out in the middle of the night in this miserable weather? Cops after you?" came his rough voice.

"No, but if they were, they sure wouldn't have any trouble catching us in this old heap," I said, trying to act tough.

He laughed. "Yeah? But there's four-hundred horsepower under the hood, kid."

I thought, *Yeah, in your dreams.*

"I'm going to San Francisco to look for work."

"What kind of work?"

"Any kind."

"I could use some help. I've got a big garden and about thirty head of sheep. You any good with animals?"

"I was born and raised on a farm and milking cows when I was in first grade."

"Yeah, and how old are you?"

"In a couple of months I'll be twenty."

He laughed and lit a cigarette that made my eyes water.

Some of the kids at school had fooled around with a joint or two and messed with their mothers' diet pills so I wasn't totally ignorant. But I didn't dare; Ma would have killed me.

"Mind if I roll the window down," I asked, "or we're both going to be stoned."

"How old are you, kid?" he asked again.

"Almost twenty," I said again.

He laughed. "I know you're lyin', kid."

I couldn't dispute it. Ma always said I was the world's worst liar.

"Yeah, you're lyin', but if you're a good worker and mind your own business, I could use some help with the sheep. They will be dropping their lambs pretty soon. Room and board—thirty bucks a month. Accommodations aren't great, but it would see you through till spring."

It didn't take me long to make up my mind.

"You know how to drive?" he asked, slanting his eyes over at me.

"Sure."

He pulled over and we traded places.

"Just stay on Four till we come to Angels Camp, then I'll drive on in."

He pinched the end of the joint and stuck it in his shirt pocket, sat back, tipped his hat over his eyes and went to sleep.

We got into Angels Camp just as the sun was coming up. I seemed to be a long way from home in this crummy little place with a gas station, post office and a sleazy-looking bar and grill. I nudged him awake. He sat up and yawned, pushed his hat back.

"You hungry? Let's get a cuppa joe and some flapjacks—sound good to you? Got any money?"

"A few bucks," I said. I hadn't even counted it. "Yeah, I'm hungry."

The flapjacks tasted like leather choked in something that resembled syrup and the coffee would have floated a horseshoe. But he picked up the tab and tipped the old guy who was both cook and waiter.

The mountains looked close, but he said it was still a two-hour drive.

"What's your name, kid?"

"Steve," I answered.

"Oliver here," he said, "but you can call me 'Ollie.'"

Handing him the keys, I leaned back and closed my eyes.

I was jolted awake as he turned into a narrow dirt road that looked as though it had been designed by someone who really loved potholes.

A cabin stood at the very edge of the forest and the dark somber mountains rose protectively around it.

He drove past a long, low building that hugged up against a big, weathered three-sided barn. As we went by, I could see the barn was almost filled with loose hay and a few random bales. He backed up to a loading chute that emptied into a large, fenced pen that contained a sizeable herd of sheep.

We got out and he pulled the bolt that released the latch. The door shoved open and the sheep crowded down to their companions. The noise was deafening.

There was no doubt as to who was the leader of that flock. A ram, whose long wool hung in dirty whorls over his little red-rimmed eyes, was almost the size of a small pony. He knocked his way through the herd to slam against the sturdy wooden panels used to reinforce the wire enclosure. Splinters flew and the sound of his head striking the wood silenced even the herd—momentarily.

I jumped back and said a couple of words Ma wouldn't have approved of, but Ollie laughed and said, "He's a mean son of a bitch, no doubt about it, and he'd be pretty rough on a guy if he ever got the opportunity. But he's a good breeder—keeps those girls happy. Never go in there without a pitchfork or a damn stout stick." As if he needed to tell me. "I take all the lambs to the Bay Area at Easter time and, of course, the wool. That and the gardens bring in a pretty fair income.

"Now, your job is to keep those sheep fed and watered, their pens cleaned every day. Take them out to the big pasture every morning and see that they're in at night so the coyotes don't get them. The ones in the shed are gonna lamb any day—or night—so keep a close eye on them. Every time I lose a lamb, I lose money and that makes me mean. You don't want that. Did you ever pull a lamb?" he asked.

"No, but I helped with a cow once."

"It's all the same. I'll help you if it comes to that."

We walked around the barn and he nodded at a little wooden building with a tin roof, set up on pier blocks, one small window.

"That's the bunkhouse. You'll be sharing it with the two Mexican guys. They've been tending the sheep, but now I need 'em full time in the garden. There ain't enough hours in the day at harvest time. They don't speak much English, but guess you'll make out. They're good workers and mind their own business. Carlos' wife does the cookin'—not bad, but a little heavy on the beans and rice—and sleeps in the kitchen."

He pointed to a path that led around to the back. "There's the shit house. Easy on the toilet paper or you'll be usin' corncobs. Get your stuff—guess you don't need any help," he said with a grin as he kicked the door open and stepped into the bunkhouse.

Ollie didn't lie about the accommodations.

A picnic table was littered with two dirty coffee cups, a partly eaten moldy sandwich, and a paper plate with the remains of rice—or was it beans. Pushed up against the walls were two double-deck bunks with rumpled blankets on the two bottom ones. A kerosene heater nestled in one corner—I guessed kerosene as I saw a kerosene lantern hung haphazardly on the corner of one bunk.

I threw my backpack on the top bunk that boasted only a thin dirty mattress. I guess he noticed my look because he said, "Well, the roof don't leak and you're only here to sleep."

We went outside, and as he walked up the path to the cabin, he called over his shoulder, "I'll send Lupe down with some blankets. The guys will be here around dark so take it easy and see you later, kid."

I went back in and climbed to the top bunk. But the mattress smelled so bad I pulled it down, dragged it outside, beat the dust and God knows what else out of it with an old broom, and leaned it up against a wall to air out.

I heard a sound behind me and looked over my shoulder to see a Mexican woman walking down the path carrying some blankets and a pillow. I walked to meet her.

She wasn't a pretty woman—looked about forty, just a couple of inches taller than I was, but at least fifty pounds heavier. She sure wasn't a lightweight.

She wore a brightly colored dress that hardly covered her knees, hung loosely from her shoulders and contained with difficulty the large heavy breasts that strained the flimsy material.

Her hair was thick and black, loosely tied, and hung down her back. She smiled and showed a wide gap between her two front teeth, very white against the brown of her skin. Small, twinkling black eyes ran over my body from head to toe, then returned slowly to do it again.

I stood like a fool with my arms outstretched and felt my face turn red. She piled the blankets in my arms. Those little black eyes seemed to glitter as her body pressed against me when she tucked the pillow under my arms. I smelled the musky scent of her as she moved against me for as long as it took her to adjust that pillow to her complete satisfaction.

Looking into my eyes, she slid her tongue slowly over her lips and reached to comb her fingers through my yellow, curly hair that I'd tried to plaster down all my life. Softly, she said, *"Tu eres guapísimo.* Pretty boy."

She turned and walked back up the path, then looked over her shoulder and laughed to see me standing there with my arm full of blankets, watching her swing those hips. She turned at the door and blew me a kiss. I got the message.

I never had any experience with girls. Ma always said, "You keep that thing in your pants till you're old enough to support a family or I'll cut it off."

Ma was handy with a knife.

After a couple of hours, I saw Ollie disappear behind the house and watched him walk up a trail that disappeared into the trees.

His truck was parked behind the barn with a tarp thrown over it. I was curious to see if he was lying about what was underneath that hood. I walked back there and pulled up the tarp, lifted the hood. My breath caught in my throat and I could only stare. I'd seen the hot rods that some of the jocks at school had and helped my stepfather work on his pickup, so I wasn't completely ignorant about what an engine should look like—but this!

The chrome pipes were spotless with a shine that almost blinded me, not a drop of oil or grease under that hood—a V8. My mind whirled as I looked at all those ponies—four hundred easy.

I gently put the hood down and backed away, almost as though it was holy.

I'd cleaned the bed of the truck after we let the sheep out, but the smell when I lifted the tarp was overpowering sheep shit and skunk—my eyes almost watered.

Ollie'd obviously enclosed the bed of the truck himself, using four-by-six slotted plywood panels. A double plywood floor had been built a foot higher than the metal floor beneath. I slid my hand around and found a cleverly concealed flap that hid the false bottom.

A person would really have to search to find it, and what cop was going to dig through the sheep shit in an old beat-up truck barely doing the speed limit.

I was more than a little scared. I knew this wasn't a mom-and-pop operation—I could only imagine the value of a load of marijuana hidden beneath the hay. Somehow I had gotten lost in a big-time operation and how in hell was I going to get out of this mess.

It was late in the afternoon, almost dusk. I was hungry and still curious. I knew Ollie's "garden" wasn't peas or carrots. I walked around the house and started up the trail—a little scared, but more curious, even though I had a pretty good idea what was up there.

The pungent smell of marijuana grew stronger with every step—it seemed to permeate even the dark trees that hung over the trail that soon had become a narrow path. I'd only gone a little way when I heard voices. Suddenly, furious barking came from nowhere and a big dog lay crouched at my feet with every tooth bared in a frightful snarl.

I froze, terrified.

Then I heard a yell and the dog backed off, still growling.

Ollie appeared, trailed by the two Mexicans.

"Where in hell do you think you're going? Does this look like a sheep pasture to you?" he raged. "You got no business up here, kid. Get the hell back where you belong and stay there—I won't call this dog off again."

Scared to death, I ran back down the trail, the branches whipping me in the face. At first I didn't feel the warm wetness on the front of my pants, but when I did, I was glad that was all it was.

I kicked open the door of the bunkhouse, breathing hard, and sank down on a bench with my head in my hands. I wanted to cry. At that moment, I'd have given anything to be in my mother's kitchen. Supper would be over by now and Sis and I would be fighting over whose turn it was to do the dishes. Then she'd be hogging the bathroom for as long as it took to put Noxzema on her pimples or curlers in her hair.

The door opened and a Mexican boy who looked about my age stepped in. He leaned gracefully against the doorjamb and I stood as we took each other's measure.

He was taller than me by a couple of inches, but very slender. His long black hair hung to his shoulders and framed the light-skinned face that was dominated by thickly fringed black eyes that appeared bottomless. I was unable to look away. High cheekbones declared his Indian blood inherited from some long-ago ancestor; a curved, smiling mouth appeared as he tentatively held out his hand and said, "Juan."

A wayward thought flashed through my mind: *He's pretty enough to be a girl.*

I held his hand gratefully and shook it with enthusiasm. I was so glad to find a friend that tears welled up in my eyes.

"Steve," I answered as I gave him back his hand.

He pointed to a bunk, made a scowly face and said, "Carlos, Papa," then made a big "O" with his mouth, pointed to the cabin, and then aimed his thumbs to the floor.

He rubbed his belly, motioned me to follow and we walked up the path to the cabin.

These "accommodations" weren't great either. A makeshift wash-stand stood outside the cabin, holding a black rubber feed pan usually used for grain. On the opposite side a hand pump, and a three-sided shower beside it with only a pipe to convey water from the well.

Juan pumped the handle and cold water gushed over Carlos as he stood, six feet three inches or more, I guessed, and naked to the waist. He cupped his hands and threw the water over the massive shoulders that would have made a bull envious. He seemed to have no hips or belly.

As he dried himself on his dirty shirt, I could see Juan's Indian blood was not that far removed. Carlos looked far more Indian than Mexican. His tawny, copper-colored skin stretched over his cheek-bones, and above, the hooded black eyes that never seemed to see me. I was glad—he scared me.

The only time he ever looked directly at me, he smiled and those black eyes glittered in the dim light of the kerosene lantern. I would never—never—forget it.

I could smell the food and I was hungry.

Ollie's rough voice shouted, "What the hell are you doing out there? This ain't the Ritz."

When Carlos went in, Juan and I hurriedly splashed some water over us and wiped off on a towel thin as tissue paper, then followed.

The kitchen didn't look much different from the bunkhouse, only that it had a stove and a better table.

Ollie motioned me to sit next to him. Remembering our last meeting, I would rather have joined Carlos and Juan on the opposite side. But I sat where I was told.

Ollie was a big man—not as tall as Carlos, but he carried a lot more weight around his belly. His hands were as big as hams. I remembered him telling me when we stopped for breakfast that he had once been a heavyweight champ.

Sitting next to him, I suddenly felt very small.

I looked across the table in the lighted kitchen and got a good look at Juan. The string that had held his long hair back must have loosened when we washed up, for now it hung close about his face, the skin only a shade darker than my own. Those eyelashes would have driven Sis wild with jealousy.

Ollie saw me staring and he laughed. "He's a hell of a lot better-lookin' than his dad, ain't he? That is, if Carlos *is* his dad. How about it, Carlos, are you real sure? He ain't Lupe's for damn sure. He sure is a pretty boy."

Carlos gave no indication that he heard; Juan never raised his eyes from the plate.

His heavy-breasted wife walked flatfooted as she dished up the food and carried the plates to the table. I noticed that she managed to brush up against Ollie as she set the other big platters down, heavy with beans and rice.

Everyone ate like they were starved. Chewing something foreign to me, I looked at Juan. He grinned and went "baa." Ollie silenced him with a look.

We ate fast and without speaking until the woman brought something in a big pan, scooped most of it on Ollie's plate, then scraped what was left to the three of us.

"Damn this flan is good. Lupe, is there any left?" Looking directly at Carlos, Ollie laughed. "Our wife has outdone herself—she's getting better in the kitchen, too."

When she turned, Ollie ran his hand over her hip and gave it a familiar slap, then looked over at Carlos with a knowing smile and said something in Spanish.

I sneaked a look at Lupe. She had a sly look on her face, but her back was to Carlos.

I caught my breath as Carlos looked up—his eyes were just black slits, hate radiating from every pore. The thick rope-like veins bulged, throbbing on his forehead; his hands trembled as if in anticipation as he pushed his plate away and left.

Ollie threw back his head and laughed.

In utter disbelief I looked at him—was he crazy? Surely he had seen the murderous look on Carlos' face. How could he be so blind?

I was glad to escape to my thin mattress and damp blanket on the top bunk. I lay awake for a long time. It seemed that all the strength had drained from my body and evaporated into the tension-filled air. Then I slept so soundly I never heard Carlos come in, except that I dreamed the dog growled.

The horrible clanging of the big rusty bell just at dawn sent us rushing up the path to the cabin. Scrambled eggs smothered in rice and beans—what else? Black coffee so bad I couldn't drink it; hardly a word was spoken.

The men walked quickly up the trail and I went down to start the sheep toward the big pasture, then went back to clean the lambing shed.

I was happy to see that twin lambs had arrived without my help, newly born, still wet and searching for their breakfast on stumbling, shaky legs. The young mother seemed uncertain as to what was expected of her and wouldn't stand for them, despite their persistent efforts to nurse.

I knelt, held that woolly body still and told her what a fine girl she was to have produced two such lovely babies. She leaned against me, relaxed, and the lambs found what they were looking for and nursed vigorously. When I left, she was cleaning her babies as though her maternal duties had suddenly come to mind.

Working most of the day cleaning that big shed and carrying manure to a pile that was almost as tall as I was totally exhausted me. Since the harvest had begun, the sheep apparently were not a priority.

Sitting against the barn for a moment's rest, I was startled when I heard that miserable old ram fighting the gate again. I realized it was late and was thankful for the wake-up call.

I ran to let the herd in and worked like hell to get the feeding done before the men came down for supper.

It was almost dark when I saw them at the washstand and I walked quickly to the cabin. Juan grinned and playfully punched me in the shoulder. Carlos never looked my way. We filed in and sat down. Ollie looked at me and asked, "Well, kid, what did you get done today?"

"I cleaned the lambing shed that didn't look as though it had been cleaned for six months, and when I counted those thirty sheep you said you had, my count came to fifty—not counting two new ones born last night."

He gave me a long, penetrating stare. As soon as the words were out of my mouth, I knew I'd stepped in it.

"Don't get mouthy with me, kid. Just keep on shovelin' shit and we'll get along."

Juan grinned and I figured he knew more English than he let on.

Ollie looked over at Carlos as Lupe started to dish up. "Hey, Carlos— next time I go to Frisco, I'm gonna buy our wife a nightgown. I don't think she's got one. What size do you s'pose?"

Carlos never lifted his eyes from his plate or let on that he heard a word.

"Lupe, bend over and let me look at that fat ass. What size, Mrs. Carlos?"

She gave him a playful swat as he ran his hands over her hips.

"Oh, hell—probably a waste of money now that I think about it. She likes bare skin. What d'ya think, Carlos?"

I watched Carlos' hands clench and unclench. The fork was bent double when he dropped it to the table.

The goose bumps on the back of my neck threatened to explode; my stomach tied in knots.

Ollie laughed as Carlos walked out—quiet as death, his feet never seemed to touch the floor.

Lupe continued to clear the table as Juan and I almost ran out of the cabin and down the path.

"Doesn't that maniac know what shit he's stirring up?" I asked Juan. He didn't answer.

Ma would have said Ollie was messing with the hind leg of a mule, but I would have said it wasn't a mule—it was a king cobra.

Mealtime was always a miserable experience. Ollie never let up on Carlos except to throw a few words at me.

CHAPTER 3

M y chores with the sheep had expanded to include digging postholes for a fifty-foot fence. It was backbreaking work—the ground obviously had never known a shovel. Plus I had to dig out the stumps that were in the way. By mealtime I was almost too exhausted to eat and food was hard to keep down. More than once I lost it along the path back to the bunkhouse.

After a couple days, I took a break to clean the sheep shed. Two more lambs had been born during the night and I was putting down clean straw, then pacifying the new mothers.

I looked up to see Lupe watching me as she leaned against the door with an egg basket hung over her arm.

What is she doing here? The henhouse is at the other end of the barn.

But I instinctively knew before she took my hand. I followed her as though hypnotized, stumbling along, my penis trying to undo my zipper—or so it seemed.

She stopped when we got past the wired bales where the loose hay was piled high. She set the egg basket aside, sat down, pulled the dress over her head, gave it a toss and lay back. Her thick brown body, her legs splayed out, those dark-tipped breasts—I could hardly breathe.

The thin sheen of sweat made her almost glow and the scent of her smothered the smell of the fragrant hay. Her voice sounded slurred and guttural as she said, "Come and get it, pretty boy."

I fell to my knees and tried to unbuckle my belt with ten fingers on each hand.

"Let me," she said.

As if in a dream, I felt the pants slide off and she moved against me, kissed a part of me that had never before known such affection. The agony was so great I groaned and uncontrollably erupted. Later—much later—I thought I had probably put most volcanoes to shame.

I wanted to die I was so humiliated. I turned away, but she pulled me back; her mouth and hands were everywhere—places I never knew existed.

Shockwaves drowned me as I lay suspended so close to Heaven I could hear the angels sing. Then exquisite agony as the entire universe exploded.

I lay almost unconscious, and still that insatiable member stood erect before I could hardly breathe—as if it was apologizing for its first premature performance.

She laughed as she whispered, "Another time, guapo, must go."

But I held her fast and in the struggle somehow her legs held me captive again. Then a rustle in the hay and she was gone.

I crawled around in the hay that wasn't stacked so neatly now, looking for my pants, wondering if I had the strength to pull them on. My boots—where are my boots?

The guys got Sunday afternoon off, but the sheep didn't observe Sunday so I took the herd to pasture and did a quick cleanup of the lambing pen. Then I could sneak a couple of hours for myself.

Juan joined me as I drove the sheep out. When they were secure, we found a sheltered place in the brush and relaxed.

Juan produced a baggie with the green stuff, then proceeded to teach me how to roll a joint. I was fascinated to see how expertly those long, graceful fingers could produce so neat a cigarette.

He took the first deep drag and held it for what seemed forever, exhaled, and handed it over.

"Bueno, bueno." He nodded.

I tried to follow his example, but thought my time had come as I coughed, choked and my eyes watered. He shook with laughter, then motioned for me to give it another try.

I did, reluctantly, and found that inhaling was easier this time, and I held it as long as I could. It was overrated as far as I was concerned. I certainly didn't feel any different, only hungry—but I was always hungry.

We passed the joint back and forth and talked. Juan was picking up English very quickly and I thought I was doing great with Spanish. We were connecting, and this time I rolled the joint.

I was tempted to tell him—brag, even—about my experience with Lupe, but somehow I couldn't find the words.

He told me of his home, deep in the mountains, where his grandmother cared for him. Later a teacher lived with them and he saw very little of kids his own age in that tiny village. He said he had been lonely all his life.

I talked about my home, of Ma and Sis, and told him about my stepfather's encounter with Ma's chicken-butchering knife and we laughed till we cried. We seemed to get the gist of each other's broken language using our hands to diagram our words.

Suddenly—or slowly—I lost track of time, ranch life got better, the rain wasn't so cold and wet, the work wasn't so miserable, and the sheep smelled good. But I sure was hungry.

Later when we brought the sheep up, I had never been so happy and the beans and rice were the best I'd ever eaten.

At supper that night I even dared to ask Ollie when payday was and, since I knew I'd been there about five months, I also asked about a raise. I didn't sign on to dig postholes. He looked at me and squinted his eyes. "You okay, kid? You couldn't be into anything—you must be gettin' loaded on the smell. Don't worry about money. God will take care of you."

Juan had sneaked five plastic bags—double-bagged to keep the smell down—of that high-grade Mary Jane. I'd stashed it in a Folgers Coffee can in a corner of the manure pile. I figured if I ever got out of there, I'd have something to compensate me for all those postholes. I knew God would take care of me, but I thought Ollie should help.

I turned my head to see the scared look on Juan's face and I realized the danger I had put us in with my big mouth. So I just looked as stupid as I was and said, "Smell of what? Sheep shit?"

And he laughed then. "Got that fence up yet, kid?"

"Not quite," I smart-alecked back. "Only got about three more stumps to dig out and about forty more postholes to dig."

"I hope I don't have to come down there and jumpstart your ass with the toe of my boot."

Then he looked over at Carlos. "I'm leavin' early in the morning—special delivery. I'll pull the truck around and you two can get it loaded by midnight—so get movin'."

"Kid, you be ready by sunup to load them sheep—use plenty of hay. And when I get home, I better see a long line of postholes—got that?"

He sneered. "Carlos, it's all yours. Don't wear it out—remember, I'll be back."

I went down to the bunkhouse and found the baggie Juan had left for me. I lay in my bunk and smoked. I didn't hear them come in, but I sure as hell heard that damned bell clanging at the cabin and it was still dark.

Ollie was gone for two days and a night.

We all slept in—what luxury. The sheep got fed late; the old ram in a rage nearly tore the fence down. Juan helped me nail it back up.

"That old son of a bitch is Ollie's real father. They've got exactly the same hateful disposition," I snarled as each nail was pounded home.

That tickled Juan. He laughed so hard he couldn't seem to drive a nail straight and I had to pull all those bent nails. Somehow his hand didn't look right curled around the handle of that hammer.

Carlos and Lupe didn't show until just before Ollie was expected back.

Juan and I scrounged around in that dirty kitchen and located the usual beans and rice, and we found the hiding place where a hen had thought her eggs were secure. So we ate all we wanted, smoked, slept and talked.

Juan held a shovel while I dug three postholes one day with a post-hole digger that I thought had probably been used to help build the pyramids.

Just before the sun went down behind those tall, dark trees, Ollie drove in, pulled up to the chute and yelled, "Take care of them sheep. Throw a tarp over the truck. I'm dead tired." Then he walked up to the cabin.

I smelled food—the first Lupe had fixed since Ollie had gone.

I was not surprised to see Carlos and Juan walking down the trail, like always—that big dog that slept by Carlos' bed following like a shadow.

At the table Ollie was quieter than usual. He turned to me. "Got that fence up, kid?"

I said, "Sure, Ollie, piece of cake. I pulled another stump, too—and added thirty-five more holes."

He looked hard at me, then laughed. "Damn. Sometimes I like you, kid. Any new lambs?"

"No, but I think one's pretty close—that old ewe has been up and down all day. I hope she doesn't have any problems."

"If she does, you come up and get Lupe. I'm so tired I don't know if I can make it into bed. Be sure to check her every few hours."

I wondered how or when I was going to get any sleep.

Then he added, "It was cold in San Francisco and I'm glad to be home. I'll have a soft pillow to sleep on tonight. How about it, Carlos? Is it still soft?"

That night I lay there, thinking about that old ewe and couldn't go to sleep. Hell, she'll be fine, I told myself and dozed off. Don't know how long I slept, but I awoke with a start thinking of that ewe.

Disgusted with myself, I fumbled for the lantern, located a couple of matches in my jeans. After a couple of tries, I got it going, then stepped behind the bunk to look for my jacket. Ma had given me that jacket for Christmas—it had a double-insulated, zippered lining. I hated to wear it out in the rain and anywhere near the crap of the sheep shed, but it was warmer by far than Ollie's ragged and filthy cast-offs that Lupe had found for me and that hung on me like an overcoat. Besides, I had my "stash"—thirty-eight dollars from my stepfather's wallet—rolled up the size of a cigarette and securely hidden, pushed up into a seam of that jacket.

The dog growled, but Carlos never opened his eyes. I knew he was awake.

I opened the door to the cold black night and hesitated. Hell, she's had a dozen of 'em. Am I crazy?

I ducked my head and ran to the lambing shed. Making my way through the sleeping sheep, I found the old ewe, stretched out, all four legs stiffly extended, straining with every contraction. I could see one little leg and what appeared to be an ear, bulging with every effort, but nothing was happening. I knew that both the ewe and lamb would be dead in the morning. I weighed that thought against the hell I was going to catch if I woke Ollie.

I couldn't stand to see the agonizing attempts of the old ewe straining to deliver a lamb that was never going to come without help.

Ollie had said to call Lupe. I ran up the path—the long shirt flapping behind me—hoping, praying she would be in her own bed.

I knocked frantically at the kitchen window. Nothing happened. I was desperate as I moved to the door and knocked again. Suddenly the door was flung open. Ollie stood there in his shorts with a double-barreled shotgun in my face.

"Ollie," I screamed, "it's me. It's me."

"What the hell are you doing up here? You're lucky I didn't blow your brainless head off. It's the middle of the night—what the hell do you want?"

"It's that ewe. The lamb is coming crooked—they're both going to die."

He turned and bellowed, "Lupe, Lupe. Get some clothes on and get down to the lambing shed and show this kid how to pull a lamb. Hurry it up."

Glaring at me, he said, "That ewe better be on her feet in the morning with a live lamb. Now get the hell out of here."

He lowered the shotgun as though he'd forgotten he held it.

Lupe was about as thrilled as I was. We rushed back to the shed and pushed our way through the disturbed sheep.

The ewe was still straining to rid herself of something that was locked in an impossible position; the front leg and little ear still showed.

Lupe knelt to examine the suffering animal, then rolled up her sleeve and wriggled her hand inside. She maneuvered in there for what seemed to me to be forever, then pulled out the little leg and another followed. She went in again, pushed the lamb back, and re-adjusted the position of the bent neck. Then the head appeared, resting on top of the front legs.

Another convulsive push and the lamb slid out as though that had been its intention from the start. I drew a shaky breath and wondered if that old girl was as happy as I was—for both of us.

"Lupe," I said, "You're a marvel—you've saved three lives tonight." I was close to serious.

"Well, did you learn anything?" she asked.

"Yeah. Never wake up Ollie again. Was that gun loaded?"

"Hell yes—did it look like an ornament to you?"

I felt like a fool. She slid her arm around me.

"If it wasn't so damned cold, we could party for a while—he won't be awake for a couple of hours."

I shrugged away. Suddenly I couldn't have been more exhausted if I had done the work for both Lupe and the ewe, who by now was on her feet cleaning her baby with enthusiasm.

I sank down on an overturned water bucket as though my legs had deserted me. Too late to go back to bed; too early for breakfast.

I watched Lupe wash her hands in the watering trough and wipe them indifferently on her shirttail.

Lupe and I had not indulged in much verbal communication and I was curious about this brown-skinned woman. Ma would have called her a "hussy" or worse.

I asked, "Lupe, how come you speak English so well? Juan can hardly say 'good morning,' and in all my time here, I've never heard Carlos speak a word. Is he mute?"

She settled herself cross-legged in the straw and looked up. A serious look on her face brought me to attention.

"Carlos mute? Hardly. His voice was the last thing many men heard before they met their Maker. Never underestimate him. He is the cruelest man I've ever known."

I felt a chill run up my back.

"But what about you, Lupe? How did you learn?"

"Ah, I'm a California native—born and raised in Concord. Went all through school there—an honor student. My grandparents raised me; I never knew my father or mother. When I was about twenty, I went to Mexico City to visit my grandmother's relatives and found that I loved Mexico, the people, the customs, flowers—and the men. I was young and pretty then."

The contented sounds of the resting sheep—their bellies full as they lay close together in a tangle of wool, the lantern's soft light and a real conversation in English almost made the night a pleasure.

"I worked in a high-class bar that catered to tourists and it wasn't long before I was living with a man, Manuel, who had a lot of money. He taught me a lot about Spanish customs." She laughed. "You can believe I was a fast learner."

"Manuel was second in command of some big organization and had a lot of respect—or even fear, I thought—for the man who headed it. I met a lot of Manuel's friends who seemed to work for the same man. They and their women, too, were a rough bunch. I didn't care as long as the money rolled in. Of course, since I was Manuel's woman, I finally figured out that it was a drug operation—and one of the biggest in Mexico.

"I had never met Carlos—he didn't associate with any of us socially. Manuel said Carlos had truly fallen in love with a beautiful gringa. She was married, but her husband had disappeared—with Carlos' help. He moved her to a magnificent estate where she lived like a queen in a villa.

"Manuel took care of business as Carlos spent a lot of time at the villa—even more when she became pregnant. She delivered a large, handsome baby boy and Carlos was beside himself with joy. But that joy soon turned to heartbreak when the gringa died shortly after giving birth to Juan.

"Carlos took the baby to be baptized, but the priest refused so Carlos burned the church and shot the priest.

"Listen, my pretty boy, Ollie will be getting up soon and I'd better be there..."

I interrupted. "Tell him we had a hard time with that ewe." I was really caught up in this story.

"Well, Carlos went completely crazy. He started a war with both the Federales and a rival gang. Eventually, he was head of the biggest cartel in Mexico, but it was paid for in blood.

"Many, many men were killed on both sides, and then three Federales were murdered. Burning churches, shooting priests and Federales are very bad things to do in Mexico.

"He and his band hid out in the mountains for a long time. He was the most wanted man in Mexico."

"Lupe, when did you meet Carlos?"

"Well, I had gone back to work at that bar when Carlos sent someone down for me. When we couldn't drive any farther, I rode a mule—me, on a mule—to some horrible little village way back in the mountains.

"My first look at Carlos made me know that I had wasted my time with other men and I guessed he'd been a long time without a woman.

"First we talked. He wanted me to be on the lookout for a suitable contact stateside and he'd leave Manuel in charge in Mexico until it was safe for him to come back. He needed help to get Juan and himself out of Mexico and help when he got to San Francisco until he could get organized. He thought that in that fancy tourist bar I might meet someone who would be of help to him.

"I agreed—many pesos later. Then we celebrated. I got high as a kite on peyote—the Indians love peyote. The next morning I woke up in his sleeping bag and someone said we'd gotten married—after a fashion.

"I went back down the mountain on the mule. I wasn't much heavier—those pesos don't weigh much.

"Sometime later, I met Ollie at the bar. He was throwing a lot of money around and asked me if I knew where he could score some really good weed. We spent a couple of days together, then he went up the mountain. A week later Mr. and Mrs. Carlos and son were on a plane bound for San Francisco.

"Carlos still has his connections in Mexico, but Ollie works this end of it. Ollie figures he's got Carlos over a barrel because of the police—I suppose they're still looking for him in Mexico.

"But Ollie is walking a damn fine line."

Lupe shifted nervously from one foot to the other—we'd both heard the muffled growl of the dog and I knew if he was out, that Carlos was up. I was glad we'd only been talking.

I grabbed her hand. "What happened to Juan all these years?"

"After Carlos burned the church, he took the baby to an old Indian woman deep in the mountains—some relative, I guess. Got a teacher for him when he was old enough, so Juan doesn't lack for an education. When he was young, Carlos spent a lot of time with him, but as Juan grew older, Carlos seemed to lose interest. Guess he had a good reason, if you look at it through Carlos' eyes. I was surprised when he brought him stateside."

I let her go and followed her to the cabin.

I was on my third cup of coffee when the bell clanged and the first sign of daylight showed through the window.

Ollie slouched into the kitchen.

"Up early, ain't you kid? How's the ewe?"

"Fine," I said. "Thanks to Lupe. I didn't study to be a vet—I'm better at digging holes."

He gave me a friendly slap that just about knocked me off the bench.

"You know you're damn lucky I didn't shoot you last night." He wasn't smiling.

CHAPTER 4

From day to day, from daylight to dark, the garden was all that existed. The men came down wet and exhausted—almost too tired to eat.

The mood at the table was tense. The occasional goad from Ollie seemingly fell on deaf ears. There was absolutely no indication that Carlos heard, but the hate that radiated from him was almost visible.

I was about halfway done with the postholes and still up at least once a night with the sheep—the cleaning was never done. One night a ewe dropped twins, but one was dead. I buried it in the manure pile and then I buried the damned shovel, too.

In the back of my mind, this thought ate at me constantly: How in hell am I ever going to get out of this mess? It was almost one hundred miles to Angels Camp and there was nothing there. And for sure Ollie wasn't going to let me go out in that truck. Actually, we were all prisoners. I was getting desperate and scared when I realized I'd been there almost seven months. The only bright spots were the stolen time Juan and I had when we smoked our way to better things and, of course, Lupe's unpredictable appearances at the barn.

One late afternoon I saw Lupe walking down the path, carrying an egg basket. I lay the hayfork down and followed her like a shadow, watching the swing of those hips and hearing her laugh. I didn't need to follow knowing that she was going to the same place where the hay was piled high in one corner of the old barn.

She set the basket aside. Before I had my pants open, she was lying there, warm and brown, waiting, her dress tucked under her chin. She reached for me, ran her fingers through my hair, which had grown so long.

"My pretty boy," she said and I fell on her as though I was starving and nothing mattered but this dark-skinned woman who brought heaven to me in an egg basket.

When we finished, again, the back of that haystack looked as though a couple of elephants had rolled around it.

I stood and tried to pull my pants up.

"Come back a minute," she said. I laughed, which took about all the strength I had left.

Suddenly she jumped up and frantically started to brush off the hay, pulled back her hair and dug for her shoes. As I looked at her in amazement, she grabbed the egg basket and darted for the opposite end of the barn.

Then I heard the dog growling at the sheep and I felt the blood drain from my face as I tried to buckle a belt that evaded my every effort to make a connection.

"Hey, Ollie. Lookin' for your sweetie?" I heard her call.

"Maybe. What the hell are you doin' down here?"

"Do you think I laid these eggs?"

"Where's the kid?"

"How should I know? He's supposed to be down in the lambing shed, isn't he?"

"Well, as long as I'm here, I may as well look in on those sheep and see what kind of job he's doin'."

I knew I was a dead man. It was a long way from that lambing shed and the shit was piled high—hadn't cleaned it yet—and no way in hell could I make it there before he did.

I heard her laugh and screwed up the courage to peek around the hay where I saw her slip an arm around him and say, "You can always look at them woolly sheep. C'mon and I'll show you something that will make you forget what a sheep looks like."

"Yeah, you're right. I can always look at sheep. I came down to get some tools, but that can wait, too."

I didn't catch what else he said, but I heard Lupe laugh and say, "That kid? He ain't old enough to have *cojones*. What do you think I am—a child molester?"

I didn't know if I should thank her for saving my life or choke her. I sank back on the hay; my legs absolutely refused to hold me.

That night at supper, Ollie said, "How're you doin', kid? You look kinda peaked. You're not goin' to poop out on me now, are ya?"

I said, "I'm so tired I can hardly walk. I hate those damn sheep."

"You're tired?" he growled. "You should try workin' like a man—like we do. You better learn to love them sheep 'cause you got a long ways to go."

"Speaking of which," I said. "I've been here nearly nine months. When am I going to get paid?" I asked for the second time.

"Paid? You got room and board, ain'tcha? You said you had money when I picked you up—you spent it already?"

He was trying to be funny—where in hell would I have spent it? In the sheep shed or bunkhouse?

Juan smuggled me a baggie a few times, but now I leaned on him for as much as he dared to steal. I'd get my wages out of that bastard one way or another and someday, someway, I was gonna get out of here.

We were all tired and irritable. Ollie had barely brought enough supplies back to feed us for three to four days, and the rest of the time, it was straight beans and rice. We were all hungry, but I figured Ollie had his own stash somewhere in the house.

Lupe didn't come down for several days, and I didn't know if I was relieved or depressed. But I figured that out when I saw her coming down the path. I was waiting in the hay.

She smiled, set down the egg basket. Although the thought *Would that work again?* crossed my mind, I immediately forgot it as she started to unbuckle my pants.

I slapped her hand away. "Child molester, huh? No *cojones*, huh?"

She laughed as she pulled off her dress. "I saved your pretty ass, amigo. He'd have killed you—and not the easy way. You'd have begged to die."

She put her mind and efforts to other things that almost left me brain-dead.

CHAPTER 5

The weeks dragged on.

The last lamb had been born; I was so grateful I could have cried. The weather had turned so bad it rained most of the time—a cold, constant drizzle. I never got warm. When I complained to Ollie, he threw us three extra blankets that helped, but not much. The kerosene heater was a decoration—there wasn't any fuel. When I brought that to Ollie's attention, he looked surprised and said, "You got blankets, ain'tcha?"

Blankets don't throw much heat—I hated him.

I asked Lupe what they had up the trail. She said, "A big tent," yet they still come down wet and cold, and Ollie was meaner than a snake. Of course, Carlos was his usual self and I felt sorry for Juan; he was so miserable.

Another dreary month passed; Friday night drew around. Ollie seemed in a good mood as he sat down at the table. He punched me playfully in the arm, hard enough to break it, and said with a grin, "Still love them sheep, kid?" I didn't answer.

He picked up his fork and shoveled the food in his mouth. When his plate was clean, he called Lupe for a refill. As she set his plate back down, he leaned his head on her breast and said, "Oh, what a pillow—I'll sleep good tonight." Then, looking directly at Carlos, his tone changed. "Tomorrow night, nobody sleeps. Got a real special order—biggest one I've ever had." For the first time, Carlos looked up, his black eyes unreadable.

"And some Mexican big shot," Ollie continued, "wants to talk. Maybe he thinks I'm crowdin' him—I'll take along a little protection." Then, with an excited laugh, he said, "Those flower children in the Haight-Ashbury are going to make me a millionaire.

"I'll pull out early Sunday morning, and we'll do the deal at the Yellow Submarine in Concord—ain't that a helluva name for a truck stop. That way I won't have to go into Frisco and I'll be home early. Kid, you better be damn quick about gettin' them sheep in—that's your department. Use lots of hay."

As he left the table, he nudged against Carlos, who coiled like a rattlesnake.

In my heart I carried the sure knowledge that he never intended for me to get out of here alive or he wouldn't have been so free with information.

The next morning the men left earlier than usual. I went up to the cabin and as Lupe poured the coffee, her hands shook. She looked like she hadn't slept or combed her hair. She flipped a couple of eggs and tossed a piece of toast on top and dropped it in front of me—not a word had been spoken. I choked down the runny eggs and cold toast as she sat down beside me with a cup of coffee.

After a while, she said, "There's gonna be trouble up there today. Ollie's got the big head—he figures he knows it all and doesn't need Carlos anymore. Carlos is no fool—he had that figured out before I did. So Carlos has got to go—it's just a matter of time. If they hadn't needed each other, one of them would have been dead by now. Everything depends on how this deal at the Submarine works out...," her voice trailed off. "What will happen to you? Guess you'll be here the rest of your life," she added.

But we both knew I shouldn't get excited about my next birthday.

"Juan?" I asked. She shrugged her shoulders.

I went back to the sheep shed and did the chores. I smoked a couple of joints, but my heart beat like a trip-hammer as I tried desperately to think of a way out. Fear took up permanent residence and crowded out any logic I might have had.

Late that afternoon, I was bringing in the sheep and I saw Lupe walking up the trail with a big basket. They got served supper up there, but for sure, I wasn't getting any—she didn't come back.

I went to bed and pulled those thin, pitiful blankets over me. They were damp and smelled bad, but hell, so did I. It seemed that I lay awake for hours and couldn't sleep—just lay there, trying to keep warm, waiting, but waiting for what?

The door opened and suddenly she was shaking the bed hard enough to loosen the hardware. I climbed down and she grabbed me by the shoulders and shook me.

"Now you listen—listen good. I can say this only once. Ollie is dead. When that truck comes down in the morning, you let Carlos see you loading those sheep. Juan will help you. When Carlos gets ready to leave, I'll call him in the cabin and you get in that truck, lie down up against the cab and get yourself covered with hay. Juan will help cover you real good. Carlos will kill you if he sees you there. When he gets to Concord, he'll stop at the Submarine to phone. That's when you gotta get out of there, some way. It's your only chance or you're dead."

She hugged me and rushed out into the night.

I was hanging on to the bunk, in my shorts and undershirt, shaking with cold and fear when Juan burst in, carrying a lantern. Even in the dim light I could see he was scared to death. He handed me my pants and shirt and pushed my jacket at me, uttering something in Spanish. I caught the name "Ollie" a couple of times and heard the frantic urgency in his voice.

I followed him, shaking with fear, up the forbidden trail. It was so dark, just the ghostly sliver of a moon.

The big trees crowded over the trail—it seemed like a tunnel with no end. I tried to talk to Juan, but he shook his head and walked faster.

The trees thinned, and then a clearing. The only thing I could see, barely outlined by the feeble light of the lantern, was the big tent and Carlos leaning against it, smoking a cigarette.

The night seemed to close around the four of us. Carlos, Juan, Ollie and myself.

Ollie lay on his back, his eyes open in an obscene stare. His mouth stuffed with a bloody piece of flesh that hung from the corner of his lip, his arms outflung, his head tilted to reveal the slash that had nearly severed it from his body. He seemed to be floating in blood.

The light of the lantern wavered over the legs, once white as the underbelly of a fish, now blood-splotched and splayed wide, his pants tangled around one twisted ankle.

Looking down in horror, my stomach revolted and I fell to my knees, puking until it seemed I'd turned inside out. I felt someone nudge me with a foot, then heard Juan's Spanish words, his voice low and urgent.

He helped me to my feet and handed me two shovels. Carrying the lantern as he held my arm, we walked back into those dark trees.

Not daring to look back, I could hear the sound of Ollie's heavy body being dragged. My knees buckled every few steps, but when I faltered, Juan jerked me along.

The image of Ollie's mutilated body was frozen in my mind and over it, all the sure knowledge that Carlos planned to leave me there, too. I prayed as I never prayed before—or after. As I stumbled along, Juan kept me upright.

The trees were silhouetted against the faint light of the flickering lantern. Only the rustle of our footsteps, the sound of Ollie's body as it bumped over the brush and fallen branches, and Carlos' muttered curses could be heard. I felt as though we were in a black, endless maze with no way out.

Carlos called to Juan and we stopped. He took the lantern from his son and walked ahead. We stood in total darkness. Sensing Ollie on the ground behind us, I prayed his dead eyes could not see in the dark.

Carlos returned with the lantern and pointed ahead as he led us to a cleared space. He drew a small track with the toe of his boot—about three by seven feet, then took a shovel from me, handed it to Juan and said, "Dig."

The leaves and rains of the past years had left the soil soft, so our shovels sank deep. As I plunged the sharp tool into the ground, cold sweat soaked my entire body.

The muted thud of the dirt as it was thrown on an ever-growing pile was the only sound I heard other than the soft, satisfied grunt as Carlos dragged Ollie close to his final resting place.

The hole was about three feet deep when he rolled the body in with a quick and powerful thrust of his boot.

Leaning weakly on the shovel, I watched Carlos as he opened his pants and pissed on the length of the dead man. I looked into the unholy glitter of those fathomless black eyes as he held mine captive. The echo of his diabolical laughter will never leave my memory.

Standing paralyzed as he walked around the hole, Carlos took the shovel from my nerveless hands. Then I knew he planned for Juan to cover me, too.

Like a shadow, Juan seemed to materialize out of the dark to stand in front of me. I felt him tremble against my body. His father cursed and I felt his hand as he grasped Juan's shoulder. Juan, legs apart, braced himself and stood firm. Then Carlos laughed and stepped back, talking to himself in Spanish. I caught the word *"cojones"* a couple of times and knew he wasn't referring to mine.

Carlos handed the shovel back to me. "Another time, señor."

The first shovelful of dirt spattered across Ollie's face, causing the head to move. Those eyes, it seemed, were fixed directly on me. I screamed, but no sound came out of my open mouth. Closing my eyes as I threw in more dirt, his head was covered when I dared to look again.

It didn't take long to fill that hole. Once, Ollie was a big man.

We shoveled until it was a heaping mound, then Carlos took the shovel and scattered the extra dirt away. He kicked some leaves and tossed some branches over the fresh dirt, and it was as if Ollie had never been.

I had no idea what time it was, but the moon was gone, so I thought it must soon be daylight.

Juan and I passed the truck on the way down; Carlos followed, carrying something. I heard the tailgate go down—apparently he was still loading.

We walked wordlessly, the lantern swinging between us. Juan kicked the bunkhouse door open and we both collapsed on the nearest bunk. I put my fist in my mouth to stifle the sobs that seemed to have gained access to my body through the soles of my feet. Juan put his arm around my shoulder and talked softly to me in Spanish. I had no idea what he was saying, but the gesture said it all.

Awhile later I took the lantern, snuck past the barn and kicked around in one corner of the manure pile until my boot connected with the Folgers Coffee can. I pried the lid off and stuffed the five plastic Baggies in the lining of my jacket, then tossed the can. Streaks of pink were starting to show in the east, so I blew the light out and ran back to the bunkhouse.

Juan hadn't moved; he was asleep, leaning against the headboard. I heard the sound of the truck pull up to the loading chute and the impatient sound of the horn woke Juan. He jumped to his feet and, as we faced each other, he put his hand out as he had the first day I was there. Pushing it away, I wrapped my arms tightly around his skinny waist and hugged him so hard he grunted. And so we stood, for one long moment.

We went out to load the sheep and both our cheeks were wet.

Carlos was checking under the hood and never looked our way until we had loaded the last of the hay. Then he came back to inspect. He frowned, so we threw in two more big bales and scattered them really deep behind the cab. Those ewes were going first-class; I was going baggage, but I didn't care how I traveled, just so I did.

I saw lights at the cabin and I prayed Lupe was making coffee.

Carlos was still tinkering under the hood as Juan and I crowded twelve reluctant ewes into the deep hay, closed the tailgate and secured the sheep door for Carlos' last inspection.

Above the noisy, milling sheep, I heard Lupe's call. Carlos waved good-bye to her, then got in the truck and started the motor. I knew it was too late. Too late—there was no way.

My knees buckled. Closing my eyes as everything got dark, I slumped against the chute.

From somewhere I could hear my mother's voice, "Oh, Stevie. Stevie, try." I opened my eyes to see Lupe standing on the path waving the coffeepot. Carlos left the motor running as he walked with long strides up to the cabin.

Juan had the tailgate open in an instant and I wriggled like a snake under the hay until I reached the back of the cab. Juan dumped another load of hay over me. How wonderful it felt to be buried deep beneath all that hay with those sheep milling around on top of me.

I burrowed right to the floorboards. I couldn't have dug any deeper or faster if I had been digging at heaven's gate.

I heard Carlos check the back of the truck, then slam the cab door. I felt the truck go into gear.

Juan and Lupe both called good-bye and I knew they called to me.

I didn't know or care where I was going to end up, but I knew hell couldn't be any worse than here.

As the truck jolted up and down over the potholes, I started to breathe again. I lay there shaking, every muscle drawn tight with the terrible fear that had blocked my senses when I thought I wasn't going to make it—my entire being pushed to the limit. I hadn't slept since Friday night. I tried to block out the events of that hellish night, but every time I closed my eyes, Ollie's face appeared and the sound of the dirt as it was thrown on his body echoed in my ears.

Thinking about my mother, it sounded as though she was standing beside me teasing, "You know, the cord has never been cut...it would stretch around the world." And now I realized she hadn't been teasing; she spoke the truth.

I would have given anything to be back in her warm kitchen sitting with Sis at that old chrome table. I could hear her saying, "Stevie, eat. Those leftovers won't kill you—eat." Then, plain as day, Sis would tattle, "Ma, Ma, look. Stevie's feeding his broccoli to the dog."

The sheep had tired of standing. I could feel them getting comfortable in the deep hay. One old ewe settled herself directly on top of me as I fought for another air passage. I couldn't complain; for the first time in months, I was warm—cramped, unable to move, but alive and warm. I thought of Ollie's words to me: "You love them sheep, kid?" Now I could answer with unhesitating honesty: "Oh yes, yes. I love them sheep." But Ollie didn't care anymore.

Gradually my heart slowed, but then my mind leaped ahead. What was going to happen when Carlos stopped to phone?

He slowed the truck. I could hear the sound of other cars so I knew we were passing through Angels Camp. Lupe had said it was about two hours to the truck stop in Concord from Angels Camp.

That meant that in a very short time, my future—or non-future— would be decided. I started to sweat. My mind started to rationalize... a truck stop early in the morning, probably lots of truckers having an early breakfast...should be some place to hide if I could escape this pickup unseen. Please God, let there be some place to hide.

The traffic noise increased and we were stopping at signals. We were getting close; my chance was coming up fast.

The truck slowed and turned sharply. Above the sound of traffic, I could hear the hum of voices, then the sudden quiet of the truck.

The old ewe scrambled to her feet. Her parting gift was a deluge of warm piss that trickled through the hay and soaked me to the skin. A random, fleeting thought: Yes, I still love you.

I waited for Carlos to get out. When I heard the door close, I started to dig out frantically. As my head cleared the hay, I looked out a crack in the side and saw he'd parked next to a big semi, the motor still running. Watching him walk toward the phone booth, my view was suddenly blocked by a car that parked on the opposite side.

Hurriedly, I plowed through the confused sheep. I heard the door to the phone booth close and I vaulted over the side and fell to my knees. I had been so cramped for at least four-and-a-half hours that I couldn't feel my feet. I crawled on my hands and knees to the big semi and hid behind one of the huge wheels. I barely noticed the odor of the exhaust; it was no competition for the stench of me. Wet, filthy, hay all over me—how in hell was I going to catch a ride out of this place? I knew Carlos' conversation would be quick. My mind was racing—where to turn? Then I heard the door of the car opening and a woman's peevish voice, "Hurry up. I'm going to piss myself. I've waited for the last hundred miles."

"Well, slide over...," a man answered. "There it is—go for it. Don't be so damned bitchy. I'm gonna get a cup of coffee. I'll pick one up for you, too, if you're dry." He laughed. The door slammed as they walked away.

Creeping around the pickup, I opened their back door only to find the back filled to the ceiling with everything imaginable—suitcases, a violin case shoved between two huge plastic bags bulging with laundry, folding chairs, a crumpled camp cot stuffed tightly against a half-folded tent and, riding high above it all, a Coleman stove.

I struggled to the floor and pulled down everything I could reach to cover me. I thought, I've survived beneath twelve sheep and half a ton of hay—this should be easy.

When the couple returned, all that was evident was a little hay that had managed to detach from my wet clothing and fallen to the asphalt. I involuntarily held my breath and squeezed my eyes shut—if I couldn't see them, they couldn't see me.

"Great grief—something stinks to high heaven," he exclaimed as he opened the car door.

"It's those animals in that awful old truck," she answered. "Let's go—where's my coffee?"

"Here—don't spill it all over," he answered and closed the door.

Hearing the pickup start and the final "baa" of that old ewe fade into the distance, I knew I was safe. Tears rolled uncontrollably down my grimy cheeks.

I lay there limp as a rag doll holding my breath, willing it not to explode. My long legs were pulled up; one arm seemed permanently locked in place to protect my face; my other arm was numb.

Every time the driver put on the brakes or hit a bump, the debris above settled a little lower. Unbearably cramped, I prayed they would soon reach their destination—I didn't care where it was.

The couple bickered constantly.

She whined, "I am so tired of them antiwar Vietnam protesters—them damn freedom marchers. Why don't they stay home?"

"You sure as hell ain't very patriotic. Almost half a million American men in that godforsaken jungle and rice paddies, over a hundred thousand killed or wounded—doesn't any of that mean anything to you?"

"That's on the other side of the world. You four-effers ought to be glad instead of wavin' the flag. I'm livin' today—right now. I love that 'turn on, tune in, drop out' sayin'. Hell, I been trippin' out and tunin' in for years. I was a hippie before there were hippies. How can any-body not love Janis Joplin or the Grateful Dead?"

He laughed. "Personally, I like Spade Cooley or Bob Wills and the Texas Playboys." Then added, "Uh-oh, we're awful low on gas."

She didn't seem to hear him, but my heart sure missed a beat. "Please, God, please," I groaned.

"My sis says livin' in a commune in a big mansion in the Haight-Ashbury is the only way to go. Free concerts, free dope, free love—all right there in Golden Gate Park. That's for me. A big love-in next week, at least thirty thousand people expected. I can't wait.

"Oh my gawd, look at that gas gauge." Her voice hit a high C. "Damn you. Don't you dare let us run out of gas."

"We wouldn't be worrying about gas or money if you hadn't insisted on a motel every night. You might miss that big love-in if we hitch-hiked. We'll get there when we get there."

"One night in that damn tent was one night too many. How in hell did you think a Coleman stove would keep us from freezing in March—and how was I so stupid to believe you? You great outdoors-man, you! I nearly froze my ass off keepin' that Coleman heater warm and cookin' over a campfire. I ain't no pioneer," she bitched.

"I've got you all the way from Maryland, haven't I? Almost a week listening to you. Damn, it will be so good to deliver you to your sister."

Suddenly she shrieked, "Turn. Turn. You're in the wrong lane—the San Francisco exit is over there."

The tires screeched and the car swerved violently. With a bang, the Coleman stove hit the back of the front seat and the tent settled around me like a shroud. I begged for breath.

Judging from the sound of the grinding brakes and wildly honk-ing horns, we must have crossed at least four lanes of traffic. Even buried as I was, I could hear the cursing drivers as they maneuvered around us.

Am I going to survive Carlos only to die in this shit-filled backseat with these maniacs? I thought.

Then his trembling voice found its way out. "You damn near got us killed. Roll us a joint."

"You're shakin' so bad you probably won't be able to hold it," she answered.

"Try me."

The secondhand smoke drifted back and even relaxed me. But the quiet didn't last long.

I could feel her bounce up and down on the seat. I guessed she'd seen the skyline and was almost hysterical.

"The sun shining through the mist," she said, "makes the city look as though it just dropped out of the sky and floated down."

He must have been impressed, too. "You're right—for once. This is a beautiful city. I've never seen such houses—and so big, built right on the hilltops, too. Never dreamed I'd ever see the famous Golden Gate Bridge. Maryland is a world away."

"Thank God," she answered. "Where is that map? We want eleven-hundred Haight Street. My sis said it's about four blocks from Ashbury."

"Will you look at those mansions? Those hippies are living high on the hog if they've got a commune in this neighborhood. Look..."

"Pay attention to your driving," she snapped. "You almost killed us once."

"Yeah? Who screamed 'turn'?" He then interrupted himself to say, "This is Ashbury Street." A few minutes later: "Haight Street—what number again?"

"Stop, stop. That's it—there on the left. Look, there's people dancin' on the porch..."

The car screeched to a stop. She leaned over and the horn sounded—seven short bursts.

I recognized that old sound: "Shave and a haircut, two bits."

"Are you crazy?" he demanded. "Maybe this isn't even the right address."

The car door slammed and I could hear her heels hitting the sidewalk. His door opened and the instant it closed, I was digging out. Finally I was on my feet—the first time I'd stood erect since Juan had pushed me into the pickup. I leaned back against the open door, feeling the sensation slowly flow back in my body. It stung so bad, my knees trembled.

I saw him start up the walk toward the people on the porch, and I staggered away from the door.

Some people were dancing, some singing; obviously, it was a party. I could see, and plainly hear, two hysterical women hugging and talking, then doing it all over again.

I got my legs under me and started up the walk behind the driver. Thinking that if everything is free and everybody loves everybody, maybe I can get a bath and a free meal.

Nearing the bottom steps, the music slacked off and the conversation quieted. I felt like a bug on a pin. I knew what I must look like with those ratty jeans I'd worn most of nine months, one filthy old shirt pulled over another one even worse, socks with my bare heels showing and shitty boots. The only decent thing I had was the jacket my Ma had given me, with the inside lining packed with five Baggies of pure Mary Jane, and the thirty-eight dollars I had lifted off my stepfather still hiding in a seam. My hair was long and stringy—the dirt had taken the curl right out of it. For that I was thankful. And how I smelled—sheep piss, manure of many days' accumulation, months of only cold showers with no soap. And wrapping around it all, the cold, clammy sweat of fear that clung to me like skin.

I stopped when the driver turned and said, "Where in hell did you come from? I could smell you before I saw you."

"From the backseat of your car," I answered, "and it sure as hell doesn't smell much better."

"Damn you, I'll have to pay someone to tow it away. When and how did you get in there? I ought to take a swing at you," he said.

"Better not, I'm in kind of a touchy mood," I answered.

Someone, some guy, came down from the porch, a guitar slung over his shoulder, and laughed. "C'mon, pilgrim, you sure can use a bath. Where're you from?"

"I just got off a mountain ranch in Calaveras County, and a bath would be a dream come true."

The crowd parted, then continued the festivities as we walked through a ten-foot doorway into an entry hung with oil paintings of old people—probably the founding fathers.

"Take off those dirty boots," he said. "These are Persian carpets and my mother is fussy. She and Dad are wintering in the Bahamas this year."

I stumbled along beside him up the stairs, then down a long hall-way separating the bedrooms. As we passed, I could see mattresses, bedrolls, blankets on the floor, as well as ornate furniture pushed up against the walls.

He turned into a bathroom that was bigger than Ma's entire house. I could only stand and stare at the big bars of pretty soap, the marble bathtub that would have accommodated an entire family.

He turned on the water and as the tub filled, I stripped. That didn't take long. He fumbled around in a drawer and found a toothbrush. "I'll be back with some towels and clothes. I'll burn these," he added, lifting my clothes with two fingers and stuffing them in a basket. Then he tossed me a brush with a long handle. "Enjoy," he said, closing the door.

I sank deep into that heavenly hot water. Only my nose escaped. Suddenly I realized he'd taken my jacket, too—my Ma's Christmas present. "And my stash—my stash," I groaned.

I leaped from the tub, the force splashing water over the walls and floor, and rushed after him stark naked, yelling, "Wait, wait—my jacket. I want my jacket."

There were people in every room, but the crowd pushed to make a path in the hallway for this crazy, naked man screaming for a jacket, on a dead run for a fellow in front of him carrying a basket with a guitar bouncing on his back. Sensing my imminent approach, the guy dropped the jacket; I caught it before it hit the floor.

I heard some other guy laugh and say, "That cowboy sure knows how to make an entrance."

A girl added, "Yes, he presents himself very well—very well indeed. I intend to look him up when he's clean."

I rolled up that jacket as tight as I could and wedged it between the commode and the wall. It had been in worse places.

I lay in that tub until my skin was so wrinkled I was embarrassed to look at myself. Although I did notice muscles I hadn't had before—guess digging postholes in the frozen ground hadn't been all bad. Now that I had scrubbed my hair until I had almost exposed my scalp, it was blond and curly again, and I had a healthy growth of stubble on my chin. I thought I had probably taken a couple layers of enamel off my teeth with that toothbrush.

Half asleep in the warm water that at last was draining clear, I was startled awake by the appearance of a girl in the open doorway—I guess they don't knock in San Francisco—carrying towels and some clothes. She tossed them on a chair and said, "C'mon down—we've got a big pot of spaghetti and Digger bread that the Diggers sent over. They bake their bread in coffee cans."

"Diggers?" I said curiously.

She hesitated in the doorway. "Oh, they're an organization that doesn't believe in buying and selling. They provide free food, clothing, a place to crash for people who need it, and even medical help. A fix, too, if you need it bad enough."

"Wait a minute and I'll come with you. Turn your back."

She giggled. "Too late for that. I saw it all in the hallway," she informed, laughing all the way down the stairs.

The huge smoke-filled room was filled with a moving sea of noisy people, and with wonderful aromas of fresh bread and hot spaghetti.

I filled my paper plate to the ultimate capacity, then piled half a loaf of bread on top of that. Looking for a place to sit, I spied my benefactor against a wall with his guitar and an empty plate in front of him, a roach smoldering in a saucer. He motioned me over.

"Sit, Cowboy. You sure smell a lot better." He grinned. "You really gave me a scare."

He played a few chords as I ate ravenously. People milled around and sang along, and traded pills of every color.

"This must be heaven," I said.

"No, this is San Francisco, man, home of the flower children." He sang, "If you're going to San Francisco, be sure to wear some flowers in your hair...You're going to meet some gentle people there...

"Turn on, tune in, drop out. Here—have a drag."

When my plate was clean for the second time, I looked up. Beads, flowers, feathers, long hair and beards seemed to predominate—I seemed to fit right in with my donated tie-dye shirt and bell-bottoms.

I hadn't slept since Thursday night and this was Saturday. I was warm, clean and so full of food, I fought to stay awake, but it was a losing battle.

"Hey man," I said, "where can I sleep?"

But as I got to my feet, I saw that he was already asleep with his guitar resting upside-down on the empty plates. I made it up the stairs and turned into the first bedroom I came to. There were several couples there in various forms of relaxation. One of them pointed to a mattress with a blanket in a corner and I stepped over and around some people, then collapsed on top of it. Hazy thoughts blew through my mind, just as my eyes closed. Did last night really happen? Did I really shovel dirt over a murdered man? Too much weed, I had to be hallucinating—never happened. And I slept.

Then I could smell that kerosene lantern. I looked up into those bulging eyes and twisted away to hide from that accusing stare and from the blood that dripped down on my face.

His voice sounded clear, the bloody gash in his throat quivering when he asked, "You love them sheep yet, kid?" Someone was screaming as I frantically threw shovelful after shovelful of that wet, black dirt and heard the soft thud as it covered his face. But his eyes never left mine.

I fought, but my arms and legs seemed immovable. As I faded back into reality, the last words I heard were, "Another time, señor." Carlos' mocking promise.

My roommates released me and went back to bed, muttering, "Where'd he score the acid? Someone ought to be with him when he trips."

My throat was raw from my own screams and I was wet with the clammy fear that only let me doze in and out of sleep for many nights to come. I wanted to go home. I wanted Ma and Sis.

CHAPTER 6

Carlos turned and drove through the rolling countryside in a neighborhood made up of white fences, elaborate barns and discreetly placed houses. The hills were dotted with sleek horses that would never have known anything but the best.

The shabby, smelly truck was buzzed through the iron gate that proclaimed the property to be a thoroughbred breeding and training facility. He pulled up to a large house that sat sequestered amid a grove of eucalyptus trees.

Before the engine stopped, large double doors were flung open and several well-dressed men strode out and deferentially, almost reverently, opened his door, enveloping him with a boisterous welcome.

The keys were tossed to a grinning workman who drove the truck into the wide aisle of a barn and parked it beside a spotless Mercedes and an equally gleaming Bentley. The tall doors rolled and closed quietly on half a million dollars' worth of grass stained with Ollie's blood.

The man who sat at the head of the table that evening was not the same man who had driven in. This man, his huge frame draped in an expensive suit, who lifted a glass of vintage wine in toast, was a far cry from the barbaric-appearing man who had arrived only this morning. But under that fine linen shirt beat the same heart.

His eyes widened, but only slightly, at the appearance of several young women, exquisitely gowned, who appeared from nowhere. None were seated until Carlos made his choice.

The festivities lasted through the night and into the next day, but on the third day, it was all business. The women, with one exception, had been sent back to the city.

The men, sequestered around a long table, were interrupted only by the appearance of food.

Plans were being made to enlarge the operation.

"I'll need at least two men to start the new field—and double the supplies. Now let your barn help enjoy the mutton."

When the truck appeared as if by magic, it was fully loaded with extra supplies and two young Mexican men.

"I'll be back soon—I liked the accommodations," Carlos said as he closed the door.

The truck pulled away and the woman waved indifferently, pulling her fur coat tightly about her. Two men in the back clutched the tarp tightly to keep themselves and the supplies out of the wind.

The windshield wipers worked furiously as the heavily loaded truck moved toward the Calaveras Mountains.

She lay asleep, her legs curled under her, her head on Carlos' thigh, his hand caressing through the long, auburn hair, then sliding about in the luxuriant fur.

The two men, wet and cold, huddled beneath the tarp that struggled to free itself from the desperate clutch of their hands, cursed the gringos, the driver, the rain and prayed for their destination to appear.

The younger Mexican spoke through chattering teeth, "I'd sooner swim the river."

"Not me, at least nobody's shooting at us."

At the ranch, Lupe agonized. What if? What if? What if Steve had been discovered? Her life would be on the line. Juan would probably get off with a beating. All too well, she knew Carlos' murderous temper.

She watched the pickup bounce up the driveway and stop at the bunkhouse, surprised to see strange men unloading supplies. *Why there?* she wondered.

Carlos was carrying something up the walkway. After pushing the door open, he stepped in and kicked it shut as he released his hold on the woman in his arms. She swayed against him, her coat slid to the floor in a soft heap around the high-heeled shoes. She smiled vacantly at Lupe.

Carlos steered her to the bedroom where she collapsed on the bed with the same vacant smile. He covered her with the coat.

Fear and rage made Lupe's voice tremble as she demanded, "Who is this woman? Why is she here?"

With a smile, Carlos answered, "She is my woman, my cook."

A fleeting memory of a time she had been all Carlos had ever needed forced the words, "Since when haven't I been your woman, your cook?"

"Since Ollie." He sneered. "You go down to the bunkhouse and cook for those new men. Help the gringo with the sheep. It gets chilly down there—take a blanket."

"Carlos, are you crazy? You know I won't sleep in the bunkhouse. I won't go—and to hell with the sheep."

His eyes glittered. "You? You'll tell *me* what you'll do?" His voice was hardly above a whisper. He stepped closer and held her by the arm with one hand; a finger of the other traced a line below her chin from ear to ear.

He dropped her arms and hissed, "Get out."

Two days later, the rain still fell, washing away the dirt that covered the roots of the hillside brush and causing streams of water to cascade down the steep slopes of the canyon. When the downpour paused momentarily, the men rushed up the eroded path to the safety of the tent.

Carlos watched through the rain-streaked window, but turned when he smelled the scorched eggs, heard the sizzle of the coffee as it boiled over.

The woman slumped at the table, barefoot, seemingly unaware of the cold. Her carelessly tied satin robe revealed the naked body beneath. Her mouth was slack, her blue-green eyes nearly closed, and her long auburn hair hung uncombed. The beautifully manicured fingers fumbled with a syringe.

Carlos cursed, then laughed as he scooped her up as effortlessly as though she were a child and tossed her on the rumpled bed. The ivory-skinned gringa lay like a silken doll—her long-lashed eyes were always half-closed in a dream sleep where he could not intrude. She was always available, accepting, but detached from his reality, rousing herself from her golden sleep only to relocate the position of the needle, then to retreat again to her world.

Better she and her heroin go back to the city, Carlos thought as he watched her insert the syringe between her painted toes, then close her eyes and turn her back to him and his world.

He felt rather than heard the door open and turned to see Lupe on the threshold. A blanket flung around her shoulders, her hair wet and clinging to her face, a long, ugly scratch showing red against her cheek.

"I told you not to come back," Carlos growled.

"Carlos," she pleaded. "I can't stay down there. I can't work with those sheep. I'm terrified of that old ram—someday he'll come through that fence at me—and the gringo is gone.

"I struggled with one of those strange men all night, but I can't stop him. He's so brutal—look at my face."

"Pretend it's Ollie." Carlos grinned.

"What I've done, I've done for you," she answered.

He gave a short, ugly laugh.

Desperation overriding her fear, she spoke through clenched teeth, "You murdering son of a bitch."

"Be careful, woman, you're a long way from home. Go back to your bunkhouse. Treat that man like you treated Ollie and maybe he won't hurt you." He laughed. "You might even break in Juan—he's old enough to need a woman. He'll be seventeen soon—almost a man now."

"A man?" She smiled. "Are you blind? That pretty one, a man?" she asked with derision in her voice.

Unwittingly, Carlos had given her the only weapon that could hurt him.

"No woman will ever seduce him. He'll never give you a grandson. Everyone has seen it but you. Are you afraid to take your blinders off? Ask him how he helped his gringo escape and in your truck," she goaded, knowing she had drawn blood.

His face remained totally impassive. He turned his head so the anguish in his eyes would not betray him, the anguish that flooded through his body with every breath he drew.

Her words finalized in his mind what he had known in his heart, the intuition he had denied for so long.

She sensed her advantage like an animal that smelled blood.

"You've been gone a long time—there are powerful men who have kept this organization going for you. What will your compadres think of their great El Jefe when your son wants to play house with their manly sons? How much respect will you get then? They will laugh at you behind your back—at their El Jefe whose son is *maricón*. I will have it better in the bunkhouse."

He stood, his back to her, bent like a great gut-shot animal, devastated by her mocking words.

Turning at last, he spoke slowly and with deliberation. "You've made it very clear what I must do. I promise you that man will never bother you again and that ram is a threat that needs to die."

He walked to the gun cabinet, chose a thirty-eight revolver, snapped the cylinder out, spun it and saw that it was loaded, then placed it in his waistband. It felt good riding against his belly.

Lupe walked ahead of him, gloating to herself. "I'll be out of that bunkhouse tonight." She pulled the blanket closer and wiped her face with one corner as she lengthened her steps to keep up with his long strides.

As they neared the fence, the big ram charged.

"Shoot. Shoot," Lupe screamed as she turned to face Carlos and looked directly into the deadly black eye of the thirty-eight. As the unaccustomed sound of the gunshot scattered the sheep, the smell of gunpowder hung in the air. Almost carelessly, he dropped her limp body into a nearby wheelbarrow and moved it behind the cabin.

The men came down from work late that afternoon. The remnants of breakfast and the empty coffeepot greeted them as they opened the door to a cold, damp bunkhouse. Juan ignited the heater and looked for the can opener.

Later that evening, Carlos lit the lantern and the wheelbarrow was pushed up the muddy path without the dinner basket Lupe had carried the last time she'd gone up there.

Carlos dug steadily, the dim light of the lantern making ghostly shadows as it moved with each push of the wind.

He hunched his massive shoulders against the driving rain as the hole grew deeper, and at last he was satisfied. He lifted her as though she were weightless and dropped the body in the muddy pit.

He looked down at her and wiped from his face the rain that dripped around the brim of his hat.

"You laid with him in life," he said with a grim smile. "Now lay with him in hell."

At daylight Juan headed out to feed the sheep. The sun broke through the clouds and a glancing ray of light glinted on an earring held fast in a congealed splatter of blood on the floor of the wheelbarrow.

He shuddered, now knowing where Lupe slept.

The tight fist in Juan's gut tensed as he sensed the presence of his father before the tall shadow fell before him.

Silently, Carlos leaned against the baled hay, lit a cigarette and watched his tall, slender son fork hay to the noisy sheep—his son who had the refined, beautiful face of the gringa woman who had born him. The large, dark eyes; the softly curved lips, the same elegant bearing. The hands that held the pitchfork with long, graceful fingers were the hands of his mother.

I loved her with every breath that I took, as I loved him when she laid him in my arms, he thought.

The memory cut like a knife, then the icy chill of revulsion flooded the past.

How could I have sired this—this man with the ways of a woman? For years I knew it wasn't true—not my son, then I thought it's just a passing phase. I knew he would change, outgrow this foolishness as he grew older. His whiskers would mark him as a man...but now I see the truth. I would sooner he be dead.

"Where is the gringo? Your lover?" came Carlos' scathing questions.

"I loved him, but he was not my lover. Now he is safe—you meant to kill him, too."

"Yes, and I am tempted to kill you, you *maricón.*" His frustration and rage struggled with his indecision.

"Yes, you could do that. But I will live in your mind as long as you draw breath."

Carlos stood, as if undecided, facing his son with only his rage and shame existing between them.

"I'll take you and that gringa whore to San Francisco in the morning, and if there is a God, I pray I'll never see either of you again, in this life or in hell," he delivered in his guttural Spanish.

"And I will say amen to that—father." The word "father" conveyed in the same scathing tone as Carlos had used for *"maricón."*

The truck was on the road almost before daylight.

Her coat pulled tight, the woman slouched against Carlos with eyes closed to the world. A small bag, loosely held in slack fingers, fell to the floor. No effort was made to retrieve it.

Juan sat pressed as close to the door as possible, staring out the window at the fleeting landscape. They rode in a strained silence and it seemed to Juan that the trip was endless.

Never had he heard the word *"maricón."* How could he have known the meaning? He had known he was different from others—he had turned in disgust from the ugly, rough talk, the casual references to sex, the unabashed nudity in the cold shower. He had closed his eyes to the blatant antics of Ollie and Lupe.

His father's accusation verbalized a feeling Juan had never consciously acknowledged, but he realized now that the feelings he had for Steve were feelings that he would not—could not—have for a woman.

As a child, he had worshipped his father and his father had returned that love. But it seemed, as he grew older, his father had put a distance between them that he did not understand. He always felt as though his father was watching and waiting. Waiting for what?

What is strange about me? Why am I different? I remember that as I grew older, I was not quite like the other boys.

Juan did not notice when the tears came; he only knew a great sense of loss, a fear of the difference that made him a shame to his father.

He had been so lonely, and then there had been Steve.

The big city seemed to fall on him like an avalanche—constant noise of cars, the thundering herd of humanity, an environment so totally different than anything he'd ever known. He felt his world disappear. Then came the paralyzing fear in the thudding of the heart against his ribs, and the cold sweat that caused his shirt to cling to his back.

Where will I go? What will I do?

Carlos pulled to the curb and Juan turned to look desperately at his father. Carlos, his face emotionless, nodded to the door. As Juan stepped out, Carlos threw a roll of bills to the sidewalk, put the truck in gear and watched in the rearview mirror to see Juan step over the money and walk out of his life.

What Carlos didn't see were the scalding tears that stood in his son's eyes; he didn't feel the wordless agony that Juan felt knowing he was not a man his father wanted to call "son."

The woman awakened and smiled. "Oh, we're here already? Just drop me off at the nearest hotel; I'll call a cab."

Carlos nodded as he stuffed some bills in her bag, then left her at the door of the first hotel he saw.

CHAPTER 7

C arlos turned the pickup toward the Calaveras Mountains and drove steadily, his mind in turmoil, fighting emotions he could not identify. The memory of the defeated, helpless slope of his son's shoulders as he walked into the park seemed to burn in his mind like an ember that would not die.

He stopped only once, at a liquor store, carried out two bottles and unscrewed the cap of one before he started the motor. After a long gulping swallow, he recapped the bottle and let it rest in his lap.

He noticed as he bumped over the potholes of the ranch that the bottle was half empty, but comforted himself with the knowledge that there was one more in the sack.

Now it was late—the never-ending rain had finally ceased. The moon crept across the sky where angry, dark rain clouds had retreated slowly behind the mountain's dark shadows.

It had been a long day, and he lay down on the rumpled bed fully clothed and buried his face in a pillow. He slept uneasily, waking often, and in his dreams Juan's face kept intruding. The stricken look on his son's face when he had flung the word *"maricón"* like a rock denied Carlos the sleep he begged for.

He looked for another bottle—he knew there was one still in the sack under the seat of the truck. He opened the kitchen door to the bright moonlight and stumbled to the pickup. He sprawled back against the seat and held the bottle to his lips, again and again. The crushing knowledge was finally accepted as it pounded through his brain as if by a giant hand—a battle that took no prisoners.

He could hear the sheep so plainly he didn't need to turn the headlights on to see their vague shadows that were scattered about the barnyard.

The deep, menacing bellow of the old ram sounded, answering the call of the undisputed matriarch.

Carlos cursed, knowing that the old ram had torn through the fence at last. He could see the sheep rampaging in and out of the barn and knew that the hay would be scattered everywhere in the morning.

"I should have killed that old bastard a long time ago," he muttered.

He staggered into the house, found his gun and lit the lantern. It would be dark in the barn.

"I'll be chasing those damn sheep all night." Then, "No, I'll get those wetbacks up...."

The light burned brightly in the lantern, unnecessary in the moonlight but essential in the barn, so dark where the moon rays didn't reach.

The snort and angry bawl of the hostile animal sounded near and Carlos' drunken mind reminded him he had better be quick with the gun.

He advanced, swinging the lantern, farther into the barn. Suddenly from the darkness, the ram exploded, knocking Carlos sprawling. As he fell, his head struck a cement pier block that held a pillar supporting the roof. The lantern flung from his outstretched hand, and with the glass chimney broken, kerosene and flame exploded and, in an instant, the dry hay ignited.

The men in the bunkhouse were awakened by the screaming sheep and the outraged bellow of the old ram. They opened the door to the suffocating smoke that coiled into the sky to watch, awestruck, the furious flames that devoured the barn.

At last, the tormented mind of Carlos was stilled.

CHAPTER 8

S tepping over the money, Juan walked away, then paused to look around. The park pulsed with humanity. It seemed choked with young people in wildly colored clothing adorned with feathers, beads, chains; they were singing, dancing...a couple lying on the grass in an intimate embrace caused him to blush as he turned his head.

The curious stares of the passing celebrants made him conscious of his heavy boots, ragged mud-splattered jeans and ill-fitting shirt, partly covered by an old, discarded jacket.

The panic kept building. *Where will I go? What will I do?* He felt the trickle of sweat slide down his back as the terror enveloped him.

He was lost in the avalanche of people in this unknown world. A desperate burst of overpowering fear swept over him and he started to run. He ran until his lungs were begging for breath, his steps slowed to a stagger, and the pavement rose up to meet his pounding feet.

He turned aside to discover a seldom-used path that led to a secluded part of the park. The steady whine of traffic and noisy voices faded into the distance.

The path seemed to end at a thick stand of bushes, a hiding place heavy with pink and white buds about to burst at the first ray of sunshine.

Exhausted, he sank down and lay back, his arms pillowing his head. The body slowly stilled, but his mind refused to be reconciled.

How have I come to this? From my grandmother who loved me—my life in that tiny mountain village. Why wasn't I allowed to play with the other children? Because "You are El Jefe's son."

El Jefe's son. How I waited for my father's visits—how I loved him. And I knew he loved me. When I grew older—thirteen? fourteen?—he came so seldom and would only watch me, not looking me in the face, and I could hear grandmother's pleading voice, his angry responses, my name, often. And all I wanted from him was his love.

Then suddenly from there to that horrible, lonely place, always raining, cold, working from daylight to dark. Me, who had never known physical work, only the love and care of an old woman.

The loneliness—I thought I'd die of loneliness...and then there was Steve. I loved him. I loved him from the moment our hands touched in that first, shy handshake. If that means I am maricón, I'll shout it to the world. I love him.

How wonderful our short time together had been—smoking a little pot, learning from each other the different languages, laughing at our mistakes. I taught Steve to roll a joint and what a cigarette that was— but he was so proud of it.

Juan smiled as he remembered how Steve had pulled the bent nails from the old ram's pen—the ram that Steve said was Ollie's father.

We laughed so hard. Steve was my only happiness. I am so grateful I could help him escape. I would have been glad to have given him my life. I'll love him forever.

Faraway sounds of the tumultuous city seemed to fade as the sun hid behind tall buildings. The same vagabond wind that sifted so carelessly through Carlos' ashes urged a heavy, damp fog ashore that covered the big town, then crept over the park, holding his son in a clammy embrace.

Juan found a more sheltered spot in the rhododendrons and lay down, emotionally and physically exhausted. He tried to get comfortable, but a cold chill seemed to seep into his very bones. He lay awake, his thoughts tormenting him, his body shaking. He slept intermittently to wake at every night sound, then fade back to a sleep that gave him neither rest nor comfort.

The sun awoke him and he lay there unmoving as the same fears that magnified in the night struggled for an answer in the bright rays of the sun.

He forced himself to stand on legs that threatened to betray him, turned his head to see two men approaching slowly, one holding a big dog by the collar.

Instinctively, Juan wanted to run—but where?

The man spoke, "Who do you s'pose that is? He's sure staggerin' around."

"Must be some flower child that got lost—probably stoned. I could use some of that. Might have a couple bucks on him, too," answered the other.

"Hell, don't bother with him. He don't look like he's got a nickel."

"Well, sometimes they hide it in their shoe. Let the dog loose," then added, "Damned if it ain't a spic. Sic the dog on him and I'll bet he'd run all the way to Mexico."

"Maybe he ain't alone..."

"Can't you count? That cheap wine makin' you see double again?"

"C'mon, let's see what he's got. There's one of him, two of us, and I got the brass knuckles."

Juan watched them with a feeling of anxiety as they moved closer.

"Hey, you. What are you doin' down there? Let's see what you got in yer pockets."

Juan didn't comprehend the words or the sudden blow that knocked him almost senseless to the ground, causing an instant flow of blood that spurted from the deep gash that opened from forehead to cheekbone.

CHAPTER 9

Yes, I want to go home—it seems like I've been gone forever. The thought nagged me. I need to see Ma and find out what Sis is up to. All these people, all this noise—I'd rather hear the sheep. I've tried to call home, but the phone is always busy—Sis, no doubt.

I wonder what Juan is doing. How is he ever going to get away? Where would he go? I miss him; he was like a brother. If it weren't for him, I'd be dead.

That damn Ollie. Why doesn't he leave me alone? All I did was help bury him. Okay, I dug his damn postholes—and tended those sheep. Why me?

"Hey, kid. How many postholes today?" And the blood—won't he ever stop bleeding? Will he ever stay dead?

I've gotta get home.

I've scared everybody so badly with my nightmares that they've moved my mattress and blanket to the servants' quarters on the third floor. Now I've got my own private room that has a door with a transom at the top. It's supposed to be a linen closet, but it's bigger than my room at home.

I lay there in the dark, afraid to go to sleep as usual. Even with the dubious aid of downers, I can sense his presence. The moment my eyes are closed, Ollie is there. I hear the words, "Hey, Kid..." bubble out of his mouth and, as his head hovers above me, I squirm away from the blood that always drips from his ravaged throat. The screams that tear from mine bring blood, too.

Somewhere, deep in my core, I know it isn't real and yet, when I fall off into that deep blackness of sleep, he is there, almost as though he waits for me—or I wait for him.

Here I was, screaming and fighting among all those people who only wanted to be happy.

After the fourth night, they zonked me with a rainbow of pills—seems like everyone wanted to donate, then they shut the door. I sank down, down into a place so black that even Ollie couldn't find me, the blanket pulled tightly over my head.

From far away, I heard muffled voices.

"Probably somebody should check Cowboy. He's been out for two nights and this is the third day."

"Maybe he's dead. You open the door."

"I'd be surprised if he wasn't—all those pills."

"Well, something worked. Wish he'd just clear out."

I lay there, semiconscious, listening. Faintly, I heard music, laughter, the door opening.

"Hey, you. Are you ready to join the living?"

My voice was only a croak as I tried to answer. I attempted to sit up, but I seemed unable to even turn my head.

"Let's get some food in him, and a cold shower. He looks like hell. How many of them pills did he get, anyhow?"

"Who knows? I was loaded myself."

"Let's get him in the shower and then drop him at the Diggers'—they'll know what to do with him."

"That's a damn good idea. C'mon, Cowboy, upsy daisy."

They half carried, half dragged me to the bathroom.

"He got the 'tune in' part right, but he's sure screwed up on the 'drop out' part."

"Upsy daisy? Hell, we'll have to lift him into the tub."

I felt the cold water hit me, then slowly cover me to the shoulders. They pulled the plug and I still hadn't moved.

"See if he wants a drink of water."

But I had already gone back to that dark hole.

"This guy sure don't look so good. The cops were just here about that dude that jumped out the window. See if you can find Alfie—he hangs out over at the Diggers when he's not at the hospital. He'll know what to do. I'm scared this cowboy's gonna kiss his horse good-bye. Hurry up."

I lay semiconscious, my uncaring brain wrapped in a thick, gray fog, dimly aware of sounds and movement that filtered through my mind but didn't connect.

"Get some blankets and let's get him out of that tub. He's turning blue."

Then a voice boomed, "What the hell is going on here? What's he doing in a tub? You've overdosed him and now you're trying to drown him? Get some blankets."

I opened my eyes to see a huge, black man bend over, put his hands under my arms and lift me to my feet. I sank to my knees, but he caught me before I hit the tile and rolled me in the blankets that suddenly appeared.

He carried me out as effortlessly as if I was a child, then sat down on the floor and leaned back against the wall, cradling most of me in his arms, rearranging the blankets.

"See if you 'boys,'" his voice pausing for emphasis, "can find some clear consommé, some milk toast—maybe applesauce? See if he can keep it down. He's dehydrated as well as poisoned. What the hell's the matter with you idiots? What's his name?"

"'Cowboy' is all I know."

I drifted. I was sick with measles and Ma was holding me...the warmth of her body penetrated the blankets and it felt so good. I heard Ma's soft voice and felt her gentle shake.

"Open your mouth, Cowboy. C'mon now—you gotta eat. I can't hold you forever. And you gotta keep it down—no pukin' on me. Hear me, Cowboy?"

Another shake. "You can do it—open up."

When Ma said, "Open up," she meant *now*, so I managed to open my lips and felt the spoon slide against my teeth, the fluid flow in my mouth. Instantly, my stomach rebelled.

"I told you, no pukin'." Ma wiped my face and pushed the hair out of my eyes. "Now, let's give it another try."

The next spoonful stayed down and the one after that tasted good. Soon I heard the spoon clink against the empty container.

"Okay, now we'll rest awhile, and then we'll have the entrée," she said. Ma never said that in her life. I didn't know what it meant, either, but it tasted like soft-boiled eggs, all mashed up.

Well, I kept that down and went back to sleep, but not before I heard her say, "You're doin' great, Cowboy. Do that good with dinner and maybe these dudes won't put you back in the tub."

I slept a soft, dreamless sleep, my head on Ma's shoulder as she rocked me back and forth like she did when I was a baby. I heard her hum a pretty tune I'd never heard before.

"For God's sake, Alfie. It's past midnight. Are you gonna sit there all night with him?"

"Nah. I'll stay a little longer and see how he is in the morning. You guys damn near killed him."

The bright sunshine and the soft snore of someone lying close behind me made me realize I was truly awake. I felt an arm beneath my head, the other flung over my shoulder, and became aware of a big, black hand that patted me reassuringly as I had seen Ma do when Sis was a baby.

As I stirred, the arms were retrieved and I turned to see this man sit up, smiling from ear to ear, his hand stuck out.

"Howdy, Cowboy. Have a good night's sleep?"

I reached for his hand and held on, my eyes suddenly blinded with tears. I had the intuitive understanding that he had ridden through my hell with me, and I knew that Ollie was dead.

CHAPTER 10

Faded-gray shingles; the peerless artistry of the gingerbread; ornate cornices; witches' turrets; leaded glass windows. Sheltering all was a steep roof upon which rested five timeworn chimneys, four of which were content to maintain their dignified demeanor. But the one at the front perched at a slant like the jaunty tilt of an old man's high silk hat. One could almost see the gold-tipped walking stick.

The house was built in 1865 by Theodore Hassé, great-grandfather of the woman who now lives there. The elegant Queen Anne Victorian stood outlined against the sky on a ridge three hundred and seventy feet above the level of the sea in a neighborhood that screamed old money, the legacy of luxury.

The Lady stood aloof, partly because of her central location on an immaculately landscaped acre of land, or perhaps because of the ornate wrought-iron fence that displayed the elaborate pattern and attention to detail that declared the artisans' skills of the past century. The recent addition of the long, low greenhouse stood unobtrusively, a blurred kaleidoscope of color faintly seen through the transparent covering.

Floor-to-ceiling leaded glass windows illuminated two floors and reflected the radiance that danced about on the cool blue-green water of San Francisco Bay. In the distance, the Golden Gate Bridge soared seven hundred and forty-six feet into the sky, shimmering through the mist that clung to it like expensive wrapping tissue.

Tall doors opened to a majestic foyer where, in years gone by, some of San Francisco's most elite had entered. A vast drawing room was separated from the lavishly decorated dining room by doors that glided noiselessly into the walls. The renovated kitchen still retained the high glass-enclosed cupboards and the old cookstove. A short hallway led from the kitchen to the cook's quarters.

The winding stairway with intricately carved railing led to the second floor, where five bedrooms, three bathrooms, and a study were located. The study was a beautifully proportioned room. On one richly paneled wall hung the paintings of several well-known artists. A long, low coffee table cluttered with magazines and news-papers, and deep overstuffed chairs stood before the fireplace that claimed most of one wall.

A book was propped open on the window seat as though someone had laid it down to gaze at the bay below. A pair of shoes, kicked off carelessly as if to relieve the owner's tired feet perhaps, lay haphazardly on the thick Persian rug.

It was in this room that Theodore Hassé's great-granddaughter, Theodora, and Sara, her lifetime companion, spent their leisure time.

Teddy's parents were disappointed when she was born. For she was not the pink-and-white dimpled baby that her mother had anticipated, a baby who cried to be cuddled, who looked so adorable in ruffles, or who lay quietly in her crib. Nor was she the son for whom Theodore had so fervently longed.

Looking down at the long-limbed, red-faced baby beating the air with her tiny fists, squalling and kicking her blankets away, he said wistfully, "She looks like a boy—almost." And over his wife's hysterical protests, he said, "I will name her after my father. Her name shall be Theodora."

She was always "Theodora-Catherine" to her mother, "Teddy" to everyone else. Theodora-Catherine, from the beginning, was very different from Teddy.

Her father accepted her difference as "just being Teddy," and stoutly maintained, "She's like my side of the family. All my sisters were big, strong women. My Teddy is a tomboy," he conceded, "but she doesn't need to wear ruffles in the operating room. Look at those hands—only a surgeon has fingers like those," he declared, "and there isn't any reason she shouldn't go into the medical profession as did my father."

Her mother never gave up hope that Theodora-Catherine would tire of this foolishness, get married and have children.

When Teddy was sixteen, her mother died and "Theodora-Catherine" was no more, thus ending the charade.

She and her father continued to live in the big house with the servants who loved the rambunctious Teddy, who was her father's entire life. She became well established in the medical field, and on the front of her office appeared the words, "Theodore Hassé Memorial Building."

Teddy was a striking five-foot, nine-inch woman: erect, slim-hipped, broad-shouldered. Her curly, once-black hair, now nearly silver, still curled around a face dominated by large expressive eyes that seemed always to have a twinkle, but a flat-level look could speak plainly to the fact that she was a woman who would tolerate no nonsense, should the need arise.

Her large, well-shaped hands held a scalpel as easily as a fork.

The strong line of the jaw, the stern curve of the lips, did not claim her to be a beauty, but beyond beauty. She was a presence that did not go unnoticed, and was considered one of the best obstetricians in the city.

CHAPTER 11

The last rays of sun dropped a glittering path across the water of the bay, and big city lights that were beginning to tiptoe scattered the darkening sky.

The woman who entered the study wore a paint-smeared smock and a smidge of blue swiped across her flushed cheek. She was carrying a bottle of wine in one hand, two glasses tinkling together in the other. A small black terrier frisked beside her.

The hair that had been pulled severely back was now struggling to lose the band that secured it.

She stopped abruptly in the doorway as she saw the tall woman who slouched in a chair, her shoes kicked off to the side, feet stretched to the fireplace.

"Teddy. You're home early. I didn't expect you." She looked down at herself. "I haven't even had time to change and I'm having a terrible time with that painting."

"Then who were you expecting? Don't I see two glasses?"

"Don't nitpick. I knew you'd be in some time."

She set the glasses on the table, still holding the wine bottle, and sank into a chair.

"This was supposed to be a surprise. Do you remember what the occasion is?" she asked.

"My birthday? Surely, hopefully, please, please. Don't let it be yours, Sara."

"Does June thirtieth mean anything to you? Don't make me drink this expensive bottle of wine by myself."

"I sense a trap here, but, no..."

"Does June 30, 1948, Carmel, bring back any romantic memories? The key word being 'romantic.'"

Teddy, laughing with delight, stood.

"Bingo. Why do you think I'm home early? Our twentieth anniversary."

She made a great pretense of searching her pockets, but finally shook her head and said regretfully, "Guess not." Pausing a moment, she reached behind her chair to produce a specially made three-foot-long paintbrush with a long, tapered point. A gold band that held a very beautifully cut stone fit perfectly over the top.

Sara dropped the bottle in the chair as she scrambled to her feet and flung her arms around Teddy.

Her voice trembled. "A blood ruby—my very favorite."

"Hold out your hand, my love," Teddy murmured, and disengaged Sara's arm to slip the ring on the third-finger left hand to nudge the diamond and whispered, "I, Theodora, promise to have and to hold, now and forever, Sara Rafferty..."

Tears streaming, Sara stood on tiptoe, her arms around Teddy's neck and added, "What God has put together, let no man put asunder." Then added, "For all these years I've loved you, and they've gone by so quickly. Double those years and it won't be enough."

The little dog pushed between their feet and tugged at the paint-splattered smock.

"Down, Sammy. You are such a bossy little dog. Do you have to be in the center of everything?"

Sara stepped away, wiping her eyes and held her hand to the light.

"Oh, Teddy, it is so beautiful. I've never seen a ruby with such remarkable color. Wherever did you find it?"

"That's a secret. You've put me through such an inquisition, my throat is parched. May I open this wine?"

"Please do. I searched the city for it. You'll remember how we danced the tango the night we discovered that wine in Paris."

"Yes, I'll never forget, nor the morning after, either."

Their glasses clinked together and Teddy spoke quietly. "Be sure to keep in mind, when you say your prayers, to ask for at least another twenty years.'

Her long fingers pushed the hair aside and she kissed Sara's upturned face.

As the level in the bottle diminished, Sara spoke of the painting that would not come together, and Teddy's face glowed as she described the hopeful success of an operation not previously attempted.

Sammy's fierce growl broke the companionable silence that rested momentarily between them as he attacked a dangerous-looking shoelace.

Sara laughed as she lifted Sammy to her lap and Teddy leaned over to scratch behind his ears.

"Sara, you've spoiled this dog worse than a child."

"I know, but he's my child. We've had him how many years now, eight? Nine? Maybe he'll grow out of it. Anyhow, what would you rather deal with—a little dog hair or diapers?"

Later, leaning back in her chair, Sara lay her napkin down and sighed. "This dinner was everything Mrs. Mackey promised. I had her make that chocolate torte just for you, but now I've eaten two helpings and I'm trying to lose weight. I don't mind getting old, but I don't want to be an old fat lady."

Teddy teased, "You're not fat. You may be a wee bit chubby—I'd even say voluptuous—and only fifty-three. That's hardly old, but what can I say about the 'lady.'"

They both broke into laughter.

Sara snickered. "Surely you must know I missed you with that cup on purpose—you brought that on yourself so don't aggravate me. Seriously, I've planned to go to the park early tomorrow to catch the morning light. There's a stand of rhododendrons in first bloom at the far end, and it will be quiet. I can paint in peace. Maybe I can bring this painting together and hopefully the walk will detour that chocolate torte before it reaches my hips. Sammy needs the exercise, too—he loves the park."

"It's bedtime for me, too. I've had a long day and that surgery is scheduled the first thing. Sammy sleeps in his own bed tonight so I can sleep in mine. He snores."

The ruby on Sara's finger shone a thousand lights when it reflected the crystal chandelier as her hand slid along the banister. They walked together up the stairway to their world.

CHAPTER 12

The grass was still wet with dew when Sara parked. Hurriedly, she deposited her paint box on the curb as Sammy barked and scratched at the window.

I'll have to come back for the rest. It's only a few blocks and maybe the extra walk will tire Sammy so he will lead like a good boy, Sara thought.

Holding the indignant, struggling little terrier, she snapped on his leash and, to his intense delight, Sammy found himself on the ground where he could lift his leg on anything that stood upright.

What a beautiful, quiet morning; the soft hum of traffic sounded very far away to Sara.

When they entered the park, the whir of wings arose as startled birds awoke and searched for breakfast; an occasional raucous call of a seagull echoed.

Picking up her paint box and holding the leash tightly to contain the terrier, which pulled and strained to be free, she walked farther into the park. Soon she could plainly see the vibrant pink and white rhodies that stood in thick clusters and seemed to present a barrier between reality and fantasy.

With a sigh of satisfaction, she paused for a moment to enjoy the beauty and relaxed her hold on the rowdy little dog. He jerked free and was off like a shot, trailing his leash, deaf to her calls.

His sensitive ears picked up the sound of some commotion behind the flowering bushes and, pushing through, he rushed furiously at a big dog.

Sara heard the outraged, vicious growls of the big dog, then the terrier's agonized yelps as she ran screaming, "Sammy, Sammy." But Sammy never heard her as the bloody jaws ripped and tore. The mastiff shook him again and again, then flung him lifeless to the ground.

As she broke through the bushes and knelt beside the motionless body of her Sammy, her hysterical screams surprised the kneeling man who stood quickly, threw a shoe aside, and cursed, "Shit, let's get out of here." But he spoke to empty air—the other man and the dog were already only a fading movement in the distance. He turned to run, then turned back to kick Juan with a steel-toed boot. "Damned wetback."

The frantic entreaties of a woman's voice screaming, "Sammy, Sammy," broke through the fog of Juan's consciousness. He groaned as he attempted to rise. He seemed unaware of the blood that spurted from the deep gash from forehead to cheekbone, but it was the stabbing pain with each breath that kept him down.

Suddenly aware of the man who lay groaning on the ground behind her, Sara turned and sobbed, "Help me, please. Help me."

Waves of pain flooded over him as he swayed, dazed and bloodied, to his feet, fighting to maintain consciousness.

Sara kneeling, holding Sammy in her arms, looked up. "Will you help me? Can you walk?" Taking his silence for consent, she said, "Follow me. I'll get the car and meet you."

She stood to place the little dog in the arms that Juan instinctively held out. Her eyes never left Sammy as she said, "Be very careful of him—he's badly hurt."

She ran until she begged for breath, her steps slowed by blinding tears, praying, "Please, God, please don't let him die," then ran again. She fumbled to unlock the car. Her trembling fingers found success after several attempts to open the door.

She drove over the curb, sped across the pristine lawn, the tires leaving deep tracks in the soft grass. As she neared the rhododendron glen, she was surprised to see the man had only gone a few steps.

The car jerked to a stop. Tenderly, she took Sammy's limp body and crooned, "You'll be all right. Teddy will fix you. You'll be your old self, my Sammy."

She motioned for the man to get in and, for the first time, realized he was badly hurt. He stood as if undecided, dazed. She opened the door and he struggled in. She lay Sammy across his lap and, with one hand, Juan cradled the little body.

Sara drove wildly through traffic. With each turn and bump Juan groaned in agony as he drifted in and out of consciousness. She parked at the rear entrance of the professional building. Carrying Sammy, she burst through the door marked "Private." Dr. Teddy was horrified to find Sara almost incoherent, disheveled, her clothing bloodied by the torn little animal in her arms.

One glance told Dr. Teddy that Sammy was beyond help.

"Teddy, Teddy, he's just unconscious. He's lost a lot of blood. I know you can save him. Stitch him up, Teddy, and he will be okay; won't he, Teddy? Hurry, I know you will bring him around. Hurry, hurry, do something," she begged.

Dr. Teddy took the lifeless little body and lay him gently on the table, then turned to put her arms around Sara. "My dear, you must know that Sammy is dead."

"No, no, no. Don't say it. I can't bear it," she cried before collapsing in Teddy's arms, sobbing uncontrollably.

Teddy held her. Slowly, Sara's sobs subsided, but the tears never ceased. A damp cloth wiped her face; the hair was pulled back and fastened with a rubber band. Sammy was wrapped in a towel and placed in Sara's arms.

"We'll go home, my dear. I'll tell Mrs. Burney to reschedule my appointments."

As they approached the car, Teddy saw the figure of a man slumped sideways; blood seemed everywhere. Alarmed, she hesitated, "Sara, who is in your car?"

Sara looked up from the bundle in her arms, bewildered.

"Oh, how could I have forgotten him? He was on the ground and bleeding when I got there. I don't know who he is, but he helped me with Sammy." Then she spoke the obvious, "He's hurt, too."

Teddy opened the door to hear Juan's agonized groans with each labored breath. As she took his pulse, she was sickened when she looked up to see the deep gaping wound in his head and the deter-mined trickle of blood.

She helped Sara into the backseat, then sped to the emergency room at Saint Joseph's Hospital.

Sara waited, smoothing the only part of Sammy that showed above the towel—his whiskered little face, the soft pointy ears. Gently, she closed his eyes and her tears dampened his covering.

It was a quiet that seemed like a damp, cold fog that lay heavy and dark, and that permeated the occupants of the study, despite the cheerful fire.

Sara, her face blotched, her eyes puffed shut, lay in a sedated half-sleep on the sofa, her head resting on her hands, an afghan tucked about her feet.

Sammy, nearby, bathed, wrapped in an old paint smock that he had loved to drag and shake, lay curled around a favorite toy as though asleep. Tomorrow he would own a tiny piece of the tremendously expensive property that boasted the best views in San Francisco.

Teddy, indifferently thumbing through a medical magazine, stood. "I'm going over to the hospital for a little while, Sara. I want to know how that man is doing and if those X-rays show what I suspect. I won't be long."

Sara slept and dreamed that Sammy was chasing butterflies in a field of yellow daisies.

For days, Sara's mood never lightened. Dry-eyed, she wandered about wordlessly, picking up Sammy's toys.

Teddy handed her a well-chewed glove retrieved from between the cushions of the sofa and coaxed, "My dear, come and sit with me."

When Sara sat down, Teddy's arm encircled the unhappy woman and pulled her close.

"Sara, my love, you must get past this and know that Sammy is in a better place—probably wearing St. Peter's robe or stealing his sandals. You know he was never in awe of anything or anybody."

She lifted Sara's tear-stained face, kissed her gently, and said, "I think I need to remind you, opening night at the gallery is only three months away and you've promised them another painting. How much time will you need to finish this one that's giving you so much trouble?"

Wiping her eyes, Sara sat up. "Awhile. I don't care if I ever finish it. The light in my studio is impossible and I'll never go to the park again. Besides, I lost all my best brushes that day and there must be tubes of paint everywhere in the grass."

"Well, that's easy enough to remedy. But I didn't realize the lighting was so poor," Teddy said, then added, "Mrs. Mackey has fixed your favorite foods three days in a row—even a chocolate torte, and you've hardly eaten a bite. She's disappointed, and Mr. Mackey is concerned about the transplants in the greenhouse. The old man worries that he is overwatering. I suspect that he thinks the grounds are all he can handle. You know he's getting old and his bad knee bothers him a lot.

"I'm going to the hospital again tonight. Won't you come with me? The nurse on the night shift is Hispanic and has learned that the young man is seventeen years old and that his name is Juan Miguel. Apparently, he's asked about you and Sammy.

"I had an excellent surgeon stitch up that nasty wound and I doubt if it will even leave a scar. The two broken ribs are another matter. One very nearly punctured a lung. He's heavily sedated; the pain is severe. He'll probably be in the hospital another week."

Sara spoke reluctantly. "Yes, I suppose the least I can do is thank him, although perhaps it should be the other way around—you've probably saved his life. I'll get a jacket—the nights are so chilly."

They walked down the long corridor in the old wing of the huge, sprawling hospital. Sara felt the years slip off her shoulders and, once again, she was a twenty-one-year-old, fun-loving nurse, trim in her white uniform, her long blonde hair tucked under the stiff white cap she had worked so hard for, her green eyes slanting as she smiled.

Juan seemed asleep as they approached his bed. The nurse was adjusting the blankets that could not conceal the heavily bandaged torso; his face was partly hidden by the fabric taped over his cheekbone and forehead.

Sara stared down wide-eyed with a look of surprise.

"Teddy, he's so young. He can't be seventeen. He looks so innocent, so vulnerable, like a little boy."

Her eyes filled with tears. She stretched to touch the thick strand of blue-black hair that lay straight and stark against the pristine white of the pillow.

"His hair is as soft as a girl's," she murmured.

Juan's hand reached up and grasped Sara's fingers. His eyes opened to look for a long moment directly into hers. He spoke brokenly, pleadingly, *"Por favor, señora, no me deje aqui. Lléveme con usted."*

Startled, Sara looked inquiringly at the Hispanic nurse. "What did he say?"

"He said, 'Please don't leave me here. Take me with you.'"

His pleading words flashed back instantly to the moment she had uttered the same desperate entreaty. Frightened, she jerked her hand away and almost ran from the room.

Teddy followed quickly. "My dear, I'm so sorry. I had no idea this visit would upset you so," she said as they hastened down the long hallway.

"We'll go home, have a glass of wine and go to bed early. You'll feel better tomorrow."

Sara didn't respond.

She lay awake, tossing and turning. The begging words echoing her own pleading triggered a scene so many years long buried in the deep recess of her subconscious, but as vivid tonight as though it were yesterday. She curled against the warmth of Teddy's back and fought the memory.

Eventually she slept to dream of the ragged, dirty little girl who sucked her thumb and sat alone with both eyes closed. The dream was so real that she heard the knock, the slurred voice of her uncle say, "It's open," and in her mind she could see his awkward attempts to open a can of beer with one hand and quiet the new baby on his other arm.

The woman who had been her savior stepped through the door and surveyed the squalor of the room: the crying toddler with the obviously soiled diaper, the rampaging, squalling older siblings, unmade beds, dirty dishes—the stench of filth.

"Well, well, well, Miss High-and-Mighty. What brings you to my humble abode? Slumming?"

"You could say that," she spoke over the screaming toddler. "Not that you're interested, but I have just come from the morgue where I identified Emily's body."

Of the harsh, embittered words, the child understood little, but she felt the undisguised anger and despair that floated just beneath the surface.

"Yeah? Please excuse the mess. The missus is at work and I'm stuck here with these damn kids. You'd think she'd never heard of birth control. Every time I hang my pants on the end of the bed, she gets knocked up. Maybe she can't resist a handsome devil like me." He grinned, his rotted teeth bared.

The woman ignored his feeble attempts at humor.

"Where is her child?"

He pointed toward the bureau. "Over there in the corner suckin' her thumb," adding, "I don't s'pose Emmie left us anything for takin' care of her kid. We've had her since before she could walk—goin' on five years."

"What care? She's skin and bones and filthy. Why is she rocking back and forth like that with her eyes closed? Is she blind?"

"Nah. She's a walleyed wonder—and her good eye is green. No wonder Emmie left her. We're tired of feeding an extra kid. Hell, we got six of our own. Why don't you take her? You nurses make good money. Sara," he bellowed, "come over here and see your Aunt Fiona."

Terrified, I crept around the big kids to stand with my eyes closed in front of this strange lady.

The woman stood speechless.

"I never said this walleyed kid was pretty," he blurted defensively.

I felt her hand tremble as she lay it on my shoulder and guided me to her. An indescribable feeling of hope, of belonging, made me tremble, too, as I grasped her fingers with my dirty little hand with one clean, wet thumb. With a voice barely audible above a whisper, I begged, "Please don't leave me. Take me with you. Please, please."

He laughed. "She's an oddball, all right. Just like you."

"Strange you should be so knowledgeable about balls, considering you haven't any," came her acid reply.

"At least I'm not a damn queer like you."

"No, you're just a damn, drunken fool."

She took my hand and, when the door closed behind us, said, "Dear

God, dear God. How did I ever escape that? Poor Emily. She's better off."

Sixteen years later Sara was a well-educated, beautiful young woman who met the world on its own terms. After three operations, the green eyes worked in tandem. Her lashes were tipped with the same gold as her hair. She flirted and danced the nights away with her numerous admirers, but they got no further than a hasty good-night kiss at the door.

Her pitiful yesterday was a memory buried deep beneath the bliss of today.

Then there was Dr. Theodora Hassé.

The next morning, Sara slept in.

As Teddy ate a hasty breakfast, she wished she hadn't encouraged Sara to see that boy. That may have been the reason that Sara tossed and turned most of the night.

Teddy stirred her second cup of coffee and stared off into space, her mind troubled.

Could she really mean her painting days are done? What a vacancy that would leave in her life. A well-known artist of twenty years hangs up her paintbrush? That can't happen. She's got to get started again, put her mind and her talents back to work, Teddy thought.

I never realized she wasn't happy with the light in that studio. She should have a room with windows on three sides—like the witches' turret in the servants' old apartment above the study, that old living room...

That fleeting thought opened the door of Pandora's box, and the ideas flooded out.

Excited, Teddy carried the embryonic plans with her to work and, at every available moment, her mind focused with amazing clarity on the image in her brain.

CHAPTER 13

The stress, poor food, hard work and the ongoing fear of the last few months have taken their toll. And now the last close call with the grim reaper has left me weak and lethargic.

I hid in my linen closet and resisted all efforts at company or to coax me into any activity.

I slept, ate voraciously, and bribed a kid from Idaho to scrounge food for me. The only time I left my nest was to raid the kitchen downstairs or go to the bathroom. With the joints I rolled to perfection, I lulled myself into a state of false complacency to keep at bay the shock treatment of the real world, the ugliness that could exist and flourish—that I had sworn never to think of again.

The partying never seemed to cease. I felt totally indifferent to the screams of laughter, the riotous sounds of conversations and the twanging music of the guitars that slid in under the crack of the door.

One morning, barely daylight, my sanctuary was invaded. The door slammed open and Alfie stomped in. He reached down, yanked the blanket off my near-naked body and yelled, "What the hell are you doing in bed? It's past breakfast time. What's this I hear about you? I saved your sorry ass so you could lay around and do nothing? Get the hell up and let's go have something to eat, a cup of coffee."

He grabbed me by a foot and dragged me out fighting for my security blanket.

"Take a shower. I'm gonna give you ten minutes, then I'm comin' in after you." His voice was only slightly lower than the sound of a locomotive.

I was ashamed that he should see me like this. I was back with no time to spare. I knew he wasn't fooling and I was about half-scared.

Somebody had left a razor out. I ran that over my face and combed my hair with my fingers.

Alfie's voice boomed. "You look like hell. Pasty-faced, pot-bellied. I need some help down at the Diggers with these crazy flower children and I'm gonna expect you down there every day for at least six hours. Got that?"

Over the next couple of months, Alfie kept me moving fast. Everybody needed something. I never adjusted; I was a square peg in a round hole. I felt like I was a hundred years old. These kids—their protests, beads, feathers, tie-dye clothes, and total lack of responsibility and direction—were as noisy and colorful as a flock of chickens.

Everything on the radio was war news. After listening to the latest bulletin, half-stoned, I said, "Where in hell is Saigon? Why are we fighting a war halfway around the world? I'm not mad at anyone."

"To stop the spread of communism, you damned pothead. If you'd leave that weed alone and come to life, you wouldn't be so ignorant. I'm going down to enlist tomorrow. I can always go back to school."

Chastened by his irritated words, I said, "Well, I'll go with you and we'll both be heroes. Besides, I don't want to get drafted."

"You may as well forget it. When they take your blood, they'll find it running green, so don't waste their time."

I went with him anyway. Of course, they wouldn't accept me and I was pissed. Even Alfie was disappointed. He was deferred because he was a medical student with high grades.

"Go home and straighten up your life. Do you think your mother would be proud of you today?"

Shamed by Alfie's scornful question, I stayed clean for a while, then went back to give it another try.

The recruiters *still* found something—even I didn't know what some of those pills were that I occasionally got in a trade.

"Go home," they advised, "and clean up."

I felt a twinge of conscience, so to comfort myself, I said, "To hell with the war," and lit up.

The nagging thought of home never left me. I didn't want to go back with my tail between my legs. And then there was my stepfather. I knew only one of us was going to survive if I ever saw him rough up my Ma again. His beer was never going to make it past the hole in his throat. A lot of water had gone under the bridge this past year of my life.

I moped around. Finally Alfie said, "Why in hell don't you go home? Go back to school, ease up on that damn pot—give your brain a chance. You think you're so much smarter than these crazies, do something with your life. You talk about your mother—make her proud of you. You're what she's traded her life for, so why don't you go home and face that bastard down like a man. You can always kick him in the balls if you're quick."

His big black hand clapped me on the back. "Go home. You're fired; your position is terminated."

I moved my head to hide the sudden tears. When I turned to him, he smiled and what I read in his eyes, made me know I could do it.

I wandered down to the pool and leaned back in a fancy deck chair thinking of Alfie and how he had saved my life twice. Watching a group of skinny-dippers in a pool as big as our backyard at home, I was strangely unmoved by the sight of naked girls; my desire was spent and lifeless.

My mind flashed back to the stocky, brown-skinned woman who

had come to the barn with an egg basket on her arm, the musky smell of her warm body as it warmed mine and pushed against me, her teasing *"guapo, guapo,"* and how fervently I kissed those dark-tipped breasts.

The rosy glow evaporated. An involuntary shudder ran the length of me as I recalled the times she had risked her life for me. I prayed, as I sat in the midst of luxury, safe and warm, that she would get out of her situation some way, somehow, alive.

My eyes closed and I lay back, basking in the sunlight, only vaguely aware of the laughter and shrieks of the skinny-dippers.

Blue smoke curled around me and my mind drifted back to the last face I had seen before the hay covered me, the strained smile like a bad photo on his face as he frantically piled the hay over my prone body and prodded the sheep back. Juan had shielded my body with his to stand terrified and defiant against Carlos' murderous hand. But what was Juan's future? Surely Carlos had better plans for his only son, now imprisoned in that hellhole.

I felt humbled and ashamed to know in my heart that I had been so paralyzed with fear that strangers had done for me what I couldn't do for myself.

I lay there half asleep, my roach pinched off, when I sensed some-one flop down in the chair beside me. I heard him inhale deeply, then ask, "Hey, Cowboy. How about a drag?"

Called back to reality, I opened my eyes to see that dude who'd driven the car in which I'd sneaked a ride.

"Sure, help yourself," I answered and closed my eyes again.

"Damn, Cowboy, you always get the good stuff. Where you scorin' this primo? I think we were smokin' shoelaces last night. I'd give any-thing for a bag of this."

I felt a stirring in my hazy mind. "Yeah? What have you got? What will you give for two bags?"

"All I've got are the clothes on my back, that old Buick you stunk up, and three hundred dollars. That car never used a quart of oil all the way across the country. It was my grandmother's and she hardly ever drove it. It's only got ten thousand miles on it and the rubber's good, too."

"Yeah? Who put the other ninety thousand on it—grandpa? And I saw the rims showing through what rubber there was. I'll bet it would take a crane to lift the oil you've got in it right now."

"Well, if you know so damn much, why did you ask? Might have a few miles on it—long ways from Maryland, you know. Guess I'll go for a dip and show these girls what a real man looks like."

"Wait a minute. Have another drag—might be your last one before they drown you. Tell you what—put new tires on it, add your three hundred bucks, and you've got two bags of something that will make you think you hear the angels singing. You can probably sell some of it and get all your money back. And you're rid of that junk heap. Make your grandma happy, too. This offer is only good for twenty-four hours, dude."

Before the deadline had passed, I had a bill of sale and some other papers tucked away with the remaining green stuff in the Baggies, a 1940 Buick with two new retreads, and a hundred dollars in my pocket.

I went over to the Diggers' tent to find Alfie. I gave him a hug and told him I was going home.

"Damn good idea, Cowboy." He hugged me hard enough to dislocate my shoulder. I offered him a bag, but he gave it back.

"Don't use that shit. I'm goin' to the university studyin' to be a doctor so don't need that shit to mess up my mind. If you're smart, you don't, either."

"Fine. I'll sell it to someone who's gonna be a shoe salesman."

"Do that," he laughed, "but look me up when you need your appendix out."

I had already changed the oil in the Buick and cleaned it inside and out. It sure smelled better—of course, so did I. I know that the angel riding on my shoulder on that fateful day nearly three months ago was grateful. I shuddered, remembering the insane crossing of four lanes of speeding traffic to reach the exit marked "San Francisco."

Now that it was known that Cowboy had the good stuff, I stuffed my three remaining Baggies back in the lining of the jacket and used it as a pillow. I planned to leave right after breakfast, but I couldn't sleep. I was up before daylight.

Everybody was zoned out except for a couple of fellows wandering around in the hall. One asked me if I'd seen his bed go by; the other one said, "Hey, man, are we still in Saint Louis?"

"Yeah, I guess so," I said, and ran down to the kitchen. I drank a cold cup of black coffee, but couldn't bring myself to eat a forlorn roll that looked older than I.

The Buick purred like a Cadillac. Traffic was light as I found my way back to the bridge and got on the freeway for home.

As I pushed the old car as fast as I dared, my thoughts wandered back to the five-acre farm where we had lived most of my seventeen years. All these years in that little faded frame house with one bath—and a privy outside that we used in summer. The house where my grandmother was born, that she had deeded to my mother as a wedding gift in a grandiose effort to impress the well-to-do family Ma was marrying into. Lace-curtain Irish, they were, from a thousand-acre wheat farm in the Midwest. Needless to say, they were unimpressed both with the gift and their son's choice, a wife they considered to be of the wash-and-wear variety.

Guess I was about nine years old, Sis almost two years younger, when our father was killed in a tractor accident. That event seemed to remove us from their Christmas mailing list.

I thought of Ma and the hardship of a young widow with two kids trying to make ends meet on a meager insurance check. She supplemented it by taking in washing, hoeing the neighbor's garden, doing their housework, and even milking their cows.

She joined a church, determined that Sis and I were going to be raised as Christians, and sent us to the church school—a very strict and expensive education.

Grandma said that Ma had loved to dance, but now she had traded her dancing slippers for boots and bib overalls. She was always so terribly tired, her curls were gone, and the fourteen-hour days showed in the lines on her face and the droop of her shoulders.

I think she married again because she thought Sis and I needed a father. I was twelve and becoming as rambunctious as I dared.

He was Dad's buddy, medically discharged from the Army. A war hero. Sis and I never did discover the exact location of his wounds, but later we laughed ourselves into hysterics when we figured he'd been shot in the ass when he ran the wrong way when the command had been to advance. Ma said I aggravated him. I sure tried.

He promised me a bike, and Sis all manner of good things that young girls love. Even brought Ma some roses that wilted overnight. Ma perked up and curled her hair.

I think he married her because she was a good cook, a hard worker, and owned her own home.

Then the justice of the peace declared them man and wife.

The honeymoon was over when Ma said, "I do."

I never got the bike, of course. Sis was told to shut up about crap she didn't need. Ma was told in very uncertain terms to forget that damned foolishness about church school and put some new tires on the pickup.

Ma hung tough on the church school.

He drank a lot of beer and never seemed to hold down a job very long. His every conversation was laced with obscenities.

He shoved Ma around. And without a moment's notice, one of his big paws would catch me beside the head and knock me sprawling.

Ma was a Sunday school teacher for years and never missed church; it was her only escape from the hell that was our home. She asked the pastor to speak to him. His response was, "You know your husband is the head of the house and you are to obey him. Are you sure you're doing as you should? Divorce? You're a Sunday school teacher. I'll pray for you, sister."

Nothing ever came of that conversation. I recall the verse that says, "Faith without works is dead," so I didn't think the pastor put in any overtime.

Sis and I quit church, but we prayed fervently every night for the head of the house—prayed he'd get leprosy and die, slowly.

Well, enough of these tender memories, I thought. It's a beautiful day, I own my own wheels, and I'm going home. I looked to see a McDonald's signboard flash by and realized I was ferociously hungry. I pulled off the freeway, found the golden arches and ordered a meal. I stuffed myself with food I hadn't tasted since I'd left home, and topped it off with a double-malt milkshake.

Back on the road, my gaze wandered to the low hills as I listened to the hum of the tires on the asphalt. I wondered what the date was. July, I think—have I missed my eighteenth birthday?

I smiled as I thought about the cakes Ma had baked for me. Always the same—two-layer chocolate with thick fudge frosting and the appropriate number of candles. Sis gloated—she always got to lick the spoon.

Then, as the wheels brought me closer, I could feel my stomach tighten, that breakfast threatening to make a quick exit. I wondered if I dared to chance a toke. No, I'd smell funny. Bad enough I'd again hidden what was left in the lining of my jacket.

I slowed to a crawl, but as I neared the turn-off, my foot pressed down on the accelerator as though it had a mind of its own. As I drove up the driveway and turned, the house came into view.

Everything looked the same. Well, almost. I laughed to myself as I saw the pickup that stood almost sideways in the door of the garage. Sis never could park that truck right. Tied to the front wheel was her old dog.

Sis' love of that animal had always been a mystery to me. All he'd ever done was whine and scratch at the door, eat, then retreat under her bed to sleep, snore and fart.

At last I was home.

The curtains were drawn, the dog barely looked at me—it was too quiet.

I gave the horn a tentative honk with no response. Worried, I gave a couple of real sharp toots. I saw the curtains move and a face peer out.

I stepped out of the car.

Then the front door flung open hard enough to crack the hinges, followed by a wild shriek, "Ma, Ma. It's Stevie."

Then it was a race to see who could get to whom first, a tangle of arms, sobs and laughter.

Ma's crumpled face pressed into my chest. I could feel the wet through my tee shirt.

"Son, son. What happened to you?"

Brushing away the tears from her face with fingers that shook almost as badly as my knees, I said, "It's a long story, Ma."

Then they were pulling me in. Sis kicked the door shut and, with hands on her hips, demanded, "Where in hell have you been?"

"Not now, Sis," Ma said. "Put the coffee on and I'll bring out the birthday cake."

Tears streaming, Sis crowded me into a chair, waving the coffee pot and shooting questions with the speed of a machine gun—despite Ma's admonition.

Ma came out of the pantry to place the cake with eighteen blue candles on the worn chrome table.

I glanced around quickly to see if there was any sign of this man I both feared and hated. "Where's what's-his-name?" I ventured.

There was a silence as Ma sliced into the cake. The sweet aroma almost made me drool. Sis handed me a fork as Ma pushed a plate toward me heavy with a huge piece of cake and said, "Son, this cake is three days old. You're late." She added, almost as an afterthought, "Oh, he isn't here anymore."

"I shot the son of a bitch," Sis said.

Ma added, "I buried the gun in the garden. We've been digging potatoes so the ground's all tore up anyway—just in case anybody ever asked about it."

My fork clattered to the floor. Nobody moved to pick it up.

I nearly choked. "Oh my God, Ma."

I leaned back; my eyes rolled upward and fastened on three flattened cardboard box tops taped to the ceiling. I stared mesmerized at the fine dust as it sifted down through the cracks and jagged edges of the exposed lath and plaster. One box top read "Rio-Visa Peaches."

Dumbfounded, almost speechless, I could only point.

Ma said, "Oh, that's just when the wind gets under a corner. I didn't get it taped very well. Probably a few dents in the roof, too, plus I found a couple of shingles in the yard.

"Sure had a hard time with the blood on the floor. Sis poured a couple of gallons of bleach on it and ruined the linoleum."

I looked down to see about half the floor splotched white.

"Yes, Sis shot that son of a bitch," Ma said, "but her aim was off."

That information wasn't half as shocking as the sound of my Ma using that kind of language. My Ma, a Sunday school teacher and a stickler for proper English, had never even uttered a "gee whiz" or a "gosh darn." Sis and I had our mouths washed out with soap more than a few times.

"He went down and lay there—bled like a stuck hog. And I kicked the shit out of him." Ma laughed, leaned over, and started to pull the candles out of the cake.

I finally found my voice and croaked, "Sis, did you really, truly shoot him?"

"She sure did," Ma said with pride in her voice. "Only I was going to say I did it. Sis, you never did make the coffee—I'll do it. Tell Stevie."

"Okay, Ma," Sis said. "Last Sunday we were dressed for church and just walking out the door when he got up, bleary-eyed, hair hanging in his face, and put his pants on. Like always," Sis began.

"He blustered to Ma, 'Where's my breakfast? You're not goin' any place till I've had my breakfast.'"

"Ma said, kinda easy, trying not to make him mad, 'That will make me late. I can't keep my class waiting. There's cereal, eggs...' Then he slapped her, knocked her back on a chair. Then he said to me, 'You damn well better get to cookin' my breakfast before I lose my temper.'

"I said, 'Sure, I'll do it. Let me get my apron.' I stepped back into the bedroom. Ma just sat there real quiet, holding her Bible, her hat all crooked."

Ma interrupted. "Yeah, I knew in my heart she was going for the gun."

Sis continued, "He was walking toward Ma, talking ugly, when I stood in the doorway holding Dad's shotgun. Ma told me, looking right past him, 'Go ahead, Sis, shoot the son of a bitch.'

"He turned his head and when he saw the gun he started to beg. 'Please, honey, Sis, put that gun down. Put it down—it's loaded.'

"I said, 'Of course it's loaded. I'm going to kill you for slapping Ma around, always making her late for church, running Stevie off. You've broken her heart; you've made our life hell. No matter what happens, life will be better.'

"Now the tears are flowing and he's pleading, 'Honey, please, I'll never do it again.'

"'I know you won't, you bastard—not where you're going.'

"I put the heavy gun to my shoulder and brought it up. He's shaking till I thought he was going to fall. I spread my feet like you've showed me, Stevie, my finger on the trigger. Then that damn old dog staggered out from under my bed to chase the cat and knocked me off balance. My finger just tightened on the trigger and there was a terrible boom— I was almost deaf for three days—and he fell on his face. Blood flew everywhere. I thought I was going to faint. I never saw a dead man before.

"The air was thick with the smell of gunpowder and blood splattered way up to the ceiling, where I saw a big hole with lath sticking out. Plaster was falling everywhere.

"Ma said, 'That was real good shooting, Sis,' took off her hat, and laid it with her Bible on the table. She stepped over the blood and plaster and gave him a good hard kick in the ass. She said, 'What are we gonna do with him, do you s'pose?'

"I said, kinda dazed, 'Ma, you're gonna be late for class,' and leaned the gun up against the wall.

"Ma looked kinda funny and said, 'I guess I'm not a Christian anymore—no need to hurry now.' Then she walked back and gave him another kick.

"That's when he sat up. I screamed, 'Ma, he's been resurrected,' and fell back against the wall.

"'Oh, shit,' Ma said. 'He isn't dead after all. You were standing too far away, I guess.'

"'You damn near blowed my arm off and my head, too. I'm blind— can't see a thing,' he blubbered. It was the truth—his face was covered with blood and there was a big hole in his upper arm. Blood was running down his naked belly.

"Ma got some towels, wrapped one around his arm real tight and with another, wiped his face, none too gently, and discovered he wasn't blind. A four-inch flap of hair and scalp hung over his ear. She sent me for an old bedsheet with yellow flowers on it, and we tore it into strips and wound it around his head and arm till he looked like a mummy. She stepped back and I snickered when she said, 'I think he looks kinda cute in yellow—don't you?'

"He crawled to a chair and I helped him up.

"'Just a little head bump,' Ma said.

"'Yeah, one inch to the right and that little bump would have been in my brain.' The tears made streaks down his face.

"Ma said, 'Head wounds always bleed a lot—not life-threatening. And that's only a flesh wound in your arm. You'll live. Too damn bad.' Her tone of voice chilled me.

"She started to clean up the mess—all the plaster and blood, but I sank down in a chair, too weak to stand anymore.

"'You two crazy women.' He pointed his good arm at Ma. 'You took a butcher knife to me and now Sis has tried to blow my head off.'

"He dabbed at himself with a towel. Ma planted herself in front of him, looking him dead in the eye. 'Too bad Sis missed. I won't—if there is a next time. Now I'm going to clean you up, pack a few things, call a cab and you can go to the hospital and get stitched up. Cause any trouble with the police and one of us will find you. You were cleaning your gun. Accidents happen—understand me?

"'You are two crazy women,' he repeated. 'I want out of here. Don't forget my shaving gear.'

"'Before you go,' Ma said, 'I want you to repeat after me in your own refined language that we've been subjected to all these years.

"'I am a foul-mouthed bully and a piss-poor lay.'

"He hesitated and fussed with his bandages. Ma picked up the gun.

"'I am a foul-mouthed bully and a piss-poor lay,' he sniveled.

"'I didn't hear a word, Ma.'

"She nudged him with the gun.

"'I am a foul-mouthed bully and a piss-poor lay.'

"'I must be going deaf, Ma. I didn't hear a thing.'

"My hearing improved after he confessed two more times.

"Ma picked up the phone and called a cab.

"We sat there—he was still blubbering snot and tears. Ma was quiet, her face crinkled up like she was deep in thought. Then she looked over at me and said with a devilish smile, 'What did he say, Sis? I can't remember.'

"He spoke right up. 'I'm a foul-mouthed bully...'

"But the rest was lost as he crawled into the cab."

CHAPTER 14

We talked far into the night. My mind was flooded with questions, as were theirs. I told them only that I had worked on a sheep ranch with some rough characters and that the work was hard. It hadn't been easy for me to dig a hole deep enough in my psyche to bury those horrible experiences and, even if I had wanted to confide, I wasn't too sure about Ma's state of mind.

I concentrated on the hippie scene in the Haight-Ashbury. Sis was fascinated, asked about a hundred questions. So the ranch episode was put to rest.

But thoughts of Juan and Lupe were never far away—both had saved my life and Lupe had served in her way a need I'd never known before. My feelings for Juan were rooted deep, far deeper than gratitude; although we were not of the same blood, I felt he was my brother and I loved him as such. Instinctively, I knew he would always be part of my life, somehow, some way.

I knew I had returned to my world when I pulled the covers over myself in the bed I had slept in for so many years. My diploma hung on the wall beside my class picture, and the valedictorian speech I was not allowed to give was framed on the dresser. My clothes were still there and the third drawer still stuck.

I pulled the chain on the bedside lamp, the dark became my own, and a great peace warmed over me.

I slept late the next morning, woke slowly to the smell of something that drifted through the open window.

I'd always hated the harsh odor of Clorox, which I now identified as my eyes watered. I groped my way to the window and, as I closed it, my bleary eyes caught sight of the jacket on the clothesline. "Please, Ma," I screamed, "not my jacket." My jacket was pinned upside down, swinging gently with the breeze.

My knees made their own choice. Horrified, I sank back on the bed.

I staggered out and followed the sound of the thud, thud, thud that the old machine was coughing up.

"Ma," I yelled. "What in hell have you done to my jacket?"

The lid was up and Ma was peering inside, fishing out bits of plastic and green stuff.

"What the hell have you done to your good jacket? I've run it through three cycles, soaked it in Clorox and I can still smell it. Now the damn washer won't drain—all that green stuff has got it plugged up."

She handed me a dripping ten-dollar bill and some plastic.

"Get me a screwdriver, damn it to hell."

The jacket that I had protected at the risk of my life, my stash that had bought me a car, put money in my jeans...and now the remaining three empty bags were floating in soapy water, the green stuff plugging the drain.

I could just hear Alfie's booming laugh, hear him say, "Well, your ma sure kept that shoe salesman straight and that machine will run for a year without electricity." I missed Alfie.

"What is this stuff?" Ma demanded. "Sis says it's marijuana, but I don't believe that. I didn't raise you to be a dope fiend. And Sis, I don't know where she gets these crazy ideas. Caught her reading *True Confessions* again. Better bring the hammer, too."

"Ma," I said, "You know Sis has always been jealous of me. Don't believe a word she says. She gets it all from that magazine.

"I've been learning to cook and we used a lot of oregano. I guess some of it got into my pockets. Why don't you go get a cup of coffee and I'll fix the drain."

Sis appeared and rolled her eyes. "Yeah, that sounds pretty reasonable. I've heard those hippies are pretty heavy on the oregano. S'pose they take those cooking classes wearing their jackets, too. With any luck, that might slide by."

She grinned as I brushed past her in the doorway.

I had just finished when she poked her head around the door and giggled. "Still here? Guess that oregano can plug a machine pretty bad."

I tried to give her a frosty stare, but I couldn't quite pull it off. I had to grin.

"You think you skidded by with that fairytale? Wanna bet?" she challenged.

That thought had been nagging at me all the time I'd been cleaning that miserable machine. Leave it to Sis—she'd zeroed in, right on target.

After dinner, Ma said, "Bring the potato fork, Stevie. I'll get a pail and let's dig some potatoes."

Sis rolled her eyes at me and said quickly, "I'll do the dishes—my turn." I knew my time had come.

With the pail rattling in cadence beside us, we walked to the garden, her hand in mine, my heart bursting with love for her. I knew I was going to catch hell.

"Stevie, you can't know how I've prayed for you to come home."

She would never know of those horrible nights at the ranch when I had so fervently prayed the same prayer.

We worked a couple of rows; the only sounds were of the potatoes clunking in the pail and Ma humming one of those old hymns under her breath. "Amazing Grace," I think it was.

When she stopped and wiped her face on the sleeve of the old work shirt, I knew where the needle pointed.

I turned to face her.

"You lied to me, didn't you, Stevie."

"Yeah."

"You know I can always tell."

"Yeah."

"If that dope is so important to you that you have to cover it with a lie...well, that breaks my heart."

"Aw, Ma. It's just a little marijuana. Just a little something for relaxation. Slows the mind, puts the brakes on..." I coaxed.

"You were an honor student, Stevie. God gave you a quick, sharp brain, a beautiful working tool, and you've chosen to dull it. For what? That's like pissing in the pure, clean water of a well.

"You've changed, Stevie."

"Yes, I've changed, Ma. And so have you. Why are you using such bad language? That's not my mother talking, and I hate it. And encouraging Sis to kill? Not that the bastard didn't deserve it."

She looked surprised, opened her mouth to speak, but then silence hung between us. I stood there leaning on the fork and waited, almost holding my breath. We never talked back to Ma.

"Well, Stevie," she said thoughtfully, as though she was searching her mind, weighing her words, "I don't rightly know how this is happening. I don't seem to hear it. I've always abhorred that kind of talk. I cringed every time your stepfather opened his mouth and now I'm doing the same thing. I'm so ashamed."

Her face screwed up and gut-wrenching sobs pounded out.

I dropped the fork and pulled her to me. I was surprised to realize in the past year that I had grown a head taller than Ma. With my arms around her, she felt so frail, so thin and vulnerable.

I begged, "Please, please don't cry, Ma. You can swear all you want— I'll get used to it."

Between sobs came halting words. "I'm crying because I've done so poorly for you and Sis. I know I haven't been a good mother. If I'd taken more time with you kids, if I'd stood up to him the first time he hit you... It's my fault—I've driven you to this, and now you're a dope fiend."

I pulled her face out of my shirt and made her look at me. "Ma, stop, stop. For God's sake, I'm not a dope fiend, Ma," I blurted out, shocked and indignant.

But she would not be comforted; the tears still flowed.

Finally I said, desperate, that good brain she said I once had in overdrive, "Ma, I promise—I promise—never to smoke a cigarette of any kind ever again."

She looked up. "Promise to God?"

"Yes, yes, promise to God."

"I'll promise, too. I'll never swear again and I'll never again tell Sis to shoot anyone. Honest to God."

And so our pact was made, with our arms around each other, standing in the freshly turned earth of the potato patch.

Neither of us has ever violated it.

Sis lay in wait for me. At the first opportunity, she asked curiously, "What happened down in the garden? Ma was on to you, wasn't she?"

Evading her question, I asked, "What happened after I left, Sis?"

She hesitated. It wasn't like Sis to be slow to answer.

"Well, that about killed her. That morning when she fixed breakfast and realized you were gone, she just turned around, closed the door and went to bed.

"I hoped you'd be gone only a couple of days and come back. When I got home from school, old what's-his-name said Ma had reported you missing to the police, but he told them you had just run off to join the hippies in San Francisco so, of course, they didn't get excited.

"Ma was still in bed when I got home. I told her I was hungry and asked her what's for dinner, but she didn't take the bait. Not that day or any of the following days. She came out of that room only to use the bathroom and days later, not even then. She didn't wash or comb her hair. Finally, I bathed her in bed. I cooked for us and forced her to eat, but that was almost nothing."

"Where was he?" I asked. I felt rage and overwhelming shame building as I visualized my mother and my sister—the ones I love and had abandoned.

"Oh, he only came home to sleep on the couch. Guess he hung out with his buddies somewhere.

"I signed Ma's name to her check and bought what we needed. I signed my own report card—I was glad she didn't see it because I dropped from straight As to Cs. I missed a lot of school, going only part time. I tried to study at home..."

"How long did she stay in bed? Didn't she say anything at all?" I asked, hardly daring to trust my own voice.

"Only if I coaxed her. She stayed in bed a couple of weeks and got so thin. Then one night, she sat straight up and asked, 'Is that Stevie? I hear Stevie.' I was so scared, I thought she was dying. I called the pastor, but she wouldn't talk to him, turned her head to the wall. Another three weeks went by..."

Sis choked on her sobs and I smothered mine as I held her, smoothed her hair, and begged, "My God, Sis—how can you love me or ever forgive me?"

She continued as though she hadn't heard me.

"Then early one morning, when it was still dark, she woke me up screaming, 'Stevie, Stevie, try.'

"I don't know how she ever made it to my bed. I pulled her down beside me and said, 'You know, Ma, Stevie isn't here.'

"Then she said, 'I see him. I see him plain as day and he's in trouble.'

"We held each other in my bed and she shook so bad it rattled.

"Then I knew she'd die if I didn't do something, so I called Dr. Burnham. You remember him—he delivered both of us, took my tonsils out, cured your pneumonia. He said she was having a nervous breakdown and called an ambulance. They kept her in the hospital for three weeks and fed her through a tube. She weighed less than a hundred pounds. They did a lot of other stuff, too. I was there every day.

"Dr. Burnham told her if she didn't get up and stay up, I'd have to go to a foster home. Seems like those were the magic words.

"She was awful shaky when she got home, but followed the doctor's orders and ate what I fixed. She did get better, but then she started talking bad—imagine Ma swearing. Then night sweats left her wringing wet. She swore the heat was coming up through the floor. You know she always hated ketchup, but now she was pouring it on her cereal. Then she hid the iron in the refrigerator. I was afraid she'd go back to bed, so I called the doctor again. He came out and gave her a shot and a bunch of pills, telling her they were vitamins and making her promise to take them. You know how she is about promises. More pills and tranquilizers. He told me she was having a premature change of life. You know, she's only forty-four. Now she's gotten almost back to her old self except for the cussing but, for some reason, it seems like she just stopped that, too."

Ma walked in and caught Sis and me hanging on to each other and bawling our heads off. She looked scared and asked, "Why are you two blubbering like babies?"

I said, "Because we're happy, Ma."

So she put her arms around us and we all cried. She looked up at that ceiling and the cardboard patch and said, "Thank you, God, for my children."

The next few days I worked on that ceiling. Ma said we couldn't afford to do the whole thing, so we had to patch it. All I knew about carpentry was when you had a hammer in your hand, you were supposed to look for a nail. I was a lot better at digging postholes.

I stood on a shaky ladder and sawed the ends off the jagged lath, trying to keep the crumbling plaster in place. Finally, I managed a square hole and filled it with strips of wood and sheetrock. The kitchen was a mess when I made my last trip down the ladder.

"Well, Ma," I said, "that's the best I can do."

I saw Ma look sternly at Sis, who was trying to smother her giggles. She was looking up at the ceiling when she said, "Ma, we can wallpaper right over those bumps—they'll never show."

Ma started mixing something in a big pan and my mouth watered. Biscuits and gravy, my favorite, I thought. But when we sat down for dinner, I discovered that Ma had been mixing flour and water for paste. I guess my disappointment showed.

"Tomorrow, son," Ma said.

The next night as I was wolfing down those golden, crusty biscuits submerged in gravy, I looked up at the daisy-patterned ceiling. There wasn't a bump to be seen.

I bragged, "Guess I'm better with a hammer than I realized."

Ma laughed and Sis sure had that eye-rolling bit down to a science.

"Son, I think you might do better in another line of work. Have you ever given any thought as to what you might want to do with your life?"

I had thought a lot about what direction my life was going, more than a few times this last year. When I was freezing my ass off at the ranch, I knew for sure what I didn't want to do—posthole digging and sheepherding were tops on that list, and now I felt I could safely add carpentry.

"I'd loved to have gone to college, Ma. I think that journalism would have been my major since I've always loved to write. Some history courses, too. But we can't even afford a new ceiling and your washing machine ate up all my ill-gotten gains, so we'll put college on hold for a while. I'm going to talk to the manager down at the market— maybe I'll find something there."

Sis interrupted. "Yeah, you were the editor of the school paper for three years. Don't you remember the principal, Mr. Wills, talked about a scholarship for both of us? Of course, that was after *I* won that big spelling contest," she emphasized as she stuck her elbow in my ribs.

"Put the pot on, Sis, and let's sit a minute."

Ma seated herself at the table. "I've got some news for you kids. When you were born, Stevie, we took out an insurance policy for your college. It matured when you were eighteen, so you've got one thousand five hundred dollars that the machine didn't eat. Sis, you've got a while to go yet, but we did the same for you.

"Stevie, I hope you didn't offend Mr. Wills because I'm going to talk to him about that scholarship. Also, I think I can swing a few votes with the minister. I taught the kids and sang in the choir for seven years. They owe me."

On Sunday morning, Ma picked up her Bible, put on her hat and went to church—on time.

Then came the bad news. The principal had conferred with the minister and they had agreed that a scholarship would not be forth-coming because of my ongoing disciplinary problems, which apparently included an irreverent attitude, questioning the Bible, cartooning the prophets, and last, but surely not least, I had graduated from church school with an unsigned diploma.

A week before graduation, the banker's son and teacher's pet had made fun of my clothes in the cloakroom. So I swung around with a wire coat hanger, catching him across the face. His blood flowed.

I found myself in the principal's office almost before I could replace the "weapon," facing an ultimatum: "Apologize or be expelled."

I couldn't force myself to apologize, even over Ma's tears.

I suppose she had to go on her knees to persuade the principal—at the last moment—to allow me to walk across the stage to accept an unsigned diploma.

Of course, no mention was made of my four-point grade average or any other accomplishment.

"Hide the shotgun, Sis," I said as Ma slept in the following Sunday. Her Bible was where it always was—on her bedside table, but we never saw the hat again.

Later I thought I recognized some flowers and part of a veil that I found in the burn barrel.

In late September, I was admitted to Oakdale Community College in the quaint little town of Oakdale, just across the bay from San Francisco.

CHAPTER 15

The unrecognizable sounds of the busy hospital intruded in the darkness of Juan's mind as he slowly drifted back to consciousness. His exploring hand encountered a wet, warm cloth moving across his face; instinctively, his grip closed over the fingers that held the towel.

Juan opened his eyes to see the small, gray-haired woman whose presence he had sensed from far away so many times in these last weeks. The fragrance was familiar.

Dropping her hand, struggling to sit up, the bed was suddenly raised and they were face to face.

Smiling, she pointed to herself and said, "Sara."

He reached for the hand that he had released and answered, "Juan."

There was a prolonged silence. Sara seemed to drown in the depth of those questioning black eyes. Juan was unable to look away.

This boy did not seem a stranger to Sara. Sitting beside him every day, she knew every curve of his fingers, every plane of that strikingly handsome face, but she could not have identified why she had the deep, innate feeling of love and connection with this tall, thin boy of different blood.

The instinctive gut feeling that flooded Juan's body, the sure knowledge of love and acceptance, the how and why—all bewildered him, but he knew he would never be alone again.

A quick knock at the door and the doctor stepped in, followed by the nurse.

Sara stepped back as the doctor examined Juan, then carefully removed the stitches from his face.

"That's healed nicely. It won't even leave a scar. His ribs are mending very well, too." He smiled. "These young ones are strong—he'll be ready to go home in a few days."

The nurse translated to Juan. He turned his head to look at Sara, a moment's desperation in his eyes.

She smiled as she spoke—the translation brought tears to his eyes as he reached for her hand.

"We'll go home, son."

At dinner that evening, Sara was in unusually high spirits.

Teddy smiled. "You seem very happy tonight. What have you been up to?"

"You know I've been going to the hospital to see Juan every day," she answered.

Teddy joked, "Have they offered you the supervisor's position yet?" Then added, "I suppose the boy will be released soon, then you'll have to go back to work, finish that painting."

Sara was quick to answer, "Bring up a bottle of wine, my love. I have a secret I'm dying to tell you."

"Then tonight is the night to reveal all. I have a secret you're going to love. I'll bring two bottles—it's a celebration," Teddy declared.

Both women were eager with anticipation and didn't linger over dinner. Hurrying up the broad stairway, they entered their sanctuary and Teddy quickly deposited the wine on the old oak table.

Turning, she put her arms around Sara. "Me first—I can't wait another minute. I have a carpenter coming on Friday to enclose that big living room in the old servants' quarters for your new studio. It has the three-sided witches' turret with three floor-to-ceiling windows," she enthused. "Perfect, it's just perfect. All the light you'll ever need, and I'm adding a bathroom, too. I want it to be beautiful for you."

Sara stiffened in Teddy's arms and stepped away. "Oh, Teddy, no, you can't do that," the words burst out. "I want that room for my boy."

"Sara, did you hear what you just said?" came Teddy's shocked voice as she looked down into a face where so many emotions ran rampant.

The unexpected outburst left Sara momentarily flustered, but then defiant. "Yes, *my* boy. I want to bring him home. That's my secret."

"That makes me a parent, too, I take it. I can't believe I'm hearing this. Why haven't you told me of your feelings for this boy? When did all this happen?"

"The first time he took my hand. I haven't told you about my feelings because I couldn't understand them but, Teddy, now I'm sure. I can't explain it, but I can't deny it. I feel as though I gave birth to him myself."

"Sara, I have no desire or need to become a parent at age fifty-five." Teddy's deliberately calm voice continued, camouflaging her shock. "And I think you've mistaken pity for love. Sammy's death has upset you more than I realized. I think you've found another Sammy."

"That's a cruel thing to say. Juan is a human being," came Sara's instant retort.

"Of course. And didn't you consider Sammy your child? I remember that cold, rainy day when you found him lying at the door of your greenhouse. What little hair he had was soaking wet and, as I recall, he had mange. Every bone was visible. You screamed for Mr. Mackey to come quick and kill this horrible big rat.

"I thought he should be put out of his misery, but you had to call a vet for a second opinion—I wasn't flattered, I may add. You nursed him back to life and for eight years he was your child.

"I could be persuaded," Teddy placated, noting Sara's reaction to her words, "to send this boy to a good school where he could learn a trade and our language and customs. And he could visit, but I'm too old to be a parent.

"Sara, you're a born mother. I wish we could have adopted years ago when our lives were ahead of us, but it seemed we were always enough for each other."

Sara put her arms around the other woman's waist. "Teddy darling, we have adopted. I gave him my word I'd bring him home. He'll be released soon. I want those rooms for Juan."

"No," said Teddy flatly.

"Surely you aren't saying 'no' to me," came Sara's astonished voice.

"Surely I am. It's been a very long time since we've differed this strongly, my dear Sara. Give it up."

Sara's anger flared. "Don't patronize me, Dr. Hassé; this is far beyond a difference. In fact, if I weren't a lady to my fingertips, I'd say I'm damn well going to have it my way. Adjust."

"And I'd say," Teddy responded, "the hell you are. I'll hammer the damn wall up with my scalpel. My German ancestors' vocabulary does not recognize the word 'adjust.'"

Teddy stalked from the room, stiff with anger.

The two battlers stood forlorn.

Tears of frustration welled in Sara's eyes. That night and the nights that followed, she slept on her own side of the bed.

An unaccustomed silence reigned and the old house seemed wrapped in loneliness until even the shingles whispered in the sudden quiet.

The undercurrent of disharmony lay just below the stilted conversation in ugly contrast with the happy exchanges and pleasures the women had taken in each other for over twenty years.

Teddy, angry and miserable, took refuge in her office, her dinner kept warm in the oven by Mrs. Mackey.

Sara spent many hours at the hospital and, as Juan's release became imminent, she realized he would need clothing.

He seemed to have grown taller in the short time he had been hospitalized and the scales showed an undeniable gain in weight.

Shopping for Juan with the measurements given by the nurse, Sara's purchases, without Teddy's suggestions, were a revelation. She gave free reign to her love of color and style.

Juan was self-conscious as he stood for Sara's appraisal. He had never known such clothing; he hardly recognized himself.

As he stood in his new trousers with a colorful shirt thrown over one bare shoulder, Sara's breath caught at the beauty of this tall, graceful boy pausing at the threshold of manhood.

Suddenly, her fingers yearned for the feel of a paintbrush. Teddy was right—she needed to paint.

The nurse smiled in appreciation and spoke to Juan in Spanish. His face clouded as he answered.

"What did you say to him?" Sara asked.

The nurse hesitated, then answered, "I said to him that he is so handsome, my daughter would like him. But he said, 'I am different. I love another and always will.'"

Sara sat quietly for a moment, then reached for his hand and pulled him to her.

"Tell him that I, too, am different."

Matter-of-factly, she tugged his hand through the dangling sleeve, then stood back smiling to observe her handiwork.

His eyes sought hers, searching for any sign of rejection.

Wordless, there was perfect understanding.

The nurse spoke again. "My daughter, who is a student at the university, is fluent in both languages. She could tutor your son. You may have a difficult time communicating when he goes home..."

Sara was delighted and scribbled her phone number with a grateful "Thank you." One problem solved.

Now that his stay grew shorter, Sara's happiness was tainted by the thoughts of Teddy's adamant decision. She could not bring her boy home until this issue had been resolved.

And how do I resolve it? she agonized.

A great sense of loss swept over her. Had she gained one love only to lose another? How will I ever find the strength to let Juan go?

Sara's foot, as though it were a separate entity, crept close to slowly caress the smooth calf of the leg that lay so near. Teddy had seemed not to have even shared the same bed these last lonely nights.

Her toes tickled as they slid over the soft skin and she felt Teddy shiver.

Her heart gave a great leap of joy as she turned.

"Is this the white flag of surrender? I warn you," Teddy said with bravado, "I take no prisoners. The carpenter is coming tomorrow."

Sara's tearful voice whispered, "I'll never, never set foot in it, so do as you please."

A long silence as both women stared into the darkness.

Defeated then, Teddy asked, "How can we resolve this? Could we not arrange it as a studio apartment?"

"That big bedroom has a large window that overlooks the rose garden and..."

Sara gave a disdainful sniff, but a wave of relief and happiness swept over her.

Teddy continued, "...redo the bathroom, repaint, some nice furniture. There's even a back stairway."

Sara didn't respond, her foot still slowly caressing Teddy's calf.

Teddy said, "My dear, that's the best that I can do."

"And a door that opens to my studio?" Sara asked.

"Of course." Teddy sighed.

"And do you think you can arrange for the hospital to keep Juan for a couple of weeks until I can get everything arranged just perfectly?"

"Of course," repeated Teddy in a resigned voice with the barest hint of laughter.

"What time is it, Teddy?"

Looking at the illuminated dial, Teddy said, "It's three a.m."

"Do you think that's too early to open the wine?"

"It's never too late to celebrate, my dearest Sara."

Four feet touched the carpeted floor simultaneously and padded to the study.

Then the pop of the cork and the laughter as the wine spilled. The happy exchange of words that had lain dormant for days now flowed freely as the glasses were replenished time and again.

They sat together, their glasses upraised in a toast.

"It's been forever since we've sat like this," Teddy said.

"At least," Sara responded and lifted her glass.

The old house sighed and settled back on the ancient stone foundation. From somewhere, a night bird sang to announce a new day and flew into the sun.

The studio was finished and beautifully done. Teddy had supervised every move of the workers.

The large room reflected the natural light that shone through the tall windows on a sunny day, and crept in when the bay so far below was only a slash of blue against the soft gray of the fog.

Fully stocked, the lovely studio boasted the ultimate in brushes, tubes of paint in every color, canvasses stacked against a wall, even a custom-made easel that replaced the old paint-spattered one now hidden in the closet.

Teddy had not allowed Sara even a peek, and at the great unveiling, she was scooped up and carried across the threshold. Sara gasped. The studio was everything she ever could have dreamed.

"Who would ever have believed you'd have done such a wonderful job with only a scalpel?" Sara giggled like a teenager.

"Put me down. I'd guess a bottle of wine and a couple of glasses are in the vicinity. This calls for a celebration. Oh, Teddy, how I love you."

"As I love you. You make my life a constant challenge. I dare not grow old," Teddy declared.

The bottle stood three-quarters empty much later as Sara examined every nook and cranny, every tube of paint.

"Teddy, wherever did you find these brushes? There are none better." Sara stood, her head thrown back, a brush held high as she read the fine print on the handle.

The small, fine-boned woman whose hair threatened to free itself from the band that held it captive; the woman with laughing eyes and a quick smile outlined against the tall window—Teddy knew that image was forever painted on her heart.

Sensing the other woman's intent gaze, Sara turned and said laughingly, "Come, let me show you what *I've* done without a scalpel," and opened the door to the short hallway that led to Juan's apartment.

The older woman followed, observing the care that had transformed the small, drab servants' quarters to the compact, colorful apartment with its simple but elegant furnishings. Intuitively, she knew that love that had gone into the placement of every object.

After a long moment, she spoke quietly.

"I'm almost jealous. Since I am involved, what is my status? Is my throne secure?"

Teddy joked, but beneath her frivolous words ran an utterly foreign undercurrent, the need of reassurance. For the first time in twenty years, she found herself sharing Sara's love.

Sara turned a shocked face. "What a strange question."

Then with the realization that Teddy's words stood out in bold type, she answered, "That throne is set in concrete, 'til death do us part.'"

Teddy hugged her tightly.

"Tell Mrs. Mackey to put on an extra place setting. There will be three of us."

CHAPTER 16

Ma had called and found out that there were two days left for registration, so we left the next day.

Ma was ecstatic, Sis never stopped talking, and I was excited, scared, overjoyed and a long range of other mixed emotions.

Oakdale didn't seem like the small town I had pictured in my mind when Alfie had described the college to me. In reality, it was a smaller version of the big city across the bay, but there was something appealing about it. Maybe it was the trees that lined the streets or the neat, old-fashioned houses that made me feel comfortable.

The college, with its stately brick buildings built on a knoll, was easy to find. The old faded bricks, mostly hidden beneath the ivy that crawled over them, gave one the feeling that they had been there forever—perhaps had grown out of the ground just to keep the eucalyptus trees company.

A sign read "Oakdale Community College, established in 1850." The campus was large and seemed like a moving multicolored carpet. Students hurrying in every direction in their bright clothing looked as though some giant hand had indiscriminately scattered a bucketful of confetti into a strong wind.

I found the sign pointing to a line, growing longer by the minute and moving with the speed of a crippled snail that led to the registrar's office. A couple of fellows stood in front of me discussing their classes. One turned around and asked me what subjects I was taking.

"Journalism," I answered.

They both laughed.

"Dowd's class. I took a semester from her last year and then transferred to English lit. Dowd knows her subject, inside and out, but boy is she rough. Got a tongue like a razor blade and loses about a third of her class the first semester. Who needs it?"

I finally reached the desk, got the paperwork and enrolled in one journalism class and six units of general education classes. When I registered, I wrote "undecided" as my major in the little box on the right. Who cared that I took only three classes? Journalism is the one I wanted, I exulted. I was a college student.

I wandered the maze of corridors in the huge building until I found the door with the right number on it. I wanted to know exactly where to go tomorrow and be there early enough for a front-row seat.

That student's comment came back to me as I stood in front of that magic door. "Who needs it?"

My inner voice answered: "Someone who wants to learn from the best and has got enough guts to do what it takes." I resolved to be that one.

Ma and Sis had been looking through the rental ads and found a little light housekeeping room above a garage. It was furnished with a hot plate, a bed that made Ma shudder, and a chest of drawers to match.

The good news? It was only a mile from campus.

My experience at the Haight-Ashbury house forever discouraged communal living—no more linen closets for me.

My first weekend home, Ma sent me back with enough stuff to furnish a three-bedroom house.

My first day in class was a complete disaster.

I was up early, did a quick shave. Not much came off, but I liked the smell of the aftershave. I grabbed a roll, a cold cup of coffee, and was out the door, excited and impatient. I moved fast even though I knew there was plenty of time.

I'd washed the old Buick the day before. Apparently the shock was too much because, as I turned the key in the ignition, nothing happened. Jiggling the key brought the same results—not even a sigh. I lifted the hood, pounded on the cables. Nothing. Shock waves swept over me as I realized that the battery was way beyond the last rites.

I hit the road running. Hell, I could make it easy—only a mile.

Arriving breathless, I flushed. I swiped the sweat with the back of my hand and tried to slick down the windblown curls that stood in defiance of the Brill Cream that I had slathered on them such a short time ago.

I eased the door open as quietly as a burglar, hoping to slither in unnoticed and find a seat in the back.

The room was crowded. No one would give me an inch.

Her eyes pinned me against the wall. I stood there as if glued.

She was a tall, bleached-blonde woman whose roots were the same color as the long black eyebrow that stretched above the piercing steel-gray eyes and dipped over a nose that was way longer than necessary.

A great shuffling of feet and muffled laughter arose as though my classmates were anticipating my demise.

"Mr. McClusky, I presume? We are so pleased you could join us. Roll call was ten minutes ago."

"Steve McAllister," I answered. "I apologize for being late. My car wouldn't start and..."

"We are not interested in discussing your transportation problem, however fascinating it may be. Perhaps another time. Seat yourself, Mr. McDuff."

I felt my face go crimson with embarrassment as I heard the room explode in laughter, and a hot flush of rage at the sarcastic put-down triggered an instant response.

"Thank you, Mrs. Dowdy," I said, finding a seat on the aisle.

A dead silence smothered the room.

Her face was a thundercloud as she stalked toward me and firmly stated, "I'd enjoy your company after class tomorrow, Mr. McDuff."

"Of course, Mrs. Dowdy."

The dressing down she gave me got my attention, but I had a mother and a sister who could have given her lessons.

The next morning the old Buick with a new battery didn't fail me. I was in class early and sat in a front row.

"Good morning, Mr. McNeil. How nice to see you."

The smile on her face never reached her eyes.

"Good morning to you, Mrs. Dowdy."

"After class?" she questioned.

"After class," I responded.

I'd come a long way—the hard way—since I'd cringed under the whiplash of ridicule and humiliation and I'd never accept that again. It was cheaper to pay the piper.

As the last of my classmates filed out, she walked over to me. Standing tall, she studied me for minutes that seemed to stretch into hours.

I returned her look with one of my own and the message passed between us.

"You do know my name, do you not, Mr. McAllister?"

"As you know mine, Mrs. Dowd."

With those words, the line was drawn and peace was declared.

"I want a fifteen-hundred-word essay on the proper, most productive way to interview the president of the United States. Due in two days. You are excused."

The first sentence of my essay read, "The most important step in establishing a good relationship with any person is to make sure you spell and pronounce his or her name correctly."

After a pause, I added, "A man's name tells you more than who he is. It tells you, in time, what he is."

I handed Mrs. Dowd my completed essay one day later. I was groggy from lack of sleep, but proud of the job I'd done.

She gave me a B minus, a grade unheard of in her class, where a C was rumored to be the equivalent of an A given by any other instructor.

"Well done, Mr. McAllister," she added.

After class I stared down the guy in the hall who called out "Ass-kisser" just loud enough for me to hear. I laughed.

Although our peace had been negotiated, life in her class was not meant to be easy. She challenged me in every possible way; her brilliant brain woke my sleeping mind to things I'd never even dreamed about and I absorbed it like a thirsty sponge.

That long black eyebrow would rise slightly on one side in a quirky gesture that would have been interesting on anyone else. But with Dowd, it was like a Doberman showing its teeth, a red flag preceding an off-the-wall question or assignment. I would brace myself for the look when her eyes finally came to rest on me.

I studied late into the night. I rewrote, researched, listened and learned—and seldom ever forgot. I truly had a photographic mind, and it had its rewards.

Once in a great while, I could best her. Then the closest thing that ever came to a smile would surface, momentarily, and leave me wondering if I had just imagined it.

As I was the scapegoat, I was also the hero—occasionally.

I heard later that there was a fair amount of wagering going on in that classroom and I cost some of those sports their allowances.

She did once say in a moment of generosity that a few of us had promise. I thought she looked at me.

CHAPTER 17

'd gotten pretty well adjusted in my second semester, but occasionally I would wake at night to the rough sounds of Carlos' snores, Juan's soft breathing just an arm's length away, and the horrific memories of that time of my life would try to push through the wall that Alfie had built. Not only the night he had rocked me in his big black arms, but the many hours we had spent talking together with the flower children at the Diggers' hangout.

I resolved once more to check the University of California, San Francisco medical school. I never knew Alfie's last name or if I did, it had long since been forgotten. I don't think he ever knew mine.

Hoping to get lucky and catch Alfie carrying a tray, I lunched at any opportunity in the cafeteria where the medical students hung out. The food was good, the room was crowded, but Alfie would be hard to miss at six feet three inches. That made him a marked man.

I used to kid him, asking, "How come you aren't pulling down the big money by playing basketball instead of ruining your eyesight trying to decipher all those big words and overloading your brain?"

His ready answer was always, "How come you ain't still shoveling shit, Cowboy?"

Giving up for the day, I stood to leave and noticed four black guys having lunch at a nearby table. Walking over, I introduced myself and asked if they might know of a big guy named Alfie, explaining that I thought he might be in his last year of medical school. I even told them that Alfie and I had worked together as volunteers at the Diggers drop-in some time ago.

Their expressions were perfectly blank.

Then one of them spoke in an exaggerated drawl, saying, "Y'all mean a big black nigga with a flat nose and kinky hair? All us niggas look alike, ya know." His companions grinned their appreciation, then shook their heads.

"Naw, ain't seen no nigga like dat," one added.

It didn't take an Einstein to see where this was going, so I said, "Thank you, gentlemen, for your time."

They laughed as I walked away, then conversed among themselves.

"Wonder what he wants with Alfred?"

"Probably one of those leftover hippies looking for a handout."

"Guess that big old boy graduated at the top of his class and is working in a big hospital on the other side of town. Now *there's* a uppity nigga."

I was pissed as I drove home. But when my anger cooled, I wondered how many times they had been humiliated—even in this upscale university where people are expected to know better.

I hated to give up my illusions, but I discovered time and again that life in the big city was hell on illusions.

My self-confidence blossomed and I matched it with a little half-hearted swagger as I walked. After all, I was a college man now.

I had gained weight eating my own mac and cheese—all I knew how to cook—and all the goodies that Ma sent back with me after stuffing me every weekend.

I hadn't seemed to stop growing. I was now pushing six feet tall and a hundred seventy pounds.

Sis said it was all in the right places, and I declared I was downright handsome now that my ears had shrunk to fit my head and my feet fit the rest of me. Of course, in the next breath Sis would ask to borrow ten dollars, so I didn't get too excited.

My experience with Lupe had educated me far beyond my years, but my sexual feelings now lay dormant beneath the excitement and commitment of college.

I thought far more about the intractable Mrs. Dowd than I did about the pretty girls who caught my eye for a fleeting hello-goodbye.

It was Friday afternoon. Classes were over and I was hurrying, wanting to get started for home.

The parking area was pretty well thinned out. As usual, I was parked at the far end because I never seemed to take the time to look for a closer space.

The Buick was at the base of a slight incline when I'd come in, so I was surprised to see a little orange Volkswagen perched at the top level. I remembered thinking, "I hope the brakes are on."

As I neared my car, I saw the two of them in close embrace—the Volkswagen had rolled back and the rear fender was in intimate contact with the Buick's bumper. Joined at the hip, you might say.

A girl with her back to me was vainly trying to pull the VW's fender loose, but the Buick held on tenaciously.

I was more than a little irritated, but rose to the occasion when I saw how incredibly lovely she was. Something jiggled in my mind, but I couldn't say what it was.

When she raised her hand to brush back the shiny black hair that swung in her face, I saw she wore a ring on the third finger of her left hand. Just my damn luck to rescue a beautiful damsel in distress who was wearing an engagement ring.

We stared at each other a moment. She looked vaguely familiar, but I knew I'd never seen her before. How would I ever have forgotten her?

Then she said, her eyes wide and disbelieving, "Cowboy? You can't be Cowboy. He was puny. But, yes, you are Cowboy. I hardly recognize you with your clothes on."

The word "Cowboy" took me back to my time at the Haight-Ashbury mansion. Seemed like a century ago. I guess I looked pretty blank because she said, "I'm the one who got you dressed—remember the tie-dyed bell-bottoms? And I cheered you on when you raced down the hall screaming for a jacket as naked as the day you were born. Well, there may have been some soap bubbles. How would I ever forget you?" She laughed.

After the shock wore off, I laughed, too.

Then the climate changed.

"Why in the world did you park way down there?"

"Why did you park directly in front of me on an incline? And didn't you set your brakes?"

She turned and was tugging at the fender with no success.

"Never mind," I said as I heard her sniffling.

I dug around in the trunk and found the jack and managed to slip it under the front wheel of that old monster—it weighed a ton. I lifted the car just enough to be able to dislodge the two cars.

The Volkswagen's fender was wrinkled and crushed into the tire.

"I don't think you can drive this—the fender is gouged too deep in the rubber and I can't make it give an inch."

"Oh, no..." The tears gathered momentum.

"Will you stop that bawling? I'll take you where you need to go. You can call a tow truck there," I said, a bit ungraciously.

"I've got a part-time job and I'm already late. And I don't really even know you. How do I know..."

I interrupted, "Do I look like a serial killer to you?"

She laughed. "I don't know. I haven't seen a naked serial killer." She blinked away the tears.

I looked at her in amazement. First she was blubbering like a baby, now she's making jokes.

"I'm Rica Vallea, and you are...?"

"Steve McAllister. Don't call me 'Cowboy.'"

As Rica got some things from her car, I pushed some stuff out of the way and piled the rest of it in the backseat. I held the door open for her and noticed she looked as good going as coming.

I maneuvered around the VW. It looked as forlorn sitting there as the beetle it was named after.

"Where to?" I asked.

"I'm embarrassed to tell you. I need to go to Pacific Heights—it's not just around the corner. I suppose you know it's across the bay."

"I don't really know San Francisco. I never got any farther than the Haight-Ashbury and I wasn't very clear then. You'll have to direct me. What's happening in Pacific Heights?"

"I have a part-time job tutoring a young man for a few months. The pay is wonderful and he is a real sweetheart...but different. They live in a mansion that makes that other place look like a tenement. He got a Mercedes coupe for his birthday so I taught him to drive. He's learned so quickly that I think my job may soon be over. I'll miss him—he seems almost like a brother. Sometimes he seems so sad—lonesome, probably."

"That's the Bay Bridge exit coming up. Stay on the right side."

It seemed like all of San Francisco was rushing home and the only possible way was over that bridge.

There were so many vehicles converging, I thought amnesty had been granted to every sinner on earth and the gates of heaven had been flung open for perhaps five minutes.

I dared to glance down for a split-second at the heat gauge—had it crept up? In moments of stress, the old clunker had been known to overheat.

As though on another planet, in the far, far distance, the vague outline appeared of the city, only to disappear again and again. The speeding cars and trucks passed around and over, horns blaring, lights flashing. I got shaky.

The great span of metal and concrete that was the Bay Bridge hung against the sky in great swoops and swirls that glinted in the late afternoon sunshine.

I was almost frozen with fear; my knuckles were white against the dark of the steering wheel as I held the car steady in a lane that I hoped was for the uninitiated.

I guess she noticed because she laughed and said, "Guess this must be pretty intimidating—your first trip across the bay?"

"It's hardly my first crossing, but it still is a bit daunting."

My heart throbbed until I thought my ribs would crack. I said, as casually as possible since my tongue was frozen to the roof of my mouth, "Oh, this isn't so much. I went over Victoria Falls in a birch-bark canoe a couple of times." But I was caught in my own lie when I stuttered.

She giggled. "This is only five lanes and there are five more on the bottom level." Then added, "The bridge is only about five miles long—actually one of the longest in the world. The scary part is that long, dark tunnel built through the rock of Yerba Buena Island."

I looked to see if she was putting me on, but her smile was so innocent that I was halfway ashamed to be so suspicious.

But then she said, "Sure would be a mess after an earthquake." And I knew.

I took a quick glance at the temperature gauge. The needle was slowly creeping up. "Please God, don't let it blow on this bridge. I promise..."

"Hang in there, Cowboy, you're doing okay."

"Don't call me Cowboy."

"You'll always be Cowboy to me. You've got a face like one of those Marlboro men."

"How about the rest of me?" I tried to joke.

"Don't know—haven't seen the Marlboro Man naked."

Damn this girl.

"Are you going to Oakdale College?" she asked. "My girlfriend goes to Oakdale and I was hoping to catch her between classes."

"Yes," I answered sharply as I tried to keep some maniac from crowding me over into the railing.

"What subjects are you taking?"

"Journalism—feature writing."

"I'm in my second year at the School of Nursing at the University of San Francisco. My fiancé graduated last year from the University of California, San Francisco Medical School and is interning there now. UCSF is considered one of the world's leading health centers."

This was more information than I needed to know.

It seemed like I had driven forever as she chatted like a magpie, when suddenly the bridge was behind us and I started to breathe again.

I fought the rush-hour traffic in the busy city and drove through some magnificent neighborhoods. I was in awe.

"You haven't seen anything yet," she said.

The tired old Buick steamed and sputtered up the hill as though it was embarrassed to be intruding into this world of luxury.

"Pacific Heights coming up," she said, and pointed to a long, winding driveway flanked by century-old trees just beginning to drop their leaves.

The ornate iron gate stood open and, beyond that, a house the likes of which I'd never even imagined stood as though it had been waiting—just for us.

I pulled into an enclosure, later learning that it's called a "porte cochere."

As I shut off the engine, I noticed the red flag on the temperature gauge burned bright. The old car was ominously silent—not a creak or a crack.

A figure ran down the steps calling, "Rica, we were worried about you. Are you all right?"

That voice—where had I heard it before? It teased my memory. I knew that voice, but who? Where?

I hesitated, then turned and looked.

My logical mind said no as I looked away. I felt a momentary sense of fear. I'd been studying late into the night, losing sleep, was pretty shook up driving over that bridge. I must be hallucinating.

I looked back again and his eyes met mine.

A disbelieving, questioning voice barely spoke above a whisper. "Steve?"

Then the wild, jubilant cry, "Steve, Steve, Steve."

Juan flung himself against me, his arms wrapped so tightly around me that I couldn't lift my own to wipe the tears that ran like a river down my face.

Together our tears wet his cashmere jacket as Rica, in shock, ran screaming to the house. "Dr. Teddy, Dr. Teddy."

Sara and Dr. Teddy stood transfixed in the doorway. Rica peeked from behind.

It was at that moment that the car from Maryland decided to expel a great explosive grunt, a long hissing sigh that rose high in the air to form a billowing cloud of steam, then passed over to wherever it is that old Buicks go to die.

CHAPTER 18

At the unaccustomed sound, Mr. Mackey, the pruning tool still in his hand, walked as fast as his arthritic old legs would carry him. He muttered to himself as he puffed with unusual exertion, "I hope the missus hasn't let that pressure cooker explode. I've told her a dozen times..."

As he threw opened the kitchen door, he saw her taking something from the oven and was reassured.

He stepped back and moved around the corner as fast as his old legs could carry him and was relieved when he spied the steaming car, but then he scowled watching the two young men embrace, stand back, then come together again and hold each other close.

Then the final straw—the Mexican held the other man's face between his hands and kissed him on both cheeks.

Outraged, he went back to the kitchen and helped himself to a handful of cookies, the vivid picture of the two men embracing festering in his mind. He chewed steadily while pouring himself a cup of coffee.

"You're awfully quiet. Are you tired? I think dinner will be a little late tonight—growing boys, you know," his wife spoke.

"I don't know about anything anymore," he growled, "but boys? Hardly. Six feet if they're an inch—they are grown men. You should have seen them out there wrapped up with each other like Siamese twins.

"I suspected that Mexican was queer, but have they brought another one home to roost? Beats me. I'll never understand—it's not right. They ought to be ashamed—in broad daylight, too."

"Henry Mackey," came his wife's surprised—and angry—voice. "You—yes, *you* ought to be ashamed. Miss Sara loves that boy and any fool can see that he adores her. Only the day after he got home from the hospital you said what a nice boy he was—for a Mexican—for working down there in the hothouse with you, his ribs all taped up. And I don't hear you complain about Miss Sara or Dr. Teddy or is that because they sign your paycheck?

"It's a different way of life, but does that make it wrong?"

She turned with her hands on her hips and demanded, "Do you understand why the sun rises in the east? What if it rises in the west tomorrow? Would you understand that? Would that make it bad? Obviously, there are lots of things about love that you don't understand. I'm here to testify to that. Shame on you.

"Get out of the cookies now. You've made me mad so get out of my kitchen, too."

Surprise and amazement were written on the faces of the three women who stood in the doorway watching the two embracing, exhilarated young men, the steaming car in the background.

Sara said, "Let's have a cup of tea and give them some privacy. I'm sure this is the friend Juan has told me about."

Rica asked, "May I use the phone to call my dad?"

"Surely, use the one in the kitchen, and would you tell Mrs. Mackey we would be delighted with a pot of tea. We'll have it on the veranda. I think I smell cookies, probably still warm from the oven."

When Juan and I had run out of breath and were able to speak coherently, I asked, "Juan, what are you doing here? Who are these people? What happened at the ranch?"

"Later. Later I'll tell you everything. Not now."

But I persisted, "How in the world did you get here?"

He paused a moment, then answered, "Mamá Sara found me in the park and now I am her son. Come."

He took me by the hand, my heart thudding, and led me like a child through those massive front doors. We followed the sounds of laughter, voices and the unmistakable aroma of fresh-baked cookies.

Two older women and Rica sat at a large glass-topped table upon which stood a pedestal plate that now held only a few chocolate crumbs.

They paused in their conversation as we stood for a moment in the doorway. Then the smaller woman motioned us to her and stood with an outstretched hand.

Juan choked out an emotional introduction with pride in every syllable. "Mamá Sara, this is my friend, my friend that I love—Steve."

Looking down at this little woman, her gray hair tied back with a colorful band, I saw Juan's love reflected in her twinkling green eyes.

Laughing, she turned to the woman beside her. "Teddy, I'm sure you've suspected that this is Juan's friend." Then she added, "Steve, this is my dearest friend, Dr. Teddy."

"This calls for a celebration," Sara said. "It's too early for champagne, but I'm sure Mrs. Mackey will come back with the tea cart."

As Sara predicted, the tea cart reappeared as if by magic, and Dr. Teddy and I reached for the cookies simultaneously.

My cookie stopped in midair as Dr. Teddy said seriously, but with a sly smile on her lips, "I must tell you how I admire your bravery in that incredible act of raw courage."

Me? She's talking about me? What act?

Noting my confusion, she added, "You know, when you went over Victoria Falls in that birch-bark canoe. I suppose the water was very wet, too."

Everyone laughed. The ice was broken.

Rica had ratted.

I looked across the table and my eyes refused to move, riveted to the picture she had made as she sat, totally unselfconscious, one long, shapely leg crossed over the other.

She didn't seem to notice—or care about the smudge of dirt that colored her skirt, a farewell gift from the dented fender.

A shaft of light from the tall window behind her shone through that long, black hair, black as the soft underfeathers of a raven's wing. I had an almost uncontrollable urge to leap over the glass that separated us to run my fingers through that silken hair and kiss away the almost nonexistent chip of orange paint near the corner of her mouth. For starters.

The sweat beaded on my forehead and elsewhere as my stomach tightened. I dropped a napkin on my lap.

Almost as if she could read my mind, her eyes slanted in a devilish wink and she raised her left hand and wriggled her third finger.

Trembling, I forced my eyes away and looked directly into the eyes of the tall woman who sat beside me and whose eyes questioned mine.

The spell was broken as Mrs. Mackey entered and announced, "Miss Rica, your father is here."

Juan sat between me and his Mamá Sara. His big dark eyes dancing with delight, the words tumbling out, his newly acquired English generously interspersed with Spanish. His excitement was contagious and radiated around the large, shady veranda that Ma would have called a front porch.

I marveled at Juan in these incredibly beautiful surroundings. The wealth and luxury was understated, but unmistakable. He looked as though he'd been born into it.

Juan poured tea for me in a tissue-thin cup and handled the ornate teapot as gracefully as his Mamá.

It felt like there were ten fingers on each hand—surely that many fingers could hold any cup securely.

Dr. Teddy and I had found a common ground. I was surprised to find out how knowledgeable she was about the intricate workings of an engine—far surpassing me.

"I thought you were a doctor, not a mechanic," I questioned.

"My father loved cars and taught both of us. He owned one of the first horseless carriages in the city." Dr. Teddy laughed, remembering, "Mother went into hysterics when I'd come in with grease on my petticoats and under my fingernails.

"Dad wanted to know what made those engines turn and so did I. We tinkered until the chauffeur had a mechanic on permanent call. I still like to know what goes on under the hood."

Watching and marveling at Juan as we talked, my mind questioned how this could be the same person.

Sitting here on this lovely veranda, surrounded by warmth and comfort, I suddenly felt cold.

Unbidden, those buried memories stirred and shook themselves alive. My mind could not release the pictures that would not fade. Once again I was back on that brush-covered hillside in the drizzling rain, my only friend teaching me to roll my first marijuana cigarette, both of us turning the corner of young manhood, shaking with cold and laughter. The smell of the potent cigarette competed with the stink of the wet sheep.

And now, *this* Juan. Has he changed inside, too?

His long, tapered fingers held the pot that filled my cup, more tea than I'd ever drunk in my life. Was this the hand that had fastened my shaking fingers around the handle of a shovel used to bury a dead man? The hand that held his murderous father back as he pushed against me? My life lay in those hands.

Is this the terrified boy who held me while I puked and pissed myself? Who half carried me down that dark trail?

I smelled not the sweet fragrance of luxury, but the ancient wet dirt that lay piled beside the black hole.

The fragile cup rattled in its saucer, then shattered on the floor.

Dr. Teddy's hand on my shoulder returned me to reality.

Instinctively, I knew that Juan had not changed. This tall, handsome young man in his elegantly casual clothes in this magnificent home was the same loving boy who had suffered with me. We had clung together as brothers for our very existence.

The cookies were long gone; the teapot was dry.

"Dinner at eight, gentlemen," Dr. Teddy announced.

In the privacy of their bedroom, as they prepared to go down to dinner, Sara said, "I noticed you and Steve got along famously. I'm so glad you like Juan's friend. I like him, too."

"I like him, but he is what he is, and that's going to break our boy's heart," Dr. Teddy responded.

CHAPTER 19

I called Ma from Juan's apartment. She was disappointed that I wouldn't be home. I told her I was staying with some nice friends and we'd just had dinner. When I added that the cooking couldn't compare to hers, she was appeased.

What Juan's apartment lacked in square footage made up in comfort. Big, soft leather sofa, matching chair, a bedroom overlooking the rose garden where Mamá Sara's award-winning hybrid roses were grown in the adjoining greenhouse.

"I help her there," Juan said proudly, then showed me through a half-open door. "This is her studio."

The easel held the unfinished portrait of a woman. There were dozens of canvases, the smell of paint, tall windows that now showed the twinkling lights of the city below.

Kicking off my worn-down shoes and sprawling on the sofa, I could contain my curiosity no longer.

"Juan, stop pacing and sit down. I want to know everything. You said Mamá Sara found you in the park. How did you get there?"

"My father."

It seemed that every word had to be dragged out of him.

"Why? Did Lupe tell him you helped me?"

"No. He killed Lupe."

I sat there stunned, my heart sick to think of her lying dead in an unknown grave. I shuddered to know how close I had come to the same fate.

Juan was up and pacing again.

"Damn it, will you sit down? Tell me, why did he dump you at the park? Surely he must have planned to come back. After all, you are his only son."

"No, he hated me. He said he should have killed me, too."

"Then why?"

He flung himself into the big chair, covering his face with his hands and sobbing, "Because I am a *maricón*."

"*Maricón?* I don't know that word. Tell me in English."

"Queer," he almost whispered, then blurted, "I have always loved you, Steve. There will never be another."

When he leaned toward me, I held up a restraining hand. The meaning of his words dumbed my senses.

We sat in silence for what seemed like an eternity. I could not have been more shocked if he had said he was a werewolf. Surely he had read the expression on my face.

"Now you will hate me, as he hated me," he spoke through his fingers covering his face.

"Do these women know?"

"Of course, they are the same."

My mind boggled. "Dr. Teddy? Sara?"

"Yes."

My mind cartwheeling, it catapulted that information into my brain—a brain that insisted "No, no, no." But in my heart I knew Juan didn't lie.

The silence hung dark and heavy.

I knew it had taken more courage to tell me this, believing that I would hate him, than he had shown the night he had stood between me and his father.

I wondered if I would have had the guts to do it.

The quiet lengthened. Walking to his chair, I slid in beside him. With my arms around him, my voice choked, "I could never hate you. I'll love you always as a brother."

His words were spoken softly, but the dark eyes were pleading.

"No, Steve, please no—not brother."

Knowing I had to do this right and do it now, I told him, "That's the only way it can ever be, Juan, my brother, my friend. We are different."

That old adage "This hurts me more than it hurts you" came to mind, but I knew it was a lie. It was close, though.

He stood wordlessly and walked unsteadily to his bedroom, then closed the door.

Sitting back in that big chair, using my sleeve to wipe the wet from my face, I tried to gather my thoughts.

CHAPTER 20

We did not, to my knowledge, know of anyone openly queer. And "gay" was a word that meant happy.

Theirs was truly a closed world. Actually, that was a subject that "nice" people didn't talk about. If there was any question of right or wrong, Ma would get the Book and find the answer.

Having been schooled in the Book myself, I knew exactly where she'd find it: Leviticus Chapter 18, Verse 22. I could almost hear her voice as she would read chapter and verse, then close the Book and that was final. No ifs, ands or buts.

My thoughts would not be stilled as my mind worried the question like a dog worries a bone—right or wrong?

When I had opened that Book, I found passages that so many more learned people than I had seemed to miss—or disregard.

In *my* Book, Jesus said, "Love one another." He didn't say, "Love only the ones without sin."

I thought Ma would probably love me anyhow, even if she knew about my exploits with Lupe in the hay, but I hastily reclassified that to myself—that wasn't "sin," that was pleasure—and comforted myself. Probably lots of people thought that way.

I didn't think that God expected us to understand that great Book in its entirety, so He made it simple. He gave us the condensed version: The Ten Commandments. A plan for our well-being so plainly written that even a child could understand. He hung the meaning of the entire Book on the first two Commandments, which to me are:

"Love God."

"Love one another."

No ifs, ands or buts.

After hours of analyzing pros and cons, I concluded that the God who made the universe was fully capable of judging it and did not need any help from me. Having allowed God that responsibility, I felt a great weight lift off my shoulders.

Waking in yesterday's clothes, a blanket thrown over me, a pillow in the vicinity of my head, I smelled the coffee perking in his fancy percolator, noted the clean clothes he had laid out for me.

Showered, dressed better than I ever had been in my life, I preened in front of the mirror. "Just call me 'Dude.'"

"No, I'll call you brother."

With a flourish, Juan poured me a cup of fresh coffee.

I was unhampered by any worry except the nagging thought about what I was going to do with that old junker cluttering up the driveway with twenty dollars in my pocket. How can I bring myself to borrow whatever it takes to get it towed away? I felt almost ashamed—that faithful old Buick had been my ride to freedom.

As we walked down the stairs, Juan slipped an arm around my shoulder. With a little twisted smile, he said, "I am so glad you are my brother."

My voice choked, "Me, too. You'll never know."

Since we were late, we had our hotcakes and various other delicious foods in what Mrs. Mackey called the "breakfast room."

Stuffed to full capacity, I followed Juan out of the kitchen door. I didn't want to see what still sat in front of the house as if waiting for a memorial service.

We walked to the garage, converted from the building that in years gone by had housed the fine carriages and the horses that pulled them.

Juan pressed a button and the doors slid open without a sound. He walked to a silver Mercedes coupe, which was elegant beyond belief.

"My birthday present. Rica taught me to drive."

Beside it sat a Mercedes sedan.

"Mamá's," he explained. "And this is Dr. Teddy's." Juan pointed as he led me to an older Bentley. "She's had it for a long time and says, next to the Bentley, she loves Mamá best." He laughed.

We went back to his birthday present and I tried not to drool on it.

"Open the hood," I said.

"Why? How? Is something broken?"

I had to see what was under that gleaming silver hood.

While looking for a release that would allow me that pleasure, a hand protruding from a white linen sleeve with a monogrammed cuff reached past me and popped the hood.

I'm sure my heart stopped at the beauty of it.

Then, of course, we discussed everything that had a motor.

Dr. Teddy taught me about fine cars while that Buick sat and waited. Its disposal finally became priority and I had psyched myself to ask for help.

As though she read my mind, Dr. Teddy said, "Don't worry so, I've already had it towed away. We'll see that you get back to class tomorrow, so enjoy the day."

I dared not look up lest she see the teardrop that hung by an eyelash. I looked away—my pride intact, my gratitude inexpressible.

She gave me a pat on the shoulder. "You've got what it takes. Some day you'll be driving a fine car. I know."

As she walked away, she left behind a burning determination in my heart. I would make my life a success, too.

In a back corner, as though ashamed to be in such elite company, sat a vehicle mostly covered but for a few random red spots showing through.

"Juan, what's that?"

"Oh, nothing much I don't think." Pausing at his coupe, he said, "Let's tour the city. Want to drive?"

"Do I want to go to heaven?"

He directed me and we spent the day exploring this indescribable city by the bay. I never wanted to leave.

It was almost dark as we drove up the hill.

The coupe had made any other car in the whole world look like a hay wagon. I was forever hooked.

We were tired and happy. We'd had such a wonderful day.

Coming through the gate, I could see that the vacancy left by my Buick was filled. Suddenly, my ears deafened by Juan's delighted laughter, I turned my head to see Dr. Teddy and Mamá Sara standing in the doorway, waiting.

I came to a stop behind a shiny red pickup. Perched on the cab, tied by a big, red bow, was a sign with a single word, "Steve."

Dazed, speechless, and paralyzed, my legs wouldn't move—only my eyes.

Dr. Teddy motioned to me. Juan nudged me out of the coupe. We walked to the truck, then he returned to stand with his Mamá.

I could almost see myself reflected in the shiny red paint. Dr. Teddy pointed to the door handle and laughingly guided my hand to the button that opened the hood.

"Don't you want to see what's under there?"

I nodded, unable to find words.

Juan and Mamá Sara watched with amazement as Dr. Teddy and I scrutinized every part of that spotless engine. It was a three hundred and fifty cubic-inch block with a four-barrel carburetor. I knew it would move out with minimum urging.

"Look," she said, stepping into the cab and pointing.

I leaned over, my eyes following her finger, to see that the truck was fully automatic.

Heaven and that Mercedes could wait.

While they explored every part of the truck that I could reach, my hands worked independently from my brain, an organ that was trying to sort out the questions becalmed in a sea of disbelief that this could be happening to me.

She handed me the keys, and Juan and Mamá Sara clapped.

"I couldn't possibly...I appreciate..." I stammered.

"You can," she said with finality.

"I could borrow it until I get my own..." My inadequate protest was cut short.

"This is your own." She pressed the keys into my hands. "You need reliable transportation until you get your Mercedes." She grinned. "We don't need it. Actually it's cluttering up the garage. I got it two years ago thinking it would be helpful for Mackey, but when he was going down the hill, he hit the gas instead of the brakes and almost scared himself into a heart attack. He drove back, put it in the garage and threw a cover over it, taking up space in the garage since then. You'd be doing us a favor."

"Yes, I can see that the garage certainly is a mess." I grinned. "Guess this is the only way to show my appreciation for all the kindness you've shown me this weekend."

I put the keys in my pocket. She put her arms around me and gave me a hug.

"Be sure to spell my name right when you're a big-time reporter." When the time came, I did.

It was a champagne celebration that evening.

Mamá Sara offered to christen my truck with a bottle—an offer I refused. We drank that bottle and then another...then I forget.

Juan and I laughed and talked way late into the night until I fell asleep drunk with champagne and happiness.

When the aroma of coffee awoke me, I found the blanket at the foot of the sofa and no pillow.

"The service isn't what it was," I complained.

Juan laughed and said, "I see you're spoiled already," as he handed me a cup.

We talked nonstop all day Sunday, taking time only to eat. We didn't discuss our time at the ranch—a raw wound barely scabbed over, but spoke of our hopes for the future. Mamá Sara and Dr. Teddy joined us at intervals and it was one of the best days of my life.

I got an early start on Monday morning—I didn't dare be late for class.

It was a happy, tearful leave-taking, with plans for the future assured.

Mr. Mackey, watching through a window, muttered, "They're at it again."

I drove my truck over the Bay Bridge, high above the water below and certainly not in the slow lane.

My mind relived the unforgettable experiences in another world— a world I never could have dreamed existed.

It had been a storybook weekend that rivaled the Arabian Nights, and was as far from my church-schooled existence as it was possible to get.

The bottom line was that Juan was still the same Juan who had survived that never-to-be-forgotten hell with me. No, he hadn't changed—only the circumstances had—and perhaps myself.

My head was still in the clouds as I scurried into her classroom. But I was late anyway—inexcusable in Mrs. Dowd's opinion.

After her acid tongue had reduced me to buttons and shoelaces, my ego landed with a thud and my normal life went on.

CHAPTER 21

W hen I wasn't studying, I'd go down to the baseball field and practice with the hopeful amateurs. I had pitched for our school games and wasn't too bad. And dribbling a basketball at the huge gym was pure pleasure. Sometimes I even got it in the hoop. But baseball was my game.

I found the college newspaper's office. It was the "Goliath" to my old school's "David." It seemed to me that's where my life began.

Hanging out there my every spare moment, bragging that I had been the editor of my school's paper for three years—I failed to mention that I had been fired, but did drop that Mrs. Dowd was giving me Bs and B pluses in her class. Anyone in the writing business knew Mrs. Dowd.

Finally the editor couldn't stand my pleading anymore and assigned me the sports column—for free.

I was ecstatic and gave it everything that was in me. To my supercritical eye, my work wasn't bad. I spelled the players' names right and got the scores correct. I knew beyond a doubt that this was my life.

My trips home became less frequent as the games were mostly on weekends. Classes, studying, writing and rewriting took all the rest of my time.

I kept in touch on the phone and the monthly phone bill grew like Topsy.

Ma was immediately suspicious of an older woman who would

give a young fellow a truck, so I dared not go into detail. She was upset, too, because Sis, now in her senior year, was seeing way too much of a guy Ma didn't approve of, especially after she'd discovered the screen that had been removed from Sis' bedroom window.

But the guy joined the Marine Corps and was now training at Camp Pendleton. Ma was relieved and Sis went back to *True Confessions*—maybe.

My friendship with Juan remained as strong as ever. I seldom got over the bridge to see him, but he would drive over regularly and we'd squeeze in as much time as possible.

Usually Rica was with him. She seemed to have a lot of time on her hands—Juan was way past the need for a tutor, but apparently Rica had adopted him. He joked that now he had a sister, too.

Rica had a great sense of humor—laughed at all my raunchy jokes, flirted like crazy with me, holding up that damn ring finger when I'd get too close.

I'd say, "Why don't you marry the guy? You're going to die an old maid."

She'd defend him with, "He's a busy man—he has his career. Mind your own business, Cowboy."

"If I was on my way to heaven, I'd take time—all the time I'd need," I said jokingly. But she knew I meant every word. I was crazy about her. She made me miserable. Both were hard to conceal.

Juan said, "Why don't you give it up, Steve. She's just not for you. Forget it."

She made every girl I took out come in a poor second. Plus, I had no time and no money for frivolities.

In a weak moment after class, Mrs. Dowd had told me that I was a natural-born writer, a sentiment I had no argument with. I was nineteen years old, full of myself, and figured the big-time was just around the corner and I could make it.

The last quarter was coming up fast and, knowing that would be the end of my formal education since I was out of funds, I badgered the editor of the *Bridgeport News,* a small newspaper nearer the city with a circulation of 25,000. Armed with Mrs. Dowd's recommendation and all other pertinent information I could dig up, I gave him no peace until he said he would consider me for the sports reporter. He had other applicants.

Some months later, when walking out of my final class, I spent my last twelve dollars on a dozen red roses and had them delivered to Mrs. Dowd with a note that read: "There is no person who has influenced my life more or for whom I have more respect. Gratefully, Steve."

CHAPTER 22

The woman who sat so gracefully in the brocaded chair had everything that screamed old money.

Completely at ease, her hands were clasped loosely in her lap, the long legs crossed at the ankle. The lovely gown draped perfectly about her slim shoulders—those shoulders that could hold a priceless fur as easily as the satin straps. Her auburn hair was piled high on a head tilted slightly to accentuate the elegant line of her jaw. He green eyes were glinting with just a hint of "Let them eat cake."

Sara painted quickly with broad, easy strokes, glancing up intermittently, stepping away only to scrutinize the painting with a critical eye.

She paused, added a color here, blended a color there, redoing a part of what she had thought was perfect at the last sitting. Trying not to show her impatience with a portrait that just would not come together, she put her brush down.

"Perhaps we've done enough for today."

The woman spoke, a little edge to her voice. "There's something about the eyes that isn't quite right and it must be perfect."

She stood and rearranged her clothing.

"When will it be finished? It's been a long time."

"Very soon. It has taken longer than I expected but, as you say, it must be perfect. Shall I ring for your car?"

As the door closed, Sara sank down on a chair. Wiping the paint from her hands, swiping at her tears, she cursed.

"This damnable portrait. Will I ever get it right? Near perfect, except for some elusive little detail. I've gone over it a hundred times in my mind. What is it that I'm missing? What?"

Exhausted, frustrated, she put her head in her hands and sobbed.

Juan had been out. As he entered his apartment, he could hear the muffled sounds from her studio. Quickly, he made tea, then knocked as he came in carrying the tray with a steaming pot.

She smiled tearfully, motioning him to sit beside her. But he deposited the tray and sat with his arms around her waist, comforting her as she alternately cried and raged.

"Truly I'm ready to burn the damn thing."

Releasing her, he poured the tea and as she accepted the cup, he walked to the easel and studied the portrait carefully. His eyes examined every brush stroke as he looked at it from every angle.

Sara poured herself another cup of tea, her emotion spent, and dabbed at her eyes while she watched him scrutinize the canvas.

He picked up a brush and turned to Sara with a questioning look.

She smiled, nodded, then walked to the closet to retrieve her old paint-spattered easel. After placing a canvas on it, she tacked on a paper cover.

"Show me. Let me be your pupil," she said, laughing, the tears still drying on her cheeks.

Returning to her chair, she refilled her cup and watched as Juan picked up a charcoal stick and started to sketch. He emphasized the arrogant tilt of the head, the miniscule slant of the eyes, then softened the curve of the cheek. With a sure hand, he shadowed the high bridge of the nose.

Sara watched, her tea growing cold, her eyes wide with disbelief, as the face became all too familiar.

Juan hesitated for a moment, stepped back, then detailed the eyes. As if by magic, the portrait became the face that Sara had been striving for.

Turning to her, he said, "I used to draw pictures of my grandmama on the wall."

He had so quickly corrected the flaw that had eluded her for weeks. The portrait had become real.

She reached for her brush and it seemed to fly as her eyes flashed from the charcoal sketch to her beautiful oil, correcting, stroke by stroke.

Juan smiled his encouragement.

Suddenly the portrait became alive. Her hand was shaking as she lay down the brush. At last—at last! It was perfect.

Holding hands, they danced like children around the portrait of the senator's wife.

CHAPTER 23

When the caller identified himself, my heart jumped so hard, I thought a rib was broken.

"Prentiss here. *Bridgeport News*. Come in and we'll see if you're as good as you say. If you are, maybe you can write a column."

"With my name at the top?" Instantly I felt my face flush at the schoolboy sound of my question and hoped he'd think I was joking.

I was so thrilled that my phone bill went up another twenty dollars—I couldn't get Ma off the line.

My first real job. Where I got paid for doing what I loved most. To be able to see my name above my article. I was ecstatic.

I was assigned a desk stuck back in a smoky corner, older than Moses, scarred with cigarette burns, and a typewriter that had certainly seen better days.

My typing skills were not great, but one of the copy boys gave me a couple of quick lessons. The hunt-and-peck system was mastered.

My brain was over the speed limit. I worked harder than I ever had in my life, pouring out the images from my mind, painting them with words to make my readers taste the popcorn, smell the hot dogs, feel the hard seat of the front row.

I considered myself a full-fledged member of the press and wore a button that said so. Unfortunately, that didn't get me into the press box. That was reserved for the announcer and his friends.

I got calluses on my ass from sitting on anything stationary. Sometimes, while trying to meet a deadline, I'd misspell a word or get the names of the players mixed up. The editor and I had some serious talks.

He didn't seem to mind that I'd only had three semesters of formal instruction —he actually said I was a "natural." I hoped he meant I was a natural writer, but the fact that I worked long hours and never mentioned the overtime may have influenced his opinion.

There were lots of adjectives—not necessarily flattering—floating around the copy room among a bunch of hardcore reporters depending on their moods. Still, I hung out there as if it was home.

"Why in hell don't you bring a sleeping bag?" some wise guy suggested.

The months passed. The truck really got a workout. I mentally thanked Dr. Teddy every time the keys turned and it leaped to life as ready to go as I was.

It seemed that I was always on the road due to my assignments covering various games from the high-school hopefuls to the state championships.

My expense account was bare bones. I met a lot of cockroaches, drank bad coffee and slept in cheap motel rooms.

I loved every minute of it.

Who would have dreamed that a posthole digger, aka sheepherder, and a penniless immigrant well-trained in the production of marijuana could have come so far—in so little time?

Maybe the Lord figured He owed us.

CHAPTER 24

The phone was ringing off the hook as I opened the door, cussing to myself. "What the hell now? That last game had been a tie and I've got to write it up before I forget anything..."

Picking up the phone, I was surprised to hear Sis' voice.

"Can you come home this weekend, Steve?"

Hesitating, I said, "Gee, Sis, I've got a game I gotta go to, and one to write up now. Maybe next week."

"Steve, you've gotta come home."

"Is anything wrong? Is Ma okay?"

"Yeah, she's okay."

"Well, maybe next weekend when I get caught up—I'm rushed."

"Steve, you've got to come home."

"Sis, what the hell is going on?"

"I'm pregnant."

"Pregnant?" I yelled. "How in hell can you be pregnant?"

"The usual way," came her sarcastic response.

"Sis, that's not funny. What's the problem?"

"Damn it, I just told you. I'm pregnant."

My mind whirled and my rage grew. The phone shook in my hand.

"Who is it?" I could hardly force the words out.

"Tim, of course."

"I'll kill that son of a bitch. Couldn't he keep it in his pants?"

"Hell, no." Her voice rose about ten octaves. "I kept it in mine.

"Don't be so self-righteous. I suppose you've kept yours in your pants just because Ma told you she'd cut it off with the chicken knife. Tim doesn't scare that easy."

"Well, what are we going to do?" I asked helplessly.

"I don't know about you, but Tim and I are going to elope to Reno and get married. He's got a three-day pass."

"Married? You're going to get married? Sis!"

"What is the matter with you, Steve? I've known Tim since sixth grade, and here's the clincher: we love each other. So do you want to come with us or not? We need a witness."

"You just want me there when you tell Ma."

"Well, yeah, that, too. Ever since Tim got caught joyriding in somebody else's car, Ma hasn't liked him. She forgets that I was in the car, too. We didn't hurt a damn thing—didn't even mess up the backseat."

"Sis!"

"S'cuse me—I forgot I was talking to a virgin. Seems to me you would want to be with your only sister—the first time..."

"What first time? The marriage, the baby, or..."

She hung up on me.

I drove home the next morning. Ma and I had a good visit that included biscuits and gravy—and chocolate cake.

"Sis is off some place with that marine. I hope they ship him off to China," Ma complained.

Knowing how upset she was going to be, I felt guilty as hell and wished I wasn't going to be involved. But how could I not? Sis and I had always been closer than most siblings—and she *was* pregnant.

Ma had always planned that Sis would have a big church wedding with bridesmaids and a long white dress. She was going to hurt, and Sis was going to need my help to defuse her.

We sneaked out early before Ma was awake.

The deed was done in a commercial-looking little wedding chapel with fake flowers and a minister who looked as though he'd had a hard night at the casino. He stunk so bad of cigarette smoke that I nearly choked.

We went to a big buffet brunch and then home to face the music.

Ma was pissed.

"You've been gone all day. I thought you came home to visit. Sis went some place, too—I s'pose with that Tim."

Ma's eyes widened as she saw him come in behind Sis, but with her usual hospitality, she put the coffeepot on and brought out what was left of the cake.

"What happened to you kids? I was going to make hotcakes and sausage, but I woke up to a deserted house. Well, sit down and be comfortable. Coffee will be done in a minute."

Shifting from one foot to another, I wished that I was in China.

Tim sat. I will admit that he looked good in those dress blues.

Sis went into the bedroom to leave her coat.

Ma said politely, "How do you like the marines, Tim? I s'pose you'll be shipped out soon. Your training must be finished, isn't it?"

"Well, actually, I've been promoted to sergeant and my orders are to stay stateside, working with a gunnery crew."

"How nice," Ma said. I didn't dare look at her.

Sis came back and gave me a desperate look.

Ma was setting the table when she glanced at Sis. "My, Sis, you sure look pretty. Is that a new dress?"

Silently, Sis held out her hand with the simple gold wedding band. I closed my eyes.

Ma gasped and held her breath so long I thought she'd turn blue, then sobbed, "Oh, Sis, you didn't...you couldn't...please. Oh, no."

Sis cried like her heart would break. I knew she was crying for Ma.

Tim stood and put his arms around Sis. I went to Ma.

Looking right into Ma's tearful eyes, Tim said, "Yes, we did, and we'd like your blessing. I promise you'll never have cause to regret it. I've loved her since sixth grade. Please be happy for us."

Ma put her arms around Sis, their tear-wet cheeks touching. Somehow Tim managed to squeeze in, so I wrapped my arms around the whole package and somehow it all came together.

I tried to call Ma as often as possible. The last time she said, "Here's some news for your newspaper—Sis is pregnant. No wonder her bedroom screen was off."

Laughing to myself, I was glad that I was out of reach.

Ma's birthday was coming up and Sis would be making plans for a celebration. My mouth watered as I envisioned the good home-cooking, and I could almost taste the chocolate birthday cake.

I had talked with Juan but hadn't seen him in over three months. The last time he had called, excited about a painting that Mamá Sara had finished, he said he was painting, too. He kept me on the phone for thirty minutes as he enthused. I could feel the grin creeping across my face—I thought he sounded as obsessed with his painting as I was with my writing.

I was excited and happy for him, my friend.

We'd come a long way.

I was still the new kid on the block, so I was flattered when the managing editor, Prentiss, sent me to interview a Vietnam vet, an old schoolmate of his.

Veterans Day was fast approaching.

I found the vet holding a can of Budweiser and waiting beside the door of a little rundown café on the corner of a small airfield. I showed him my press card; he transferred his beer to the other hand and we shook.

"Just call me Al," he said in a slow, quiet voice.

He was shorter than me with hair that had started to gray under a greasy cap, about a two-day stubble of beard on his chin, and blood-shot eyes that looked like he'd just come off a big one and wished he hadn't. A sweatshirt was pulled over a belly just beginning to show, and his jeans apparently had been overlooked when the laundry was done.

"C'mon, let's sit in the plane where we'll have a little privacy."

He led the way to a small plane that seemed dwarfed between two larger, obviously newer aircrafts. As he climbed in, he said over his shoulder, "She ain't pretty, could use some new paint and probably a good tune-up, but she's mine."

I followed him in and settled myself in the passenger seat, my feet resting on a six-pack.

"This one's dead," he said, tossing an empty can behind his seat. I heard it rattle with the others.

Pushing my foot aside, he retrieved another can and popped the cap.

"Yeah," he continued, "I saved my pay in 'Nam. Hell, there wasn't any place to spend it except on booze, drugs, whores...of course, those came cheap: a candy bar would do it; a pack of cigarettes would get you as much time as you wanted.

"I had a good-sized bundle when I got stateside and spent most of it on this old girl. She was beautiful and shiny then. I spent the rest on flying lessons and went into the charter business. I can under-stand how Prentiss got hooked. Up there, it's only you and God and the wild blue yonder."

"Are you married?" I asked.

"No." His face clouded. "A near-miss once."

"How old are you, Al?"

"Older than God," he replied with a sound I thought might be a laugh.

"Tell me about Vietnam, your experiences."

"What do you want? The movie version or the way it really was?"

Then he went on as if he'd never asked, tossing another empty one to the back. I moved my feet as he reached over for the next full can.

"Prentiss, your boss, ended up a pilot. Of course, he came up through the ranks. Made corporal in about six months. I remember because it was my birthday and we got roaring drunk on some home-made hooch that damn near killed us." Al closed his eyes and leaned back with his memories.

"He learned his ABCs working on them big planes, but he wanted to fly. Said he didn't like the grease under his fingernails. So after he got his sergeant's stripes, he put in for OTS—that's Officer Training School—and got through all the paperwork. Said that's how he knew war was hell.

"He had a lot of scalps on his belt when he damn near went down with the plane and took some bumps himself. Got out on a medical.

"So now he's in the newspaper business. Good choice—he was always full of bullshit, but a good joe. Glad he made it.

"I'm still thirsty. Anything left down there?"

I shook my head. "Sorry."

"Damn. Well, then there was Mickey McGuire, that poor son of a bitch. He got the infantry. Both legs were blown off by a land mine—lost his manhood, too. They sent him stateside to a veterans hospital where he tried to commit suicide, so now he's in the psych ward and he ain't no crazier than the rest of us.

"And then, of course, there's me. I could talk the rest of your life and wouldn't cover even a chapter of Vietnam."

And so he talked, pausing only to light a cigarette from the glowing butt of another, and the cans rattled behind him every time he changed positions.

For two hours I saw the horror of Vietnam through his eyes—the nightmare nights, the rain-sodden days, the screaming of the wounded and dying, the creeping jungle, the rotted feet in shoes that never dried.

His whispering voice continued. "Yeah, three boys just out of high school, little boys grown tall." He laughed. "Trained to kill and do unto them as they did unto us. Then we were shunned if we made it home. We were crippled mentally and physically and kicked around like an empty beer can."

I was in a cold sweat. There was a growing certainty in my mind that I had been given this assignment because no one else wanted it.

I had to get out. It was more than I could endure, so I lied to him.

"Al, I have to go. I've got another assignment. I appreciate..." For once in my life, I could not find the words.

"Oh, wait a minute. I want to show you some pictures. There's only three of them—just take a minute."

His hands shook as he dug around in his back pocket for his billfold— turned it inside out. He finally squirmed around to drag a tattered old knapsack from under the beer cans and pulled out the creased and faded photos.

The first picture was of three laughing boys on the verge of manhood, their arms around each other's shoulders. Their uniforms appeared immaculate—the knife-sharp crease in the trousers, their caps square on—absolute regulation.

Even through the worn paper of the photo, I swear I could feel the vibrant life of those boys as it burned in my hand.

"That's your boss on the end. Bet he doesn't have as much hair now. Haven't seen him in a while—guess we don't travel in the same social circle."

The second picture was a close-up. I recognized Prentiss. He was obviously drunk—his flyboy hat on backward, a bottle held high, one arm around the shoulders of a man with a cap of sorts pulled low on his forehead, his mouth turned in a grim smile. I knew it must be Mickey. He was holding a gun as though it were a toy.

"That's an M16," Al said, pointing. "Hell of a good gun. The best—if it didn't get hot and jam just when you needed it most."

Around Mickey's neck hung something on a string I couldn't immediately identify.

"What's that?"

"Ears. Eight or ten of 'em—don't remember now. A lot of that went on then—no big deal. We didn't send those pictures home to Mom." He laughed.

My stomach did a slow churn. "Al, I really have to go…"

He put a restraining hand on my arm. "You gotta see the last one," he said as he pushed the picture of a boy with a wide smile, his hat at a jaunty angle, his uniform without a wrinkle. A pretty girl, laughing, looked up at him, her arms around his waist.

The picture had been torn in pieces and somehow the ragged edges fixed together.

I pushed Al's hand away and stumbled out.

Arriving home, I felt so terribly tired and flung myself on the bed, cursing my editor and closing my eyes tightly, as if that would erase this hideous afternoon from my memory. For the first time, I questioned my career choice.

There was no escaping the images that chased around my brain, so I got up and put on a pot of coffee and made a sandwich, which was promptly rejected by my stomach.

I picked up my pen and put it all down the way it was. My story, finished just as the sun came up, was good.

When I handed it to Prentiss, he asked with a straight face, "How did you and Al get along?"

"Just fine, but you sure weren't very photogenic."

On the way home I picked up a good steak and onions and kept it all down.

I took a quick shower and slept all day. Sometime later—it was dark by then—the phone rang and rang. Groggy with sleep, I picked up the receiver to hear Juan's voice leaping with delight over the wires.

"Steve. Mamá Sara is having a big, big party—a hundred and fifty guests—next Saturday. You must come. It's the first showing of her most recent painting."

"Juan," I interrupted. "I don't have the clothes for a fancy party— don't even own a necktie. And I'm tired and not good company. Maybe another time..."

But he would not be denied. "Steve, I've got enough clothes to open a store and we're the same size. Come early. Rica will be here."

CHAPTER 25

Mr. Mackey sat at a small table in a corner of the kitchen. His wife placed a plate of food before him.

"Hurry up," she urged. "I've got a dozen things to do—all these people coming in with the buffet and I'll have to see that everything goes right."

"This must be an extra fancy party. We haven't had one this big in years. The whole property is lit up like a Christmas tree."

"Yes, Miss Sara is premiering that painting she's just finished for someone real important, I'll guess. I heard her tell Dr. Teddy it was Juan's introduction to the art world, too. Says he's an undiscovered genius, that he should be teaching her."

"That's pretty high praise coming from someone as well known as she is. Guess I've lost my helper—he was awfully good with the roses, even if he is a queer," admitted Mackey.

"That boy has brought Miss Sara so much happiness," Mrs. Mackey snapped, "and it looks like Dr. Teddy has adopted the other one. He's sure driving proud in that truck. Those boys sure have fun when he visits. It's nice to cook for someone who really digs into meat and potatoes. Nice to have young people around."

Mackey looked up from his food. "I don't see where that girl fits in with two queers. A looker like her—seems to me she could do better with one of her own kind. Or is she one, too?"

"You know, you're going to be out selling pencils on skid row if you don't get off this 'queer' business," his wife said disgustedly. "Can't you understand friendship? Or have you never had a friend? I think this might be a good time for you to get out of my kitchen. Here..." She pushed a piece of cake on a plate toward him. "Take it with you. Go home. Maybe you can find a prizefight on TV. Watch a couple of macho idiots beat each other's brains out. That you understand."

CHAPTER 26

A s the lavish event at the mansion drew near, I reconsidered. Reluctantly, I agreed to go, but the images of that war-torn Asian country a continent away left a residue in my mind that I could not shake. I was not in a party mood.

As if my thoughts had reached Juan, the phone rang.

"I thought you were going to come early," he said in an aggrieved voice. "Hurry up—I've got something I'm dying to show you."

It was late when I crossed the bridge and traffic was heavy. It was near dark when I started up the hill. In the distance I could see the line of colored lights that danced along the lengthy driveway like a stand-up comic before the main event, pointing to the old house standing regal and tall at the top of the hill, brilliant as a diamond in the sunlight.

Juan must have been watching for me. Almost before the ignition was turned off, he was opening my door, a billboard grin across his face. With one arm around my shoulders and the other hand carrying my bare essentials, he almost pushed me into the house. I looked back to see a uniformed valet parking my truck.

Laughing and talking, we passed the bustling maids. Mrs. Mackey was supervising, giving orders like a four-star general.

I glimpsed the buffet table laid out and ready for the great unveiling, and myriad other signs of preparation.

Juan was as happy as I had ever seen him. He took the stairs to his apartment two at a time. "Come on," he urged. "What are you waiting for?" His happiness seemed to rub off on me and my mood lifted. I was glad to be here.

"This is for starters," he said, handing me a cold beer, then pouring one for himself. It seemed to me that his drink disappeared before my glass was half empty. He was in a flurry of excitement. As I swallowed the last drop, he stood quickly and walked to the door, flung it open and stepped into the studio.

He switched on one light, and then another that centered on a paint-stained easel that held the mostly finished painting of a face I had memorized in my heart and one that had visited me often in my dreams. It was Rica, and it was beautifully done.

When I could speak, all I could come up with was, "Damn lucky for you it wasn't a nude.

"She poses for you?" came my half-jealous question.

"Of course," Juan said. Noting my expression, he added, "You know you don't need to worry about me. I'm waiting for you."

He turned his face away as the impulsive words tumbled out of his mouth, and I thought to myself that we were both embarrassed.

"What's to eat? I'm starved."

"I'll bring up some sandwiches," Juan answered as he left the room.

Standing there, I was not smelling the oil and turpentine, but the lingering fragrance of her hair and remembering the teasing, lying promise in her eyes.

I was in shock, too, thinking of the Juan who had spent his formative years in a tiny remote village in the mountains of Mexico. His old grandmother, schooled in the ways of her grandmother, his only contact with the outside world. Later a local woman had taught him the rudiments of the English ABCs, but a God-given talent was crowned this night.

When he returned, I said with honest awe in my voice, "I hope that

I will someday write as well as you paint." He blushed at my praise and his smile raced from ear to ear.

A quick knock at the door and his Mamá Sara stepped in. Resplendent in a flowing chiffon dress, a jeweled headband holding her hair. Over her arm was an extravagantly ruffled shirt with jeweled cufflinks dangling from one sleeve.

"Steve—I'm glad you came," was delivered with a hug and returned in kind. "I got this especially for you." Sara beamed, holding up the shirt. "I know it will fit you."

"I laid out your clothes," Juan added. "Hurry and get dressed. I'll change in the bathroom."

Escaping into the bedroom with my finery, I dressed quickly and stepped out. Miss Sara adjusted the cummerbund as Juan, in an elegant tux, dodged around to straighten my tie and insert the studs, then helped me into the finest jacket I had ever worn.

They had such fun dressing me, turning me this way and that, that it was my pleasure to accommodate them. I looked down at my black silk stockings in the patent leather shoes and knew my feet would forever sneer at cotton.

As Juan adjusted his cufflinks, I could tell it wasn't the first time he'd worn a tux. I thought he was the handsomest man I'd ever seen.

As we stood together in front of the mirror, I felt like Cinderella. Miss Sara clapped her hands and said, "Such a handsome pair. You could be twins if Steve didn't have that curly blond hair."

I was complimented, and while gazing into that mirror, I thought, Steve, you are a long way from the farm.

"Hurry down," Sara said. "I must go—the guests are starting to arrive."

Her footsteps were noiseless on the thickly carpeted stairs.

A few last-minute adjustments and Juan and I followed. Walking down the wide, curving stairway into the incredible luxury of this other world overwhelmed me. The drawing room was now teeming with San Francisco's elite.

I spied Dr. Teddy who stood greeting guests, and marveled at her appearance. She was conspicuous in the simplicity of a satin tuxedo cut almost exactly as my own, the exceptions being the sequined lapels with a hint of ruffle at the throat and the jeweled studs I didn't doubt were real.

The trousers that hung from her slim hips emphasized the long line of her shapely legs. Diamonds that blazed from beneath the short, curly hair caught the brilliance of the chandeliers.

I wandered about. A maid, in a frilly apron that would have made Ma laugh, paused beside me with a tray of something that appeared so beautiful in the long-stemmed glasses that it seemed almost criminal to drink it. But as it lingered on my tongue, my taste buds declared that crime did pay. And when she came back, I felt it was a kindness to lighten her burden at least twice more.

I was definitely not tired and my mood bordered on the hilarious.

I caught glimpses of Juan as he circulated through the celebrants. Watching as women of all ages vied for his attention, he was trying to get past the reserve that marked his indifference. I was amused to see a man, later identified as a famous landscape painter, seemingly grow fast to Juan's elbow.

The trapped look on Juan's face brought Miss Sara to the rescue. They joined the group who were excitedly discussing her painting that sat high on an easel in the center of the room.

Posing beside it, the senator's wife was smiling at the attention, holding a cocktail glass high. Her gown attested to the skill of a well-known designer; a fur carelessly thrown over her shoulder would have paid for a tropical island.

Then the attention turned to Juan as Mamá Sara proudly introduced him as her protégé and promised that the next showing would be his.

Wandering through the rooms, I hadn't seen Rica. Juan had assured me that she would be there. Then the door opened and I knew why I had come to this party.

A maid took her wrap and my breath caught in my throat at the beauty of this woman. A low-cut strapless sheath clung to her every curve and revealed more of her than I had ever seen. Her black hair was piled high and secured with some kind of jeweled pins, her big eyes dancing with excitement. I moved toward her.

Then came the crushing disappointment. That damn fiancé, who was *always* busy, apparently had not been too busy to escort her to this prestigious party.

I stepped back quickly, but too late.

Smiling, she walked to me and formally extended her hand. I held it until she pulled away.

Turning to her fiancé, she said, "Doug, I'd like you to meet Steve, Juan's friend."

He didn't offer his hand and I was glad. He had a bored, superior look on his face as he glanced around, seeming to appraise everything. Finally his eyes came back to me.

"So this is Juan's boyfriend." His eyebrow went up, and with a knowing smirk he added, "What a cozy arrangement."

Rica tugged his arm and said sharply, "Please, Doug."

I felt the blood rush to my face hard enough to break a vessel. As he turned away, he gave a limp-wrist wave. "See you later, boyfriend."

My foot slid out almost as though it weren't part of me—a schoolboy trick reminiscent of the third grade. He tripped, half sprawling.

"My goodness." I grinned as I helped him up and straightened his tie. "Better go easy on that booze."

He glared at me and slapped my hand away. Rica gave me a look that would have frozen a polar bear. As they walked away, I called after them. "The buffet is wonderful—try the caviar."

Juan, who had been talking to some lady dripping diamonds, was looking past her and laughing so hard I could see his tonsils.

As the evening progressed, I wandered around watching the colorful scene before me, wishing with all my heart that Rica's companion would get an emergency call that would delay him forever.

I seemed like a magnet to all those maids in their frilly aprons. As I was busy exchanging glasses, a pretty redheaded woman took my arm and said, "You look lonesome. Want to dance? My name's Peggy."

"Dance? Sure—why not."

I loved to dance. Ma and Sis had taught me, and Sis and I had won a couple of contests when we sneaked out at night. I was smarter than Tim, though—I replaced the screens.

My patent-leather shoes slid over that polished floor with ease. Peggy was a good dancer and followed my fancy steps. I was almost enjoying myself.

Looking past Peggy's cleavage, I saw Rica dancing a slow waltz, looking bored as her fiancé pushed around the dance floor like an old plow horse with bad feet. I waved at her and she stuck out her tongue.

"Peggy," I said. "Would you do me a favor?"

"Anything." She giggled and did a suggestive little dance step that Ma hadn't taught me.

"I'm going to dance over to that couple," I said, pointing. "I'd like you to tap him on the shoulder and say 'tag,' then take him away and keep him happy. He's very rich."

"Really?"

"Oh, yes, really," I lied.

"My pleasure," she said. "Don't hurry."

Doug looked surprised, but recovered quickly and stepped back.

I moved in and pulled Rica into my arms. She fit into me just as I had always known she would.

"That was a pretty put-up job, Cowboy," she said as we danced away.

"You're a pretty put-up job yourself," answering as I held her close, then closer still.

"Cowboy, you're drunk," she accused.

"I am, I am," came my elated answer. "Wonderfully, happily drunk." Then I sang a few bars of "The night is young, you in my arms" until I realized that wasn't what the band was playing. And I was also very off-key.

"I think we better sit this one out," Rica told me, pulling away and taking my hand. "Let's go out on the veranda until you cool off. There's a glider porch swing in the little alcove. You might even catch a wink. You don't want to embarrass yourself."

"Sure, why not." But my sparkling conversation ceased as my patent-leather shoes betrayed me. As we turned the corner, I stumbled and fell, pulling Rica with me. By sheer luck, we landed in the swing.

A golden opportunity, my mind declared. Holding her tight, I bent my head to kiss that soft, perfumed spot, somewhere beneath her ear. I'd like to say she swooned in my arms, but she retaliated with a stinging slap that almost sobered me up.

Then came her sarcastic response, "Your aim is way off, Cowboy. Those bad guys are safe with you." So saying, she untangled herself and stood.

"Damn it, that hurt," I cried indignantly, lifting my hand to the cheek that stung. Then I grabbed her, pulled her back and held her down as she struggled.

"How long have we known each other?" I demanded.

"Who the hell cares? Let me go."

"I care. It's been sixteen months, three weeks and two days. I don't count the hours. And all these months you've teased and flirted and tried to make a fool of me."

"You've done a pretty good job of that yourself, country boy."

Apparently she hadn't noticed that after my time with the "boys" in the copy room and elsewhere, there wasn't much "country" left.

"Well, let this country boy see if he can improve his aim." I shifted my grip, holding her arms tightly to her sides. I pushed her back against the swing and kissed her the way I'd wanted to since the tea and cookies on this very veranda—long, slow, searching kisses that started with her tightly closed lips and traveled down her throat to the cleft of her breasts, where I buried my head in that ivory darkness and kissed a soft white mound. When the pink nipple stood firm against my invading tongue, I thought I would suffocate—and welcomed the possibility.

She was kicking furiously. I moved to hold her hands in one of mine and pulled the pins from her hair with the other, then buried my face in that soft, fragrant hair as it tumbled down her shoulders.

I caught her foot before she could damage me and her shoe came off in my hand. Then I let her go.

She blazed at me in a killing rage. "Give me my shoe, damn you. My pins—you'll pay for this."

Holding her shoe high over my head, I challenged her. "Come and get it—I dare you." Turning, I hooked the heel over the decoration that hung high on one of the pillars that supported the roof—safely out of her reach.

Laughing, I said, "Guess I'm just too drunk to know what I'm doing. Probably won't respect myself in the morning." Somewhere in my mind I congratulated myself on such original lines.

"Seriously, there is only one way you're going to get this shoe back and this is how it's going to happen. I'm going to stand here and you are going to walk over like a lady, put your arms around my neck and kiss me like you really mean it until I am a quivering mass of jelly and beg you to stop."

"You can go to hell, you damn fool. I'll never do it."

"Okay, sure enjoyed my part, even if you can't kiss worth a damn.

You'll make quite the entrance with your hair all over your face, limping along with one shoe on. I'd say you'll be a sensation." I turned and walked away.

She started to cry. "Steve, wait. You can't do this to me."

"Don't underestimate a country boy." I took another step.

"Steve, please. What will Dr. Teddy say? Or Sara and Juan? We can't embarrass them—this party..."

"Aha. So now you're taking a little responsibility? I agree it would cause a lot of bad publicity, so you better get started. The terms are the same, but could change if you keep me waiting."

"Steve, you are a real bastard." She hobbled over, put her hands in my hair, and pulled my face down and kissed me as she had in my dreams, and kissed me and kissed me.

"I love you, Rica, love you." My arms were around her, pulling her close, so close an onlooker would have said there was only one person on that veranda.

She trembled against me, but my knees had turned to water and somehow, someway, we stumbled to the porch swing—a glider, I think it was.

Somewhere in the distance I could hear the orchestra, but there seemed to be a discordant note. Or it may have been the creaky noise of the springs.

Later we found a valet, retrieved my truck and I took her home. She held the pins in her hand, but she wasn't barefoot.

I was ecstatic...I knew she must love me to have responded the way she did—no-holds-barred, a passionate return of everything I'd given her. Then there were her murmured words, "Hold me, Steve, hold me."

My mind floated in the clouds as my truck soared like Pegasus over the bridge.

CHAPTER 27

Waiting to hear something from her, I stuck it out for three days. Even though I had never known her phone number, I thought she might have gotten mine from Juan. So I called him to ask.

"Have you seen Rica?"

"Yes, we've just finished her sitting and she's gone home."

Despising myself for asking, I asked anyway, "Is she still wearing that damn ring?" knowing for sure that the answer would be "no."

"Of course, why wouldn't she be? They've set the date."

"Set the date? The date for what?" My confused mind refused to accept those unbelievable words.

Juan sensed my desperation and gently said, "Steve, let it go. You can live with it. You know I have, don't you?"

I hung up.

I didn't need to check the dictionary for "heartbreak." The hurt was so deep I sobbed soundlessly without tears.

"Country boy," she'd called me. Guess she had that right. And guess it was just a one-night stand for her.

My work went to hell. I couldn't concentrate. My coworkers stayed clear of my nasty mouth and Ma called to ask why she hadn't heard from me.

Prentiss called me in, a scowl on his face.

"What in hell is wrong with you? You're a real prima donna lately.

Or to put it more plainly, a real pain in the ass. You need to get out of here before you get lynched.

"I'm sending you to Centerville, Kansas. There's been a tornado there that almost wiped out the town. Hit three other states, too. Should be some good stories there and you're the man for the job. Wire me something I can use on the front page."

He handed me an envelope. "Here's your ticket and some mad money. Don't waste any time, the flight's at two thirty. I'm probably saving your life."

It was a short flight into the airport near Centerville; I arrived only hours after the destruction of a town with a population of eighteen thousand. I rented a car and drove the forty miles on a road straight as a string and bordered on both sides by a golden sea of gently waving wheat.

Nearing my destination, the reality became a nightmare. That golden wheat lay flat as though trampled by the giant feet of a madman. The black, muddy earth screamed through the scattered broken stalks. The sun had come out; the sky was cloudless as though the heavens were trying to make amends.

The road became increasingly impossible. Fighting their way through were ambulances and fire trucks, along with heavy equipment pushing aside telephone poles canted at impossible angles, their dangling wires rolled into a tangled mass—like a ball of yarn pounced upon by a playful kitten.

I parked the car on a wall that lay somewhat flat beside the road— the frame that held it together gouged deep in the mud, set the brakes and prayed the car would still be there when I came back. It was.

Carrying my suitcase with my typewriter in a bag, I hitched a ride with an ambulance driver. He had passed me but stopped when I yelled and waved my press card.

Progress was slow and his voice shook as he cursed two cows that lay across the road bloating in the sun. He gunned the motor only to see the mud fly when the wheels spun as we dug our way around the cows. Then we encountered an overturned tractor and a refrigerator.

With a cigarette hanging from the corner of his mouth, his fingers brown with nicotine, his words flung out as if to rid his mind of the image of black body bags, the names printed in white, that lay in neat rows on the torn grass of the makeshift morgue.

"It was hard, punishing rain pounding down and the wind had picked up, but hell, that ain't unusual." His voice roughened, "But suddenly, without warning, the black roiling clouds, twisting that hideously colored funnel straight from hell..." He paused to light another cigarette. "The goddamn wind was a hundred seventy miles an hour." He took a long drag. "And there was no time, no time, no place to hide."

I could see it vividly in my mind, this horror that had settled over this town like a hungry animal with its prey. Then, its appetite sated for the moment, it moved on.

"I'll let you out here. It's as good a place as any."

An immense pile of bricks, tall shards of glass, a steeple buried amidst the splintered pews identified it as a church. A little boy's shoe, the strings still tied in a bow, lay on a step.

Two boards, nailed roughly together to form a cross, leaned uncertainly as if it was inappropriate to stand where so many had kneeled.

"Eight people died here, three of 'em kids and a five-year-old boy still unaccounted for," he said. I closed the door.

Walking down the broken concrete path that was the sidewalk, I saw the rows and rows of raw black earth that showed where houses had stood. A foundation here and there, a standing fireplace like a sentinel spared. Furniture broken and scattered marked the places where only yesterday ordinary people had lived their ordinary lives.

Pausing beside a group standing quietly by a gigantic uprooted tree, I heard someone say, "Two hundred years old..."

Something moved with the breeze in the fork of a bare branch.

Looking up I saw a doll in a ruffled bonnet, one eye hanging loosely by a thread, then my gaze followed a pointing finger. Barely visible beneath a massive limb lay an old man in bib overalls with white hair caked in red. His arm flung protectively over a small woman with hair the same color.

The hush was broken by the sound of a chainsaw.

A feeling of utter desolation lay over the town. The inhabitants walked slowly, staring vacantly or digging through the fallen timbers and corrugated tin of their former lives. Occasionally I heard a muffled sob or a curse as this incomprehensible horror grew into reality.

As I talked to the survivors—walking with them for almost three days, sharing food and coffee at the Red Cross wagon—I took notes. I heard things, saw things I never dared to think about.

Writing my first report by the light of a borrowed flashlight, I sent it out the next morning with an ambulance driver who promised to fax it to Prentiss.

That night I slept in a donated sleeping bag on a porch that had no house. Somewhere in the distance, I heard the mournful howl of a dog.

The next day help was pouring in with food, tents, water and a large shelter erected for the medics.

Huge earth-moving machines and tractors were scooping up the remnants of the townspeople's previous existence. Piles of debris grew high outside the desolated town. Reporters and photographers swarmed everywhere.

On the outskirts of town, I passed by one of the few remaining houses that still stood upright. It was settled snugly beside its foundation; a woman stood inside, looking out a window with no glass.

The woman ran out to me, followed by a man who was vainly trying to hold her, begging in that broken voice I'll never forget, "Robbie, Robbie, did you find Robbie?"

The man disengaged her frantic hands from my arm and she

screamed hoarsely, "Robbie, you come home this instant, you hear?"

I think we all knew the unspeakable truth. Robbie *was* home.

Hurrying away, I heard the discordant clang of a bell. Following the sorrowful sound, I rounded a corner and saw a belfry perched unsteadily on the broken back of a small clapboard church. The bell sounding intermittently, swinging aimlessly as though it had no place to go but couldn't bear to leave.

It seemed somehow appropriate.

I wrote my second report under the light of a single bulb that dangled from a cord wrapped around the one remaining beam that had held a roof only yesterday.

It was not the sound of an orchestra that I heard, but the metallic clank-clank of a generator that denied me the sleep that would give me the distance for which I prayed. I left late in the afternoon, stopping long enough to spend my mad money on everything from shirt to shoes, then caught the red-eye flight and sat way in the back. It seemed that the odor of death clung to me like that of dirty underwear.

Three hours before the paper went to press, I was back in my sane world. My report made the front page. Prentiss was delighted to have scooped the *Kansas City Star.* Somehow it didn't matter to me.

Coming home to my apartment, I had an overwhelming urge to kneel and kiss the floor. After showering until the hot water ran cold, I slept for twenty-four hours between clean sheets.

One of my stories had caught the eye of the senior editor of the *Bay City Chronicle.* His name was J.W. Marteen—J.W. to his associates. He offered me the job of news reporter with a sizeable increase in pay and benefits, plus a desk in the newsroom—a dream come true.

It was a giant leap for me and I was apprehensive. This was the second-largest paper in the city. This was *Big Time.* Wildly excited and scared at the same time, I stuttered when I said, "Good morning."

I would be working with men who had formidable experience

and education—Harvard and Yale no less. And me, in my twenties, with just one semester of journalism on my resume? Well, I had reason to be scared.

J.W. later told me that he knew about my brief encounter at the small college, but he weighed that against my "natural talent and originality"—Prentiss' kind words.

Prentiss' confidence in me gave me the reassurance I so badly needed and, settling in, it entered my mind that this may be the closest I'd ever get to heaven.

Prentiss held a going-away party for me, which I vaguely remember. Then came the reluctant good-byes.

Prentiss was a patient man who taught me a lot about life that Mrs. Dowd didn't know—or didn't tell.

CHAPTER 28

F
our months flew by in a whirlwind of work. No need to search for anything to write about in this enormous city teeming with life. The streets, my hunting grounds, provided the raw material.

Whores who called me "Sonny" offered services at a reduced rate. The wretched homeless were ever-present. At first, it was impossible to resist an outstretched hand, but as time went on, it became easier for me to walk with my eyes straight ahead. Then there were the gangs that fought for dominance and would kill for a pair of shoes. The downside of a beautiful city.

What a thrill to get an approving nod from J.W., to see my name in print in the byline on the front page. Time slipped away.

Then I was jolted back to another world by a scalding letter from Sis.

"You haven't been home in almost four months," she accused. "Just because you think you're a big stud in the city. Telephone calls don't count."

"Stud?" Apparently her vocabulary had expanded since she'd married that marine.

Counting on my fingers, I figured she was getting close to the arrival of that little person who would call me "Uncle Stevie." I knew I needed to go home.

Only yesterday we were fighting over everything, and Sis tattling to Ma that I'd taught that miserable old dog to hump every stationary shoe. I had to admit he was an enthusiastic student.

I called J.W. and told him I had contacted leprosy and needed some time off. He agreed that my immune system was probably down and gave me four days to recover. I made plans to go home.

I hadn't seen Juan for months either and, as Sis said, phone calls don't count. Her letter slowed me down and brought me back to another world.

Despite Sis' snide remark about phone calls, I promptly called Juan. Hearing his happy voice, I realized how much I missed him and how deep was our friendship.

"Juan. It's my party—find us the best restaurant in the city. We'll have lunch and talk all day. I miss you."

His delighted voice never hesitated. "The Grotto on Fisherman's Wharf. Tomorrow at eleven. Don't be late—I have so much to tell you."

Parking was a challenge, but after a half-hour search, I found the only parking space available in the entire city.

Hurrying to the discreetly elegant restaurant of Juan's choice on the wharf, I found him waiting for me, seated at a table overlooking the water. His long-ago words, "I'm waiting for you," crept out of the depth of my subconscious, and I loved him for his innate sense of decency and his loyalty to a hopeless cause. I almost wished things were different, and wondered: Will a woman ever love me as much?

He stood, my arm around his shoulders, our hands clasped, with sad resignation in his eyes that contradicted the ear-to-ear smile on his handsome face.

We sat down at the table with spotless linen.

A slight nod brought a white-coated waiter. Juan waved the menu away and ordered something I couldn't pronounce and a bottle of sauvignon blanc. My taste buds came alive.

"What's good?" I asked.

"Lobster—the best in the city."

Silence held us for a moment as we looked at each other, then both spoke at once. Laughing, we started over.

He was excited and thrilled to tell me that "The portrait of Rica won top honors at the best shows on the East Coast. Now it's here on exhibit at the Jon Bergmann Gallery on Grant Street. I know you've seen it, but it looks so different in a gallery. Let's drop by later—I want you to see it again..." And the story raced on with his contagious enthusiasm.

All I could do was nod with my mouth full. The food was everything he said it would be, the wine magnificent. My tongue was looser than usual as I shared my hopes and dreams. I knew that this party would cost me a month's wages, but it was worth every penny. I ordered another bottle.

Looking up from the lobster that Juan declared to be "the very best," I met the eyes of a good-looking, red-haired girl sitting across the room at a table with an older woman.

My mind fumbled. She looked familiar and yet I couldn't place her red hair. Where did I know her?

She smiled and waved, then walked over, bent down and put her arm around my shoulder, nodding to Juan.

She obviously noted my confusion and, with a hug, she said, "Remember me? I'm Peggy. I want to thank you."

"For what?"

"For my future husband, Doug. You remember the party in Pacific Heights? You told me to tag him at the dance? You were right—he is filthy rich. He's the only son of a multimillionaire shipping magnate on the East Coast." She gave me another hug. "He can't dance like you can, but he has some good moves. I can teach him to dance." She laughed as she continued, "We're going to be married in June. I'll invite you to the wedding."

She looked up to see the old woman glaring at her. "Uh-oh, I'm a live-in companion girl Friday for that old harridan—I read to her, run her errands. She wants to make sure she gets her money's worth and she's got lots of it."

A resounding whack on the table interrupted the girl and, blowing a kiss over her shoulder, she turned back.

Juan grinned. "You sure don't have much luck with the ladies. Another Doug in the way, huh? This one must not be as slow as Rica's Doug."

Obviously, Juan had not known the meaning of "tag" and had not put two and two together.

My mind whirling, I managed a weak, "Guess I've struck out twice. What's for dessert?"

Lunch finished, Juan urged, "C'mon, I can't wait. Where's your truck?"

"Damned if I know. Somewhere over there," I waved my hand, "thataway."

It wasn't only the wine, but Peggy's words connected in my somewhat fuzzy brain. One part of me, a finger of shame, pointed at me for my part in it. All the rest of me danced a wild jig of complete abandon and shouted, "Hooray."

My pseudo big-city sophistication left me like a dirty shirt on a Saturday night and I was just what Rica had said I was—a country boy.

Juan coaxed me. "C'mon, can't wait to show you. I'll take my car and we'll come back for your truck." He chattered all the way.

"I'm doing another portrait. Rica may decide to do full-time modeling. She's already quit nursing school and is moving to an apartment. She and her father aren't getting along. She's had the flu..."

Through clenched teeth came, "Juan, I don't want to talk about Rica. She's a real pain in the ass most of the time."

Her portrait that stood on the old paint-spattered easel had been enough to take my breath away when I first saw it in the studio. But here, framed, and with the proper lighting, it dominated the show— everything else was just fine print.

Juan had painted not only her vibrant image, but he had also dug beneath the surface of a capricious, provocative girl to capture the essence of the real woman in the direct, honest gaze that would own me forever.

Standing there wordless, looking at those sedately folded hands, the remembrance of those fingers in my hair pulling my face down to those warm parted lips four months ago was so vivid I gasped.

Turning to leave, Juan followed. We paused outside the door where I drew a deep breath.

"Aren't you ever going to get over her?"

"I don't think so," I answered, choking on the words.

Juan drove us back to find the truck with a ticket under the wiper.

"Damn it to hell," I said. "First ticket I ever got."

Juan laughed and stuck it in his pocket.

"I'm going to go on home—it's only a few hours' drive. I'll sleep in my own bed tonight, and in the morning Ma will make hotcakes and eggs scrambled just the way she knows I like them. Eggs from our own hens. We'll probably enjoy a chocolate cake at lunch."

Impulsively, I asked, "Why don't you treat yourself to a little country air and come out? We could spend a couple of hours at the local watering hole, have a few beers..."

"Sounds wonderful—I've gone as far as I can with this new painting until Rica gets back. Save some cake." He waved good-bye.

Got home just at dark. Sis met me at the door. "Hey Ma, the city slicker has come to call." She threw her arms around me. Standing as close as she could, she added, "'Bout time."

Stepping back, I looked at her. "'Bout time is right. You're big as a barrel."

Ma stood, her hands on her hips, smiling. "First time I ever saw you two that close together and you aren't fighting."

Then it was a loving, three-way hug and Ma led the way to the kitchen and put on the coffee pot.

It seemed like I'd been gone forever and it was an overwhelming warmth that melted into my very bones as I sat in my mother's kitchen. The warmth of her love would sustain me throughout my lifetime.

Looking up at the ceiling, Sis' eyes followed mine and she grinned.

"Well, guess the ceiling has held up pretty well, but the wallpaper looks pretty shoddy," I said, grinning at Sis.

"Why wouldn't it hold up? My son did the job." From the pride that filled my mother's voice, she was certain there wasn't anything impossible for me.

Her confidence always made me feel the same way—at least for the moment.

"My bedtime," Sis said. "S'pose you two will talk all night." She blew a kiss and closed the door.

And talk we did. It was ten o'clock when I pulled up the covers.

But, despite the long day, sleep eluded me.

The moment I closed my eyes, my mind was consumed with thoughts of Rica and that night I was so sure she loved me, followed by the unbelievable knowledge that it was real only to me, an unexpected happening for her.

The long hours I spent at work—and I begged for every assignment—were the only relief for me from the vile words: "They've set the date."

The wall I put up to distance myself from this unbearable pain was built of bricks made from anger, frustration and despair. And it crumbled every time my eyes closed.

Neither Juan nor I had spoken her name these previous months as he seemed to instinctively feel my efforts to get past this and rejoin the human race. The wall was shattered the moment I walked into the gallery; now to start reassembling the bricks.

The illuminated dial on the bedside clock glowed four a.m. when I untangled the blankets and located the pillow. My eyes squeezed shut and my nightly mantra repeated.

"I am not a bricklayer. I am a writer. I am a damned fool wasting my time. Feeling sorry for myself will stop. She is not the only woman in the world."

I didn't believe a word of it.

Awakened rudely when the covers were yanked off my sleeping body, Sis snickered. "This ain't room service, Mr. Big Time. Get up—breakfast in ten minutes."

Smelling bacon and the tantalizing aroma of coffee, I spared her life.

Breakfast was a lengthy affair. Sis was bursting with talk of the coming baby and her excitement was barely contained as she waited for Ma to break the news.

"Son, I'm going to sell the farm and move to Fort Worth, Texas, with Sis and Tim. The neighbor wants to buy it—he has the money and it's a done deal. Tim has been transferred and promoted, so we'll join him as soon as the baby is old enough to travel. I'm tired of farming and Sis will need me."

Incredulous, my shocked voice exploded. "Ma, this farm has been in the family for three generations. How can I come home if you're in Texas?"

Suddenly I knew how those baby birds felt when they were pushed out of their nest. My face must have reflected that abandonment.

Ma laughed. "Stevie, you don't live here anymore. You have your own life now. You're doing what you love to do—you'll probably own that paper in a few years. You'll get married and have your own home...stop looking like that."

Sis snorted. "You're still dragging your blanket around sucking your thumb, you big titty baby. Time you get married and make your own home. Don't be so selfish."

My brain caught up with my mouth and I quickly amended. "Sorry,

Ma. Sis is right—for once. "Texas is a big state. There will be room for me to visit and Sis will love John Wayne and the cowboys..."

A wet dish towel that didn't miss its destination interrupted me. My face now dripping, I heaved the towel at Sis, but she caught it in midair.

"Why don't you two go outside and fight? Help your sister with the chickens—that old rooster has turned mean so it will be chicken potpie shortly. And I want to bake a cake in peace."

"We've got baby lambs," Sis said as we walked down the path to the barn. Then she stopped talking, turned and threw her arms around me. "Ah Stevie, we'll miss you so much. Promise you'll come visit right away."

My eyes got misty and she sniffled, so I promised with a weak laugh, "I'll meet the train."

The smell of Ma's incomparable chocolate cake wafted through the air as we walked back, Sis' apron caught up by the corners, full of eggs resting on her belly and moving every time the baby kicked.

In the bathroom washing up, I heard Ma call, "Stevie, your friend is here."

Hurriedly running a comb through my hair, I ran to the door. Standing beside Juan stood Rica.

"Oh, he's brought his girlfriend," Ma said.

I stood in shock.

"Well, for goodness sakes, invite them in. Where are your manners?"

Standing back with a sick smile on my face, Juan nudged Rica ahead.

"I hope I'm not intruding," Rica said to Ma, "but when Juan said he was driving to the country, I insisted on riding along."

Juan looked at me with an almost imperceptible shrug of his shoulders and a raised eyebrow.

Smiling at Juan, I put my arm around his shoulder. "Glad you made it. Ma, I want you to meet my best friend, Juan."

Juan ignored her outstretched hand and, smiling, put his arm around her with a hug, saying, "Steve has told me so much about you. If I did not have a Mamá, you would be my choice." Then he kissed her on the cheek. Ma lost her heart in less than a minute.

"And this is my friend Rica, who makes my paintings beautiful..."

Juan was interrupted as Sis emerged in a clean dress. I introduced her to Juan and then to "Juan's friend Rica." Then I pointedly ignored Juan's friend.

Sis had struck up an immediate conversation with Rica and they disappeared into Sis' bedroom to look at baby clothes and talk whatever girls talk about.

Juan declared, "I smell chocolate cake," and led Ma into the kitchen, pulled out a chair and sat down in my place at the old chrome-legged table as I trailed along. With a delighted smile, Ma handed Juan a plate and fork. As I watched, he cut a piece of cake that covered a large part of that plate.

"Mind if I join you, or am I an orphan?"

"Of course, be my guest," he answered, not missing a bite.

He and Ma were having such a good time talking and laughing, I might as well have been back in the city.

Holding out my own plate and utensils, Ma cut me a sliver.

"Girls," she called. "If you want any of this cake, you'd better hurry."

"That's the best cake I've ever eaten," Juan declared.

Ma whipped that cake off the table, wrapped it in waxed paper, and said, "Take this home with you."

"Hey, Ma—what about me?" I asked as I forked up the last crumbs.

"You're tired of cake—try a cookie," she said as she set a plate of cookies on the table.

Juan said, "I'll put this in the car so I won't forget it or Steve will eat it all."

Ma called again, "Cookies, girls."

As they came out of the bedroom laughing, Sis said, "Cookies? Where's the cake, Ma?"

"The boys ate it all," she said.

Juan came back and had a cup of coffee and a cookie with the girls, Ma included.

Rica and Sis were still talking about diapers and formulas, and Ma was saying, "Juan, you better stick with painting—you'll never make it as a cook. It's *four* eggs and *one* cup of sugar, not one egg and four cups of sugar."

Everyone was laughing and enjoying the camaraderie. Almost everyone—seemingly my tongue had been lost.

When the last cookie was gone and the pot was near empty, Ma said to me, "Why don't you show Juan and his friend the baby chicks and the lambs?"

"I will," Sis said and led them to the barn.

"Ma, I better go down to the chicken coop and shut up that rooster. We don't want any casualties."

"Good idea. Oh, Steve, I'm so glad you have such a wonderful friend. How could you not just love him? I'll stack these dishes and come down, too."

As I walked down the path, I was glad for the brief respite. I needed to sort out my conflicting emotions—the anger boiling just below the small talk, and yet that other feeling pushing back... The question drummed in my brain: Why? Why had she come?

I shoved the belligerent rooster into an empty cage and fastened the latch. The mother hen indignantly clucked her babies away from my big feet.

The door opened just as I turned. Rica stepped in. Wordlessly, we looked at each other, then my anger exploded, wanting to hurt her as deeply as she had hurt me.

"Rica, why are you here?" My voice was so thick I could hardly force the words.

"I want to talk to you," came a shaky reply.

I replied, "After four months, you have a word for me? How nice. Perhaps to invite me to the wedding? What the hell do you want from me? Is Steve a play toy?"

She stepped toward me, but I held up my hand.

"Doubtless that asshole bores you to death, but get your kicks from some other witless fool. I did my time." Adding a crude lie, I continued, "And it wasn't that good—I've had much better. But here's one for the road and don't let me keep you."

I grabbed her and pulled her close, heard her gasp for breath as I kissed her—hard, bruising, insulting kisses. Her arms went around my neck and she melted into me.

The creak of the hinges on that old henhouse door jolted me back to the here and now. Lifting my head, I looked directly into Juan's shocked eyes. He leaned into the doorjamb limply as though he'd been drowning and I had pushed the lifeline away.

Suddenly I saw Ma's disbelieving face, with Sis behind her.

Rica turned her head, her arms slipped from my shoulders, and she pushed her way out. Juan followed. Then came the sound of the car as it drove away.

I stood drained and dazed. What could I say?

"Well," Sis said, always ready with a comment. "What did you do? Steal his wallet?"

Ma, who could contain herself no longer, demanded furiously, "Steven, how could you do that to your best friend? The moment Juan's back was turned, you had his girl wrapped up tighter than a Christmas package, kissing her all over her face. You should have seen Juan's face. Shame on you."

"Well, Ma," my talkative sister interposed, "Guess you missed the look on Rica's face. They're *both* in love with Stevie."

Ma turned a bewildered face to her. "I don't understand. What are you saying?"

I glared at Sis, but there was no shutting her up.

"I'm saying that Juan is a homosexual, Ma. I said something about his pretty girlfriend and he told me straight out—right there in the barn—that she was only a friend and that he was gay." Sighing, she added, "Such a gorgeous man going to waste."

I was enraged with Sis. I would have told Ma in my own time, knowing how straightlaced she is, but Sis had ruined that opportunity.

Ma stalked to the house and we followed. Sis, knowing by the look on my face that she'd better do a disappearing act, said, "Sorry, Stevie, didn't mean to get you in trouble. Guess I'd better take a long walk. Doctor's orders, you know."

Sitting down with a cold cup of coffee, waiting for the sky to fall didn't take long.

"Steven, what is going on with that hussy? I hope he drops her like a hot potato. I don't believe he's queer—Sis is trying to be funny. He is such a gentleman and treated me like a queen. He meant it, too. I could tell if it was a put-on." She paused to catch her breath.

"I know in my heart that he is not one of those. Sis has just about spoiled my day with her silly idea of a joke. She'll hear about this— she's not above a good switching if she wasn't pregnant."

Interrupting, I said slowly, "Ma, I never wanted to tell you about the year up there on that mountain. It was a living hell, and a man was murdered. Juan and I were forced to dig his grave. The next one was for me, but Juan stood between me and the man who held the knife—even though he knew it could mean his life.

"I wouldn't be drinking coffee in our kitchen if Juan hadn't put his life on the line again to help me escape. He is an honorable man and I love him like a brother. If he grew horns and had a forked tail, he would still be my brother, and that's the end of it."

"That Sis," Ma said. "I knew he was a decent man."

CHAPTER 29

The silence was broken only by the quiet hum of the car as it sped homeward.

Juan's knuckles whitened on the steering wheel. His face had no expression—a mask that covered the agony of his longing that he finally accepted would never be. The unbearable knowledge nurtured the almost paralyzing pain.

With a distance between them, Rica sat with her mind in chaos. She sensed his torment and her heart ached for the part she played.

But Juan had to know that somewhere in Steve's virile young life, he was going to love a woman and she prayed that somehow, somewhere, Juan would find the love that would make his life whole.

She moved to Juan, lay her arm across his shoulder.

No response. Juan was lost in despair.

Who are the people who have the right to love? Why am I different? A wall of no understanding built by unseen hands. There is nothing strange in my loving Steve—it is as natural as breathing.

Strange is that he cannot love me as I love him. Yes, strange is the love that is only acceptable to those who are fashioned in life's rigid pattern.

I, who would give my life so freely—must I go through life empty-handed as a beggar pleading for alms?

The God who designed me has destroyed me.

The quiet lengthened.

Rica's arm tightened about his shoulder.

"Juan, it has taken me some time to accept the very real truth that I love Steve." Hesitating, she added, "And what the future will bring lies before us. I know that we both love him—not the way you want him to love you, but what we offer you is our love, always. Perhaps that is a sorry exchange, but you must accept the fact that Steve can offer you no more. Juan, isn't it better me than someone else? We're family."

Juan's lips twisted around his words, "Yes, let's keep it in the family."

"Juan has been very quiet—I'd almost say depressed since the day he spent with Steve in the country."

Sara spoke with concern to Teddy as they lay together in the big four-poster bed.

"Do you think they quarreled?"

"I doubt it, my dear. Do you remember the day they were reunited? I told you I liked Steve, but that he would break your boy's heart? It was inevitable, Sara, they are what they are. East is east and west is west and never the twain shall meet—if I may quote Kipling."

Juan had not painted for several days. Explaining to Sara, he said, "Rica has been unavailable and I have gone as far as I can with this. I'll see if Mr. Mackey needs any help with the roses." He was gone before Sara could respond.

Sara painted by herself, missing Juan's laughter and warm companionship. Later, the hurrying steps that sounded made her smile expectantly, but it was a distraught Rica who stood in the doorway.

"Rica, come in. I was about to take a break. I'll make some tea."

"Thank you. Surely I would enjoy a cup of tea," responded Rica, wiping at the tears that shimmered in her eyes.

Seating herself, listening to the tea preparation in Juan's so seldom used kitchen, she wondered at the friendship that had entered her life so unexpectedly and had grown into a near family relationship.

As Sara returned with the tea tray, Rica's shaky voice appeared. "Thought I'd find Juan here and I wanted to talk to him. He was so terribly upset when we left Steve's. Please tell him how sorry I am to have held him up for over a week — and what a week it's been."

As Sara poured the tea, she asked, "Can I help? You look so sad. What's happening?"

"Everything. The good news, the wedding is off. The bad news, Mother is heartbroken and Dad is furious, not only about the wedding, but because I had quit school. In fact, he's angry that he's disowned me. Told me to find myself another place to live since he had wasted his money sending me to school..." She forced a weak smile. "Mother helped me find a small apartment and paid the rent for six months, so I guess I'm only half disowned. Do you want to hear the rest of this sad story?"

Sara nodded.

"Well, the wedding was only six weeks away and I was more frantic every day. I knew if I told them it wasn't going to happen that there would be a terrible scene and mother's dream would become a nightmare.

"Our mothers have been best friends since grade school and they have been matchmaking since Doug and I were in diapers. Of course, at first it was exciting. I had a schoolgirl crush on him — he was an 'older man,' by eight years actually — and when he noticed me years later, I was flattered and our parents were very pleased. His dad was even going to buy us a house for a wedding present." She paused as Sara refilled her cup.

"Doug was interning at UCSF medical school and always too busy or too tired. And I was in nursing school, so we didn't have much time together. My crush on him wore thin, but he didn't seem to notice. He spent more time with his friends than with me."

Sipping her tea, she continued, "Our mothers were having a great time making all the plans. His mother even set the date to accommodate her New York relatives. My mother chose the color of the bridesmaids' dresses. I was praying for the courage to tell her."

Interrupting herself, she said, "Miss Sara, sorry to be bothering you with my problems..."

"Rica, you're practically family so you're not bothering me—you've piqued my curiosity. Apparently you found the courage—and I'm sure it did take courage."

"I didn't tell them. Doug did. And Dad almost threw him off the porch." She laughed and continued. "Doug took me to dinner and, between the martini and the hors d'oeuvres, he told me he had fallen in love with someone else. He added, 'The wedding is off. Please tell me I haven't ruined your life. Be strong.' Then he patted my hand and said, 'Since this is my decision, I will break the news to both our parents.' Then he ordered another martini.

"Such an indescribable wave of relief swept over me—a reprieve as the trap door was about to be sprung. I covered my face and laughed hysterically, the tears running through my fingers. Of course, he thought I was crying and begged me not to make a scene. 'Here drink this,' and pushed his martini toward me.

"He seemed delighted to tell me of this other girl—said she'd evoked feelings in him that he'd never had and added that they had met the night of your party. He told me that she lives with her very sick grandmother in the house next to this one, and 'She is a very beautiful person, the only heir, but the money she will inherit means nothing to me.'"

Rica set her cup down. "Guess it was the thought of that heiress that gave him the push to tell our parents—the martini probably helped. I spent the night at a girlfriend's house. Mother said that Dad threatened to punch him right out on the front porch and all the neighbors could hear. Poor Mother." Rica sighed.

Sara said thoughtfully, "If 'next door' means the house that is the nearest to us, that would be Mrs. Bradbury, a descendant of one of the old families. We know her well. She and Teddy played together as children. She has been a widow for many years—never had children. I wonder if that 'granddaughter' could be Mrs. Bradbury's live-in girl Friday who drives for her occasionally and runs errands. Perhaps you should let Doug discover that for himself."

They giggled like two schoolgirls.

"Why are you feeling so badly? You don't look well."

"I think it must be the flu. I'm so nauseated, nothing stays down. I've lost three pounds. Plus it's all this stress, and moving."

"You should see Dr. Teddy. I'll ask her if she has any time tomorrow. More tea?"

CHAPTER 30

"Mrs. Mackey definitely has a way with a rack of lamb. I think she knows when I've had a long day," Teddy said, sniffing appreciatively as they seated themselves at the elegant table where her father once sat.

"Good food, vintage wine and a love like no other...oh, Sara, we have a good life."

Leaning forward, Teddy poured the wine.

"Ah, Teddy, why won't you slow down? You have no need to work such hours. You're nearing your sixtieth birthday."

Reaching out, Sara clasped Teddy's hand and held it to her cheek.

"Such a beautiful hand that has brought so much comfort to others, and given me everything."

"I love my work," Teddy responded, "second only to you. This is my life and I've had it all."

"Not quite all." Sara smiled as she gave Teddy her hand back. "Mrs. Mackey has a chocolate torte for dessert. She is a jewel, but I can't say I care much for her husband. Juan has been helping him with the roses. Speaking of Juan, he seems so unhappy. I pray that someday he will find his happiness as we have found ours. And Rica—tears and more tears. Her parents are angry and very disappointed that the wedding was canceled and she has moved."

"Really?" Teddy raised an eyebrow. "That decision may give her an additional problem. I examined her this afternoon and she is almost four months' pregnant."

"Pregnant? Oh my."

"That girl was so shocked and scared. She acted as though she didn't know how that could possibly have happened."

Teddy leaned forward to replenish the wine. "So much for the age of enlightenment." Then added, "Frankly, I was shocked. The only time I met her fiancé was at your party. It occurred to me that he was hiding in the closet, that Rica was only window dressing. I'd guess Steve had a finger in that pie."

"Finger?" Sara laughed. "Teddy, you do have such a way with words."

The question nagged me. Why had Rica driven out with Juan? What had she wanted to say?

The shame kept building for the hateful things I'd said, but I tried to comfort myself with the excuse that "She hurt me, so I hurt her back." But somehow I couldn't bring that off. I was raised better than that.

My conscience gave me no rest. I'd have to apologize, but I'd held out for three weeks—that should show her that I was a man not to be trifled with. Yeah, sure. Had to laugh at my own pitiful attempt to detour the feminine psyche. Hadn't I retained anything I learned from Ma and Sis?

I did hold tough to one decision: I was going to find out if I was at bat or on the bench. This "kiss and run" tactic was no more.

Ma was mad at me, I'd insulted Rica, and the look on the face of my best friend had cut me like a knife. I sure wasn't on the best of terms with myself, so when J.W. called, I hoped he'd send me to the Arctic to interview a polar bear.

Opening the door to his sanctuary, I saw his bald head with its untidy fringe of iron gray hair above the straggly white brows that met above his eyes, and those piercing eyes that could reduce the most hardened reporter to a mass of quivering jelly with a look.

He sat behind a desk piled high, the perpetual ashtray in a prominent position, a still-smoldering cigarette lighting the one dangling from his lip, the wastebasket overflowing...

"Steve," he growled, "sit down." With a sweep of his arm, he cleared a chair and I sat.

He took a long drag and eyed me speculatively. Then his gravelly voice announced, "I've kept you pretty busy and you've done a damn good job. Don't let that go to your head. A good job for a kid who has only three semesters at college to brag about and slides by on natural talent—so says your old boss, Prentiss." He chuckled, then added, "I've decided to throw you a little candy.

"How would you like to spend a few days in Los Angeles to cover the National Bathing Beauty contest? Should be right down the alley for a young stud like you. A lot of hoopla and bullshit, but a beauty in a bikini is always good press. Wrangle some backstage interviews, background stuff. Who knows," he grinned, "you might get lucky—on your own time, of course. But business first. I'll expect something that will go on the front page, so don't disappoint me.

"Won't take long to drive down. Leave tomorrow morning."

He shoved an envelope toward me.

"Go easy on the expense account. Have some fun, live a little. You look like hell." With that, he waved me out.

CHAPTER 31

Writing for a major newspaper had always been my dream. Ma's faith in me, along with opportunity and countless hours of doing what I loved to do best, had earned me a spot as the youngest reporter on the second-largest paper in San Francisco.

I had proven myself as a featured writer where thousands read my words on the front page, my name on the byline.

Is this success? Sure wasn't failure. But now it was only half of the equation. I wanted the other half: Rica. Even as my frustration grew, I could feel her presence.

What the hell, I thought, pounding on the steering wheel. She's not the only woman in the world. Forget her; find someone who will appreciate me—no sweat.

Ma's words sneaked back into my feeble brain. "I can always tell when you're lying, Stevie."

Speeding along that breathtaking coastal scenery that was Highway 101, my emotions ran the gamut; no less tumultuous than the tossing whitecaps below.

Finally arriving in the City of Angels, I felt my way, trying to read the street signs as they flashed by in that brawling, frantic traffic.

L.A. made me feel welcome with the universal middle-finger salute.

With heartfelt relief, I found the hotel, which surprisingly had an adjoining restaurant, complete with patio and bar. J.W. had booked a room for me much nicer than I would have dared to put on the expense account.

Checking in, the bored voice of the clerk informed me, to my delight, that the convention center where the beauty pageant was to be held was within walking distance, then turned wearily to repeat the same information to the next person in line.

Coming from the cool, sophisticated city of San Francisco, whose misty skyline was so often blurred by fog covering it like a soft blanket and obscuring that which was not good to look upon, I was not prepared for this great, golden city that lay like an overfed cat, sprawled lazily in the sunshine of an open doorway. The Sierra Madre Mountains stood guard in the distance.

City of Angels. Red-tiled roofs, palm trees standing tall against the startling blue of the sky. Purple bougainvillea, the raucous blare of horns, ricocheting traffic, where gang wars erupt upon sighting a jacket of a different color and prostitutes fight for their corner on Sunset Boulevard.

"Drugs? You name it, bro." Available to rich and poor alike.

Chauffeured limos, Rodeo Drive, Bel Air, Beverly Hills mansions looking down their stuccoed noses.

Home to the beautiful people.

The "Hollywood" sign that dwarfed the hillside announcing to thousands that this *was* the end of the rainbow.

Movie studios, starlets, young hopefuls seeking fame and fortune in this make-believe world that really was the end of the rainbow for most.

Hollywood Boulevard, the street of broken dreams, and in this bawdy, teeming city of exotic mix, woven somewhere in between was the tenacious thread that held the fabric together: the ordinary people with their ordinary nine-to-five jobs.

With my few clothes quickly unpacked and hung, the nagging thought of a tall, cold beer urged me to the elevator. It stopped a couple of floors down to admit two women. One, a bleached blonde with a swinging, bulky camera bag over her shoulder competing with a dangerously bulging purse. The other reminded me instantly of the one I had promised myself to forget. I think it was the black hair that hung over her back, or perhaps it was wishful thinking.

As the elevator touched down, I noticed that they had preceded me to the bar and, as I ordered, they walked past me carrying a tray with glasses and a pitcher of something that momentarily erased beer from my mind. They were heading for the near vacant patio.

With a beer in hand, I stopped at a table partly obscured by a large potted plant and carefully seated myself on a spindly legged chair that hopefully would sustain my hundred and eighty pounds. Lifting my glass, it hung frozen in midair as I heard clearly the laughing voice, "...fat-assed Miss Alabama...got a few good shots of her. She's a thirty-eight/thirty-eight/thirty-eight if my camera doesn't lie." Their voices choked with laughter.

My mind went into overdrive. This was the back door that J.W. had pointed to. I leaned over farther as the voice snickered. "...and the tits on Miss Ohio..." The rest was lost as the damned chair collapsed. Fighting to maintain my balance, I found myself swiping frantically and uselessly at the beer cascading down my front. "Son of a bitch," I cursed as I kicked the three-legged chair and its orphaned leg behind the flowerpot.

The women laughed uproariously and clapped. Then the blonde said, "I shoulda had a picture—my editor would have loved it."

I gave a weak smile and continued the vain attempt to dry myself.

The dark-haired woman drawled, "You know they'll probably bill you for that chair. Maybe you'd better sit with us. We'll cover for you." She smiled and patted the chair beside her.

I was in. Her foot held the door wide open.

Gratefully, I sank down in the chair beside her as she pulled it closer and motioned for another glass.

"My name is Amy, and this is Janella. What should we call you— 'handsome'?"

"Just call me anytime," I flirted. "Steve Smith for now. I'm a salesman just passing through." Anything, anything—keep them talking.

"Janella is a big-time photographer for the *L.A. Times*—she's covering the beauty pageant that my sister is going to win at the convention center tomorrow," Amy said confidently.

Turning to Janella, I said innocently, "You're really a photographer? That must be an interesting profession, taking pictures of beautiful women. Wow."

"They're not very beautiful in the morning, although the plastic boobs stand up pretty well. Already shot two rolls today—human interest stuff."

"My sister's boobs aren't plastic. She was always beautiful even when she was nursing a kid at fifteen and living on a dirt floor," Amy said defensively.

"Fifteen?" Janella's eyebrows raised. "Thought that was illegal."

"Not down on the border where we lived. People didn't notice stuff like that. After we moved to the hill country in Texas, everybody thought the kid was our mother's.

"We're doing better now that EmmaJean—of course, that's not her real name—won the Miss Abilene when she was seventeen, Miss Texas at eighteen. In Phoenix, she was runner-up—the lighting was really poor there. I always do her hair and makeup so I flew in last night. She'll win this one; I know she will."

"Doubt she's prettier than you," I said gallantly. "Bet you could beat her."

She smiled and patted my knee as she generously filled my glass.

I got all the details right down to the thirty-four/twenty-two/thirty-four C-cup in that honeyed drawl that was beginning to send shivers down my spine.

All the salt on the rim of that frosty glass was keeping me thirsty. Janella motioned to the barkeep who arrived just as she poured the last drop—while Amy's foot played with mine under the table. I began to sweat.

"That Miss Michigan—her ass is as big as Kansas and her tits look like parts left over from Frankenstein. Miss Arizona—isn't she a mess?" Amy asked, turning to Janella. Not waiting for an answer, she continued, "The lighting was great in Tucson where she came in third..."

The shop talk and information flowed so fast I couldn't absorb it all, so excusing myself, I found the men's room to make copious notes on my forearms, then rebuttoned my sleeves.

Amy chattered for two more hours. My eyes glazed as she caressed my thigh—or close to it. I endured this torture manfully. Anything for the story that would bring joy to J.W.'s wicked heart and my byline to the front page.

Janella excused herself—it may have been apparent that Amy and I were joined at the hip, and we practically were. She had moved her chair so close she was, to a casual observer, sitting in my lap.

The patio had filled with a noisy crowd; the air was blue with smoke. My head was spinning and I was eager to get away, eager to put this story together knowing it would take all night.

Finally I stood. "I gotta go."

"What room are you in, Sugar?"

"Six-thirteen," I lied.

"Will I see you later?"

"Of course. Knock three times on the ceiling." I fled.

High above the noisy crowds and congested traffic, I rang for coffee, made myself comfortable and pulled the cover from my typewriter. The words seemed to flood the paper.

Writing steadily, the hours flew by and my story came alive. I knew that it was good.

Amy had been a goldmine of information—her candid descriptions of backstage activities left little to the imagination. Where there was a lapse, I took a few liberties—a writer's prerogative. It was three a.m. when I added the last period.

I routed the sleepy night clerk from his dreams to fax my night's efforts over the airwaves to join the morning coffee on J.W.'s desk.

As I showered the priceless information from my forearms, my thoughts were not of the attractive, talkative woman with whom I had spent most of the day, but of a woman in San Francisco who disturbed my dreams and told me nothing of what I so desperately wanted to hear.

I was about to work myself into a righteous rage when I fell asleep.

Waking late, I sent down for coffee and read the *L.A. Times* that came with it.

I marveled at the publicity that this pageant was getting—why hadn't J.W. sent a photographer with me? Damned penny-pincher. I could smell another good story here and pictures would have nailed it down.

Had lunch in the ridiculously overpriced restaurant and lingered over dessert. My mind cringed at the thought of the look of J.W.'s face when he checked the expense account and saw the tag on the apple pie à la mode.

My press card saved him the admittance charge at the convention hall—small comfort.

I pushed my way to the front seating. Although still early, the building was nearly full. The hoopla and bullshit that J.W. had predicted were certainly right on the money.

The blaring announcements, the orchestra valiantly competing, the sound of voices that thundered against the walls—all seemed as perpetual as waves breaking against the shore. As latecomers banged the seats, finally the curtains rose and the lights dimmed.

Despite cynical appraisal of various contestants by last night's companion, I was enthralled. They were all beautiful. I didn't envy the judges, who took notes carefully as each contestant performed.

Never had I seen so much of so many.

If any of it was plastic, to my inexperienced eye, it was a damned good job. But who could tell; who could care at this distance?

I scribbled furiously, but my arm was constantly bumped by a man who overflowed his seat. My notes became unreadable and I bumped back. He gave me a frosty stare and muttered, "Damn tourist." I wondered how he could tell.

The last contestant appeared, climaxing the pageant.

She seemed oblivious of the suddenly quieted audience as the spotlight followed her across the darkened stage, then blazed to show a petite woman in a ten-gallon hat atop a forest of red hair, high-heeled boots, a bikini almost as large as my handkerchief, and a guitar.

She strummed slowly for a moment, paused to adjust something, then pushed her hat back. It was then that the first words of that unforgettable song, "Ave Maria," sounded.

It was as though every person in that huge auditorium held their breath and exhaled only as the last hauntingly beautiful note faded. Shivers chased themselves across my back. I couldn't control the pen. The walls shook as the crowd roared and stood as one.

"Encore. Encore," yelled the audience as Miss Texas grinned—the same grin I'd seen on Amy's face. Then she belted out a foot-stomping, yahooing version of "The Eyes of Texas."

Looking around the near-riotous crowd, I could see the placards with the Texas star waving everywhere high in the air. I could hear Amy leading the chant, "Texas, Texas, Texas." I was excited for her and her sister, remembering her assured "She'll win this one..."

Jostled by the crowd, I finally found the men's room and locked myself in a stall. Adding to my almost unreadable notes while seated most uncomfortably, I heard a gruff, threatening voice.

"If you don't come out of there right now, I'm coming in to get you. Are you constipated?"

Sliding past a guy who looked like a professional wrestler and avoiding his scowl with an apologetic, "S'cuse me," I escaped to hear Amy's shrill voice above the thinning celebrants. "Hey, Steve—over here."

Hoping my good luck would hold, I dodged the noisy groups and, as Amy grabbed my arm, asked, "Do you s'pose you could introduce me?"

"Are you crazy? Just look." She pointed at the mad scramble surrounding her sister.

"There's a big-time movie producer and that's a guy from CBS and look at the photographers..."

Realizing my luck had run out, I bolted through a side door and made a death-defying trip through the parking lot. Racing for the hotel, the words already forming in my mind, I found the sanctuary of my room.

I typed and retyped, crossed it out and did it again and again. Changed a paragraph, added and deleted. My fingers were numb, but it had to be perfect. And at last my instincts told me it was all I had.

I had typed steadily, skipped dinner and now it was dark—my watch indicated ten p.m.

The elevator was too slow; I took the stairs two at a time.

Shaking the night clerk awake, I disregarded his hostile, "Not again."

The airwaves were smoking when the last page was en route.

The elevator traveled its usual speed going up and that was fine with me. My mission was accomplished. Kicking off my shoes and socks, I collapsed across the bed, almost instantly asleep.

A loud, persistent banging on the door floundered through my sleep-numbed brain and I croaked, "Who is it?"

"Amy. Who the hell do you think it is? Open up."

"Not a chance—go to bed."

The pounding intensified. Cursing, I struggled to the door and opened it an inch, only to have it pushed open. I jumped back to avoid facial reconstruction.

"Hey Handsome—party time. C'mon. I've got munchies and Jack Daniel's in my room. Hurry up."

I could smell that she had already made Jack's acquaintance. Her voice was insistent and sleep had fled. Realizing there was no escape, suddenly a celebration on my last night here didn't seem like such a bad idea. One could always sleep. Hadn't J.W. said to live a little?

I'd written a fabulous report, Rica was a long ways gone—perhaps the hair of the dog? I assured myself that indeed a celebration was in order.

Having justified myself, my bare feet followed Amy like a shadow.

"So," she said triumphantly. "I've tracked you down and you are now my captive."

"How did you find me?"

"When I knocked on the ceiling, that guy was so mad he called the room clerk. I told him I was your wife and that you often got numbers confused, and he said the only Steve he had on the books was in Room five thirteen..."

Still chatting, she slipped the key in the lock and the door opened to an empty room.

"Where is everyone? The party?" I stuttered.

She leaned against me, nibbling my ear and whispered, "We are everybody. Are you ready to party?"

"Not quite yet. Let's have a drink first."

"Consider this foreplay," she said as a drink appeared like magic a moment later.

Manfully, I slugged it down. My eyes watered and my curly hair straightened like the tail of a cat at the sight of a strange dog.

She pushed me down on the bed where my recovery began. The

kisses lengthened as our tongues had a lively conversation and I cooperated with enthusiasm. Somehow she had shed her clothes without breaking contact.

I could feel my pants growing tight enough to cripple me. Apparently she had noticed. Her hand had just found the zipper when a deafening bang-bang sounded on the door.

"Oh, shit—who can that be?"

"Janella here—open up."

"I don't hear anything, do you?"

"Hell no. I'm deaf as a post."

Again her mouth sought mine.

I thought the door would fly off the hinges.

"Damn it to hell. I know you're in there. Open this door before I kick it in."

Amy fumbled with her clothes and opened the door. Janella stalked in, tossing her purse on the nightstand.

"My, aren't you cozy."

I held a pillow on my lap.

"Hope I didn't interrupt anything," she said innocently, kicking off her shoes and seating herself in the only chair. "I won't stay long."

"Bitch," Amy said under her breath. "I hope yours grows together."

"It would serve her right," I muttered. "She talks too much."

Amy looked at me in amazement.

"Steve, you can't possibly be that dumb." She started to laugh.

Janella's laughter joined ours. "I don't know what's so funny, but I've sure livened up this party. Somebody fix me a drink."

I crawled off the bed to do her bidding, and wondered if she would fly when I pushed her out the window. That would liven up my party.

"Had a bad scene with my boss. I lost that last roll of film that I took at the pageant with all my best shots. I would have gotten the Pulitzer. I'd already given him three so he didn't need to get so nasty." She started to cry.

"Stop sniveling, Janella. I hate a crying drunk."

"Shut your big Texas mouth. I'm not drunk yet."

"Sitting by myself playing solitaire isn't much fun. Thought you might like to play a few hands." Then, wiping her eyes on her sleeve, she added, "Hand me my purse, will ya?"

Digging through her cluttered bag, she pulled out a wad of Kleenex and with it came the roll of film.

She leaped to her feet with an ecstatic whoop.

"Omigawd, it's my lucky day." Laughing and crying, she cavorted about the room, Jack Daniel's sloshing in one hand, the film held higher in the other.

The film—my heart lusted for that roll, but I knew it would take a king's ransom to part her from it. My story would make the front page, but it would go over the top if I could add those pictures. My mind cleared as I schemed and plotted to no avail.

Holding her over the railing by her feet tempted me, but I discarded that plan when I realized she'd take the film with her.

Amy was sulking, giving Janella a sour look. "C'mon, c'mon. It's getting late. This ain't no ladies aid society. You brought the cards, now let's play."

Then she brightened. "I know. Let's play strip poker. I'll show you how a Texas girl can strip a guy right down to his spurs and make him look forward to it."

With a wicked smile, Janella answered, "I'm not so bad at that myself, and if it's a draw, we'll play a hand for his spurs."

J.W. had said I might get lucky, so why was I so nervous?

"Wait a minute, ladies," I stalled. "Let's have a drink."

My brain wrestled with indecision. I could leave, but I wanted that film. I had to figure out a way to get it. Then, too, Amy was no afterthought.

My grandfather had been a hellfire-and-brimstone traveling preacher, traveling by horseback to joust with the devil regarding sins of the flesh. Dancing was intercourse set to music, smoking was a deadly sin, and cards were an invention of the devil. Ma had never learned to play, although she had bent the rules of dancing; consequently, Sis and I had never been allowed. We hid our Monopoly board in the barn.

In college I had picked up a little information, but really had no interest. I couldn't even classify myself as an amateur.

Now I was feeling like a minnow in a small fish bowl with two hungry sharks.

Amy moved her chair back and sat with crossed legs in the lotus position on the carpet, making it more difficult for me to concentrate. Janella positioned herself against the wall. I folded my long legs beneath me and pushed up beside the bed.

Amy was shuffling the cards, running them up her arm, flipping them, and various other maneuvers.

"Show-off." Janella snorted.

"Here, cut 'em, Handsome, bring you luck," Amy said. Handing the cards back, I knew I was going to need all the luck I could get.

The cards blurred as they flew past me.

"Wait a minute—hold on," I said. "What are the rules?"

"'Rules'? That's a dirty word in Texas. You're playing with the big kids now. You're on your own."

Gingerly, I picked up the five cards in front of me. Amy snatched up hers. With an "Oh shit," she tossed two back and picked up two more.

Janella considered hers, smiled and said, "Pass."

Looking at me expectantly, she said, "What you got?"

I laid my hand down hopefully.

"You lose, sucker. You, too, Texas. Take it off."

I undid my watch.

"Hey, you can't do that. Against the rules."

"You said there were no rules."

"Well, any tenderfoot knows the fundamentals."

"What's the difference between rules and 'fundamentals'?"

"Damn it, are we playing cards or having a philosophical discussion?"

Amy slipped out of her halter top and the two unconfined breasts bounded to freedom.

Removing my shirt, I felt Janella's fingers smoothing my arm. "Nice," she said.

"Keep your hands to yourself," Amy snapped.

Frowning, Janella shuffled, cut the deck and handed it to me. "Deal," she demanded.

Shaking as I reached to take the cards, they slipped through my fingers and scattered. Grabbing for the runaway deck, my elbow knocked over my glass and the liquor splashed.

The women cursed and quickly removed themselves.

"Son of a bitch! Steve, pay attention. Don't be so damned clumsy."

There were other niceties that I ignored.

Amy was attempting to wipe the cards with a towel and dry the carpet. I made a half-hearted effort to help her, but the look on her face told me to stay out of her way.

"Lucky I brought another bottle. Say good-bye to Jack," said this woman who had announced earlier that she wouldn't stay long.

She was opening her bag, and while one eye was watched avidly for the sight of that precious film, my other fixated on the rosy-tipped breasts that winked every time Amy dried a card.

Janella nudged Amy to her feet and bent to whisper something that caused both of them to convulse with laughter.

Why was I so nervous? Why wasn't I having fun like any red-blooded man sitting with two good-looking women drinking their liquor—one of whom was half-naked and openly on the make—and having a friendly game of cards?

Of course I was having fun.

The cards recovered and were reasonably dry when the game resumed.

Amy dealt the cards so fast that they flew through the air. "C'mon, let's get this show on the road."

Their cards hit the carpet like hail.

Fumbling for a card, Janella's hand found my thigh.

"Keep your paws to yourself. I told you, I'm teaching this class," came Amy's angry voice.

"Well, I've been known to break in a few beginners myself," responded Janella quickly. Her cards bounced as she threw them down and chose two others.

I looked helplessly at mine, my Monopoly experience useless. This hand couldn't even buy a hotel.

Amy laughed and threw down the winning hand, looked at me and purred, "Take it off, Sugar."

Reluctantly, my undershirt came off.

"Now for the pants and shorts," Janella said.

"Won't be long now," Amy added.

Both women laughed hilariously.

As Amy refilled my glass, her breasts managed to brush against my face. A moment later, Janella's hand was admiring my biceps.

It was obvious that this was a game between two women and I was up for grabs. The future looked grim. Grandpa was right—this was a wicked game. I could feel the devil's hot breath—or was it Amy's? I was confused.

Again and again the cards slapped the carpet. The insults and laughter comingled. I was miserable, feeling like a fool.

I thought if they got drunk enough, Janella might fall asleep. I'd grab that purse and make a run for it. Amy wouldn't care. But then my conscience rose up. Steve, have you sunk to that? It's the devil tempting me, Grandpa, you were right. Lord help me.

Amy gave an ear-splitting rebel yell and I knew I'd lost my pants.

A furious knocking on the wall quieted them momentarily.

"Steve, if you could play poker like you can put away drinks, you'd be a millionaire."

I was thankful they couldn't see the wet stain under the bed where I'd been spilling out the liquor.

"You must have some hidden talents," Janella slurred.

"I'm sure he has, and I intend to find out right after this next hand. Janella, you look tired—I'm sure you'll want to go home."

"Wait a minute, don't count your chickens. The game's not over..."

Lord help me. I thought I heard the devil chuckle.

I sat there and shivered in my paisley shorts. Ma had given me three pairs at Christmas.

Janella dealt with a sure hand. Amy picked up her cards. I just pushed mine around. All hope fled as I sent a last despairing plea speeding through space.

He didn't hear me. I lost.

"Take 'em off, Sugar," Amy purred as soft as velvet, then, "Good night, Janella. See you later."

"Wait, wait," I begged. She just can't leave with that film, my mind screamed.

"Amy, let's have a nightcap. Fix a good stiff drink and I'll take 'em off."

"Great idea," Janella said. "I think it's only fair that I see the great unveiling. Do you really think it's great?"

"Must be—he can't be totally without some assets."

"Well, speaking of asses, his was pretty neat."

So the ribald comments bantered back and forth at my expense. But Amy hung tough. "We're playing by Texas rules—take 'em off or we will."

Janella added, "And we won't be careful."

I begged to play another hand, but there was no mercy.

Finally, I slid them to my knees, and with one powerful yank, Amy sent my shorts sailing across the room. Now naked as a newborn babe, I quickly covered myself with my hands.

"Ladies," I said desperately, "let's be civilized and have a drink to celebrate this, um, great unveiling."

"Okay." Amy giggled. "Just one, though."

Then the rattle of glasses sounded and I knew she was looking for the ice. Janella leaned her head against the wall and closed her bleary eyes.

On my knees, I inclined myself along the bed to reach a pillow. In an instant I was safely covered.

Amy returned with the drinks. Her eyes widened with shock as she furiously poured the drinks over my head and screamed, "You can't do that—it's against the rules."

Janella's eyes opened. "What the hell is going on here?"

Again came the indignant pounding from the other side of the wall.

Janella stumbled to her feet. "Gimme that pillow, you conniving bastard," she yelled, but my hands held the pillow so tightly a gorilla couldn't have moved it.

Amy ranted. "That's cheating. In Texas we hang horse thieves and card cheaters."

My mind was frantic. *Lord, Lord, this is my last chance. I'm begging You.*

Stalling for time, I managed a weak, "Now, now, girls—let's talk about this. Tell you what, Janella, I'll play one more hand. I'll bet this pillow against that roll of film. Is that fair?"

She didn't hesitate. "It's a deal—hell, yes."

"Honest? No reneging," I pressed.

"Believe it."

She spat on her hand. I spat on mine and, holding the pillow firmly with one hand, I shook with the other.

"With his luck, my ass will sit on that pillow and what he's got under it is mine, too."

"Over my dead body." Amy gritted through clenched teeth.

"Why don't we draw for it—save time," Janella suggested with a diabolical grin.

"Why not," I said, with all hope gone, wondering almost hysterically when the cops would be called to catch a naked man racing down the street with two women in hot pursuit, and if the headlines would get back to J.W. before I did.

"I'll hold the cards," Amy said as she shuffled, then extended the deck to Janella, who pulled a card.

"The winner," she gloated and laid it face-down on the carpet.

"Your turn, Sugar," Amy said as she turned to me.

I saw the card peek out of the deck as if beckoning. As it attached itself to my finger, I mumbled a prayer.

Tenderly, I laid it down.

Janella's hand shot out and turned her card.

Laughing triumphantly, she held it up. "Queen of hearts—I win." She reached for the pillow.

"Not so fast, you bitch. Turn it over, Sugar."

Trembling, I reached and turned the card.

It was the ace of spades.

"You cheated—I know you cheated," Janella shrieked, stamping her feet.

Amy stood between us. "How in hell could he cheat? Where would he hide it? Besides, he's too dumb to cheat and I held the cards. Pay up."

In a fury, Janella dug in the bag and flung the roll so hard it could have fractured my skull. It flew straight as a homing pigeon to my waiting hand.

Cursing, using words even I hadn't heard before, she grabbed her belongings and slammed out so hard the picture on the wall rattled.

"Give me my pillow," Amy demanded as she plucked it from my unresisting hand and pulled the bedclothes back. The springs groaned as our bodies made a perfect landing.

With the priceless film clutched in my fist, my other hand removed a strip of satin that slid away quite easily. Opening one eye, I saw it fly through the air like a bird.

Our over-eager bodies intertwined feverishly. This time, there was no banging at the door to interrupt our increasingly passionate moment.

But to my horror, I suddenly realized that there was an interruption far worse. I was growing limp.

My frantic mind implored, Lord, please—not payback time now, not now. To no avail.

Even as she moved against me, I knew it was a disaster. Her seeking mouth and coaxing hands embarrassed me.

She giggled, peeking under the covers. "Where did it go?"

"I guess I must be too drunk," came my feeble excuse.

But in my heart I knew that witch in San Francisco had put the hex on me and she was laughing, too.

Rolling out of bed, I pulled on my pants, carried the rest, and made for the door.

"In Texas, we'd call that an assault with a dead weapon." Amy's laughter followed me out and chased me down the hall.

CHAPTER 32

It took me only a moment to throw my things together for the drive home.

Stepping off the elevator with my uncombed hair and bloodshot eyes, the typewriter bag bouncing off my hip, brought a delighted grin to the face of the night clerk. His hopeful "Checking out?" confirmed I'd worn out my welcome.

On the fast-moving Interstate 5, even stopping briefly for gas and a burger, it was still an eight-hour drive. I had plenty of time to think.

As comforted as I was by the thought that Ma probably would be over her anger at me by now, the look in Juan's eyes wouldn't leave my mind, even as I rationalized that his unspoken, heart-filled dreams had to die. But in my cowardly heart, I didn't want to be the one to draw blood.

And then there was Rica. There could be no more gray. It had to be either black or white, and I would live with her decision.

At last the misty outline of the city came into view. Rushing into J.W.'s office without even a knock, I threw the film on his desk. His gruff "What the hell" turned to "Bless you, my son" as his mind registered what he held.

The pictures were everything Janella had said they were. I told J.W. that I had sacrificed my virginity for these and he returned my lie with "I told you you'd get lucky, didn't I."

Then I came clean.

"I won that film from the *Los Angeles Times'* best photographer with an ace of spades and a lot of help from the Man upstairs."

"The hell you did." He pounded his desk, elated to know that his rival newspaper had picked up the tab.

"You musta thrown in a good word for me, too." He grinned. "We both got lucky."

He crowned me on the spot: I was now a national correspondent high on the ladder of my dreams—and still reaching, which came with a substantial increase in salary.

Dr. Teddy was in her downstairs study and waved to me as she saw the pickup winding up the driveway. The grand old house seemed almost like a second home to me.

She opened the door as I raised my hand to knock. With her arm around my shoulder, she brought me in.

"What adventures have you been on lately? We haven't seen you in weeks and we've missed you."

Briefly telling her of my time in Los Angeles, I asked the question on my mind.

"Where is Juan? I thought I'd find him in his studio."

"Oh, he's with Rica helping her hang pictures and arrange furniture. She's moved and hasn't been feeling well. Don't suppose you knew?"

"No, I didn't know. I haven't seen Juan for a couple of weeks. I miss him—and we need to talk."

"That's a good idea. He hasn't been painting for a while and that isn't like him."

Caught in a web not of their making, Dr. Teddy thought despairingly. *Steve will find his happiness, but Juan will never surrender his love for Steve. It lays buried, but will never die. Steve is a decent man. I know he loves Juan, but he cannot give what he doesn't have. God alone knows the answer to this. Breaks my heart as it will break Sara's,* Teddy's soliloquy concluded.

Dr. Teddy seemed uncommonly quiet, but now she answered my unasked question.

"She's at the Ocean View Apartments over on Forty-Seventh Avenue. Apartment eight, I believe. Bring them back with you. I'll see what Mrs. Mackey is planning for dinner."

She hugged me good-bye.

The apartment was in an area of old converted homes and stood on a gentle slope that almost overlooked the ocean. I could smell the salt air and hear the swooping, noisy seagulls.

The little orange Beetle shone in the sunlight, its tires turned against the curb, but there was no sign of Juan's car.

I knocked on the door while mentally rehearsing what had been churning in my mind those many hours on the road. I would, of course, apologize; would not for any reason lose my composure. No country boy here, I reassured myself. I am a gentleman, but the answers had to be straight. No more gray.

The tension built even as I knocked—a little harder than intended.

The door opened. Rica's eyes widened in surprise and one hand flew to push back her hair. My eyes followed it. If there was a ring on that finger, I'd bite it off.

Suddenly my good intentions were shot to hell and all reason fled.

"Am I holding down the bench or am I in the game?" the words ground out.

"You are the game," Rica almost whispered.

With those four simple words, she had disarmed me. I felt the anger slip out of me like air from a pricked balloon.

"I tried to tell you, but you were so angry. And nasty, too, I might add."

Speechless, I felt my eyes fill with tears. My body ached with an incredible feeling of love that flooded my every nerve as I heard her say the words I had waited to hear for too long.

Standing transfixed in the doorway, suddenly afraid I had misunderstood—until she found her way into my arms. I didn't know a woman could be the origin of such profound ecstasy. Without leaving my embrace, she closed the door.

The moment seemed too intense for words but finally, between kisses, the words stumbled out almost incoherently. "Rica, Rica, you know I want to marry you."

Gently pressing her fingers on my lips, she said, "Wait, wait…"

She stepped away and pulled her dress tight across her body.

I stared, not understanding.

She tugged the dress higher and tighter.

Finally, shocked and disbelieving, I saw the thickening waistline and swell of her belly. Counting back, and for a split-second considering another possibility, I hesitated. Then her tremulous voice whispered, "Aren't you going to say something?"

"I already have—weren't you listening?"

"Does that question still stand even when you don't know who the father of this baby is?"

"It's part of you and your love makes you mine. So it's our baby."

"You would marry me thinking the baby was not yours? I love you more than you can ever know for that. It is your baby, Steve."

She sobbed against my chest, the hair falling into her face. I kissed the back of her neck and led her to the only chair big enough to hold both of us.

"Is that what you came to the farm to tell me?"

"No, I didn't know then. I came to tell you that sham romance was over, to tell you I loved you, but you were so angry and didn't want me anymore."

Holding her so tightly against me that I could almost feel the baby move within her, it seemed as though we were one body. The world was mine—I had it all.

"Let's get married right away."

"We have to get a license first—that takes three days, Steve."

"That's too long."

"Three days? I haven't a thing to wear that fits..."

We had breakfast in Reno the next morning. Her dress was a little longer in the back, but it didn't matter. She's got great legs.

A commercial wedding chapel with canned music didn't seem right to me. We wanted a church wedding.

On the very outskirts of town I found a little brick church with a steeple and belfry. Beside it was a cottage with peeling white paint competing with a climbing rose that reached for the roof.

I knocked.

A white-haired lady answered with a smile and a welcoming, "Come in—it's hot in the sun."

We explained our mission. A twinkle in her eye suggested an explanation was unnecessary.

"Please sit down. I believe the man you're looking for is in the garden."

She called from the back door. "Dear, there are some folks here who would like to talk to you."

He appeared promptly, holding two roses in one hand, pruning shears in the other. Listening to our request, he said, "I'll need to tidy up a bit." Handing one rose to his wife and the other to Rica, he excused himself.

When he reappeared, his hair was neatly combed; instead of pruning shears, he held a Bible. As we took refuge from the world in the holiness of the sanctuary, a great peace prevailed. Soft light filtered through two stained-glass windows, casting a rosy glow throughout. The wooden pews were our silent witnesses.

We were not surprised to see the minister's wife seated at the organ. I could almost hear the choir singing Ma's favorite song, "Amazing Grace."

The music, a lovely complement, was a backdrop for the ceremony that was short and heartfelt. Never had I heard such beautiful words.

Rica extended her finger to accept my class ring and I smiled to myself seeing her slyly insert a tissue under the band to secure it.

When the magic phrase was spoken, "I now pronounce you man and wife," I thought my heart would burst, and looked to see Rica's radiant tear-stained face as she held it up to be kissed.

The minister prayed for God's blessing on our union as we sat in the peaceful quiet of the rose garden.

The table before us was set with lemonade and freshly baked tea cakes. And so we celebrated our nuptials.

The document tied with a white ribbon was made out to Steven and Rica McAllister and it never left her hand all the way home.

That night as we lay in each other's arms, her black hair tangled across my chest, her body molded to my every contour, I knew that she had been made for me. I gave my fervent thanks to God who had given me my ace of spades again.

I invaded my savings and spent my raise before it was in my hand. Spent it lavishly on a five-day honeymoon in a luxurious suite eighteen floors above the clattering machines, shrieking winners, losers' despair and, of course, the eternal optimists.

The penthouse above us was an elaborate suite of rooms that sheltered in utmost privacy the really big-time spenders—those who lost or won thousands on the turn of a card. Little did they know that I was the winner and she was warm in my arms—my ace of spades.

We luxuriated in the splendor of these rooms.

Propped up among the pillows, I was almost intimidated by this huge piece of furniture that seemed to cover half an acre. I had slept in a twin bed all of my life.

We loved and played like children. Sometimes we slept.

The first ring of the phone brought room service that spoiled us with extravagant choices. We tried everything on the menu. Rica's "flu" seemed to have succumbed to the lobster.

I think about the third day, sated with love and good food, we talked and thought about our future. Rica called her mother—there were tears, of both delight and disappointment. I was too selfish to share my happiness just yet.

We decided to find larger accommodations after the baby was born—a place with a yard.

Rica was excited and thrilled about her pregnancy and as she chattered, I tuned in on, "...we really shouldn't spoil an only child. I think at least two more children, don't you?"

Still trying to assimilate the sudden knowledge that I was going to be a father and that someone would be calling me "Daddy" in the very near future, I was apprehensive. But my courage prevailed and I said, "Well, we may as well get started."

On the fifth day we shopped, and my love now wore a gold band with a two-carat diamond on the finger on which I had always kept a watchful eye. We decided a plain gold band would mark me as unavailable.

The trouble-free red truck, whose odometer read close to a hundred fifty thousand miles, had not a dent and was rewarded only by new tires and periodic oil changes. It had transported me faithfully to the work that I loved, and now carried the three of us back to reality.

Thinking of Ma, I laughed and remembered her threat of surgery with the chicken knife. I thought I was safe now, and in an enviable position with a good salary—and a marriage certificate.

Depositing Rica in the apartment, I drove to collect my few belongings from the little housekeeping room above the garage.

It seemed unbelievable that nearly four years had passed since Ma had found that room so close to the university where I had learned my ABCs from the indomitable Mrs. Dowd.

Upon opening the door, the flashing red light on the message machine could not be ignored.

"Where are you? Call," came Ma's usual salutation.

"Dammit to hell, pick up the phone," were Sis' irate words.

J.W.'s gruff voice, "Got a good one for you. Call."

Call? Hadn't he just given me a good one? The truck's engine hadn't even cooled and he wanted me to call?

Juan's disappointed voice: "Thought you were coming for dinner. You missed a good one. Call."

Dr. Teddy's urgent voice: "Steve, Steve, call."

Instantly I knew that Juan had called Rica's mother when he hadn't found Rica at the apartment, and her mother had told him what I had wanted to tell him in my own words.

The dark premonition that had been hiding in the deep subconscious of my mind came flooding to the surface with Dr. Teddy's voice. Instinctively I knew then that when Juan learned the door was closed and locked with no key, he would know the anguish, the frantic denial that I had known when he had told me, "They've set the date."

But I had found the key that he would never find.

I had wanted to be with him to say the words—but what words? What could I say? Not the words that he prayed to hear, but I could cement what had always been his—my love and respect that would sustain our friendship forever.

My fingers dialed, but the phone clattered to the floor. Dialing again, there was no answer. Finally, on the third try, Mrs. Mackey's strained voice directed, "Dr. Teddy said to tell you Saint Francis Hospital. Intensive care."

I stopped for Rica and as we sped through the traffic, she sobbed. The tears falling down my face finally turned to cold sweat as I begged God for my brother's life.

We found Dr. Teddy at the nursing station, her usual composure hovering on the precipice.

"Sara?" Rica asked.

Dr. Teddy nodded to the sign on the door that read "No admittance." "She's hardly been out of there for three days. Dr. Myers is with him, too."

My eyes asked what my tongue couldn't articulate.

"He was in an accident three days ago. Internal injuries, lacerations, concussion. A terrible loss of blood. Hasn't been conscious."

Dr. Teddy paused, the words choked out, her shoulders shaking.

"He has a rare blood type and we can't find a match, so he's hanging by a thread. It will take Sara with him if he goes."

Something flared in my brain. Remembering a long-forgotten argument with Sis when she had said, "You are so weird, you even have weird blood..." followed by Ma's quick remonstration, "Sis!"

How would she know? But she and Ma talked about a lot of things to which I wasn't privy.

"Test me, Dr. Teddy. Please."

"We've tested so many, and checked all the other hospitals. That blood type seems nonexistent. The odds are astronomical, but let's try." She nodded to a nurse.

Turning to Dr. Teddy as she walked unsteadily with us, I took her hand and drew her close. Speaking with absolute surety, I said, "Mine will be a match."

As the needle slipped painlessly into my vein, I knew in my heart that God had heard my prayer.

It seemed to me that we waited a lifetime with only a murmur of voices in that quiet room. Waiting for the results of the test that could determine life or death for Juan.

Rica sat with her arms around Sara, with Dr. Teddy chafing her cold hands. I stood at the window gazing at the horizon with unseeing eyes.

The door opened and an exuberant voice seemed to shake the walls. "It's a match, it's a match. A perfect match."

Turning, I saw this huge man. The ebony black of his smiling face shone above the white jacket that stretched across his massive shoulders. It was Alfie. I stood speechless.

Dr. Teddy stood, holding Sara, who was sobbing uncontrollably. "Thank God, thank God."

Rica slumped back in her chair exhausted.

The doctor stood before them, his deep voice explaining, "Now he has a fighting chance. The next couple of days should give us the answer. It will be a long journey, but he'll make it." He gave Sara a comforting pat. "Get some food into this one. Where's the donor?"

Dr. Teddy's nod turned him to me and as our eyes made contact, his incredulous booming voice cried, "Cowboy!" as he wrapped me in a bear hug. That voice that had so softly sung me back to life tethered me to reality in another time.

Dr. Teddy's discreet cough interrupted. "Obviously introductions aren't necessary. Steve, we'll take care of Rica for you. Thank you, Dr. Myers. I know you'll keep us informed."

"Of course, Dr. Hassé."

"C'mon, Steve. It is Steve, isn't it? We've got work to do."

With his arm around my shoulder, we hastened to start the procedure that would restore my brother, my friend.

For two more days, Juan lay comatose, attached to a machine whose tentacles brought the nutrients that preserved his life. His lashes were black against the pallor of his face; his head was swathed in layers of gauze.

Time blurred as Sara and I kept our vigil while my lifeblood flowed into his broken body.

"What happened?" I hardly dared to ask, not wanting to know.

In a hushed voice, Sara told me. At breakneck speed, Juan had fled down the great hill as if to escape the irrevocable knowledge. Somewhere, miles away on the coast highway, he had veered from the road and smashed into an abutment at the end of a bridge. A smear of silver paint crushed into the cement was all that marked his passage.

She would not look at me as she whispered, "There were no skid marks."

I closed my eyes as if to blind myself to that unbearable understanding.

We were there when he regained consciousness for the first time in five days. His eyes focused on my face with a steady gaze. Holding my breath, I knew instinctively that with that look, he was trying to free himself, trying to accept the inevitable.

His head turned to Mamá Sara. I was happy for him. At last he would have peace of mind. Yet it seemed that I'd lost almost a physical part of myself. That feeling clung to me as my feet carried me down the long corridor.

Rica had been at the hospital daily, but our time had been strained and interrupted. Both Dr. Teddy and Sara had urged me to go home, but I could not bear to leave until I knew that Juan was going to live. The stress had taken its toll on all of us.

Then the magic words were given with a beaming smile; the words that reduced all of us to tears: "I believe he's out of the danger zone. He'll make it now, but it will be a slow process. His vital signs are good and he's breathing on his own."

Alfie clapped me on the shoulder. "Let's go have a cup of coffee."

With a quick nod to Dr. Teddy and Sara, he turned, my feet following as though they had grown wings.

Our coffee break lasted over two hours as we reminisced. He told me that he'd never heard my last name, only known that I had really gone home. He had wondered about me many times.

I filled him in, telling him of my work at the *Bay City Chronicle*, my new promotion, my marriage. I wanted him to know that his faith in me was justified. Then I told him how Ma's washing machine had eaten my marijuana stash—it seemed so long ago.

"What?" Laughing, he asked, "The shoe salesman didn't get it?"

As we rose to leave, he leaned in to say good-bye and give me a hug. But I grabbed his hand and hung on saying as clearly as possible while choking, "You saved my sanity and jolted me back to the real world with your big-foot-up-my-ass method of encouragement. Made me know that I could justify my existence and leave a mark on the world. And I love you for it, Dr. Myers. I am so proud of you. You've earned the right to wear that white jacket and you look damned good in it, I might add."

His eyes brimmed with tears, but he smiled. "Love you, too, Cowboy. We've come a long way together and we're not there yet."

And so we parted. I went home to my wife. She let me know that the honeymoon was just beginning.

Later, when I had found the strength to lift the phone, I tried to reach Ma. A recorded message informed me that the phone had been disconnected. That brought my head out of the clouds.

Knowing that they hadn't planned to leave until after the baby was born, I worried and decided to make a quick trip to the farm. Then, too, Ma should know about our marriage.

Recalling her instant assessment of Rica when she had surprised us in the chicken coop on that visit months ago, I was more than a little apprehensive.

Just as Rica and I were preparing to leave, the phone rang. That damn phone.

It was my boss.

"I'll call you back, J.W...."

"Wait, wait, hotshot. There's a telegram here for you."

My heart sank, envisioning a problem with Sis' pregnancy. Rushing down to the office, I was ripping it open even as he was handing it to me.

Ma's terse message: "Call 887-4143."

"Ma. Where in hell are you? What's wrong? How's Sis?"

"Calm down, Stevie. Nothing's wrong. Well, nothing much. Tim broke his arm in two places and Sis is spoon-feeding the big sissy marine. We're in Fort Worth—Texas, of course. Got a nice little three-bedroom house..."

"Ma" I interrupted. "I've got a new phone number. Got a pencil?"

In the pause that followed, my mind tried frantically to find an easy way to break the news. With my usual tact, I blurted, "I'm married, Ma."

"Married?" her shocked voice asked. "You're married? Not to Juan's girlfriend, I hope. That hussy."

Absolving me, of course, of any responsibility.

"Easy now. You're talking about my wife. Your new daughter. We've loved each other for a long time, Ma."

Then came a prolonged silence while she digested the news.

"Ma, say something. This phone call is costing me money."

"Our address is seventy-seven eighty-four Alamo Drive. When can you come visit? Sis liked her so guess I must have missed something."

"You don't know the half of it. I love you, Ma."

I was sweating when I hung up.

CHAPTER 33

O ne week later, the phone rang. Ma's voice was jubilant. "It's a boy, eight pounds, ten ounces." Then the phone was held close to the peevish complaint of a baby.

"See how smart he is. Already he can say 'Uncle Stevie' plain as day."

After congratulations to Sis, I made my own announcement.

"Well, Ma, get lots of practice with diapers. Rica is expecting in a few months."

Sis' voice came from the background. "Wow! That old rooster must have told him the secret down there in the chicken coop."

Ma's snort of laughter told me she was happy.

Her original lack of enthusiasm was matched by Rica's mother at our first meeting. It was obvious that a newspaperman and a Reno wedding were not what she had envisioned for her only daughter. She did, however, thaw out somewhat when she learned that the rent would be taken care of.

Rica and her father were happily reunited. His welcome was considerably warmer as his eyes fastened on the unmistakable mound of her belly and the hand that lay upon it with the sparkling wedding band.

Juan's homecoming was a joyous celebration. With our arms around each other's shoulders, no words were needed.

The tears that Sara shed were tears of gratitude and spoke for all of us. Happiness reigned at the big house.

Juan healed on the side presented to the world, but I knew the scars on his heart were permanent. The courage he displayed when he stood between me and his father's knife was the same he now presented to the world when he resumed a life newly empty of hope, but accepting at last the ghost of his dreams.

He was painting again, and one of his previous oils had sold for an amount that made my eyes grow big. He was definitely one of the big-time, sought-after painters and Rica was his favorite model.

As her pregnancy advanced, he said she grew more beautiful. He captured her radiance on canvas. Always he was available to drive her to appointments or spend time with her when I was on assignment on the other side of town. Their close association reminded me of Sis and me, but without the bickering.

"How wonderful," a spoiled Rica laughed, "to have a brother so available and the Dr. Teddy, the best obstetrician in San Francisco."

Before I had the chance to tell J.W. of my marriage, I was summoned to his office. Scowling at me from under those bushy white eyebrows, he reproached me with "Married, huh? I had to read it in my own newspaper?" He rose and shook my hand, adding, "Maybe that will settle you down."

Sensing his good mood, I took a deep breath and asked that I not be sent out of town for the months of January and February.

"For what reason?" he asked with a piercing look.

"Well, uh, my wife is pregnant."

"Since when is it required that a man hold her head for morning sickness?"

"Well," I mumbled, "she's a little further along than that."

"When is it due?"

Looking over his head, admiring the wall, I stuttered, "Uh, in a while."

"No more bullshit," he thundered. "I asked you when."

"In about three months," I whispered.

He looked at me in amazement and then laughed. "I'll be damned." His fist banged the desk.

"You didn't have to do it all at once, stupid. Guess I haven't kept you busy enough. I'll remedy that."

And he did, but at least there were no out-of-town trips.

It was rumored among my peer group in the pressroom that I was the favorite son, which did not gain me any favors there. However, J.W. was tough on me if he felt my work wasn't as good as it could have been. But those times were seldom since I had to please myself first.

My life with Rica in that crowded apartment was all I ever dreamed it could be. To lay my hand on her belly and feel the new life that stirred so vigorously beneath, caused a thrill that consumed me, especially knowing it was part of me.

"What shall we name him?"

"Him? It's a girl—I should know. Let's name her 'Margaret' for your mother, or 'Mary' for mine. That should gain us some points."

"I think 'William' for my father. 'William McAllister' has a nice ring to it," I coaxed.

"Betcha." She giggled.

"Betcha," I answered with a kiss.

We shopped for baby things. I never dreamed such a small individual could require so many clothes. Rica chose pink ruffles; I chose blue, but also found to my delight a tiny red baseball cap with "SF 49ers" embroidered in gold thread.

"That will look silly on a girl," Rica declared, but I persevered.

The one thing that we really needed was a crib and we found a most beautiful white piece of furniture fit for a royal prince.

"Princess," Rica insisted.

The price was fit for royalty, too, so we settled on a bassinette that would fit next to our bed.

Our happiness made time fly; soon we were counting the weeks.

True to his word, J.W. kept me in the city, available at a moment's notice.

"I guess you think your mother is the only woman in the world who can make a chocolate cake," accused Rica.

"Well," I responded peacefully, "I'm sure you could do as well—she just measures the flour and adds eggs and ..."

"Now you're going to give me a cooking lesson—my coffee is weak, the tacos are burned..."

"Darling, I love your tacos; they were a little brown, but on the third day you had them absolutely perfect."

"I didn't know cooking was a requirement—my mother did that. She didn't raise me to be a cook."

The tears flowed; I kissed them away.

I came home early the next day to find all the windows open, the fan whirring—and the distinct odor of smoke.

My wife was in a blazing tantrum.

"There's the damn cake," she said, pointing to the charred chunks of chocolate stuffed back into the box of mix in which it had arrived—flung in the general direction of the garbage can.

I took a tentative step forward and slid on the sticky remains and broken shells of a hen's best effort.

"And damn those chickens—their eggs roll right off a countertop," she continued.

"I'm fat and ugly and I know my ankles are fat, too, even if I can't see them. Look what you've done to me. And now you'll hate me because I can't cook." She threw a mixing spoon that clattered off the wall.

"You'll never make the team with a pitch like that, my beloved."

Casting caution to the wind, I grabbed her and pulled her down with me in our big chair.

"Rica, Rica, my darling. I've never told anyone this before, but I've been so tired of chocolate cake all these years." Then came the fleeting recollection that Ma always knew when I was lying.

"You make wonderful tacos. Anyway, it isn't food I'm thinking about when I'm with you. And in a few weeks, you'll be holding our baby. Your ankles won't be swollen; you'll be slim and beautiful, as beautiful as you are now." As I held her close and wiped away her tears, I said, "You've never been so beautiful to me. Now blow your nose."

With her arms around my neck, she said, "I love you, Steve."

A quick knock at the door interrupted us. "Anyone home?" Juan called.

The door opened and he stood there with a big smile lighting up his face, two men behind him with a large box almost too big to squeeze inside. Well rewarded, the men left and Juan stood grinning expectantly. "Surprise."

Rica's curiosity overpowered her baking disaster. She ran to Juan, gave him a hug and shook the box to no avail.

Together Juan and I dismantled the heavy cardboard carton to reveal a magnificent baby crib that brought on another flood of tears. The crib fit very snugly between the foot of the bed.

Glancing discreetly around the apartment, Juan said, "I've been wanting to try this new place where the food is rumored to be wonderful. Rica, powder your nose and let's go to dinner. C'mon, Steve."

Surely there was no man in the world as rich as me.

Dinner wasn't a gala affair, although the food was excellent, the

surroundings beautiful. Rica picked at her food. I knew she was uncomfortable and exhausted. Suddenly her belly seemed to have grown
larger.

"Maybe it's twins," she worried. "Perhaps I should have had that
sonogram. Another week or so to go. I'm glad the bag is packed; I'm
tired of waiting."

Juan drove slowly, carefully, as I held Rica close in the backseat of
his new car.

"Dr. Teddy said I should try a Bentley and I really like it. What do
you think?"

"I guess I'll have to get one, too," I joked, "now that I'm a family
man. We'll crowd that truck."

"Country boy," Rica murmured, cuddling closer.

She was so tired and it had been a long day for me, too. Bed was a
welcome refuge.

Finally, after much tossing and turning, she lay quiet and I drifted
off into a dreamless sleep. Slowly awakening, I was vaguely aware
that something...what was happening? I peered at the clock. The
illuminated dial showed 2:30 a.m.

My pajamas were clinging to my body. I felt a strange sensation—
something warm and wet, very wet. Slipping my hand tentatively
between the sheets, I discovered Rica was saturated. Realizing she
had wet the bed and knowing how embarrassed she'd feel, how could
I wake her?

Then her hands were shaking me. "Steve, Steve, wake up. I think
my water broke and I hurt," she groaned. "I think the baby's coming."

"No, it can't," I said stupidly. "It isn't due for eight days—maybe ten."
We abandoned the bed and dressed quickly.

"Call Dr. Teddy."

Then she was in the shower.

The sound of Dr. Teddy's sleepy voice did nothing to slow my heartbeat, despite her reassuring words.

"Don't worry; she's got lots of time. Take her to the hospital where they will make her comfortable. And drive carefully. I'll be there shortly."

Rica was struggling to get into her clothes, but then gave it up and pulled on my robe. She was excited, happy...and scared.

"What if something should go wrong? It's too early, Steve."

With a sharp intake of breath, she took my hand.

"Dr. Teddy told you she couldn't give you the exact time. Don't worry. Where's your bag?"

"Over there. I need a towel. Just think, at last, at last we'll have the baby and my ankles won't be fat. Hurry, Steve," she gasped.

Driving perhaps faster than necessary, I parked in front of the brightly lit hospital, both of us glad to be there.

"I don't need a wheelchair. I can walk."

"Sit," a no-nonsense nurse instructed.

"Now I suppose she'll want me to roll over," came Rica's irritated aside to me. Then she gasped and held her belly.

With the paperwork finished quickly, I followed the wheelchair through the maze of corridors. Abruptly, it stopped and the nurse pointed to a room.

"You can wait in there."

"Can't he come with me?" Rica cried out.

"No, later maybe."

My shaky legs were glad to deliver my body to a chair. There were two other people in the room, obviously for the same reason. A boy, who hardly looked old enough to grow whiskers, trying not to act as I felt, was pacing up and down the small room, an unlit cigarette hanging from his mouth.

An older man sitting with an unopened magazine in his lap and a look of irritation crossing his bearded face spoke in a low, angry voice. "You damn kids. What the hell do you expect? Sixteen years old and now she's got a baby. I'm not supporting them. You damn well better have a plan and you damn well better get a ring on her finger. She's the last of my five kids and I'm not raising yours. Tires aren't the only things made out of rubber, you know—or ought to know."

The kid lit his cigarette with shaking hands and didn't answer.

Time seemed to crawl. I looked at my watch; it was nearly six. I needed a cup of coffee, but I didn't want to leave.

The kid was still pacing and I almost laughed when I found myself in perfect step beside him.

At last a nurse appeared at our door. The boy's expectant face turned to her, but she nodded in my direction and I followed her into the delivery room. I didn't even like the name—it sounded like the end of a loading dock.

Everything was white, including Rica's face. Wet with sweat, only her big brown eyes and black hair tied back showed color.

She reached for me and I bent down to hold her. When she groaned and strained, my body involuntarily strained along. She managed a weak smile as she relaxed and squeezed my hand.

"I'm okay, Cowboy. Dr. Teddy is taking good care of me. Don't worry—our daughter is on the way."

Dr. Teddy appeared. "She's coming along, Steve, but it will be awhile. Don't worry." She showed me to the door.

I walked back to the waiting room to hear the gruff voice, "Why in hell don't you sit down? You're driving me crazy. You shoulda been on your feet nine months ago. Relax—we've got the best baby doctor in San Francisco."

As if on cue, Dr. Teddy appeared and motioned to the boy, who almost crowded her into the doorway in his haste.

The man sat quietly for a while. "This your first?"

"Yeah."

"The first one is always scary, but it gets easier with the next one."

Easier for who, I thought with the image of Rica's contorted face before me. I didn't answer.

"You raise them up the best you can—the wife's been dead ten years.

Twelve hours a day on the job to buy their clothes, feed them, keep a roof over their heads. Try to teach them right from wrong, pay their speeding tickets, educate them." He paused. "This one was the baby. She never lacked for anything—got everything she ever wanted. Except this baby, of course."

He sat for a moment, then added, "Now this boy. His family has disowned him, kicked him out. Wrong religion—Jewish. You know how they are with their different customs. My girl, my baby girl— she's been in there eight hours."

He put his head down and the sound of great gulping sobs slid through his callused hands.

Like he said, the first one was scary.

The boy came back and put his hand on the man's shoulders. "The doctor said she's doing real good and it won't be long now."

I watched to see the man's hand reach up and clasp the boy's hand.

The hours dragged on. I was walking the corridors; I couldn't go back into that room. I found the cafeteria and ordered coffee that I couldn't seem to swallow, a sandwich that all but dried on the plate. I tried to read, but the words were only letters on a page.

Dr. Teddy hadn't been back for a while or perhaps I'd missed her. Rica had been in that room for over nine hours.

I talked to Sara on the phone. She said that Juan was in Los Angeles for a show; told me not to worry.

Eleven hours had passed. A sense of foreboding crept in and smothered those tired words, "Don't worry."

On my return, I caught sight of Dr. Teddy and another doctor at the nurse's station and ran up to them.

Dr. Teddy turned to me and, with her arm around my shoulder, spoke gently, "Steve, Rica is having complications. The baby has changed positions and is unable to move along. It is too far advanced in the birth canal to do a caesarean. We may not be able to save the baby and we are concentrating our every effort on Rica."

I slumped up against the wall. Dr. Teddy led me to another room and quickly left me alone. I almost fell into a chair fighting for breath, feeling as though I had been punched hard in the solar plexus.

"Oh, God, Oh, God. Not Rica—please God, not Rica."

In my agony, I bargained with Him. "The baby. Not my wife."

I heard the suitcase drop and felt Juan's arms as he kneeled beside me, his eyes brilliant with unshed tears. Mine were frozen within me.

Sara was standing back, smudges of paint on the face she hadn't taken time to wash.

We all sat in silence, yet our thoughts were completely attuned to each other.

My tongue was unable to bring a single word to life.

The torturous thought of Rica lying in that bed, fighting alone to bring our baby alive, was intolerable. I stood and my footsteps sounded on the polished floor with Juan's steps echoing beside me. We walked together as we always had.

Fourteen hours after I had brought my wife and unborn child into the hospital, an inner peace enveloped me. I resigned myself to the bitter knowledge that the little body torn from my beloved wife was at peace.

Dr. Teddy stepped in. Her shoulders were slumped, her body drained of every resource. With her mask hanging against a bloodied uniform, a smile denied her exhaustion.

"Rica?" I begged.

"Sleeping peacefully. All is well."

Then she added, "Steve, we have your boy, and the little warrior is going to make it."

I fell to my knees; the tears that had frozen in my heart flowed like a river.

CHAPTER 34

Following Dr. Teddy's explicit orders, I lay down in a quiet waiting room to rest until Rica awoke. My mind numbed, my body betrayed me and I slept.

When I felt a hand on my shoulder, I sat up so suddenly the blood rushed out of my head; the blanket that someone had thrown over me slid to the floor. Untangling my feet, I stood unsteadily. My watch indicated that two hours had passed.

"She's awake and waiting for you."

I ran after the nurse, brushed past her at the door. Rica's eyes had the hint of a sparkle; her lips formed a tremulous smile as she held out her arms to me.

Leaning, I wrapped my arms around her and tried to speak but, wordlessly, we clung together.

The discreet cough of a smiling nurse interrupted, then came the unfamiliar sound of a baby's whimper.

I moved aside as the nurse laid him in Rica's outstretched arms and quietly closed the door behind her. Rica moved the blanket aside and together we saw our son for the first time.

His tiny red face turned from side to side as though searching, indignant at the delay. One little pink fist was in his mouth, the other flailing in the air.

After Rica positioned the nipple, the only sounds were those of his sucking and my sniffles as Rica murmured endearments to both of us.

That room was no longer a sterile white, but glowed with a soft radiance that warmed me to my soul.

Later, the sleeping baby lay quietly, having relinquished his hold on the nipple, and was reluctantly surrendered to the nurse. She carried him to the sanctuary of the nursery with a bubble of milk still clinging to the corner of his lips.

Rica's hand relaxed in mine. Her long lashes that lay dark against her pale cheeks told me that she, too, was fast asleep.

The hustle and bustle of this huge hospital seemed muted, and the world seemed far away as I sat there overwhelmed by the flooding emotions of the last interminable hours.

The nurse returned and held the door, apparently an unspoken invitation for me to leave.

I stepped into the long corridor and suddenly wanted to be sitting at that old table with Ma, telling her face-to-face, "We have a boy. His name is William Manuel McAllister."

Juan fell in step beside me smiling, jingling a pocketful of change, and pointed me to a pay phone.

Laughing, I watched him feed the phone but, abruptly, my voice broke the instant I heard Ma's voice.

"We've got a boy, Ma..." I choked. "Rica's fine."

My tears of relief wet the receiver.

"So what are you crying about? I think that's wonderful. What did you name him?"

"William Manuel McAllister...for Dad and Rica's father."

"Oh, Stevie," came her tearful voice.

"So what are you crying about, Grandma?"

I was delighted to pay her back in her own coin.

"I've just got a little cold."

"Yeah, sure Ma. Me, too. Tell Sis I love her." Juan nudged me. "I'm almost out of change, Ma. We'll come for a visit as soon as we can. Bye, Ma."

Handing me a handkerchief, Juan grinned. "When do I get to see the other baby?"

I ignored the remark and put an elbow in his ribs.

We found Rica's parents in the small waiting room that had been witness to so many emotions.

Dr. Teddy appeared in a clean uniform, but the dark circles under her eyes and the strain in her voice testified to her fatigue.

Speaking quietly, she said, "I think it would be in Rica's best interests if you would all wait until tomorrow to visit. She and the baby are doing well, but she has had a very hard time and needs to rest." Turning to me, she said, "Steve, I'd like to keep Rica here for a few extra days to monitor her more closely."

"Of course..."

"And I suggest you go home and get some sleep."

With a quick hug for me, she nodded her goodbye and turned away.

There was a momentary silence as Dr. Teddy left, then Rica's mother hugged me and my hand was shaken vigorously.

"Has he been named?" her father asked.

"Yes, we've named him William Manuel McAllister."

I could feel my stock go through the roof as my hand was returned after a bone-crushing handshake.

"You must have endeared yourself to Dad," Juan teased after their departure.

"Yes, and I picked up a few points with Mother, too."

Feeling utterly drained, I accepted Juan's offer to drive me home. Along the way, I asked myself why everyone always thinks that fathers get off easily. Then the pain-contorted face of Rica flashed through my mind—and I knew.

As she sat in her big chair that evening, Dr. Teddy seemed unusually quiet. Sara knew she was exhausted.

"Medical science still has its mysteries," Teddy spoke thoughtfully, almost as though she was speaking to herself.

"The delivery was progressing normally, but when the baby was far advanced in the birth canal—too far for a caesarian section—unexpectedly it was presenting a breech position. Despite our every effort to reposition it, the situation seemed to worsen.

"As the hours dragged by, the strain grew unbearable as we saw our every effort fail.

"Rica's contractions slowed and finally stopped. She became unresponsive except for an occasional convulsive push. I heard myself say, 'We've lost the baby.'

"The shine of tears showed plainly in the eyes above the mask of the surgical nurse. I hoped mine didn't.

"I remember saying that if we are to save the mother, we must take the baby surgically and do it now.

"Dr. Fuller gave an approving nod. Suddenly Rica gave a desperate push—it was almost frightening. The baby moved as if powered by another force. Rica pushed again and then the agonizing finale—the baby crowned."

Dr. Teddy paused as if re-creating the scene in her mind.

"Now he was in my hand. As if from far away, I heard my unbelieving voice utter, 'This baby has a heartbeat, a strong heartbeat.'

"'Thank God the bleeding's stopped,' came Dr. Fuller's heartfelt exclamation.

"We looked in amazement at Rica, completely sedated, her eyes closed, but she was smiling as if she had known something we didn't. Then the muffled sobs of the nurse turned to hysterical laughter as a baby's lusty cry broke the sudden hush."

I called J.W. with the good news, and he generously gave me a week off with his heartfelt congratulations, adding, "Keep in touch." That had a worrisome sound to it, so I decided to use the pony express should the need arise.

I slept until the phone awakened me. Juan asked, "Are you up? I'll be right there—I'm anxious to see the baby."

Hurriedly, I shaved and showered, embarrassed to realize that I'd slept away last night's visiting hours. Arriving at the hospital, we walked quickly to Rica's door. After knocking quietly, we stepped in.

Her pale face lit up and she lifted her face for a kiss, laughing as we bumped heads.

The nurse stood with a disapproving look and said sternly, "Dr. Hassé said no visitors, only your husband."

"This isn't a visitor, this is my brother."

With one hand, Rica pulled the blanket away from the little form cuddled in the crook of her arm.

"Look, Juan. Isn't he beautiful?"

Juan bent to stroke his little hand.

"Ah, yes, yes. How beautiful, so perfect."

Rica looked up at me.

"Steve, you haven't even held him yet. Hold out your arms."

Before I could utter a word, Rica said to the nurse, "Will you hand our baby to my husband."

Instinctively, I put out my arms as if to ward off a blow. The nurse placed this tiny bundle of life, with only a downy halo of gold showing above his blue blanket, on my stiffly outstretched arms.

Panic flooded through my every cell and I stood as though paralyzed.

"Don't drop him," came the nurse's irritated voice.

"Hold him close for goodness' sake. He won't bite, you know," instructed Rica.

I suddenly turned and thrust the baby at Juan, whose arms received him and held him so closely, so tenderly, as though they were melted into one.

Relieved, embarrassed and, yes, jealous, I looked everywhere except at my wife.

Juan seemed not to know that we were even there. He had found the little toes and almost crooned when he counted, "...eight, nine and ten..." His face was beatific.

One hand held the little head and the downy soft hair curled against his fingers while he murmured endearments in Spanish.

I tentatively offered a finger and stood at a safe distance.

Juan lifted a rapt face. "Look, look, he's smiling at me."

Sure enough, the corners of those rosy lips turned up.

"All right," I said, suddenly possessive. "I'll take him now."

"Not so fast," Juan said, turning. "See, he's laughing."

I noticed the baby's fingers holding Juan's thumb.

Rica's arms reached out. "If you two are going to come to blows over my baby, bring him to me."

As Juan reluctantly returned him, my son delivered himself of a distinct, unmistakable sound.

"See?" Rica laughed. "Only gas."

"Not so," Juan countered. "That boy gave the very first smile to his Uncle Juan before that."

"The baby really should go back to the nursery now," the nurse declared.

Juan held the door for her and, with a disapproving sniff, she carried the boy to safety.

"Uncle Juan will see you tomorrow, Steve." Juan grinned as he closed the door behind him.

I could tell that Rica was regaining her strength rapidly as she turned her gaze to me. Her tart comment followed: "On a scale of one to ten, I'd say you rated a two-and-a-half—at the most."

I pulled my chair closer to the bed and put my arms around her.

"Rica," I pleaded my case, "I don't know about babies. He's so little.

I'll do better. If you can keep that nurse out of here, I'll spend the whole day with you. I'll hold him."

"Not likely."

I heard the decisive voice of the nurse as she appeared noiselessly from somewhere.

Despite my early arrival the next morning, I met Juan coming out of Rica's room.

"Beware the witch," he muttered as he passed me. "Meet me later?"

I nodded.

The room was fragrant with the many arrangements of red roses. The old nurse grumbled as she positioned the vases.

"Why didn't I think of that?"

"Because you're a country boy," teased Rica.

Did I imagine that nurse adding, "...with cow shit on his boots"? No, I thought, those words were unknown to that proper lady.

When I bent to kiss Rica, the blanket moved and I looked in wonderment at this tiny replica of myself, his eyes looking up at me as if making a decision. I hoped that Rica had put in a good word for me. Fearlessly, I slipped my arm beneath him, a hand holding his head.

How hard can this be? I thought, psyching myself up while frantically trying to remember in which hand Juan had held that downy head.

Quickly I sat down, holding him close. He seemed to snuggle into his chosen position and, oddly enough, we were both comfortable. With one little fist in his mouth, he closed his eyes, seemingly satisfied with his decision.

I sat with my eyes closed, too, thanking God, then Rica, for her recommendation.

I met Juan an hour later as he read a day-old newspaper in the little room where I had spent some agonizing hours. He stood, grinning from ear to ear.

"How lucky can I get. At last I get a little uninterrupted time with you. It is a happy day," he declared enthusiastically.

"Yes, I've never been happier," I said. "I held my son for an hour and he laughed out loud. He probably would have said 'Daddy' if that thoughtless nurse hadn't whisked him away. It is a happy day."

"Steve, you have everything in life that counts except money..." Pausing, he added, "But I have that, so we're both happy, aren't we?"

The tone of his voice had changed. Disturbed, I glanced at him. He was smiling, but the smile never reached his eyes.

I spoke with perfect truth. "Let's eat—I'm starved. Dinner last night was a can of chicken soup with not a cracker in the house."

I wasn't dawdling over lunch, but Juan rushed me anyhow.

"What's so important that I can't have dessert?"

"Drink your coffee and I'll show you."

Juan drove carefully through the busy city, picking up speed as he started the climb up a hill. A smile seemed to tug at the corners of his mouth, and I could sense his excitement.

"Juan, where are we going?"

His smile widened. "It's a surprise."

I allowed myself a brief memory of my first experience in this magnificent part of the universe. Terrified, filthy, reeking of sheep shit, and hiding behind the huge wheel of a semi, I prayed for deliverance. Deliverance came in the form of a battered old Buick where I found sanctuary buried in the backseat, hidden beneath a crumpled tent, folding chair, Coleman stove, dirty laundry and more.

In the front seat, two zoned-out would-be hippies were looking for their dream at eleven hundred Haight Street.

Now it seemed never to have happened.

I suddenly laughed. "Juan, I've come a long way."

"*We've* come a long way," he corrected. "We still have a long way to go."

"What is all this secrecy about? You know you're dying to tell me, so let's have it."

His grin plastered across his face.

"Well, Dr. Teddy told me that I must invest some money or it will be heavily taxed. My last two paintings sold to a woman for a ridiculous price. Now she has commissioned me to do a portrait of her and her daughter...money is no object, of course.

"Real estate is the best investment. Dr. Teddy said that God doesn't make any more of it, the population is growing at a tremendous rate, and the city isn't keeping up, although some redevelopment has started. So I've been doing a lot of research and I want to show you what I've found."

His excitement seemed to grow with every sharp curve.

A winding tangle of streets threaded over an increasingly steep hill. Appearing momentarily were traditional houses, both stucco and wood frame, clinging to the hillsides and adding splashes of color as we continued our climb.

Finally, when it seemed that we could go no farther, Juan turned down a little twisted path, an indication that there had once been a driveway. Seen dimly through the old eucalyptus trees stood a weathered gray house and, as we drew near, Juan turned off the motor and we sat, just looking. I was speechless.

Juan's face had the look of a man in love. He saw the incredible beauty of a bygone era, still obvious in the graceful lines and steep roof of the Queen Anne Victorian, which was similar in structure to the Hassé house in Pacific Heights, even to the canted chimney on one end.

What I saw instead was the abandoned remains of a house that must have been spectacular even in its time, still standing proudly as if to say, "Do what you will, I'm still here."

The windows were gone or hung in great broken shards; what was left of the tall front door stood open. One slim ionic column was all that supported the richly decorated portico that sagged in despair as if waiting for the count of nine, but game to the finish. And this was only the front.

"Juan," I gasped. "You couldn't have invested any money in this."

He didn't answer, but opened the door and got out.

"Are you coming?"

I followed.

"Juan, where in hell are we? All those twists and turns...I don't know east from west."

"We are in the center of an acre on Telegraph Hill near North Beach, which is a hangout for artists, poets, Bohemian intellectuals. There's plenty of nightlife and expensive little shops and cafes there, but Telegraph Hill is much quieter and this house is insulated on this beautiful land. Many of these old homes up here have been bulldozed, but I got here first." And he laughed as I had not heard him for a long, long time.

"The Spaniards named it 'Loma Alta,' then it was known later as 'Goat Hill' by the early San Franciscans. The hill now owes its name to a semaphore—a windmill-like structure used to signal to the rest of the city the nature and purpose of the ships entering the Golden Gate...the history is fascinating."

His head thrown back and arms outstretched, he spoke almost with awe. "You've never seen such beauty—the view is forever. Look, the Golden Gate Bridge seems to hang from the sky, and there's Treasure Island. If you look past Coit Tower, you can see Alcatraz. The murals at Coit Tower make me want to burn my brushes, they are so beautiful. The entire city lies beneath us—imagine what it looks like at night. Steve, say something."

I laughed. "Watch where you're walking, Juan. Your head is in the clouds. You're in love with an acre of dirt, a beautiful view and a house that the bulldozer missed."

I saw the disappointment in his eyes before he turned his head. Instantly, I was ashamed to have hurt him, to have rained on his parade.

Flinging my arm over his shoulder, trying to soften my words, I said, "You may as well show me everything. What is that building over there?"

He brightened. "That's the old carriage house and stable. Can't you just see a fine old buggy drawn by a high-spirited horse?"

He was walking quickly and I stretched my legs to keep up, wondering how he knew about buggies and horses, while I stumbled over a length of iron fencing concealed in the weeds.

"This must have been a lily pond—see the beautiful stonework and the unusual shape? Surely there must have been formal gardens."

We walked over a large part of the land. I was growing tired, but Juan never slowed.

"You haven't seen the inside yet, but be careful—some of the floor has been torn up. Vandals have carted off everything they could."

As we approached the house, I saw it was surrounded by a sea of old boxwood trees, azaleas and wisteria all growing together in a tangle, the wisteria seeking to invade every crevice.

"Can't you see them all in bloom this spring? The fragrance will be heavenly."

Juan pushed open a back door—the servants' entrance, I assumed.

I felt glued to the threshold, horrified at the devastation of this fine old Victorian. The house had been raped. Ornate woodwork had been defaced, windows were broken, and there were gaping holes in the high ceiling where the crystal chandeliers had hung and shone their light on a different generation. The magnificent fireplace looked naked without the mantel that I knew had once surrounded it.

We walked from room to room and Juan painted a visual picture of his plans. His enthusiasm was contagious, but my mind could only see the tremendous amount of work, time and money that would be required to restore this aged beauty.

As if reading my thoughts, Juan said, "I have the time—and the money. I'll have the best craftsmen in the city."

"Yes, that would be a good idea." I laughed. "Remember the bent nails I pulled out of that old ram's pen?"

His look darkened. "I probably can use a hammer as well as you can use a brush." Touché. "I love this house. Even the walls whisper to me."

Looking at the wide carved stairway, I saw that the elegantly shaped bannisters had been spared. We tread lightly as we walked up and paused on the second-floor landing. Looking down for a moment, I could almost see the rooms refinished through Juan's enamored eyes...but, oh, the work, the time...

"Probably needs a new foundation and roof, too."

"No, the foundation doesn't even have a crack. Rock, of course. Haven't been on the roof yet, though. You probably don't know, but many of these old houses were built of redwood. It was plentiful, cheap and has the rare ability to withstand rot and insects."

Juan's determination fought with my common sense.

Slowly, reluctantly, my objections and criticism seemed to leak away like sand through a sieve and I began to see the old house and feel the call as Juan had.

Common sense made a last desperate try.

No sane man would buy a house in this condition. After all, it's only an acre of dirt and a view, so I pushed away Juan's vision. But why did I smell the fragrance of azaleas and boxwoods—and spring was months away.

"Juan, have you forgotten I have a wife waiting for me?"

As we drove down the hill, I asked, "Have you discussed this with Dr. Teddy?"

"No, I wanted you to see it first. Why don't you come to dinner tonight?"

"Aha. You just want reinforcements."

He didn't deny it.

But anything Mrs. Mackey fixed was going to beat chicken soup out of a can again, and I knew that Juan needed me.

Back at the hospital, I found Rica sitting up, a beatific smile on her face as she held the sleeping heir to the McAllister fortune. I stooped to kiss her and she raised one arm to pull my head down for a kiss that warmed me to my very bones. Can life get any better than this?

Pushing the blanket aside, she extended a leg for my inspection. "Will you notice that thin ankle?"

My quick response was "I'd like to see more of that leg before making a decision."

And we giggled like two teenagers, ignoring the indignant look from the hovering nurse.

We would need to get a larger apartment—perhaps a house with a yard. And I was going to need some different transportation what with almost two hundred thousand miles on that truck. So we talked and planned until her eyelids got heavy and the baby had been carried back to the nursery.

It was late afternoon as I drove through the city, Juan's dinner invitation lurking in the back of my mind.

Traffic thinned as I started up the long drive. In the distance I could see the lights of the big house. The truck slowed in second gear and slowly made it to the top.

With the addition to my family, a different mode of transportation was going to be a necessity, but how could I part with this faithful old friend?

Even as Juan opened the big door, I could smell the delicious aroma and I knew Mrs. Mackey had done it again.

"Someday I am going to make Mrs. Mackey a better offer and *you* can eat chicken soup out of a can."

After a quick hug, I heard Dr. Teddy's voice respond, "I doubt that—after twenty-six years."

She led the way to the dining room that was bigger than my entire apartment.

We finished a dinner that probably ruined me for tacos permanently when Juan announced, "I'd like to show you some pictures of a property I've been looking at, adhering to your advice, Dr. Teddy."

We followed him to the library. I lagged behind and refused to meet Juan's eyes.

He spread the pictures of the outside of the old house on the library table, then the interior photos, room by room. Pictures of the land lay beside them.

I hadn't known about the pictures and the damage to the rooms looked horrifying in the cold media of black and white.

Sara gasped, "Juan...you didn't..."

Their questions were quick; Juan's answers were slow.

"I know the house is in terrible shape..."

Dr. Teddy interrupted. "Where is this property located?"

"Telegraph Hill."

"The location is good. What do you plan to do with the land after you demolish the house?"

Juan looked at me.

I heard myself answer with a confidence that came from a previously unknown part of my psyche.

"The house has been badly damaged, but the foundation is perfect and the roof is good. Most of the harm has been done to the first floor. With Juan's eye for beauty and some competent contractors who are experienced in restoration of these old Victorians, this house would reclaim its original beauty. I'd guess it would double the original investment."

I stopped for a breath, then plunged in again.

"Then, too, it is positioned in the center of very valuable acreage.

The view is breathtaking—matchless. This property has unlimited potential and, as you say, Dr. Teddy, it also has an excellent address."

With Sara beside her, Dr. Teddy studied the pictures.

As Sis had often said, I could talk my way into heaven. Suddenly I thought, what if it really is just a piece of dirt and a view? Maybe I'd talked myself out of friendships that I treasured. My self-confidence retreated to wherever it was that it had come from. My knees trembled.

The look that Juan flashed at me told me without words: Win, place or lose, we walked together.

"When can we see it?"

"Anytime—I own it."

"Juan," Sara gasped. Dr. Teddy laughed.

I choked on the memory of a terrified, penniless, skinny boy teaching me how to roll a joint while sitting on a lonely, wet hillside in the drizzle of that rain that never seemed to stop. A million miles from this reality.

Mamá Sara's tremulous voice asked, "What will you do with it when it's finished? You don't plan to leave, do you, Juan?" Her big eyes searched his face.

"I'll never leave you, Mamá," came his quick answer.

Sara burst into tears and Juan's arms encircled her and pulled her close.

Teddy's arms found their way around Juan, and I smelled the fragrance of Sara's hair as I somehow got enclosed in the circle.

The next morning, as I was walking down the corridor to Rica's room, a chance meeting with Dr. Teddy provided me with the happy announcement.

"I think Rica can go home tomorrow. She seems to be doing very well and your boy couldn't be better—he's gained three ounces."

She shook her head. "I don't understand how she could have gone from such a near disaster and suddenly pushed that baby from an impossible position."

"You would understand, Dr. Teddy, if you had eavesdropped on my conversation with the Lord."

"Well, perhaps. Your oratory skills regarding Juan's house certainly impressed me. Maybe you should have been a politician."

We parted laughing and I pushed the door open to Rica's room, bursting with the good news.

I encountered the nurse's stern stare.

"It's very early. We are just ready for our bath."

My enthusiasm would not be dampened. "That's wonderful. I'd like her to be clean when I take her home tomorrow—and I'm sure you'll enjoy your bath, too."

Rica's snort was somewhere between a giggle and a whoop. "Home. We get to go home—I can't wait."

"And more good news. Your mother has tidied up the apartment and Dr. Teddy has invited us for a coming-home dinner. Juan will pick us up."

Bending down, I kissed her and said, "Let me see that leg. Is the ankle as good as the other one? Just think—tomorrow I get to see them both at once."

We snickered at the nurse's shocked expression.

"Don't let us keep you from your job—I assume you are a working man," came her icy voice.

"Oh, yes, I work for a newspaper."

"Oh, one of those. Why is it that none of you fellows can ever land my paper on the porch instead of the lawn?" She held the door.

I took my whipping like a man and left quietly.

Rica had been home for three weeks and it seemed that with the addition of one small person, our need for larger quarters escalated.

The walk to the kitchen was a hazardous journey. A middle-of-the-night trip to the bathroom was fraught with disaster.

Rica's mother had given her a changing table that took up most of the hallway. One misstep or slight bump could cause baby oil, talcum powder and various and numerous other articles to fly through the air, awakening both mother and baby with dire results. Baby was easily pacified with a warm breast; Rica not so easily.

The crib stood at the foot of the bed, guarding the dresser. To tunnel through fourteen inches of space to get a pair of shorts was a challenge.

We desperately needed more room, and almost as badly, we needed better transportation. The truck was needy, too, especially with its ever-increasing mileage.

I felt like I was deserting an old friend when we decided to put the money in a newer family car. Juan directed us to a used Chrysler station wagon—top-of-the-line with low mileage. Affordable, too. The wagon was great for my line of work and Rica loved the luxurious interior and the roominess.

Sis or Ma would call about every week; when they missed, I called them. Always the same question: "When are you coming to visit?"

Now the calls intensified. Sis sounded edgy.

"Is everything okay, Sis?"

"Well, not really. Ma has been going to church and one time her car wouldn't start. This old guy gave her a ride home and now it's every Sunday."

"How old is this 'old guy'? Is he a danger at the wheel?"

"Oh, I guess around fifty—'bout Ma's age. Wish you'd tell her to take her own car. Tim fixed the starter.

"He brought her home from the church picnic—the *church* picnic—and it was ten thirty. Nearly midnight. They stood so long on the porch that I turned the lights on and saw them holding hands."

"Well, Sis, I think you ought to leave her alone and let her have a little fun—she's earned it."

"Well, it's really too bad you haven't any time to look after our mother's best interests."

The phone went dead.

Sis was the originator of the guilt trip.

It seemed like our life had been on hold these last months and now everything was happening in double time.

Since J.W. had given me such a hefty raise, he almost doubled my workload. I loved my job, but I was exhausted, sometimes finishing late at the office or taking the work home to work on a small cluttered table.

At home, I was the odd man out—Rica's attention revolved around the new master of the universe.

He grew round and pink with golden hair that Rica curled around her finger and stuck bobby pins in as fast as I pulled them out.

Juan was completely captivated with Billy, who held out his arms and drooled with delight at the sight of him.

The first tooth appeared at four months, which gave Juan the excuse to bring a boxful of toys that we had no room for. The majority of them went under the bed.

"I'm surprised he didn't bring a bicycle," I groused.

Rica hadn't given up her search for a house, but the houses we liked we couldn't afford.

Juan stood by, frustrated. "Why won't you let me help?"

It hurt my "manly ego," so said Rica, to let another man put a roof over my family's head.

Juan devoted his mornings to his painting in the studio at the big house, where he and Mamá Sara worked side by side.

He wanted to finish his commissioned portrait as quickly as possible. The brush was in his hand, but his every thought was on the work that was happening on Telegraph Hill.

Juan, with Dr. Teddy's help, had located John Carter, an old-time contractor, and lured him from his retirement with the challenge to completely restore the ravished Victorian. Plus, it was love at first sight for John as it had been with Juan.

Carter handpicked his crew—the best craftsmen, some of whom had worked for him in his earlier years.

He and Juan spent many hours together discussing plans and changes and became fast friends.

CHAPTER 35

B illy was a good baby with a big dimpled smile that displayed six teeth. He was an active boy, crawling almost as fast as I could walk. Leaning back on his chubby little bottom, he would raise his arms, guaranteeing instant transportation.

Those wide, unblinking eyes peered from beneath the brim of the 49ers cap, the one that I had bought so many months ago, and almost hid the stray golden curls that tried to escape.

Juan stopped by to play with him almost every afternoon. I confess I was jealous. Billy would settle for me, but at Juan's appearance he would hold out his arms smiling with delight, and I was abandoned.

I was happy that Juan was so involved, but deep down there was a nagging little hurt—wanting my son to know who was daddy. Then I was ashamed. I had so much that Juan would never have. "Share," my brain insisted, but my heart was a holdout.

I was working long hours and when I got home, Billy was ready for bed. Rica said Juan had been by earlier to tell her about the work at his house and to kiss Billy good night.

Juan had numerous friends in the art world where he was well-known, but they were really acquaintances. Mamá Sara, Dr. Teddy, Rica, Billy and I were his world.

Rica still sat for him occasionally, loving the reprieve from the apartment and Mamá Sara loving her time with Billy.

My conscience bothered me. It seemed that my job interfered with my family life. I often wished there were two of me, especially when Juan was filling my chair at the table. The feeling that I was missing a large part of my son's first year nagged at me, but J.W. was not paying me for baby talk. I was making a good salary and he wanted to know that I earned every penny of it.

Then, too, Rica's every attention was for Billy and it didn't seem as though our honeymoon would resume until the boy's every care was finished. Then Rica was tired and so was I.

I wrangled an afternoon off and Rica and I had been discussing a house that she had found. She was disappointed that it had no yard.

We heard a quick knock and Juan stepped inside. He was puzzled. "Where's Billy?"

Surprised, Rica and I exchanged glances. Where *was* Billy? We had been so engrossed in our conversation...

A quick search found him clinging to the bedpost, having pulled himself up. Balancing on his little pink feet, every dimple, every tooth on full display, he surveyed his audience.

Rica had promptly sat on the floor, holding out her arms. Juan and I followed, arms outstretched.

"I'll bet you dinner that he comes to me first." Juan laughed.

"You're on," Rica declared.

But I sat silent, knowing we would go out to dinner.

One, two, three tentative steps toward Juan, who scooped him up, hugged him close, and murmured endearments. The absolute expression of love on Juan's face was unlike any I'd ever seen.

I knew that I was Billy's father and knew just as sure that Billy was Juan's son.

Crowding the empty feeling in my heart was the knowledge and gratitude that I was able to give something to my brother that his money couldn't buy, something of myself.

CHAPTER 36

The phone rang.

"Son, aren't you ever going to come? It seems like forever since I've seen you. And don't tell me you're busy—we're all busy. But I'm your mother; don't I count?"

She'd been taking lessons from Sis—the old guilt trip.

"Ma..."

"Don't interrupt me. In ten days, I will be fifty-one. I'm not getting any younger. Some folks are having a party for me, so won't you please say you'll be here? I'd like to get better acquainted with my new daughter and my grandbaby. Will you please come, or do I have to beg," her voice quivered.

"Ma, of course we'll come, even if I have to shut down the presses. Don't you dare cry; Sis has put you up to this, hasn't she? What do you want for your birthday?"

"I've got it," she said and hung up.

Approaching J.W. with a handkerchief in my hand, I stammered, "J.W., I need some time off," while passing the hanky over my eyes.

"My mother...my mother..." I blew my nose; my words failed.

He got up and put an arm around my shoulder. "Of course, son, of course. We only have one mother. Will a week do it?"

Ma had reserved a suite at a nice little motel not far from Sis' home, which didn't have enough beds for all of us.

Billy was tired from traveling so he went to sleep early. I reminded Rica about our honeymoon in that hotel in Reno and we reminisced. The next morning I whistled as I tried to work that funny little coffee-pot in the bathroom.

There were tears, hugs and kisses, and more tears that day. Ma was still "home" to me, even if she moved to China.

"You sure look great, Ma. What have you done to yourself? Texas must agree with you; you're slim as a girl."

"Well, for starts," Sis chimed in. "She's cut her hair and I know she colored it and she's been wearing lipstick to church."

We spent the day catching up. Tim barbequed and we drank beer. The girls compared notes on childcare and current fashion, and Ma played with her grandchildren.

When a battered old pickup pulled up late in the afternoon, Ma ran out the door to greet the man who drove it.

Watching out the window, Sis said triumphantly, "See there? See that? He actually hugged her in broad daylight right in front of her children."

Tim interrupted with, "Well, if her own daughter hadn't been hiding behind the curtains..."

Ma opened the door, her face radiant. She came directly to me.

"Charles, I want you to meet my son, Steve. Steve, Charles Kearney."

His big hands gave a firm handshake and his piercing blue eyes looked directly into mine with an easy smile. Above his ruddy complexion was a rumpled thatch of hair just starting to gray. I thought he probably spent a lot of time outdoors.

He wore a plaid shirt that looked like it knew what the inside of a washer looked like, and jeans that shared the secret.

Ma turned him to Rica and Sis, whose acknowledgment was frosty. But Rica smiled and returned his handshake.

Tim stepped forward, extending his hand. "Glad to meet you. You've been very kind to our mother. Would you like a beer? Steve and I have been working on a six-pack."

"I'd love one, but later. I'm helping with this party and, since Margaret has offered to help, too, I've stopped by for her."

"But the party is tomorrow," Sis exclaimed.

"Well, it's a big house with lots of rooms. She can find a place to sleep, I'm sure. A car will pick you up tomorrow. You'll probably want to stay over, too. A Texas party can last a few days. Delighted to have met y'all. Are you ready, Margaret?"

Ma whispered something in Sis' ear and then they were gone.

"What did Ma say?" I asked.

"Said to get dressed in our very best. It will be a big celebration."

Sis was beside herself. "How dare he call her by her first name. Why should we have to get dressed for some cowboy whoop-de-do."

Tim said, "I noticed she changed into those handmade boots he gave her. Handmade boots usually start at about four hundred dollars."

"He probably sold the cow." Sis sniffed.

"The party starts at three. It will probably be a barbeque to celebrate the end of the roundup," she added.

"It's nice he's providing transportation," Rica said. "How far is it from here?"

"I really don't know. We'll crowd his truck, so we'll probably travel in a horse trailer."

"Well," Rica said, "I'm going to dress up. I'm tired of everyday clothes. If it's a party, I'm going to whoop-de-do in something pretty."

"Me, too," I added. "I brought a white shirt, a sports jacket and new slacks."

"Sounds like fun," Tim said. "Wish I could go in my dress blues and show those cowboys what a tough marine looks like. We haven't been out to a party for ages. I'm ready."

"Okay, I'm outvoted," Sis said. "I've still got that dress I got married in, so it's off with the gingham and homespun. I should borrow something from Ma's closet. She bought three new dresses last week and one real fancy one. Don't know what those church folks will think about that." She laughed. "Don't know what's gotten into her, a woman of her age."

"Sis," I protested, "she's only fifty-one."

"That's old. She should act her age."

"I hope I look that good when I'm fifty-one," Rica said.

"Outvoted again. Tim, pick up your cans and check your fire."

The next morning Tim and I were put in charge of the two children. Sis' boy was five months older than Billy and quicker on his feet. Billy was still uncertain. He played rough—reminded me of Sis and me as kids. I was older, but she was bigger. By lunchtime, Tim and I were ready for their nap.

Rica had brought an overnight bag with a quick change for me in case we should stay over, and Billy's stuff. Sis thought that was a good idea, too.

After lunch we decided to think about getting ready for the grand party. The boys were dressed first and, once again, Tim and I babysat. They looked adorable and squirmed to get down, but Tim said, "Then we'd have to dress them, so hold tight."

Rica walked out of the bedroom and I caught my breath. I hadn't seen her really dressed up for months. She was gorgeous in a gown that clung to every curve. She had been a beautiful girl, but now she was a voluptuous woman. Motherhood became her.

Sis appeared and I could tell she was pleased with herself, pleased that she could still get into her wedding dress. She, too, was a woman to be proud of. Sis had no need now for Noxzema or curlers, her blonde hair curled naturally around her face. She was striking. I thought Ma had probably looked like that when she was young.

"Your sister sure got all the looks in your family," Tim said as he feasted his eyes. He nudged me and added, "S'pose we could skip that other shindig and do a little partying ourselves? I s'pose if you even suggested that to these beauties, they wouldn't leave us enough to party with."

Sis looked out the window. "Oh my God," she shrieked. "He's sent a hearse."

I rushed to the window and recognized a black limo I guessed to be about fifty feet long. I gasped, "Come in," when the chauffeur knocked.

"May I take your bag, ma'am?"

Wordless, Sis handed him her overnighter.

He held the door to the limo and we settled ourselves comfortably.

The babies slept all the way in our arms, Tim's and mine. The girls didn't want to get wrinkled.

We sat almost in shock as the limo sped across the Texas prairie. Then I mumbled to Sis, "Not bad for a horse trailer," which earned me a wicked dig in the ribs.

The limo threaded its way in and out of the wide sweeping turns as we neared the low-lying hills. It seemed to me that we had been on the road for a long time—or else I was just impatient.

Leaning forward, I asked the driver, "How far is it to this shindig?"

"About seventy miles to the big house," he answered.

"That seems like a long way to go to a party," I said.

"Not if you're on a good horse," he drawled.

"Not me," I said. "Personally I'd prefer rubber beneath me."

"Well, guess Mr. Kearney does, too. He's still partial to that old pickup he drives."

"I've never seen so many hills," Rica said to the driver. "I feel sorry for the cows—where are the cows?"

Catching her eye in the rearview mirror, he said, "They're all in the winter pastures now. Those hills are a cow's heaven. You should see them in the spring with all their calves. The hills are green; it's beautiful," his voice softened.

Then he continued, "This is a part of Texas that's known as the hill country. Big cattle ranches, mesquite, oil wells. Oh, and rattlesnakes, too." He laughed. "Mr. Kearney owns a big part of it. One of the biggest ranches in Texas."

A shocked silence behind him as we digested this information. I didn't dare to look at Sis. Her gasp told me for once in her life she was speechless, but I wasn't going to let her off easy.

Speaking quietly, I said, "Well, Sis, what do you think?"

"I think I shouldn't have been so quick to turn that porch light on." She sighed.

Finally, the outline of a house appeared like a cherry at the top of an ice cream sundae, nestled on the low rise of a hill. Even at a distance the long, flowing lines of the residence appeared impressive.

"Doesn't look like a cook house to me," Tim whispered. I heard him grunt as Sis' elbow found its mark.

As we moved slowly up the driveway, I could tell that the party was already in progress. Through the open window, we could hear the band tuning up, shouts of laughter, and, oh, the mouthwatering aroma of roasting pork.

Ma had been watching for us as I knew she would. She ran down the broad steps of the veranda before the limo came to a full stop.

Charles followed with a broad smile on his face as he said, "Glad you're here. Now we'll have that beer."

Billy was now wide awake in Rica's arms and squirming to get down.

Ma threw her arms around me. Looking down to see the love and the tears competing, I didn't care if the press ever rolled again.

Sis squeezed in. "See, I always knew she loved you best."

"And the most," I answered, repeating a ritual we had perfected since childhood.

"Come along, gentlemen," Charles said. "Allow the ladies to do what they do best. Let's see if we can find a snack somewhere to go with that beer I promised you.

"I've got two wonderful Mexican ladies here to care for the babies so you needn't worry and we can all join the party."

So we went our separate ways.

Tim and I followed Charles down the long shaded veranda, then stepped down to the tiled courtyard. A brightly colored canopy kept the hot afternoon sun from the big table groaning with Charles' "snacks."

"This is just to keep our strength up until dinner." He grinned. "Grab a plate."

I could smell the porker roasting on a spit somewhere nearby, and I knew from whom Billy had inherited his drool.

Wide wooden gates opened from the courtyard to a newly constructed flat surface, obviously a dance floor—I saw band instruments and a fellow tuning his guitar.

The courtyard was large with tables and colored umbrellas scattered randomly about, some pushed against the low adobe wall that hung heavy with vines and flowers.

"Charles," Tim said, almost running to keep up, "Your driver said something about not being far if you had a good horse?"

"Well, sometimes it seems like a fur piece." Charles laughed, lapsing into the twang and jargon of the locals.

We found an empty table and set our heaping plates down.

"Now for the beer. Tim, get on your horse."

We struggled back through the growing crowd and found the real party at the bar. We pushed through and it was easily apparent that Charles was surely among friends—backslapping, hand-shaking greetings from every side.

A voice called, "Hey Charlie, when are you gonna get rid of that old junker you drive? It's an embarrassment. Gives Texas a bad image."

Another voice added, "Now that you've got that new gusher, you can afford to buy a new one. Heck, you can buy one for all of us— how about it?"

Above the din came Charles' announcement. "Hey, you bronc busters, give me a minute. I want to introduce Steve..." He put his arm over my shoulder, "...and Tim, a Marine who keeps you boys safe from the bad guys. Treat 'em right."

Then turning to me, he said, "I'm gonna leave you on your own with these hooligans. I've got to get this party started."

I thought if it moved any faster, I'd be late.

Two large tubs of ice were packed with cans of beer brands I'd never heard of; two barkeeps were rushing to keep up at the heavily stocked bar.

Everyone wanted to stand us a drink, but I begged off. "We're waiting for our ladies and we promised to be sober." We compromised with a beer in each hand as we slowly found our way to the table where our food waited.

Tim stopped chewing long enough to ask, "Did you hear that guy say something about a new gusher. Does that mean oil?"

"Yeah, but s'pose he was just BSing."

I looked up from my food to see a fellow approaching our table. He seemed a bit unsteady, a can of beer in each hand. When he reached the table, he put a beer down and extended his hand.

"Bob Morris here, one of Charlie's neighbors about fifty miles east. Can I *set* with you guys a spell till my legs get used to walkin'?"

"Yeah, I lost my horse, too," Tim joked.

Full of food and icy cold beer, we stretched our legs and leaned back. A loud blast from the mariachi trio that was circling around quieted us for a moment.

Talking above the strident music, Tim said, "That sure is a beautiful house."

"Yeah," Bob replied, "My great-grandfather helped Kearney's great-grandfather build it, in 1890, I think it was. The outside adobe walls are three feet thick. Six bedrooms—those old-timers had lots of kids."

He pulled a cigarette from a crumpled pack, lit a match with a swipe of his hand across his pants, then took a long drag.

"The kitchen is twenty feet long and the pot rack is hung with many of the old handmade utensils. Guess it will last forever. Charles has modernized it, of course. The inside walls are all aromatic cedar— sure smells good," he added as he took another long drag. "Took thirty Mexicans over a year to build it. Kearney built that little church in town, too."

Tim and I listened in silence; Bob was a fountain of information.

"His wife died about twelve years ago. She was a great lady and he took it awful hard. Nobody saw him for a month and he sure looked like hell when they did. Heard he's courtin' a lady from his church now."

Tim interrupted, "Well, she's another fine lady. I know because she's my mother-in-law and there's none finer."

Bob looked dumfounded. "Didn't know you were kinfolk." He ground out the remains of his cigarette with the worn-over heel of his boot.

"I s'pose you've heard they're gonna run Charlie for governor next year. A gusher that just come in will probably finance his campaign. That makes three wells he's got. Ol' Charlie ain't hurtin'."

He drained his last beer, fumbled for his cigarettes and struck another match. Standing, he said, "Good to have met you boys. Guess I'll amble over and see if the bar's still open."

We sat in stunned silence, looking at each other.

"I'll be damned," Tim said. "Ma's struck oil."

The band, composed of a drum, saxophone and two guitars, hit a few tentative notes, then opened up.

People scrambled to their feet and stampeded to the dance floor. The music pounded to rock 'n' roll.

"Where are our women?" Tim demanded.

"Probably Ma is showing them through the house. Rica is wild for a big house so now I'm in trouble again."

"Oh, here they come, the both of 'em. They look just as good coming as going." Tim grinned.

I walked to meet Rica and fell in love all over again. Sis and Tim joined us.

"Where is Ma?" Tim and I spoke in unison as though we had rehearsed. Sis pointed to the dancers.

My eyes found Ma, held closely in Charles' arms. There was such an expression of love imprinted on his face that I knew Ma had found something far more valuable than oil.

We immediately joined the boisterous group, pushing in between the stomping boots and whirling skirts. The festive mood of the crowd was contagious and we were having a wonderful time.

I tried to cut in on Charles, but he laughed and swung Ma away from me. Worse still, she waved a happy good-bye.

Well, Rica, looks like you're stuck with me, I thought. But when I went back to join her, she was gone. I spotted her dancing with a big good-looking guy and immediately tried my luck again. I tapped him on the shoulder.

"No way, Jose," he said with a devilish grin.

I said through clenched teeth, "Damn it, that's my wife."

Rica slipped from his arms into mine, her eyes sparkling.

"Better not leave me alone. I'm helpless around these good-looking Texans."

"You'll pay dearly for this when the lights are out tonight," I threatened her.

"I certainly hope so," she said without an ounce of resistance.

The floor shook beneath the flying feet of the dancers. But when the music became soft and slow, Rica cuddled close to me. I thought I might pay the musicians to play all night.

Then I saw Charles talking to the leader of the band. Suddenly, the tempo picked up—a tune I didn't know.

I heard somebody's voice, loud and clear, shout, "Hey—that's the 'Chattanooga Choo-Choo.' Heard that just before I went overseas. Jitterbug king, I was."

I turned to see some gray-haired man dancing funny by himself. His forefinger waving in the air and singing at the top of his voice, "Chattanooga Choo-Choo, won't you choo-choo me home!"

Well, I supposed you could expect anything at a Texas hoedown. Rica stepped back and nudged me.

Charles had Ma out on the dance floor. When he twirled her around a couple of times, the crowd moved back.

Sis was scandalized. "That fancy dress is flying way above her knees. Her legs are in full view."

"Legs? I didn't know Ma had legs above her knees," I interjected.

Rica laughed and clapped, yelling, "Swing it, Ma!"

Then everyone clapped and whooped and hollered.

Charles flung her out, pulled her in, whirled her back into his arms; now they were dancing side by side. I heard the jitterbug king yell, "Shag—they're doin' the shag."

Fancy little steps, then quick steps, now back to back—now she's close in his arms.

The crowd was laughing, clapping, stomping, and shouting encouragements, although I didn't think any encouragement was needed.

Charles waved to the band—the tempo slowed and the birthday song began. With his arm around Ma, he announced, "I want all of you to sing 'Happy Birthday' to my wife, Margaret. We were married six days ago and I'm a very happy man."

We stood stunned. Sis said petulantly, "She could have told me."

"She probably wanted to surprise you," Rica said. "Besides, she knew you'd give her trouble—marrying a guy with an old truck and manure on his boots."

Ma did a little dance step over to us and laughed. "Surprised you, didn't I?"

Then sing we did. I had never heard that song really sung before I heard it sung in Texas.

Pandemonium prevailed. I had to stand in line to kiss my own mother.

Then Charles' voice lifted above the hubbub. "Now let's have dinner. If you're going to dance all night, you'll need some reinforcements."

The "dire consequences" that I had threatened earlier that night never happened. I made the mistake of closing my eyes as Rica went to check on Billy. When I woke up, the sun shone brightly.

Rica rapped on our door. "Are you gonna sleep all day? Breakfast is almost ready so hurry—we've got to leave early. Tim has the duty first thing tomorrow—a group is coming in for training."

What a breakfast it was. And the conversation was a jumble of voices, fast and funny.

"Ma, where did you learn to dance like that? That dress showed your legs, way up."

"For your information, daughter, I was young once. And who taught you to dance?"

Charles added, "You sure can see those legs through that see-through nightgown..."

"Sis," I said, "you probably should, no, I think I should...

Tim interrupted. "Charles, where could I buy a nightgown like that? You know the apple doesn't fall too far from the tree."

Billy, from his secure position on Rica's lap, wanted his share of attention. He brought the palm of his hand down hard in his cereal bowl, spattering both Charles and me.

"Little man." Charles laughed as Ma brushed oatmeal from his shirt. "I know exactly what pony you are going to ride when you come to visit Grandpa."

With breakfast over, the limo waited. Walking down the steps, Ma had tears in her eyes, but a smile on her face as she kissed us all good-bye.

"Son," she spoke to me with an arm around Rica. "You've made a good choice."

Sis, with her arms around Ma, asked, "What are you going to do in this big house?

"Honeymoon," Charles boomed, then "Y'all come back" as he shook my hand. He looked me in the eye and said, "You can't know how much I love her and she'll always have the best," adding with a twinkle in his eyes, "including me."

As the limo pulled away, I looked back to see Charles' arm around Ma and there was peace in my heart to know she had, at last, gotten what she deserved.

The limo was full of happy people and the chatter never ceased. I'd guess that driver was wishing for a good horse.

Tim went to work the next morning and we left, too. J.W. would be waiting for me. He'd ask about my dear old mother. I thought I'd tell him that she'd had a full recovery.

Driving back, we stayed one night in a nice motel. Rica said, "If we're going to honeymoon, I want a nightgown like Ma's."

I promised her one. I'd have promised her anything.

CHAPTER 37

When we arrived at our destination, it was a shock to see how the apartment had shrunk.

Rica said, "I'm sorry I've been such a nag about this apartment. I am resolved to wait until the right place comes along and then we'll both be happy."

"Billy looks tired; shouldn't he be in bed?"

She looked at me for a moment, said something about "motel madness," whatever that meant.

She hardly had time to put his pajamas on and sure enough, he went right to sleep. I intended to raise his allowance at some later date.

It seemed as though our brief stay in Texas had given us a little fun time together—time that we needed. Now we felt closer than we had ever been.

I put in two extra long days to catch up with work. J.W. was pleased that I was back and that my mother had shown such improvement.

On the third day, I took off at noon and wasted no time getting home, with Billy's afternoon nap on my mind.

Juan's car was parked at the curb. I found him sitting on the floor with Billy, building a house out of brightly colored blocks that the laughing boy scattered time and time again.

"Hey, how come you're not up there doing your own building?"

Juan grinned up at me as he laid a blue block on a red one and said, "I've got a good crew doing just that." Holding Billy back with one hand, Juan added another block.

Standing to his feet, Juan said, "C'mon, let's all take a ride. I want to show you something."

"Well," I said, "that sounds familiar. I remember the last time you 'showed' me something. I don't think..."

"Oh, Steve," Rica interrupted. "Let's go. I've been stuck at home for days."

With that, she grabbed a blanket, wrapped Billy so snugly that all that could be seen were two sparkling brown eyes and a little pink fist still holding a block.

As we pulled away from the curb, I asked, "Where to this time?" wondering if he meant to show Rica his house.

We started up the hill. The trees announced the entrance of a late spring as the soft buds unfolded and presented to the world the soft green beauty of the misty city.

Rica was enchanted by the magnificent views as the car climbed higher. Her declaration, "Ah, Steve, this is just a step below heaven— can't we find something here?"

That stung. I wanted to give her the world and I couldn't even give her a house with a yard.

I was surprised as Juan ignored the path that had now become a circular driveway leading to his house. Looking through the trees I could see the workmen's trucks and equipment.

"Hey, where are you taking us? Surely not through the back door."

He didn't answer, but turned left at the next intersection, then proceeded down a winding, overgrown green-canopied driveway. In front of us stood a large two-story house. Looking past the tangle of crepe myrtles and old boxwood trees, I could see the back of Juan's house. I realized that the backyards were separated only by a low fence now overhung with pink climbing roses that had chosen to scramble haphazardly rather than climb.

The house was not Victorian, but many of the traditional accents of that era were evident. It was obviously vacant. No smoke was coming from the faded red-brick chimney that guarded one end. The soft patina of the gray, weathered shingles wrapped the big house in a protective embrace.

The big rain-streaked windows, like tears on the unwashed face of a child, looked desolate. Wisteria vines arched over the portico, bathing the area with a fragrance almost overwhelming.

"Whose house is this and why are we here?" I asked, knowing the answer.

"I have the key," Juan replied. "Let's look."

He unlocked the door and we stepped into a wide entry hall with a cold, musty smell that told me it had been empty for a long time.

"Oh, it's beautiful," Rica enthused with a look on her face as though she had glimpsed heaven.

Walking with Juan, I sensed a trap.

"What do you plan to do with this house?"

He was vague. "I may rent it as an investment. I got such a wonderful deal on it that I couldn't refuse."

"Yes," I said as we walked from room to room. I could hear Rica's heels clattering ahead of us.

"This is a lovely house. I can see where you would get a very good return."

"Depends on who I rent it to," Juan replied, not looking at me.

The trap was set.

I felt a quick rush of anger and stared at him, but something outside the window seemed to have claimed his attention.

"Juan, there is no way I can afford this house."

"Steve, please don't be so pigheaded. I have so much—why won't you let me share it with you?"

"I'll be damned if I'll let another man put a roof over my family's head."

Carrying this baby, who had awakened and was now wriggling like he wanted down. Now, I heard Rica call, "Oh, Steve, come look..."

Juan was holding out his arms. I deposited Billy and walked toward Rica's voice. Looking back, I saw Juan's dark head bent over my boy and heard the soft murmur of his whispered words as he put Billy down and bent to hold his hand.

One look at Rica's enthralled face told me that this already was her house, and my intuition told me that Juan had planned it so.

Rica was ecstatic. We walked quickly from one room to another.

"Oh, Steve, look at this bedroom. It even opens to a small room— I'm sure it was a nursery. How perfect."

"This house has got to be four-thousand square feet. It's much too big for us...and five bedrooms—that's a bit excessive."

"That's a library—for your office," she answered quickly.

"This kitchen is huge—and you don't even like to cook."

"I'll learn, I'll learn. I promise."

"All these big windows. Who will wash them? And that fireplace is big enough to roast a buffalo."

"Think how nice it will be to sit in front of it, maybe even make love on a bearskin rug," she added with a sly smile.

"Oh, now you're resorting to bribery."

"Steve, we'll have more children. We'll need those bedrooms. Please, Steve, this is my dream."

Damn that Juan. He'd left me to do the dirty work.

"My darling Rica, it is a beautiful house, but you know that there is no way we can afford it and I will not—will not—take Juan's charity."

The instant tears and sobs that followed made me feel inadequate, less of a man.

Yes, Juan's trap was sprung.

Furious, I retraced my steps to Juan. Billy had gone to sleep on his shoulder.

"Well, you have my son in your arms and my wife is heartbroken in your house. I used to think I had it all, but you make me feel as though I am still digging potholes and herding sheep. I'll live in a tent before you'll give me this house."

Walking past him, I said, "I'll catch a ride, don't wait up."

I walked across the connecting yards to Juan's house and caught Mr. Carter leaving and happy to give me a lift.

"Just drop me off at the *Chronicle*. I have some things I need to finish."

But once back at my desk, I couldn't concentrate. So I walked down the street to a little bar where the guys who work on the paper hung out and where I occasionally stopped in for a beer.

I wasn't in a beer mood. I ordered a shot of bourbon on the rocks from the cute little redheaded barmaid. That shot burned all the way down. I ordered another with the same result. Then the barmaid kept them coming—I think.

Turning my head, I saw Juan walk in and go to a pool table. When I looked again, I saw two of him playing with one cue stick. That's when I realized I was definitely over the top and thought I'd better leave. Juan walked over and said, "Let's go home. You're going to have a big head tomorrow."

"I'll go home when I please. Why don't you mind your own business." I had the pleasure of seeing his face flush.

The little redhead said, "Say, honey, I'll take you home and we can stop at my apartment for a nightcap. I'm just going off shift."

"Good idea," I slurred as I tried to get upright.

I hung on to the bar, slid off the stool and got both my feet headed in the same direction. She put her arm through mine and we made a couple of false starts toward the doorway.

Juan caught up to us there, put his arm around my shoulder and pulled me close. I tried to move, but the three of us seemed stuck in the entry.

"C'mon, sweetheart, don't stay mad just because we had a little disagreement," he said as he planted his lips on my cheek.

I tried to push him away, but I was held mostly vertical by the girl, the doorjamb, and now his arms around my waist holding me tight.

"You know you and I go back a long way, sweetie. What would we do without each other? Let's go home and get some sleep. I'll even make you breakfast in bed."

The girl looked from one of us to the other, then realization dawned. "You're gay," she exclaimed.

"Honey," Juan laughed, "we are so gay we are probably the happiest men you'll ever know."

In a second, she had untangled herself from my arm. Without her support, I started to fall. Only Juan's arms kept me upright.

Struggling to regain my balance and free my arm so that I could take a swing at him, I finally got one arm to respond and swung a haymaker, which he merely pushed away with his hand. Then my legs betrayed me and I collapsed in a heap on the floor.

Picking me up, Juan flung me over his shoulder, stuffed me into the car and took me home.

I woke up slouched down in our big chair and managed to call J.W. I told him not to stop the presses because I had food poisoning. His response to that bit of information was ominous.

"You had better make me believe that or I may reconsider the raise I gave you a few months ago."

Rica was outraged and not speaking to me. She took Billy and the car keys and was gone all day, completely ignoring my sudden close relationship with the commode. She remarked unsympathetically, "You may as well say your prayers; you're in the right position."

I was going to remind her of that part of our wedding vows that said "in sickness and in health," but she was already out the door.

For the next few days, I worked overtime. Just as well; it seemed that I was an outcast in my own home.

Finally, after days of solitude and dinners of tacos and beans, the silence was broken. Shattered, really, with Rica's shocking statement.

"I've bought a house with a yard."

I choked and coughed until the prospect of widowhood entered her mind and she gave me a glass of water. When speech returned, I spoke furiously, only a few octaves below the mating call of a bull alligator.

"You can't be telling me you've spent our savings on a house I've never even seen or we've even discussed. You *can't* be telling me that."

I stood so suddenly from the table that a plate splattered to the floor.

With a voice as cold as an Arctic glacier, Rica said, "Sit down, Cowboy. I'm in the saddle. I'll lead you to water and if you don't drink, you'll die of thirst. I'm moving and you're sure going to get thirsty in that tent.

"Yes, I bought a house from an old lady who recently acquired it, but then decided she didn't want to move. The payment is the same as our rent and there is no due date on the deed."

In my mind, a tiny seed of suspicion sprouted.

"Where is this house?"

"Telegraph Hill."

"Does it happen to have five bedrooms?"

"No, four bedrooms and a library."

"I guess Juan wants to see me sleep in a tent."

"Juan has no part in this. It was put together by myself, with your mother's encouragement, and Sara Rafferty."

"How did Sara come by this property?" I asked.

"Juan said that he had no use for it and gave it to her to do with it what she pleased."

"And she was pleased to sell it to you with such incredibly generous terms?" I asked, not without sarcasm.

"Yes, and your mother offered to make a down payment, which was refused. Mamá Sara suggested that the monthly payment be put in a special account for Billy's college."

Apparently, I had been bested by three women. Three women whom I loved.

But in my heart, I knew that Juan had made it happen.

With complete disregard for my feelings on the matter, Rica had gone over my head and bought the house—and then dared to give me an ultimatum. I had no choice in either matter—I would move or I would live in a tent.

And how many times had I told her not to call me Cowboy. Who was wearing the pants in this household?

Adding fuel to the flame was the knowledge that Juan had made all this possible. Momentarily, I shuffled his goodness to the back of my mind—even the fact that he had saved my drunken self from disaster only days ago. Then there was my deserter mother.

With my thoughts in a civil war, my anger simmered.

Slowly, the unbidden thought pushed its way into my reluctant brain. Okay, this did seem like a golden opportunity—Ma had said so—that I had brushed aside. I wanted to be angry until it was clear that decisions stopped at my desk first. An apology from Rica might get things into perspective again.

But then the right side of my brain appealed. "Why are you spoiling this for her?" Answering myself, my manly pride shouted, "Because *I* wanted to find the house. *I* wanted to do it."

The apartment was so quiet; we spoke only when necessary.

Juan's car had not stood at the curb for a week. Billy was irritable and whining, probably cutting a tooth, I lied to myself.

Like the drip of a leaky faucet, the steady knowledge that I had made an ass of myself persisted. Still, my stubborn pride did not know how to put Humpty Dumpty back together again without losing face.

Dr. Teddy solved the problem.

She called me at work. "Let's have lunch, Steve. Meet me at that little café around the corner from my office."

After a quick hello, we ordered coffee and a sandwich. Then she fired from the hip. "Steve, how long are you going to act like a spoiled child?"

"Dr. Teddy, you sound just like my mother."

"I've been thinking I should call her," she replied.

That brought me to my knees.

"Steve, you've put your pride before Rica's happiness. You ought to be proud of your wife. She made a sound decision. Sara has made herself happy in the process. Sara's happiness makes my life complete. I'm sure Rica's happiness is your priority as yours is to her. You and yours are Juan's life—don't hurt him. No one will ever love you more.

"I find it almost impossible to believe that a man of your intelligence would allow macho pride to hold Rica's happiness hostage."

Surely macho pride doesn't rhyme with manly pride, I thought.

"I love you, Steve. Take off your spurs."

Driving back to the office, I felt thoroughly chastised. Dr. Teddy had forced me to tell the truth. No stalling, no excuses, just the plain, unvarnished way it was.

I had shattered the happiness that had been Rica's dream—the house that had been given with such love. My foolish pride had stolen her pleasure with the house. I was so ashamed and embarrassed to have made such a fool of myself.

Now, how to make amends?

"Face up to it like a man," I heard my mother's voice as clearly as if she were standing next to me.

On the way home I fumbled around in a florist shop and chose two dozen long-stemmed roses. As the girl behind the counter wrapped them, she laughed. "Got caught, did ya?" I felt myself blush as red as the roses.

I knocked on the door of our apartment. *She will probably tell me to go to my tent. Then what will I do with all these damn flowers?*

I knocked again and the door opened. Rica looked at the flowers, then up at my face, then threw her arms around my neck.

The flowers fell to the ground and I heard them crunch beneath our feet. With my face buried in her hair, I whispered, "I'm so sorry, so ashamed."

She stopped my words with her kisses. "I love you, Steve. Love you, love you..."

I whirled her around and kissed her every place I could reach.

"Shh, you'll wake Billy."

"You mean he's actually asleep?" I whispered, disbelieving my good fortune.

She sat down on the bed and pulled off her shoes.

"Sound asleep," she said as she held out her arms.

The phone finally woke all of us.

It was Sara. "Mrs. Mackey has made a soufflé like no other. Please come over. Let's see if it's as good as she says."

Sara met Rica and Billy at the big door in front, but I made a dash for the back entrance and bounded up the stairs to Juan's apartment. I pushed open the door to the room and found it empty, then opened the door to his studio. There he stood, holding a paintbrush and looking surprised. He reached his hand out in welcome.

I pushed his hand aside. "Juan, I'm so sorry," I mumbled as I hugged him with both arms around his waist until he grunted.

He laughed and held me off saying, "You weren't nearly this affectionate the last time I saw you."

I had the decency to feel that prick of conscience for the ugly things I had said to him then. Trying to speak again, Juan stopped me, holding up his hand.

"Don't say it. Don't tell me something I already know.

"Let me tell you about this house situation. Of course, I wanted you to have it. It's perfect for you both—and close to me." He smiled. "But how to go about it? I know your stubborn pride. Rica went to Mamá Sara in tears about her stubborn husband. Her heart was broken and she was angry with you. At that time, Mamá Sara turned to me and asked me if that house wasn't actually hers. I told her that, of course, it was—because how could I refuse her anything? Then she put her arms around Rica and told her not to cry, that she would deed the house over to her tomorrow and everyone will be happy. She added that Steve may find that 'pride goeth before a fall.'

"So...exit Juan and Steve—we're in the clear."

I had to laugh. We'd both been outwitted. And when I allowed myself to think about that lovely big house, I knew it would be perfect and that we'd never leave it, nor would we forget the generous gift.

When Juan and I walked out, the company below looked up to see us—both tall, but there the resemblance ended. He so dark, so graceful; me, blond and broad. A study in contrasts.

We moved as one down the wide, curving stairway, his one hand sliding lightly on the bannister, the other on my shoulder. The love that was manifested between us was the same, only different.

It was a wonderful occasion, a family reunion of sorts. Rica and Mamá Sara, their heads together, enthusiastically reviewed the plans for the new house as their food grew cold.

"Of course, it will be repainted..."

"The floors are worn and should be replaced..."

Juan reminded them not to forget about the plumbing fixtures.

Dr. Teddy caught my eye.

"Look at all the fun they're having. I can't remember when Sara has enjoyed herself so much. She has never decorated a house before. And look at Rica—she is positively glowing. I love our family."

Her face lit in a devilish smile. "Steve, you seem so much bigger without your spurs."

CHAPTER 38

Rica wore the key to the house on a ribbon around her neck, supposedly for fun, but I knew in her heart that she was dead serious.

At every opportunity, we would bundle up Billy and drive to "our" house. I knew she had generously put my name on the deed.

The workmen were coming soon, but we wanted to have the house to ourselves first. We examined every nook and corner.

Rica discovered a large space behind the bookcase containing many old magazines. I found the wine cellar complete with empty bottles. We roamed from room to room and, even empty and cold, they were beautiful in their spaciousness. So well arranged, they seemed not to be even a foot too large.

In the garage behind the house we found a wealth of Persian carpets, all rolled carefully and covered. Upon Rica's ecstatic examination, they seemed not to have a worn spot anywhere.

I gained my knowledge of carpets from the braided rag rug at the farm, and that was as scant as the ragged rug. Obviously my opinion was not sought after.

Juan said, to Rica's delight, that the carpets had probably cost more than the house.

I got raised eyebrows and amused glances when I asked, "Are you really going to cover those beautiful new floors?"

Rica laughed, answering, "You'd better start shopping for that bear-skin rug."

I gave that some serious thought and concluded that bare floors weren't all that appealing.

I was in my cubicle at the newspaper every day at J.W.'s beck and call and couldn't spend much time at the house.

Acting on the advice of Mr. Carter, Juan kept the various contractors busy at our house. There wasn't much more than cosmetic work to be done, other than the reflooring, so the project moved quickly.

The house started to glow. The musty smell of empty dissipated; instead, the odor of fresh paint that brightened the rooms greeted us when we opened the door.

We settled in more quickly than I could have dreamed. I guess luxury is easy to get accustomed to—I didn't give much thought to the cramped little farmhouse in which I was raised.

The windows sparkled, the floors gleamed. Now it wasn't just a house—it was fast becoming our home.

Sara and Rica had kept a relentless eye on the progress. I'd guess that the workmen sighed with relief when the job was completed.

Rica caught up with a reluctant Billy who was skidding across the shiny new floors, but his tears turned to smiles when Juan appeared and scooped him up.

"This is an amazing boy," Juan declared. "Already walking, and he's only a year old. Well, almost. And the words he can say. I've just realized that he was born at the same time I signed the papers for my house. Next week they will both be a year old. We need to party."

And party we did. Except that the guest of honor fell asleep before we cut into the three-tiered birthday cake.

Juan's work crew was surprised to see a catering truck appear with a luncheon that few had ever imagined. A bottle of the finest champagne for Mr. Carter with the laughing admonition, "Don't christen anything but your throat."

The day before the party had found Juan painting a colorful mural on the nursery wall—the imaginary adventures of Humpty Dumpty, Little Bo Peep and others came beautifully to life.

Billy stared in amazement, then pushed his little hand in a leftover pail of paint and planted a perfect imprint as high as he could reach.

Juan was delighted. "See, I knew he had artistic abilities."

Lifting Billy, Juan left little handprints on the wall at random.

The adjoining folding doors that kept Billy's sleep undisturbed were painted on the inside with a fierce fire-belching dragon, a golden-haired, laughing little boy astride.

This perhaps brought more joy to me than Billy. The indignant rattling of the crib bars, faintly audible through the closed doors, sometimes indicated my pleasure and his frustration.

CHAPTER 39

I can imagine what the spirit of the house—had there been such a thing—would have thought as it looked askance at the meager amount and condition of the furniture we brought with us: an old bed with a change of sheets, a wooden table and three rickety chairs, and a chest of drawers. The only things of value were Billy's crib and our big overstuffed chair.

"Rica," I said in a burst of enthusiasm, "I think we can do better than this. Let's use some of our savings and buy some decent furniture. A really nice bedroom set, a table that has four legs all the same length, a comfortable sofa and chairs that match. We'll have to forgo the bearskin rug temporarily."

"Well," she said, those brown eyes teasing, "I can probably make do with a new bedroom suite."

She cajoled the store manager with the promise of payment in full for next-day delivery.

We arrived at the house the next morning to find all new appliances in the kitchen, a formal dining-room set, and the service porch complete with washer and dryer. In Billy's nursery were a wardrobe, a well-stocked toy box, and a tricycle. The ornate crib that Juan had given us earlier now stood in a corner.

A big sign on the dining room table read, "Don't give me any trouble. This is a housewarming gift, a customary practice among civilized people."

Rica hissed through her teeth, "You damn well better be civilized."

I was. No more tent time for me.

We opened a door to a fully furnished bedroom. Rica said, with a knowing look, "This looks like Dr. Teddy's work. Very elegant and spare. Done with a wave of her stethoscope, no doubt."

Then the mailman brought a check from Ma and Charles. "We're coming to visit and we will need a decent bed and proper accommodations."

I went into the bathroom to hide my tears and compose myself. Even through my bleary eyes, I admired the beautiful towels that I suspected Sara had thoughtfully provided.

"For goodness' sake, what's taking you so long?"

I didn't dare wipe my eyes on those fancy towels, and used toilet paper instead.

I stopped in at J.W.'s office to give him my change of address.

"Telegraph Hill?" he asked in surprise. "That's my neighborhood. That's about eight blocks from my house. Your rich uncle die and leave you an inheritance or did you marry money? Now I can drop in and give you my condolences when you're sick—food poisoning, snakebite, things like that—or even say hello to your bedridden mother." He gave me a sly wink.

I couldn't contain my grin. We were fond of each other.

"Steve, stay close. I've got a big one for you coming up."

So what's new, I thought.

We had been in our new house for a few months when Rica found a cooking school in nearby North Beach. To our mutual delight, she loved it. Tacos and beans soon became a thing of the past.

Juan was always happy to keep Billy while Rica was gone six hours a day, three days a week. Billy was all his.

The workmen became accustomed to seeing this tall, dark-haired man conferring with their boss or sketching out a plan, with a watchful eye on a playful, curly-haired toddler riding on his shoulders playing "giddy up horsie."

Billy now had several more teeth and was stumbling over new words every day, even some in Spanish.

Juan adored this miracle that had grown into such a lovable, delightful little person, and made no secret of this fact.

Glued to my desk, or off to the "big one"—they were all "big ones" to J.W., I was weary at the end of the day and not really up to playing horsie on my hands and knees until Billy's good-night kiss. And so our prime time vanished.

Of course, on occasion we romped and played, but I was no competition for Juan, whose time was his own and it was only a short walk from his house to ours.

"Juan," I said, joking on the square, "You are stealing my son from me."

He returned my look, gazing directly into my eyes, a slight smile on his lips.

"Not so, Steve. You placed him in my arms the morning he was born. You gave him to me and I shall never give him back."

"Billy will always have the best that life can offer. When he is grown and has a family, I will love them, too. He is as close to you as I can ever get."

And there lay the naked truth.

A long look floated between us, then he turned one way and I the other.

I didn't speak to Rica about this. My instinct told me there was no need. She had known it from the beginning.

Driving by daily, I marveled at the changes that seemed to happen almost overnight to Juan's old house. The landscaping crew had recovered the beauty of the land, the trees were heavy with bloom, and the fragrance they had promised over a year ago filled the air. The ornate wrought-iron fence was barely visible beneath the clinging roses.

I left the office early with a throbbing head, which seemed to have been going on for a couple of days.

As I passed the house, Juan hailed me and I stopped.

He said, "I want you to see the progress we're making."

He pointed to the rosy pink of the newly cleaned chimney, then turned to point out the graceful symmetry of a turret, shingled insets, and ornate cornices framed above the tall lead-glass windows. "Gingerbread." Juan smiled.

This old house stood proud.

Through the beautifully carved doors now open, we could see the new floors that supported the scaffolding, hear the noisy sounds of the workers and smell the sawdust.

My eyes kept coming back to the incredible workmanship on the doors.

Juan exclaimed, "Mr. Carter, those doors are magnificent."

"Yes, carved by one of my best men—an artist in wood, but he has some finishing to do. He has been off for two weeks due to an abscessed tooth, he thought, but he was so sick a doctor finally declared it to be mumps. Very contagious—hope he took it all home with him."

"I hope so, too." Juan smiled.

I tried to smile, but my jaw had become so swollen and painful. Surely it couldn't be an abscessed tooth. I'd never had a toothache in my life, thanks to Ma's mania for brushing three times a day.

As I bent my head for a closer look at the doors, a pain so exquisite shot through my entire being. When I gasped, Juan looked closely into my face.

"Steve, are you all right?"

He pulled my collar down. "You're so swollen. I thought you've just been putting on a little weight. You've got to see a doctor."

The pain was so intense that I didn't give him an argument.

It didn't take long for the doctor to diagnose an acute attack of mumps. Writing out the prescription for the vilest tasting thing I ever put in my mouth, he said, "Nothing much you can do now but tough it out. Take a pill every four hours, use ice packs, and stay in bed. Mumps are bad news. Sure can play hell with your manhood so take care. Don't worry about infecting anyone—that would have happened a long time ago. Mumps has an eight-day incubation period."

That cheered me right up.

Despite the doctor's information about the contagious period, I went to bed upstairs.

My face had swollen to the size of a basketball—at least it seemed so. I was unable to open my eyes.

Unbelievably, another part of my anatomy was so swollen it would have made a donkey blush.

Dr. Teddy arrived, bringing with her more of those blessed ice packs and medication. "This should bring the fever down."

Juan toiled up the stairs with a rollaway cot riding sidesaddle on his back.

Vaguely, I heard Rica's voice at various intervals and felt the straw pushed between my lips and tasted the broth. Every four hours, Juan would awaken me for the pills, sponge my sweaty face and reapply the ice packs.

Retreating then to my dreamless sleep, I was comforted by the knowledge that my best friend slept on a rollaway at the foot of my bed.

Several days later, I could open my eyes, the swelling in my jaws had subsided, and my testicles had reverted to their normal size.

It was then that I knew there was life after death.

I had lost weight during the mumps ordeal; even J.W. showed a little compassion when I returned to work.

"You look like hell. Better take it easy for a couple of days. Here," he said as he shoved a pile of paperwork at me, "you can work on these at home."

That did give me some extra time with Billy.

Looking across the breakfast table, I was struck by the sight of the oatmeal bowl upside down on Billy's head, the cereal squishing down through the long golden curls that hung below his ears.

"Rica," I howled, "Will you look at this kid? He needs a haircut. He is a boy. B-O-Y. He's almost two."

"Well, I thought you were helping him. Can't I turn my back for an instant? He is not a boy, he's a baby. B-A-B-Y. He is not going to have his curls cut off. Forget it—get your own haircut."

Rica and Billy disappeared in the direction of the bathroom, Billy waving "bye-bye" over her shoulder.

That afternoon when she went to cooking school, I outmaneuvered Juan and took Billy to the barber's.

Billy was entranced with the scissors and never shed a tear. I saved curls for Rica and Juan, feeling very generous. Now that the deed was done, though, I felt a little nervous.

I heard the door close and immediately became engrossed in my paperwork. But I was totally surprised at her shriek.

"Steve, damn you! Oh, my baby, my baby," she cried and damned me again for my sacrilege.

It was tacos and beans for me three nights in a row.

Hell hath no fury like a woman who comes home from cooking school to find her baby has become a B-O-Y.

Even Juan looked pained and tucked away the curl I'd saved for him without even a thank you.

Billy, who had been a bit dubious about the tricycle, now bravely flung a chubby leg over it, seated himself and pedaled away.

The floor lamp was the first casualty; fortunately, it fell in the opposite direction from the little speedster.

In the coming months, he seemed to have grown an inch, could hold a fairly understandable conversation and had toilet-trained himself with very little help. "Unkie Juan's" pride in this achievement was surpassed only by Rica's relief.

"Just when you had finally mastered the diaper thing," teased Juan.

Billy was a happy, loving boy and anything within reach lived a short life—with the exception of the small, shiny silver fork and spoon given to him by Sara. These were always on the tray of the high chair—Juan's latest gift.

Perhaps it was the shine that caught his eye, or perhaps the fact that he could spear anything within range of his chubby little arm with the small fork that made mealtime an adventure to sit at the same table.

On Billy's third birthday, in the privacy of our bedroom at a moment I would have promised her anything, she whispered, "Steve, I want a baby..."

"Can we talk about this later?"

"No."

The flame flickered and died.

"Isn't one little hellion all we need—for now?"

"No. I don't want to raise Billy by himself. I want our children to grow up together."

"'Our children,'" I echoed.

"Billy needs a companion, a playmate."

"Well, maybe. I'll think about it. We've got lots of time. Possibly in a few years."

The tone of her voice should have warned me. "Steve, you're not hearing me. I want to start a baby now. I haven't taken any precautions for several months. If you have, stop now...or it's back to the tent for you."

"Surely you can't mean that," came my dumbfounded response.

"Believe me. Go to sleep. I have a headache."

I got lots of sleep—more than I needed. Then it suddenly occurred to me that perhaps Billy really did need a playmate.

Every month she waited. Every month she cried. Several months went by with nothing happening. Rica consulted with Dr. Teddy, and we tried everything, including the obvious. Sex on command seemed almost like a duty sometimes. Could her first difficult delivery be causing the problem? The answer was no; Rica was in perfect condition.

More months passed with no results. We'd been trying for almost a year now. Then came Dr. Teddy's disturbing words to me: "You should be checked, too, Steve."

That prospect didn't thrill me. Hadn't I already sired a child? I was in the peak of good health. But I'd do anything to make it happen. Maybe there was some magic potion.

What Rica wanted so badly, I wanted her to have. Her happiness was my happiness.

Dr. Teddy sent me to a specialist who checked me thoroughly and efficiently, with test after test, until the bad news was apparent. Mumps had destroyed any hope of another child.

"You are producing no viable sperm," the doctor announced, "and it would take a miracle for you to impregnate your wife. You know, adoption is an option."

The diagnosis was disheartening and unbelievable.

Compassionate as ever, Dr. Teddy said, "Steve, I think you will have to accept this doctor's opinion. Perhaps you should consider adopting."

Rica was heartbroken. She had been painting over Billy's artistic attempts with Crayolas on the nursery wall. Now she abandoned the partially painted wall and put the paint in the garage.

We sat in front of the fire one evening, Rica holding Billy who had gone fast asleep. He fit quite comfortably in her lap if you didn't notice that his feet touched the floor.

I teased her about her "mama's boy," but she threw back an irrefutable truth: "There never was a bigger mama's boy than you, than you *still* are."

"Steve, let's talk. I have an idea I want you to consider. When Juan needed your blood, you were happy to give it. Now you need something he has, and I know he'd be happy to give you anything."

"Do you mean what I think you mean?"

"Yes."

My mind whirled. I couldn't quite get a grasp on that idea. "Just my brief experience with those doctors' procedures convinced me that it sure isn't a picnic, and I would guess it would be very involved. It's such a new idea. I really don't know how I feel about it," I answered, stalling for time.

"Well, will you at least think about it?"

My Rica, carrying another man's baby? My brain countered: *Not just any man, it's Juan.*

A wicked thought almost made me laugh. Turnabout is fair play. Rica had carried my baby, but undeniably, he was Juan's boy. Sometimes I thought Billy was about to call me "Unkie Stevie." Of course, I knew this was a stretch...I think. Now, if she carried Juan's, this one would be mine.

The next morning at breakfast, Rica wasted no time. "Well, have you decided?"

"Rica, we just talked last night."

"So? It's either yes or yes. That shouldn't be so difficult."

"Instant gratification, thy name is Rica," was the best I could come up with.

"I've waited long enough."

There was no doubt in my mind that she was sure it was going to happen.

"Why don't you discuss this with Sara and Dr. Teddy before you go off the deep end," I suggested.

"Of course, if you insist."

In spite of her words, I knew that Rica *was* going to make it happen, and now.

Rica asked Juan to dinner, and he innocently accepted the invitation. The last bite of a really good dessert was still on our tongues when Rica went right to the point.

"Juan, I'm sure you know how badly I want a baby and the difficulties we're having. Would you help? It would mean so much to us."

"Of course, you know I'd do anything, but I don't understand what it is you want from me."

"It's called 'artificial insemination,'" Rica explained.

He looked confused, then flushed red and turned to me. "Steve? You know that I am a confirmed bachelor."

"No physical contact required, Juan, just a lot of procedures. Dr. Teddy can give you all the details."

"It can be only you, Juan," Rica pleaded.

"How much time do I have to think this over?"

"You've had it." Tears filled her eyes.

"I'll talk to Dr. Teddy. Don't cry," he said.

That night Rica was ecstatic. "I know he'll do it."

I hadn't seen her so happy in months. The next day she had the pink paint and was finishing up the wall. "This time it will be a girl."

And, of course, Juan didn't disappoint her.

The testing, both physiological and physical, he endured with patience.

The first two months produced nothing but Rica's tears. The third month she was almost hysterical, laughing and crying, and counting on her fingers.

Juan had taken the news very calmly. He gave Rica a hug and punched me in the arm, saying, "It's all yours, Daddy."

I was so happy for Rica, and I knew it would be a beautiful baby— if it resembled either parent.

"It's only fair," I devilled him. "You've taken my only child; now you can give me one that will be all mine."

His eyes that looked into mine gave credence to his words: "I love him more than life itself, and am thankful more than anyone could ever know that you have shared him so generously. I have something in my life to live for—the joy of being part of Billy's life. The fear of loneliness is almost as bad as the reality." Juan's voice was hardly audible.

I was at the top of my profession, a journalist for *Bay City Chronicle*, doing what I loved best. J.W. accused me of casting covetous eyes at his chair, but I was happy with my own.

Time seemed to fly. I thought probably I had all life had to offer and now a new baby on the way.

The first two months of Rica's pregnancy were miserable, but borne with a smile.

"Happy to be miserable," she said as I gathered her up in my arms and held her in our big chair as I had when she was pregnant with Billy.

The third month was better. Rica looked at herself and laughed. "I look like I swallowed an olive." I couldn't see it, but she could.

Sara came often. They had a very close friendship—few secrets, laughing together like schoolgirls. Sometimes they walked over to Juan's "playhouse" as they teasingly referred to it. Billy always tagged along.

Juan's house, nearing completion, was everything he dreamed it would be. Rica had described the kitchen as a cook's heaven. The third story, which had been servants' quarters, was now the perfect studio. The long curving stairway, now divided at the first landing, led upward to the most elegant bedrooms and study. The original bannister, after cleaning and refinishing, seemed to point the way. The carriage house was now a delightful little cottage.

So much seemed to have happened in our lives these past years. Last month Sis had another baby, a girl this time. Ma was now the governor's wife, a far cry from the lady with the shovel in the potato patch with whom I'd had difficulty convincing I was not a dope fiend a century ago.

Juan had taken up his brush again. Rica and Billy sat for a painting in which Billy's former curls were restored by Juan's brush. The portrait, titled "Modern Madonna," sold for a very large sum to a gentleman in England.

We seemed to have evolved into a tightly knit family group.

Sara was delighted with the prospect of another baby and planned with Rica for a girl.

Dr. Teddy said quite seriously, "I never thought I'd end up as a grandma. Yesterday there were just two of us. Where did all these damn kids come from?"

Dr. Teddy had come home early, eaten a light dinner and retired with Sara to the study. She kicked off her shoes, stretched out on the overstuffed sofa with Sara at the opposite end. Sara spoke softly, "You look so tired tonight, love. Let me rub your feet. You must slow down— we're not that young anymore. There are those who would say we were past our prime—way past."

"You're rubbing the wrong foot, my dear," Teddy interrupted. "It's the other one that hurts. Anyway, I can't retire now—I've got to see Rica through this pregnancy. I'm curious as to how this will all turn out. I hope Rica has a boy since Steve shared his first-born son so completely. There is such a bond, such a great love between these two men. Reminds me of David and Jonathan," she remarked. "You know, Saul's son in the Old Testament—Samuel, I think, where it says that 'Jonathan loved him as his own soul.' I don't doubt the baby will be beautiful; how could it not? It is wonderful to see Rica so happy again. She has an appointment with me tomorrow."

Rica was pleased when I offered to drive her to Dr. Teddy's office the next morning. Her enthusiasm was contagious. She seemed to sense something that was, as yet, a mystery to me.

The atmosphere was much more pleasant, I'd even say peaceful, at our house since her pregnancy.

Billy was nearing his fourth birthday, had long ago begun dressing himself after a fashion—his, and had long since tired of his tricycle. "For goodness' sake, don't mention it to Juan," I advised, "or he'll replace it with a motorcycle."

Juan had arrived early, poured himself a cup of coffee, pleased to entertain Billy until we got back. They were busy with building blocks as I waited in the car.

I had been involved in this pregnancy from the first. With Billy, I had been four months late. For some reason, this pregnancy seemed to touch something within me that the first one missed.

As Rica danced down the walkway laughing, I marveled again that this lovely woman had chosen to be mine—for better or for worse.

We were early and the waiting room was almost empty. Rica was shown in without delay. I sat, it seemed for hours, thumbing through every baby magazine ever written. The room slowly filled and I felt like a scarecrow in a cornfield.

Dr. Teddy finally came to the door and motioned me in.

Rica was sitting up on a table, her gown pulled high to reveal the belly she was clasping with both hands. Dr. Teddy had a broad smile tugging at both corners of her lips. She slipped the stethoscope from around her neck to mine and positioned the end on Rica's belly, plugging the other end into my ears. I could hear the steady thump, thump, thump of something within. The puzzled look on my face brought a whisper from Rica who was so overcome she could hardly squeeze out the words.

"Steve, it's twins. Twins, Steve."

Hopelessly, I tried to erase the words.

"Don't joke, Rica. Be serious. Is everything all right?"

The radiant look on her face told me the truth.

Twins? I hadn't gotten off on the right foot with the first child, and now two more? My mind fogged at the image.

Dr. Teddy pushed a chair behind me just as I collapsed.

Juan grinned when he heard the news. He said, above the clamor of the women, "Be careful what you wish for..."

For once I was utterly speechless. I called Ma, always my refuge of choice. She added her voice to that of the others. It was obvious who walked alone.

Confused, scared—yes, scared. My thoughts were troubled: Would I be up to it? I hadn't done such a great job with the first one.

Rica was happier than seemed possible. Now there was no weeping about the fat ankles or back pain, even though I knew she was uncomfortable as the months passed. She gained a lot of weight and it caused her usual graceful movements to be awkward and unsteady. Still, I heard her singing as she moved around.

Mrs. Mackey recommended a woman who lived in North Beach who could come four days a week to help out. This gave Rica some rest and free time, time she used to plan and prepare for babies not yet born. I teased her about everything being color-coordinated.

We decided against a sonogram and opted to be surprised. A boy for you, and a girl for me, and together we shopped accordingly.

At this point, all I wanted was an easy delivery and healthy babies.

Juan was thoughtful as always, but from a distance. I had the feeling we were on our own with these babies.

Earlier I had found the bearskin rug that now made itself comfortable in front of the warm fireplace. Originally, Rica was concerned that it would frighten Billy with its ferocious head and glaring eyes. Her fears were unfounded as he bravely decided it could double for a "horsie," and rode it to complete submission. It now contemplated its world with one glass eye and a loose fang.

At present, it was of no interest to him since it didn't whinny and was slow on the "giddyup."

Billy's tricycle limped along, one wheel considerably out of alignment. I warned Rica half-jokingly that motorcycle oil would make an awful mess on those Persian carpets.

Billy's fourth birthday had passed and I knew Juan was probably making a list for the next one. All Billy had to do was point a chubby finger. What he really needed now, since Rica had decided that his crib could easily accommodate two tiny babies, was a bed. We decided to shop for a youth bed and we laughed that he would grow into it. His size was already above average for his age.

Before any action could be taken, a small bed that would have sent any antique enthusiast into a frenzy was delivered to our door complete with bedding.

Sara confided that Dr. Teddy had searched the attic to find the bed that she had slept in as a child, handmade and elaborately carved by her father. The bed they had shared all these years was a replica.

Now Billy slept in a child's bed that was old and priceless. Priceless, too, because of the loving generosity in which it was given to us.

The time was growing closer. It seemed that we stood on the sidelines, holding our breath, waiting for the main event.

Rica was the exception. She seemed ready, calm and starry-eyed.

Now our house contained as much happiness and anticipation as it had tears and unhappiness only a short time ago. I must say I welcomed the change even as I stumbled down this scary, uncertain path. I prayed that when the time came, I would miraculously become the perfect father.

Now we were counting the days.

In the back of my mind lay the horrific memory of Billy's birth, but I smothered those thoughts with Dr. Teddy's assurances.

I rubbed fragrant oil—guaranteed to prevent stretch marks, then laid my ear against that sweet-smelling swollen belly.

"This one will be a linebacker," I said as I felt the vigorous push and the roundness became a peak.

Rica laughed. "Two ballet dancers in pink tutus."

"I suppose if one is a boy, his tutu will be blue?"

"Go to sleep," Rica said. "I'll coordinate the tutus."

Despite Dr. Teddy's assurances, I still worried. She comforted me with the suggestion that "perhaps Rica should come in a few days early." Against Rica's protests, I fell back on my second line of defense, "Dr. Teddy said..."

Rica was soon established in a private room and looking very comfortable.

J.W. was more than generous after a gruff, "Twins, huh? I suppose next time it will be triplets. How many times am I expected to put up with this? I'm not keeping you busy enough. Two weeks I'm giving you."

As I backed out, he called, "Relax, don't worry; it's wimmen's work."

CHAPTER 40

At one a.m., the phone rang. Rica's excited voice cried, "Steve, my water broke. We're on our way. Are you coming?"

"Of course I'm coming—leaving now," I said as I managed to put both feet into one pants leg, hopping around, trying to fight my way out for another try.

We had planned to leave Billy in Juan's care, but we had not expected anything to happen so soon. By all calculations, this was three days early.

I was looking forward to Juan's stay at our house. It seemed as though we never got much time together to talk and have a beer.

I called him in a panic.

"Don't worry, relax. I'll be there in twenty minutes."

As I was ready to turn the key, he drove in. "I hope you left the bed warm for me..." The rest was lost as I sped away.

Arriving at the hospital, I found Rica's bed empty. She had already been taken to the delivery room. I was allowed to see her for just a moment. The pains were constant but several minutes apart. I heard the same old refrain, "Don't worry."

I sat in the waiting room, closed my eyes for a moment, and awoke six hours later when Dr. Teddy nudged me. She said with a smile, "I guess I won't have to tell you not to worry."

I walked down to the café for a cup of coffee, suddenly wondering about the man whose young daughter was about to give birth, and with whom I had shared the waiting room just yesterday, it seemed.

Drinking my coffee, I scanned the newspaper and was pleased to see a rerun of an article I had written some years ago. I smiled to myself. J.W. was getting mileage out of it.

In the back of my mind, I asked myself some questions. How is Rica doing? It's been six to seven hours. What if it takes twice as long? Dr. Teddy had assured me that they had ways to control the pain.

I called Juan. He and Billy had just finished breakfast. Juan said, "Thought I might take him shopping for his birthday present."

"Don't do that," came my quick reply. "Why don't you take him to Sara for a while if she isn't busy?" Then, half joking, I added, "Am I expected to go through this alone?"

"You are such a baby. Rica doesn't need another one with you around. Billy and I are going shopping."

My best friend and he couldn't be here when I needed him.

An hour later I looked up from a magazine dated two years earlier and gazed at Juan's laughing face.

I couldn't stand that waiting room another instant. It was nearly noon and I hadn't seen Dr. Teddy for a couple of hours.

"Let's see if there's anything good to eat at the cafeteria. I haven't had any breakfast."

Sitting in the café looking at a leftover sweet roll, suddenly, I heard my name paged. I almost ran down the corridor. Juan followed, telling me, "I'm going back. I promised Billy and I know he's waiting." He waved me on. "You don't need me."

I found Dr. Teddy waiting for me. "She's nearly ready to deliver, Steve; stay close. Everything is as it should be."

I sat down on a chair. The months of trying, the unhappiness, nine months of waiting, and now, at last—at last—the culmination of our dreams.

The feelings struggled within me, but I determined children are not for the faint of heart.

Shortly thereafter, Dr. Teddy appeared with a huge smile stretched from ear to ear. "Well, Daddy, Rica has given you two beautiful little girls, healthy but small. One weighs four pounds, the other weighs three-and-a-half pounds. Rica is fine but heavily sedated. We'll bring her to her room shortly. You may as well wait there. The babies will go to the nursery for a final check."

"Twin girls? Pink tutus?"

I don't care, I don't care. Everyone is all right.

I heard the almost noiseless wheels of the gurney when Rica was moved to her bed fast asleep. I got a wet cloth from the bathroom and wiped her sweaty face, found her brush and pulled her hair back. Her eyes never opened. The long black lashes lay against the pallor of her skin.

I moved a chair close to her bed and sat holding her hand for a couple of hours, my mind contemplating the future.

Dr. Teddy appeared. "She's worked hard and needs her rest. I'll keep her and the babies for a few days. They will need special attention they are so small. The nurses will take good care of her. I'm going home for a while."

Two hours later, those big brown eyes opened. I put my arms around her, holding her tight, unable to say a word. Her arms found their way around me.

"I love you, Steve," she whispered. "Ring for the nurses—we want to see our babies."

What words can describe the miracle of childbirth? Wrapped in pink blankets, the babies were brought in by two nurses and laid at Rica's breasts. We marveled at the closed eyes with black lashes, the tiny working mouths, perfect little faces, downy black hair covering the tiny heads like a doll's cap. Carefully, we unwrapped these little creatures, counting fingers, and toes—all perfect.

"How will we ever tell them apart? They're identical."

"I'll know," Rica answered with a tremulous smile that quivered on the edge of tears. I let mine drip off my nose.

They were so tiny I could have held one in each hand. But they were so fragile-looking that I was actually glad when the nurses took them back to the nursery.

Juan and Sara came later. Sara's heart burst as she admired the babies through the nursery window. Juan was very reserved and outwardly almost disinterested as he arranged a mound of red roses.

Sara laughed and cried as she and Rica clung together.

"What have you named them?"

"I have named the larger baby after my best friend, Sara—Sarita."

Juan turned his head away quickly, but Sara's tears overflowed.

"Steve has named the smaller girl Margarita for his mother, who said it was the most beautiful gift she had ever been given."

"Then they look exactly like you, Rica. I wish them health," declared Sara.

Juan stood quietly, then leaned over and whispered softly, "Your babies are beautiful, Rica. I wish them health and happiness always."

Dr. Teddy spoke seriously. "These babies are so tiny, they will need to stay here in an incubator with supplementary feedings and around-the-clock supervision until they are safely stabilized and gaining weight.

"Rica, mother's milk is by far the best. You will need to use a breast pump."

Noting the look on Rica's face, she added, "These babies are healthy, but absolutely must have every chance to maintain and gain weight.

"You can wear a hospital gown and help the nurses so you won't be isolated from your babies."

The time seemed to pass so slowly and we tried to be patient.

We understood, of course. Rica was keenly disappointed; comforted later with the time she spent in the nursery and the feel of their closeness as she held them.

I was secretly grateful, content to see them in her arms through the nursery window, marveling at this living part of her and the life they had drawn from her body.

The babies did seem to grow a little each day and it wasn't just our imagination. The scale didn't lie.

Billy's fifth birthday was upon us. Hoping to beat Juan to the punch, we bought Billy a small two-wheeled bicycle, a baseball and a bat.

Sara and Dr. Teddy came to dinner bearing a beautifully wrapped package. I cringed as I watched Billy rip the expensive paper away from the fancy pair of cowboy boots. I thought perhaps a broomstick horse was hidden somewhere.

The dining-room door had remained shut to keep the balloons and gifts a surprise. Billy's eyes grew big and round as he heard the birthday song, and his laughter and excitement were contagious.

Juan hadn't arrived so we waited dinner, a dinner that included Billy's favorite, mac and cheese. The birthday cake, three layers of decadence, was a thing of beauty.

Then Juan walked in, carrying nothing but his coat. "Sorry I'm late."

No present? I eyed him suspiciously. Instinctively, I knew that our bicycle was outclassed.

The dinner was delightful. Sara declaring not even Mrs. Mackey could have prepared a better roast. Finally, we laid down our forks and leaned back to watch Rica light the candles. Billy was fascinated with the dancing flames. I instructed him, "Make a wish for something you want very much and, if you can blow out all the candles, you will get your wish."

Juan coached him with a few practice puffs. "Now blow really hard." With the next effort, the candles were sputtering smoke.

"Now, what did you wish for?"

"A horse," he said clearly.

"A horse? A horse?"

He looked me right in the eyes. "Yes, I want a horse."

Juan slid his chair back and quickly walked out of the door.

Rica looked puzzled; Dr. Teddy and Sara exchanged glances.

My razor-sharp mind knew he had a broomstick or something similar outside.

When the front door opened, Juan entered, leading a small spotted pony, complete with saddle. There was a moment of shocked silence. Walking across the Persian carpet, Juan handed the reins to a chubby little hand that shot out with the speed of light to receive them.

Juan lifted Billy into the saddle and somehow I was not surprised to see how perfectly the new boots fit in the stirrups.

"We're both going to take riding lessons and he needs a real horse," Juan explained halfheartedly.

I wondered if I could get my money back for the bicycle. I'd take the loss on the ball and bat.

I marveled at Rica's composure. More than once I had been instructed to take off my shoes. "Those are Persian carpets, you know." Now Juan was leading the pony from room to room, receiving no such admonition. Amazingly, the little hooves left no indentation on the deep carpets.

Billy's whoops of delight and his "giddyup, giddyup" kept all of us rooted in our chairs, wordless.

Then Rica shrieked, "Not the kitchen, not the kitchen," and broke the spell.

"The pony is tired now. More tomorrow," Juan promised as Billy dismounted, his smile beatific.

I glanced at Juan. The look on his face told me that he didn't know anyone was in the room but the three of them: Billy, the pony, and Juan. The rest of us were laughing and clapping.

"What will you name him?"

"Horse," Billy said with finality. "His name is Horse."

The pony's quarters had been built behind the cottage in a fenced area. It was just big enough to accommodate a stall, a tack room, and a haymow for three bales of hay and a sack of grain.

Juan took Billy to an equestrian training school and we grew accustomed to seeing him riding confidently down the path that connected our properties, shouting, "Giddyup, Horse" to a pony that never got past a slow trot. It seemed unreal to see a five-year-old child eat his breakfast quickly so he could run to the barn to feed his pony the correct amount, then rake his stall. Responsibility in someone so young caused me to brag shamelessly, but I'm sure it was common knowledge who had done the teaching.

On my time off, I taught Billy how to throw a ball or catch one, but he was more interested in showing me from which side to mount or to explain what a farrier is.

Billy was tall for his age and I thought that Horse's time was limited. But I was wrong—Horse died in his stall at the age of eighteen.

Even though I had returned to work, I managed to go by the hospital daily, sometimes gowned so that I might enter the nursery where I nearly always found Rica with a baby in her arms.

So many incubators in the nursery, but I could find my girls almost by instinct. For whatever reason, the smaller of the babies always seemed to find her place in my arms. Not that I noticed, but she had gained a pound. Her big dark eyes looked up at me unblinking as she seemed to melt into every beat of my heart.

Now I understood perfectly the feelings that had taken Juan prisoner when I had put Billy in his arms. The indescribable love that engulfed me at the feel of her tiny body in my arms made me feel even closer to Juan.

I loved Sarita the same, only different.

As I was about to leave the hospital one day, I saw the black hair with just a hint of gray above massive shoulders, and the long, unmistakable stride of Alfie—Dr. Alfred Myers, so dignified in his white coat.

I ran to catch up. "Alfie," I called, "slow down."

He turned to me and a great smile split his face. "Cowboy, what are you doing here?" As he wrapped me in a bear hug, my ribs screamed for mercy.

"Twins," I bragged, as if the idea had been my own. "See the shoe salesman hasn't got me yet. Got time for a cup of coffee?"

For two hours we dawdled over empty cups. He was busy and loved his work. My sentiments echoed his, except that I had a wife and children. His talk turned to politics, and then to a war he predicted was imminent and his desire to enlist.

We recalled the time he had tried to enlist when the Vietnam War was in progress. He had been refused because he was a medical student with an A average.

Alfie said, "I'm guessing they will take me now. I want the Marines—no back at the base crap. I want to be with the troops on the front lines."

His enthusiasm spurred my imagination. What an opportunity as a foreign correspondent. What an adventure: front-page material, dramatic photos—a chance to see the real thing close up. We parted, promising to stay in touch.

CHAPTER 41

At last, we were bringing the babies home.

For the first year, it seemed that all they did was sleep and eat. It was seldom that I saw Rica without a baby at her breast. They were mine to burp or change. Our lives revolved around the girls.

Billy had difficulty pronouncing "Margarita," and since I often referred to her as "Baby," he shortened that to "Babe." So that was the name she was known by. Actually, from the beginning she was "Daddy's Babe," and in later years, when knowledge increased and tongues grew sharper, she became "Daddy's Pet." This really wasn't true; it was only that I loved them differently.

They walked at thirteen months. With her first steps, Babe bypassed her mother and fell into my arms. I thought my heart would burst. Sarita was loyal to her mother.

They had such fun sitting in their high chairs throwing food at each other. Our experience with Billy obviously was a test—nothing prepared us for these hell-raising, angelic-appearing little cherubs. If these were the terrible twos, I shuddered for the coming years.

"Rica, we've got to get away from these kids once in a while. We are not required to give up our lives for their constant attendance," I insisted.

She agreed, but nothing changed. The tickets I bought for a play I thought we'd both enjoy somehow got mislaid.

Then Rica joined the Women's Literary Guild in North Beach, making the acquaintance of other young women with similar interests.

I fell asleep in my big chair, dreaming of places far away.

Our neighborhood was older and mainly occupied by a childless population. There was one family with an eight-year-old girl who occasionally came to play with Billy, but that friendship faltered when she insisted that Horse was "only a pony."

Now it was time to think of Billy's education. At Juan's suggestion, we enrolled him in a small private school with excellent credentials in North Beach.

Billy—fun-loving, outgoing, wise beyond his years, having been raised in a mostly adult world—had no difficulty finding his place at the top of his class, a position he maintained until he graduated high school.

When living is easy, the years slide by.

In high school, Billy was a sports addict—captain of the basketball team, fast man on the track, and pitcher for the softball team. Juan and Sara never missed his games. Dr. Teddy said she would rather read about them in the newspaper.

Rica, the girls and I cheered so loudly when he made a basket that he said we embarrassed him.

Rica said it was no more than she expected, but Juan's pride knew no bounds.

Billy, at that upscale academy for boys, was home on weekends and holidays. "Home" could mean Pacific Heights, Juan's "playhouse" or his room.

The house now resounded with girls' giggles or the boisterous noise of Billy's friends.

When did Billy get so tall? He grew so fast, tall and skinny with close-cropped, curly blond hair, not to mention the pimples. And his voice was already changing. The years had blurred by—I could hardly remember his fifth birthday. Ah, yes, how could I forget that pony.

"Thanks a lot, Pop, for this contribution." Billy always reminded me as he tried to slick down an errant curl—like I once had.

I could see myself in Billy at that age. My hope was that he should travel faster and go further than I had.

From birth, Billy had the best, with never a hand laid on him in anger. I smothered the intruding scenes of my childhood and knew that it was my mother who had given me whatever it took to make me the man I was.

Juan's attitude toward the girls was completely different—I don't believe I ever saw him hold one in his arms. He was always kind and thoughtful, but distant—as though they were the children of strangers. Sometimes I wondered if this was a form of self-protection on his part.

Juan had profited hugely from Dr. Teddy's advice and was now the owner of some very fine properties in the downtown area of San Francisco. He had maintained his studio in the house he had so beautifully restored, and in his sanctuary, stacked against the walls, were many canvases—some half-finished paintings leaning against the wall, another on the easel—and the smell of turpentine, brushes and paints.

Billy's gym equipment was in a corner. A basketball hoop was fastened high outside where Juan and Billy practiced and I joined them on occasion.

From Juan's, it was a short walk on a beaten path to our house, from where that delicious smell of food emanated most evenings.

Juan, fundamentally the same skinny boy who had taught me to roll a cigarette, was now a man in an expensive suit, a little older, a little quieter, but the same feelings between us never changed, except perhaps to have grown deeper with maturity. And I knew he loved Billy as though he was his own son.

As they grew older, the two identical black-haired girls were replicas of their mother. Juan had marked them, too, in ways not so easily seen, but recognized instantly by those who knew him well.

The girls did not betray the beauty of their inheritance.

Sarita was more outgoing. Her dark hair swinging around a face that nearly always was about to break into a giggle. Her feet never walked, they danced—sometimes clomping awkwardly in her mother's high-heels or twirling in pink ballet slippers.

With all the "Lookit me, Dad, Mom. Look," came wet sloppy kisses, and screams of agony at the sight of broccoli. "Not again."

"My" Babe, quiet, quick-witted, sensitive, and usually with her nose in a picture book, was devoted to her more adventuresome sister who frequently got Babe involved, too. A stern look from her mother would send her flying to my lap, her sanctuary. This was always followed by Sarita's teasing "Daddy's Pet," while explaining to her mother with such perfectly logical reasoning why she was made up like a burlesque queen, ignoring the powder covering the floor.

These girls made the "terrible twos" seem mild. We were pleased and relieved to get them enrolled in a good private school.

The girls loved to visit Gramma Sara and she loved to have them. Dr. Teddy watched with bemused eyes as Sara played with the girls as though they were paper dolls. She took them shopping and they brought back everything Rica had forbidden—lipstick, high-heeled shoes, eye shadow. Had Rica dropped in, she would not have recognized these two young girls, still in grade school, dressed in the outrageous clothing and makeup of runway models. Tottering in their high-heels, they played and paraded with abandon, but left their treasures behind when, newly scrubbed, they came home.

Sara had loved the twins from birth—she loved their youth and enthusiasm and, of course, the knowledge that they were of Juan.

After a long day in a busy workday, my reward was Babe waiting for my car to turn in the long driveway and walk with me to the door where Sarita stood and chanted, "Daddy's Pet, Daddy's Pet." Then the three of us would walk into this lovely home. With a beautiful ten-year-old girl on each arm, I would smell the pot roast. Woe betide me if I didn't produce some little goody—even if it was no more than a chocolate bar concealed in a pocket.

Soon I would hear the plaintive cry, "And what do you have for the mistress of the house?"

I always answered with a leer and, "Later, Mistress, later."

CHAPTER 42

N ow that Charles had finished his second term as governor, he and Ma had been living it up, traveling in a motorhome as big as a boxcar—a far cry from the "horse trailer" that Sis had predicted would transport us to the whoop-de-do that had announced Ma's birthday and their marriage.

They had yet to spend more than a few days at a time with us since I was usually on the job. And now that they had surprised us with plans to visit, J.W. called with another "big one" for me.

For the first time, I rebelled and screwed up my courage to confront J.W. I asked, hat in hand, if someone else couldn't do the job as well. I was almost—almost—ready to add "better," but couldn't bring myself to say it.

I promised an in-depth interview in the near future with Charles Kearney, recently retired governor of Texas, who had his eye on a seat in the senate.

I skidded by on that.

The following week was unforgettable.

Ma and I sat up late with time that was our very own. She was indulged by Rica's culinary skills and impressed with the beautiful kitchen. Charles and I talked politics and drank lots of beer.

Ma was, of course, entranced with our identical twins who delighted in confusing her as they pretended to be each other.

"I would have thought one of them would have looked like you, Steve."

"Sure, Ma, the next time you're here, Babe will have blue eyes. They change as they grow older, you know."

"How would I know? No one in our family ever had black hair and brown eyes. Sis and Tim's three-year-old girl has curly blonde hair and big blue eyes. Cutest baby that ever walked," Ma declared.

To cover Ma's misspoken words, Charles and I exchanged glances and changed the subject, nearly outshouting each other about the price of oil. I was grateful that Rica was in the kitchen.

Charles added that Tim had received another promotion, and that there was talk among the military of an American interaction to discourage Iraqi violation of Kuwait territory.

The night before they left, we were invited to dinner at the big house in Pacific Heights. And what a dinner it was, as usual, and in such impressive surroundings.

Charles and Dr. Teddy were deeply engrossed in the subject of cars. Ma and Sara bragged about their sons, and Rica attempted to interrupt with Billy's latest achievements. Juan and I hid out in his studio.

I wished that Sis and Tim could have been with us to make the evening even more perfect.

But there was a serpent in the Garden of Eden.

I was disenchanted with the same old routine of everyday life, and increasingly bored, even with the job that I loved.

My wife, my kids and my job. As much as I truly loved them, this was my entire world from day to day.

Now, I did have my Saturday-night poker game with the fellows at the paper, and Rica had her clubs and activities with the girls, plus a new Chrysler station wagon, in which she was always picking up or dropping off someone. She acted like a girl herself and I loved her—that never changed.

So why wasn't I content? Sometimes I felt alone, what with Rica and the girls off to their various events, and Billy and Juan almost inseparable. Just reading the Sunday funnies was all the excitement I thought I needed.

I got fat and lazy.

"There's got to be something more," I told Rica.

She laughed at me. "You're young for male menopause. What more is there? You have beautiful children, a lovely home, a good job, a devoted wife and friends who love you. There isn't any more—you've got it all."

"I know, but for some reason it isn't enough." Thoughts of an exciting faraway adventure blocked everything else out.

Then came breaking news that grew like Jack-in-the-Beanstalk of an invasion by Iraq into Kuwait, a land rich in oil that Saddam Hussein maintained still belonged to Iraq. This claim was violently disputed by Kuwait and supported by the United Nations.

An ultimatum to withdraw Iraqi troops from Kuwait was ignored, and so the Persian Gulf War exploded with over one hundred thousand sorties flown, eighty-eight thousand and five hundred tons of bombs destroying both military and civilian structures on the first day.

At that, my mind instantly snapped back to my last conversation with Alfie, and how it had fueled the flames of my imagination.

As I sat by my warm fireside dreaming, I did not know how fine the line is between a dream and a nightmare.

Everything else paled beside the news of the war. Every newspaper, every television program centered on reports of the Gulf War.

Inwardly, I both raged and wept—and here I was home "walking the dog."

I called Alfie, only to be told that Dr. Myers had joined the military.

Shortly after, I received a short note from Alfie telling me that "Now is the time" and giving me his location.

My heart leaped—this was my chance to be involved in something really big. I imagined my magic pen could win me the Pulitzer Prize if only I could get to the real war. I would probably get enough material to write a book—oh, and the pictures taken on the spot would go down in history books. I'd never have another opportunity like this—I couldn't miss it. I was going to go come hell or high water and nobody was going to stop me.

I knew the real battle would start at home and that was a feeble understatement.

When I approached J.W. with the hope that he was going to be supportive, that hope died a quick death.

"You're like a damn kid. You think war is all glamour and excitement like it is in the movies. I can tell you it is not. I was in the Second World War, and that hell I don't dare to think about. Blood, guts, brains—not from the assholes that plan it, of course, but the little guys in the field." He waved away any interruptions.

"What's this noble war all about? The poor people in Kuwait? Hell, no," he spewed, stubbing out his cigarette hard enough to put it through the desk. "We want the oil to feed our fancy cars. Those people have been fighting over there before the ground was dry in Noah's day and they will be fighting as long as this world exists. We'll get our men back in pieces, dead, crippled—mentally as well as physically. And the bombing will probably kill thousands of their innocent civilians, too."

His disillusioned old eyes were almost hidden under leathery wrinkles; his growly voice was only getting deeper with age.

"Why do you want to go to some hellhole across the world to get your ass shot off? Find some excitement closer to home. You won't get my blessing, and if you go, don't come back here—if you ever come back at all."

I called Juan, hoping that he would understand.

"Got a minute?"

We met at a little coffee shop near the newspaper office. I figured I'd just been fired so I laid it all out for my friend.

When I first started to tell him, he laughed. Then, judging from the look on my face, he realized that I was dead serious.

"Steve, you can't mean that. What about Rica and the kids? You've got a good thing going here—why go halfway across the world to get involved in a war that means nothing to us? Please reconsider. Don't go, please don't."

That night after dinner and the kids were asleep, I carefully approached Rica with my intentions.

"What the hell are you thinking of? Yourself? Sure isn't your family. Why? Why are you doing this?"

How could I explain?

"I'm going to call Ma," Rica stated firmly.

Before I could intercede, she was on the phone with Ma, raging.

"Put him on now," Ma told Rica.

"Steve, you cannot do this to your family—it's insane. Promise me you'll forget this foolishness. You're working too hard to think clearly. Bring Rica and the kids and come down to the ranch for some rest for a while."

"Talk to you later, Ma," I said as I hung up the phone.

Two days later, J.W. called. "Steve, if you're fool enough to do this, you'll need a lot of paperwork to prove you are an accredited journalist for this paper. My nephew is a pilot on one of those transport cargo planes. He could probably help you with transportation. Here is his name and phone number. I told him you'd call. Take care, Steve... and come home."

When I picked up my papers from him, there were tears enough for two.

Doubts rose up in the night to torment me. I knew the war would be dangerous, but that knowledge blurred with my determination.

What of Rica and my kids? What if anything should happen to me? I agonized at the thought that some other man would become a father to my children, would comfort my wife, his shoes under my bed. After all, Rica was a beautiful woman. But I comforted myself with the knowledge that nothing, of course, would happen to me.

We seldom quarreled, but I knew this final round was coming very soon.

In the light of day, I rationalized. Rica had everything she wanted. She had wanted a fine house, she got it. Children I couldn't give her, but I gave her all my support. Now she had the girls she wanted. They were everything to me, too, but I had wanted her to be happy. I had wanted her to have her dream. And she had it: a lovely home, children, a husband who denied her nothing, who loved her.

Now what of my dream?

I appreciated what our life was. My mother, Sis—how I loved them. Our beloved friends in Pacific Heights, the man I loved as a brother, even my fire-snorting old boss who sometimes thought I hung the moon...sometimes.

But there was a piece missing in this jigsaw puzzle of my life. There was something else. Yes, there was—there had to be.

I wanted one last fling in my life. Then I would come home and once again the last piece would fit and we would all live happily ever after.

Over the following days, I got my gear ready: lots of film, note-books—everything I could think of that I might need. Packed in a duffle bag, I left it in the garage.

The girls cried and I made extravagant promises. Billy thought of it as an exciting adventure and wished that he could go. My only supporter.

Rica alternated between tears and recriminations, finally to lan-guage I'd heard only in the newsroom.

"Rica, darling..."

"Don't darling me."

"I promise I'll be gone only a month and I won't leave the base."

"Don't lie to me."

"Rica..."

Two days later I got a message from John Owens, J.W.'s nephew. "I'm leaving on Tuesday at five a.m. Call me if you're coming with me and I'll give you the details."

Coward that I was, late Monday night, I sneaked to the kitchen to call a cab. Waiting, I tiptoed to the girls' room and pulled their blankets up, kissed Sarita, smoothed the hair from Babe's face and whispered, "My girls, I love you the most and the best."

My girls were sixteen, almost young women now. Sarita, outgoing, with a vivacious laugh and dancing feet, was a carbon copy of her mother. My "Babe" had Juan's unmistakable stamp upon her and yet was still "Daddy's Babe." My beautiful girls.

Billy had spent the night in Pacific Heights.

As I left, I looked back at this huge part of my life that I was putting on hold. I tucked the letter I had written under the coffeepot where Rica couldn't miss it, then added a P.S.: "I promise to come home."

After paying the driver, I walked toward the biggest plane I'd ever seen. John intercepted me as I was halfway across the runway. Taking my duffle bag, he said, "Glad you're early. I was hoping to get an earlier start. Go over there to the flight crew," he directed and motioned to a group of men near a large pile of boxes. "Give them a hand. Then carry a box into the plane and stay in the crapper until we're off the ground."

When I joined the men, one welcomed me with "You got here just in time—we're almost done."

Laughing, I carried a box, followed a man who carried the same and watched as he delivered it to the fellow waiting, standing in the doorway of the plane's belly. I brought two more boxes, and then went up the steps with another in my arms. Depositing that, I retreated to the crapper.

I sat down on the stool and promptly fell asleep. I hadn't had much rest at home since I had been holding down our big chair due to the hostile reaction to my announcement.

I was awakened by a thunderous knock on the door.

"Hey, are you alive?" came the copilot's irritated voice.

I could tell the copilot was not impressed by my presence, but he eventually warmed and we talked with the pilot off and on for about eighteen hours as the flight crew played cards and slept.

I was thrilled beyond words. My mental notebook was bursting.

"We'll set down shortly. Where are you off to?"

"The field hospital near the First Battalion of the First Calvary Division."

"We can probably get you a lift. Some of this stuff is for them."

My luck was running strong, I thought. See? I was meant to do this; everything is going perfectly.

When that big cargo plane rolled to a stop, all I could see were camouflaged men and khaki-colored sand—and lots of both, and big trucks and every kind of equipment. I was about to get into a waiting loaded truck when an officer approached me.

"Hey you. Who are you and where do you think you're going? What are you doing here? This ain't fucking Disneyland—no tourists allowed here."

I stood up tall, my heart pounding. Oh no, not now.

Looking him dead in the eye, I said, "I am an American citizen and I am an accredited journalist for the *Bay City Chronicle* in San Francisco. I have a right to let my readers know what is going on in this country, and I have a right to be here. I've been cleared by top authority."

J.W. would have been pleased by that promotion.

The driver of the truck was revving his motor.

I added, "I know my material will be subject to military approval and I respect that. If you'll excuse me, I have an appointment with Major Alfred Myers."

I stepped past him and climbed into the truck. He gave me a baleful stare and waved us off.

My luck was holding, I assured myself.

From the youthful truck driver, a young kid who didn't look much older than Billy, I learned enough about the war to fill a book. He dropped me off right in front of the field hospital.

I walked inside and asked for Dr. Alfred Myers and waited a moment. Then a voice boomed, "Cowboy, where's your horse?" Standing as big as a mountain, Alfie's arms enveloped me.

My dream was coming true.

"You got here just in time. This war is about over. The Iraqis are about done, deserting back into the desert. The fires are burning at seven hundred oil wells, and four hundred million gallons of crude oil have been dumped into the gulf to keep the Marines out. Of course, there's still some last-minute, last-ditch fighting." He paused. "But they are at a big disadvantage with old, very poor equipment, poor training and not much motivation. And our men, excited about our new armored tanks and Humvees, thermal site lasers, and range-finders, are eager to use them. Rumor has it that we're pushing the Iraqis down to the last tank."

He put his arm over my shoulder. "You should get some incredible pictures of the oil wells, especially at night."

I felt my state-of-the-art camera dance with anticipation.

"We haven't had many casualties, thank God, but let me show you what a mine can do."

I followed him to the back of the tent. On a stretcher lay a body. Alfie pulled the blanket back. The body was that of a young man who had no legs, and some of his internal organs were exposed in the torn abdomen. His bloodless hands were crossed on his chest as if in prayer.

I turned my head, my stomach rebelling, but I made a desperate effort to keep everything down. Alfie pulled the blanket up.

"Are you gonna faint?"

"Of course, I'm not gonna faint. Do I look like I'm gonna faint?"

"Yes. Don't go outside the perimeter."

"This is where we put the dead and the 'expectants.' Those are the ones we expect will die immediately. When we have to choose quickly between those we can save and those we can't, it's a horrible decision. The ones who are alive but need immediate, extensive surgery are airlifted to a hospital in Landstuhl, Germany, in a special cargo plane."

As we walked back, he said, "There is a huge armored convoy of tanks and Humvees going down the Iraq-Kuwait highway to clean up Kuwait. The Iraqis have mostly gone. Now that you shouldn't miss. That will be the end. You should be able to get enough pics and material there that you'll never have to work again. But you'll have to figure a way to get into one of those tanks. Act cool and keep that camera out of sight; it won't be easy."

"I will, if I have to buy it," came my cocky response.

"You can sleep in my tent. Did you bring a sleeping bag? The sand fleas will eat you alive."

I slept soundly that night despite the sound of far-off guns, and dreamed of ways to get into that front tank. I was here and I was safe and heaven could wait.

A day later, there was a tremendous amount of activity—looked like an anthill that had been disturbed. I tried to sneak a few pictures without much luck. A big guy noticed me and said, "Get your ass in gear, soldier. This ain't no picnic."

Somehow Alfie had found me a camouflage uniform, but my longer hair betrayed me. I heard snickering as I walked around. "Pretty Boy" was the nicest thing they called me.

Since it was an open secret, I knew the big push was going to start early in the morning when the 1st Marine Division, 1st Light Armored Infantry would head for Kuwait City. I couldn't sleep—excitement was at fever pitch.

Alfie embraced me and gave me his Kevlar vest. "Cover that camera and don't take chances. When we get back home, we'll have a party that will make the Fourth of July look like an ice-cream social. Take care."

I had never been so excited in my life—nothing mattered to me today but going to Kuwait in that tank.

Loading started at daylight. I edged my way up to the big tank. Watching my chance, I climbed up to the turret and pushed in close behind another guy.

"Hey, you stupid asshole. This ain't your ride out."

I was shoved out so fast I thought maybe I had sprouted wings. But it was only a size-twelve boot. Shit.

Taking another tactic, I walked boldly up past a guy waiting to climb up. He said, "That you, Mickey?"

"Yeah," I grunted and figured I had it made.

"You ain't Mick. Who the hell is this shit-for-brains? Don't even know his own name."

Again I got a rough shove and sprawled in the sand. I started to panic. I was going with this damn convoy if I had to ride on the roof.

The Humvees were loading their last men. Slipping among some guys who were bullshitting each other, I elbowed in and crowded between two soldiers, then put my head in my hands and held it down.

"What's the matter with you?"

"I'm sick to my stomach. Leave me alone or I'll puke all over you."

"Oh, shit, just my luck to sit next to a puker."

The column was moving and picking up speed. I raised my head to look out the little slit from which the guns worked.

"Hey, who the hell is this?"

"Dan Smith. O'Brien gave me orders."

"That son of a bitch throws his surplus off on us like we're not already sardines."

The men all talked at once—arguing, chatting about all the fun they were going to have in Kuwait, cursing the crowded quarters and O'Brien.

We had been on the road about two hours. It was hot, noisy and stank of sweat and worse. I put my face up to the narrow slit and up ahead I saw a good-sized hump of dirt, probably knocked out from a bomb blast, with a little depression behind it. I drew in a breath of fresh air and my seatmate said, "Sit down, stupid. This ain't no sightseeing tour."

It was then that a deafening boom split the air. There was sudden, shocked silence. We all lurched forward as the brakes were floored.

Then someone—the driver?—screamed hoarsely, "Oh my God, the lead truck is blown all to hell. Must have hit a mine. Oh my God, there goes a tank."

Voices clamored all at once.

"Thought this road was cleared—must have been replanted."

"The whole thing's on fire. All that ammo they were carrying."

"Nobody got out alive."

Now we could smell the smoke.

The radio was crackling orders.

"This was the perfect place for an ambush with all the shit they left behind—bombed-out tanks, LEDs. Can't go forward; they're behind us, too."

Abject fear, indecision, rage, shock and terror written on the faces of the men. The radio squawked, then the smell of roiling black smoke enveloped the tank.

I struggled to the door.

"Sit the hell down, you damned fool. Are you crazy?"

But I had the door handle clutched tightly. The curses and screaming efforts to stop me were useless as the vision of the pictures I could get of the burning tank fueled a superhuman effort. In some faraway place in my mind, the horror of that body engulfed in flames that hung from the twisted turret sickened me, but did not part me from the craving for a once-in-a-lifetime shot that would make the front page.

I opened the door and jumped, instantly hearing the unfamiliar sound of bullets hitting the sand. As I ran, as I had never run before, I stumbled over the top of the hump and fell into that shallow indentation of the earth, wishing it was ten feet deep.

My pants were clinging to my legs and I realized I had pissed myself. There goes my badge for bravery, my conscious mind informed me.

I lay there panting, my nostrils filled with the smell of the burning tank.

The thud of big shells suddenly erupted around me, and the chatter of machine guns ripping the sand paralyzed my thinking. I curled up in a ball, holding my camera to my chest. My thought process returned with the realization that I was alone somewhere in a place where people were trying to kill me.

I was too far away from home. What am I doing here? Why am I out here in the middle of a desert on my ass in the sand? For a moment, the camera and the pictures didn't seem that important. My wife, my kids. What in hell have I done?

Yeah, my conscience sneered, *but you just had to be a hero. This trip was for your ego, Steve—for your pleasure. Life at home with wife and kiddies wasn't enough for you.*

I saw a grenade drop and roll out just past me. The smoky trail was evident and didn't conceal the pineapple-shaped killer. Frantically, I rolled away, using every ounce of strength to push myself from this deadly horror.

Then it blew. I felt a flash of heat and light, and tasted the bitter chemical ignition as I felt myself driven far into the ground.

A voice bellowed, "Medic. Medic."

As the medic administered plasma, his eyes assessed the shrapnel-riddled body, blood-soaked on one side from hip to what was left of a foot.

"That vest probably saved his life or the full force of the explosion was deflected by the hump and blasted up and out. Those poor devils in the tank should have been so lucky."

He moved to take the pulse, and Steve's head rolled. The medic saw the fried flesh around the opening of a hole in the exact center of the forehead and muttered, "Poor devil. I'm probably wasting my time and the plasma here."

Dr. Myers and Dr. Francis heard the heavy vehicle approaching and stood with the nurses and other personnel watching and waiting to bring in the wounded.

The back of the big truck opened to reveal the bloodied, crying, screaming, cursing wounded, and the dead.

The doctors indicated which of the injured would go into the tent for emergency treatment and who would go to the back.

Dr. Francis looked at Steve's mangled body and turned to Alfie, muttering, "This one has a pulse, barely, and a hole in his head. He's lost a lot of blood. 'Expectant,' I'd say." He nodded to an aide. "Take him back."

Later the nurses talked.

"That Dr. Myers, big as a tank and black as night, screamed 'No' and just gathered that guy up in his arms like a baby. Carried him out, and I swear I heard him singing."

"I wonder if the good doctor isn't cracking up."

From another world, I could see Alfie's contorted face and hear his anguished voice.

"I told you to come to me when you needed an appendectomy, but no, you had to go to that damn shoe salesman." He rocked me as he had in that other lifetime.

In the quickening darkness, I heard him humming that old song I'd heard Ma sing a hundred times—something about amazing grace.

Drawn by an unseen hand, the darkness covered me like a soft, warm blanket.

"Sir, the plane is ready for takeoff."

"Hold it—hold it. Put this man on."

The plane's wheels had hardly left the runway when Dr. Myers had Dr. Hassé on the phone.

"Steve is in the hospital at Landstuhl, Germany. I pray to God that he will still be alive when you get there."

Sara and Dr. Teddy drove to Rica's, finding her in her garden. When Rica reached out with a huge bouquet of flowers and said, "I was just going in to make a cup of tea. Now I won't have to drink alone."

A sense of foreboding suddenly overcame Rica as she looked closely at Sara and their eyes met. The roses fell to the ground.

"It's Steve, isn't it? Isn't it?"

Sara didn't need to answer.

"Where is he?

"Germany. Juan has sent me for you. He has chartered a plane to bring him home. Go, Rica. I'll call Steve's mother and take care of everything here. Go."

Dr. Teddy said, "I would be glad to go, but I don't feel qualified. There is a young neurosurgeon here—the very best. He's on vacation, but I'll see if I can locate him. His name is O'Connor."

Within hours, the plane—piloted by a man who marveled at the resources of the rich—was in the air with three passengers, a copilot and flight crew.

On the way over, Rica sat by herself, numb with grief and conscious of nothing but her love and need. She never noticed the vast expanse of land and water. When she closed her eyes, all she could see was Steve asleep alone in their big chair.

Juan and Dr. O'Connor spoke briefly, then silence prevailed.

The plane rolled to a stop ten hours later in the busy airport of Landstuhl, Germany.

Juan gave the pilots instructions.

"Get what you need and have the plane ready to depart. We won't be long."

The weary group followed the red line that led to a big gray building that wore a sign reading "Customs." Inside, the line was long, but moving. Then they stepped out into the morning sunshine.

A taxi pulled to the curb and the driver quickly opened the door. Juan gave him the address. The driver had made many trips to the Landstuhl Regional Medical Center where war casualties were taken and grieving relatives followed.

The driver brought them to the door of the huge, intimidating building. Rica faltered, but with Dr. O'Connor and Juan on either side of her, she composed herself. Holding Juan's hand, she walked in.

Their presence was announced and a doctor in a spotless white coat walked to meet them, introducing himself as Dr. Brenner. Three other doctors who had followed did the same.

Dr. Brenner turned down the hall, and Rica, Juan and Dr. O'Connor followed him with the others.

"He has not recovered consciousness, nor have we expected him to," one doctor spoke as he opened the door where Steve lay swathed in bandages. The only exposed parts of him were his swollen, bruised face and his hands that lay white against the white bandages.

Rica fell to her knees, her head against the bed, and clasped Steve's cold hand. Juan stood wordless, his hand on her shoulder.

Dr. O'Connor spoke quietly to Dr. Brenner, then Juan pulled Rica gently to her feet. They were led to the doctor's office.

Dr. Brenner pulled out a chair for Rica and motioned for the men to find a seat, then stood as he spoke, quickly and plainly.

Addressing Dr. O'Connor first, he said, "Your man has been evaluated per an urgent request from Dr. Myers. It was difficult because of the short notice, but thorough. We have the best team of neurosurgeons in Germany." His praise was given with no embarrassment or hesitation.

He paused. "The man is terminal and we are not miracle workers."

Rica sat with closed eyes. Dr. O'Connor put his arm around Juan's shoulder as if to steady him for the doctor's next words.

"The wounds on his body are ugly and severe, but not life-threatening. The foot can possibly be saved. Understandably, there has been a tremendous loss of blood.

"The major problem is a sliver of shrapnel embedded deeply in his brain. It is my belief that an effort to remove it would cause his death. Better to let the shrapnel go with him."

The other doctors nodded their agreement.

Dr. O'Connor stood. "Dr. Brenner, I would like my patient to have an immediate blood transfusion. I have a donor." Meeting Dr. Brenner's disbelieving stare, he added, "Immediately."

"Of course. This must be a very important man. Who is he?"

Juan's voice shook as he replied, "My brother."

The sound of the plane as it flew high over the turbulent black sea failed to erase Dr. Brenner's words. They had held no meaning for Rica at the time. Words—just words, sounds hanging in the air, the words of a stranger that passed through her mind.

Of course, Steve wouldn't die.

But as the dark hours passed, she sat by the silent, motionless body, unresponsive to her touch, and doubt crept in.

How can I tell the children? How can I face your mother? Oh, Steve, you are the other half of me. How can I live without you? Why would I want to?

"My Steve." She sobbed with her arms around his blanketed figure. "The price was too high for your dream."

Her voice brought Juan to her. Tenderly, he loosened her arms and held her as Steve once had.

CHAPTER 43

"We've been in the air for ten hours. What's taking so long?" Juan asked impatiently of the pilot as the other man slept.

"Headwind is very strong. Two more hours and we're home. Sorry." Juan looked at his watch. Twelve a.m.

The plane's wheels had hardly touched down when a waiting ambulance pulled up. Steve was carefully lifted out, and with lights blazing and sirens blaring, he was taken to the University of California, San Francisco Medical Center.

Ma, Sis, Dr. Teddy and Sara anxiously waited, only to see the gurney with its near-lifeless figure roll quickly past. Following at a slower pace were the exhausted Juan, Rica and Dr. O'Connor.

After a few moments of excited questions, the doctor motioned them to a private room and spoke quickly.

"As long as you are all here, it will be easier if we can discuss Steve's condition now. Time is vital and I know you are anxious to hear. These are the facts. The doctors at Landstuhl are considered by the medical profession to be some of the best. They found a sliver of shrapnel deep in the front of the brain, as well as other wounds. They believe any attempt to remove that steel from his brain will be fatal, and that he is terminal.

"I would like the opportunity to examine him for my own satisfaction. Perhaps my fellow neurosurgeons and I can find something that the Germans have missed. I feel there is a chance and Steve is entitled to it."

Deep silence hung like a shroud, broken by Rica's muffled sobs, and Ma's broken-hearted, "My son, my son." Juan stood speechless, his face drained white.

"Your decision must be made quickly," the doctor continued. "He can't last. Three blood transfusions have helped keep him alive this long. He has never regained consciousness."

"He is in God's hands and Those hands will guide you," Ma said. Sis, with her arms around her mother, nodded her agreement.

Rica was sobbing on Sara's shoulder and they spoke as one. "Yes."

Dr. Teddy said, "You can do it. I have every confidence in you."

Juan's voice choked, "Don't let him die."

Wearily, Dr. O'Connor's said, "I have three specialists in this field who will work with me. The operation will be a lengthy one. He must heal slowly, so I will have him in an induced coma for at least a couple of weeks afterwards. I am grateful for your confidence and we will give him his chance. You folks go home and say your prayers and I will say mine. We will operate as soon as it is humanly possible and I will keep you fully informed."

After a lengthy conference with the operating team, elderly Dr. Bowers said confidentially to Dr. O'Connor: "This patient must be a very close friend of Dr. Hassé and a beloved friend of Mr. Miguel—if you know what I mean.

"I've known Dr. Hassé for years. Her father and my father practiced together before we were born. Goes back aways, doesn't it? She is very highly thought of despite her sexual preference. A queer, you know."

The younger doctor spoke quietly, as if to himself: "How wonderful to have a beloved friend like that—I would trade places with the patient if I could."

"Pardon me, Dr. O'Connor, I didn't hear you."

"Oh, talking to myself. Since I live alone, I tend to do that a lot. I hope people will think as highly of me some day, despite my sexual preference. I believe the honest word is 'homosexual.'"

Dr. Bowers flushed. "Sorry, I didn't know. Didn't mean to embarrass you."

"I am not embarrassed—but it appears that you are. Shall we get back to our patient?"

Teddy and Sara went home. As they undressed for bed, Teddy said, "Better pray for both of us. I haven't been in very close touch with God for a while."

"I always do," responded Sara.

At home, Rica lay on her back holding Steve's pillow close to her, gazing at the ceiling. She prayed that once again Steve's head would lie on that pillow and that she would hear his teasing voice, "Later, Mistress, later," and see his impish grin. Then her eyes closed and she slept.

Sis and Ma had tossed and turned, but finally dropped off in an agitated sleep in the bedroom that Dr. Teddy had designed.

In the morning, the sitter had readied the girls for school. Their cereal bowls were still on the table beside Babe's forgotten lunch money.

Rica was awakened late in the afternoon by the insistent ring of the phone.

Juan announced that "Steve's been in surgery since ten this morning, but I've heard nothing else. Me? I slept at the hospital in a chair. Don't worry."

Rica heard Ma's and Sis' voices in the kitchen. She walked in in her nightgown and gave them Juan's message. She poured herself a cup of coffee and patted Ma's shoulder as the older woman cried without tears.

"I think that's good news," Sis said. "He's still alive."

Rica became increasingly despondent, her hope fading, angry that against all pleas, Steve had done this to them, to all of them—her, the children, family and friends—for what? And she prayed fervently that he would recover. *How can I live without him? Damn this man who couldn't be satisfied with having had it all. Steve, Steve, come home. Please come home. You promised.*

Dr. Teddy received an update from Dr. O'Connor.

"We have removed the front of the skull and discovered what the Germans missed. The shrapnel is embedded exactly between the lobes of the brain—a hair's breadth on both sides is the reason he's still alive. If that can be removed without disturbing that almost nonexistent margin, his chances are good."

Dr. Teddy did not reveal this information. "If" was too strong a word.

Instead, she sent a car for Steve's family and they sat down to a dinner that under ordinary circumstances would have had Ma begging for the recipe.

Most of the food went back to the kitchen.

Conversation was subdued, with everyone immersed in his or her own thoughts.

Billy, who had cried his tears on Juan's shoulder, now sat in the library thumbing through a book with his eyes closed.

The hours dragged by. Why doesn't Juan call? They knew he had been staying at the hospital, coming home only to shower and change clothes.

It was late. Sara urged Ma, Sis and Rica to stay in a guest room.

Sis, with her arm around her mother, retired.

Billy had fallen asleep; his book had fallen to the floor. The girls were asleep on the sofa. Sara covered them and marveled at their resemblance to her beloved son.

Rica demurred. "I can't sleep; I'll be comfortable in this chair."

Rica's eyes brimmed as she looked at her long-legged daughters crowding the sofa. *My beautiful girls,* she thought. *How quickly the last sixteen years have rushed by. Soon they will want their own lives; already boys are calling. Oh, Steve, my Steve, you can't leave us. We need you so.* She closed her eyes, but there was no sleep.

It was now one a.m.

The operating room door opened and Dr. O'Connor stepped out, holding his cap in one hand, rubbing his tousled hair with the other. His eyes were tired, his shoulders slumped. He was still in his blood-stained scrubs.

In spite of knowing that Juan would still be there, he was startled at Juan's almost instant appearance and asked, "Where did you come from so quickly?" Then jokingly added, "Have you been listening at the door?"

Juan pointed to a chair he had pulled from an alcove.

"Let me show you something," the doctor said, and stepped back into the operating room.

He returned with a tray. On it lay a two-inch ribbon of steel. Juan looked at the death on a tray and shuddered. He put his head against the wall and his shoulders shook.

The doctor gave him a playful shake. "Stop or you'll have me there beside you and that will ruin my professional dignity. Call his wife."

Dr. Teddy reached for the ringing phone, but Rica had it and listened while the rest held their breath. She dropped the phone, turned, and said in a voice she didn't recognize as human, "Thank God. They got it out and he's alive."

The floor rose up to meet her. Ma caught her as she fell and held her as a child. "She is Steve's love—I must keep her safe for him."

That night, Teddy said, "I'll say my own prayers tonight and I'll put in a good word for you." She turned off the light.

Sara smiled to herself in the darkness.

The next morning the family met with the doctor and he explained the process they followed and added, "He also has a severe concussion and is probably deaf. His hearing may be partially regained. His foot is repaired, but he will always have a limp," he smiled, "to remind him not to go to war again. We took out a lot of shrapnel. I have him in an induced coma for a couple of weeks or more to allow that head to heal with no movement.

"The Man upstairs did indeed guide my hand, but extracting that steel has taken years of my life—it was a difficult and scary surgery. He's in intensive care and you may visit briefly, but you won't see anything but bandages."

He nodded to Juan. "Would you like to join me for coffee?"

Juan walked with him down the hall. He was impressed with this tall, lanky doctor who had the coppery red hair and blue eyes of the Irish. "The best surgeon in the city," Dr. Teddy had declared.

Impressive, too, was the excellent personal treatment plan and interest shown. Steve lacked for nothing—he had the best that money could buy.

There was something about this doctor that caught Juan's interest and wouldn't go away. Was it the way his hands moved so surely, or the questioning look in those blue eyes?

Steve had been in an induced coma for two weeks, and Juan had spent part of every one of those days at Steve's bedside.

Dr. O'Connor frequently came by at the same time. The two men slowly built a friendship that gave comfort to both of them. It was during that time that Dr. O'Connor became "Shaun," and Mr. Miguel became "Juan."

Another week went by. The doctor shook his head and spoke quietly. "We took him off the medication a few days ago. He should be showing some positive signs by now. The shrapnel in his head came out in one piece. Pray an infection doesn't develop or that there isn't another sliver farther in. I dare not go back into the brain any deeper."

Shaun saw the stricken look on Juan's face and laid a compassionate hand gently on his shoulder. His touch brought tears and the broken words, "I love him so."

Utter desolation clawed at the hope that had begun to grow in Shaun's entire being. Pity followed for Juan who would never know the love he craved from this man who had a wife and a life so different from their own.

But hope dies hard, although the mute question in his eyes went unanswered as Juan's emotions conflicted and sought their identity.

Shaun's touch caused a strong, hot current of desire to flash through Juan's veins, and he struggled with feelings of guilt that he knew were ridiculous, but that place in his heart had always been inviolate for Steve.

As always, Shaun lingered, reading the charts, taking notes, waiting for Juan to appear.

Why can't I admit to what I feel? It's love. Why can't I just say it? Shaun's reason demanded. *No, I won't run a poor second. It will have to come from him. It's too soon—there's still time.*

The conflict in Juan's mind grew. *How can I love two men? I'll always love Steve, but I can't let Shaun go. I've been waiting all my life for someone to love me as I want to be loved. I feel Shaun loves me—it shows in every glance and hidden word.*

Dr. O'Connor's professional cool betrayed him. The staff whispered: "He stumbles over his words." "He doesn't hear a word I say." "His mind is on another planet."

Dr. Bower supported his associate with, "I think he's not well and is working himself to exhaustion, probably coming down with something. Give him a break."

Dr. Teddy often accompanied Juan to the hospital and usually had long conversations with Dr. O'Connor about Steve. Her wise old eyes missed very little. She felt the tension between the two men and the reason was obvious.

She left her clinic early and drove home. Sara was painting, but pulled off the paint-spattered smock as Teddy arrived.

"Sara," Teddy said as she tossed her coat over a chair, "can you please see if Mrs. Mackey has anything good to eat down there, and find a bottle of wine." She walked quickly up the stairs to the study.

With the poker, the coals were quickly stirred up and, when a log was thrown on, the fire crackled. Teddy found her favorite place on the sofa that Sara teased had the full imprint of her bottom forever indented in the cushion. She kicked off her shoes and leaned back as Sara appeared with a plate of cookies and the wine.

"Fresh cookies. These should spoil your appetite for the roast Mrs. Mackey has in the oven."

"Sit down, my love. I'll pour the wine. Where are the glasses? Or must I drink out of the bottle?" Teddy asked, looking about.

"On the table beside you. You sound like you've already tasted the fruit of the vine. What makes you so happy?"

"Happy? Astounded. You will be, too.

"The unbelievable has happened. I strongly suspect that Juan is in love with Steve's doctor, and it's obvious, at least to me, that the feeling is mutual." She paused to fill her glass.

"Dr. O'Connor is the best young surgeon in the city with a great future. I am so happy for Juan. I know Steve will be happy for him, too. Breaks my heart, though, that Steve is still swathed in bandages, many of which should be ready to come off, yet he's still comatose. They took enough metal out of him to build a railroad, but it's that piece that was in his head that's causing the problem."

"I don't want to talk about Steve's problems now that you've opened Pandora's box," Sara said as she moved closer. "Tell me, hurry," but then she interrupted herself. "I could see such changes in Juan. His painting—what little he does of it—has completely changed. Wild, crazy colors; he's just smearing his canvas. Everything is so different from what he's always done. Of course, I have attributed that to his concern for Steve.

"This would be the first man who has ever captured Juan's interest, and there have been many who tried." She paused to refill their glasses and pulled the cookies closer.

Teddy sipped her wine, her eyes following the reflection of the fire in her glass. She spoke thoughtfully. "It is obvious to me that there is a very strong attraction there. I know Juan feels guilty. It has always been Steve and Steve needs to cut the cord. It is choking Juan's future and Steve would never want that.

"I pray he will recover consciousness. He has had a rough time; it is miraculous that Dr. O'Connor has kept him alive."

Laughing, Teddy added, "Juan acts like a schoolboy. After all these solitary years, happiness is within his reach. I think they are both afraid to face it squarely, afraid of the hurt that rejection would bring.

"Of course, Dr. O'Connor is aware of Juan's feelings for Steve. I feel he is waiting for Juan to get that into perspective. They are very formal in my presence, like two schoolboys in the principal's office, but I can tell."

She turned and laid her arm around Sara's shoulders to pull her close, then spoke softly.

"Sara, I know how you love him, but do you love him enough to push him out of the nest?"

Sara looked up, surprised. Was that a flash of anger in her eyes? She pulled away.

Teddy, unruffled, continued. "He promised that he would never leave you and only you can let him go. Let him live in his own house and have the life we all dream of. Deep down, he is a very lonely man.

"All our love cannot fill that void—that emptiness—that cries out for someone to wake up with in the morning.

"Sara, we've enjoyed that happiness for more years than I can remember. Give him his chance now, for a life that we've lived with such peace and happiness."

Sara was troubled. Of course, Teddy's words made perfect sense to her. Juan could travel the world over with someone that he loved, but she would always have her place in his heart, as he would live in hers.

Teddy seem so sure that the doctor is seriously in love with Juan and I see it in Juan's actions, too, Sara thought, and knew she would not stand in the way of his happiness.

That evening at dinner, after the general talk of the day had dwindled, Sara turned to Juan.

"Teddy has surprised me with the good news that she is retiring in thirty days. We are going to do what we've promised ourselves for a long time. We're going to travel before we get too old. We may even winter on the French Riviera. Won't that be wonderful?"

Juan looked shocked. "Mamá, this is so very sudden. I don't know that I can do that. I have a very big deal working and, of course, there's Steve. I'd like to, but..."

Sara got up and put her arms around him. "My dearest son, this isn't about you. This is for us—two old ladies having their last fling. We plan to close up this big house. Mrs. Mackey has been wanting to move in with her sister. Mr. Mackey is ready, too—these big grounds are too much for him now. You have your lovely house close to Steve and Rica. What would Billy do without you? And what about Dr. O'Connor?"

At the sound of his name, Juan flushed. "He's just a friend."

"Teddy says he'd like to be more than a friend."

"Mamá, you're embarrassing me." But he couldn't keep the smile from his voice.

"We've scheduled our flight already. In five weeks, we'll be in the air. Our first stop is Paris. Wish us well, my son," she said as the tears wet her cheeks.

Teddy had never loved her more.

"Now I must spend some time at my own house. The kitchen needs a different color and my yardman is slacking on the job." Juan's voice had a lilt that Sara had never heard before.

CHAPTER 44

I opened my eyes to the light. Where was I? That thought found its way through my foggy brain. My mind whirled around. I sought safety in the darkness. My eyes closed and shut out the reality.

Slowly I regained consciousness as I heard, from far away, the sound of voices. It couldn't be Juan, could it? Then his hands were on my face and he was calling my name.

"Steve, Steve, wake up."

Opening my eyes to Juan's tear-streaked face. I knew I was home.

It seemed seconds later that Rica's arms tenderly, carefully wrapped around me. She was kissing me and crying softly as I drifted back to sleep.

Dr. O'Connor spoke with a huge smile on his face. "His vital signs are all right where they should be. He's doing better than I expected."

As I opened my eyes to the morning sun, I heard the click-click of high-heeled shoes and turned my head to see two beautiful girls: Daddy's Babe in the lead, then Sarita, who were followed by my equally lovely wife.

Bringing up the rear was my tall son, who was nearing his twenty-first birthday. He bent over to hug me and grinned. "Pop, you looked better the last time I saw you. Have you been sick?"

But he couldn't quite bring it off. When he straightened, his cheeks were wet, as were mine.

Rica had her arms around as much of me as was possible and stifled her sobs in my pillow.

Each girl held a hand.

We were afloat in a sea of tears. Tears of gratefulness and joy.

"You shouldn't have so many visitors—you're recuperating," admonished a nurse.

"So many? Never, never can I have too many of the people I love and who love me back."

When Dr. O'Connor came in later, I mumbled through my bandages. "Would you get in touch with Dr. Myers and tell him the party is still on? Since this is where he worked for years, I'm sure they will have his address."

"Of course. He was a very respected doctor here. Sorry I never got to meet him."

I liked this Irish doctor. He was with me often, sometimes to talk, to visit, even though my hearing was gone in one ear. Gradually, I noticed that a lot of his visits coincided with those of Juan's. It was then that I became just an audience.

Sis, Ma and Charles flew through the door, and once the hysterics were over, my helpless condition did not shield me from Sis' assessment of my previous intelligence. Her stringent comments were accompanied by Charles' laughter and Ma's remonstrative, "Now, Sis, now, Sis—Sis!"

The bandages on my body were being removed one by one as the wounds healed. I always kept them covered because I couldn't bear to look at them myself. The foot remained in a cast. I was told that I would always walk with a limp. When I complained that the bandages on my head looked as though I was wearing a turban, the nurse replied tartly, "At least you've got a head to put in on." I concluded she was right.

More and more I was aware of the restrained courtship happening almost at my door. Juan had never shown interest in any of the suitors who had tried their luck. This was different.

Dr. Teddy came by one day and got right to the point.

"Steve, it is you who must cut the cord. You have always been his only love. He is tortured by the decision he must make. I know he hasn't committed himself to Dr. O'Connor, but I also know he is deeply in love—as I'm sure you've seen. You must break the cord.

"I know you love him and this is his chance for the happiness that you and I both have."

The thought occurred to me that I should have figured that out myself.

Dr. Teddy continued. "Have you and Rica ever had a honeymoon? Now is the time. Take the kids; travel is an education. Did I tell you I have retired? Sara and I are going to Paris—for starters. Let's give Juan some room. I'll wager he will be honeymooning when we get back."

She leaned over and kissed me on my bandaged forehead. "We love you, too, Steve. You'll always be family to us."

I was shocked, honored and humbled. I'd never known Dr. Teddy to kiss anyone but Sara.

Later that evening, with visiting hours almost over, Juan and Rica came to visit. Rica looked so lovely that she took my breath away.

Sis had come over earlier to say a tearful goodbye. She was lonesome for her kids and Tim. She said she was leaving me in good hands. Dr. Teddy took her to the plane. Ma stayed a few days longer.

Rica laughed a little and said, "Well, I guess Ma's been converted."

"To what?" I asked.

"You'd never guess," she answered. "Well, we were just talking and sipping tea. Then she got really quiet and said, 'You and Steve are so fortunate to have such wonderful friends. Steve could never have a truer friend than Juan. They are like brothers. And those women are as concerned about Steve as though he were their son.'

"'Yes,' I agreed, 'we've known them for a very long time—around twenty-five years.'

"Then, of course, I couldn't resist a little jibe, knowing Ma's previous adamant beliefs.

"'You know, of course, they are homosexual,' and waited for her reaction.

"She'd been giving this some thought; I could tell by her quick answer.

"She said, 'There never was a better man than Juan and those women have lived together for forty-five years. Sara told me, and I believe these are her exact words, '...and I have loved her for longer.' Who can quarrel with that? The same God that judges them will judge me—judge not lest ye be judged.'"

"That's my Ma," I said. "God's in his 'heaven and all's right with the world.'"

Dr. O'Connor happened by. "Stopped to see how my patient is doing."

We all chatted for a short while, then, kissing the hand I was holding, my words tumbled out.

"Rica, when I get out of here, let's you and I go on an extended honeymoon. We'll take the kids—travel is education. We can be gone for as long as we like. I'm sure I don't have a job anymore. Teddy and Sara are going to Paris. Why should they have all the fun?"

Rica giggled like a girl. "Quick, Doctor, I think Steve is having a relapse..." Then, turning to me, she asked, "Honest? And take the kids?"

"Sure, why not?"

She flung her arms about me and kissed me all over my face, bandages and all.

"Ireland. That's the place to go," Dr. O'Connor suggested.

I looked at Juan's flushed face, and the emotions that chased themselves back and forth told me that, indeed, this was the time.

He stood. "Doctor, if the cafeteria is still open, let's have a cup of coffee. Excuse us."

"Juan." My voice stopped him at the door. "I wish for you, my brother, all the happiness your heart can hold."

That night Juan's heart tuned out the world. There was only himself and Shaun.

With the morning light, Juan turned his head to see tangled covers thrown back. The fragrant aroma of coffee drifted in and with it came a happy whistle that echoed in his heart.

I was sitting up when J.W. blustered his way past the nurse. He took my hand and his face twisted to what I knew he intended to be a smile. He pulled out an old tattered handkerchief from somewhere and blew his nose so loudly that the nurse scowled. After a few aborted starts, he spoke.

"Well, you damn fool, I'll give you credit. You did make it home. I've got an opening for a copy boy. Do you think you could handle that?"

He released my hand as if surprised to find he was still holding it.

When he had gone, my own tears flowed; J.W. had said "I love you" in the only way he knew.

Then I blew my nose and the nurse said, "What is this? An epidemic?"

After two more weeks, the doctor reluctantly released me. I promised to take care and Rica guaranteed it. "Nothing strenuous," she emphasized.

My hair had mostly covered the scars on my head, but a dimple still appeared in my forehead. I walked with a cane into our home that now rivaled Heaven.

Everyone was at my beck and call and at last, I was master of my domain. Rica and I had time for each other for long talks, cuddling in front of the fireplace when the kids were in school, and planning our future. But first our honeymoon.

A big plate of cookies one evening set the scene. The fireplace was a rosy glow.

Rica called, "Kids, it's a party—cookies and ice cream."

She didn't need to call the girls twice and by the time Billy pried himself from his auto mechanic magazine, inroads had been made on the cookie plate.

Rica laid the maps and the travel folder on the coffee table, smoothed the wrinkles and gave the kids the news.

"We're all going on a three-month cruise."

"When are we leaving?" asked Billy.

"Maybe they'll have a good-looking lifeguard for the pool."

"Yeah," said Billy, "and I hope it's female."

"Now can I have a bikini?"

"Will we have a room with a view?"

The questions were endless, coming thick and fast.

Rica was as excited as the kids and I felt a very strong desire to cry. I asked myself why we'd never done this before.

Finally, it was bedtime. Apparently, though, it was not sleep time—we heard the muffled sounds of conversation and laughter from the girls.

Billy's muted voice on the phone could be heard—a voice that had started to change so long ago, and now sounded so...so adult. How quickly he had grown up.

The cane leaned beside the bed and watched without surprise as I kissed my wife goodnight. I didn't hear when she said, "nothing strenuous." I'm half deaf, you know.

ABOUT THE AUTHOR

Dorothy Durando is the author of *And Yesterday is Gone, Beyond the Bougainvillea* and *Out of the Darkness*. She gained deep intuition for the diversity of human nature as a licensed psychiatric technician for more than forty years in various mental hospitals. She served on mental health advisory boards, both in California and Oregon, with fourteen years as a board member of *ASSET,* a nationally published magazine, for which she wrote short stories. She retired at seventy and moved to Oregon, where she has been writing, painting watercolors, and sculpting. She lives independently in a cottage on the doorstep of Grayback Mountain in Williams, Oregon, with her corgi and two cats.